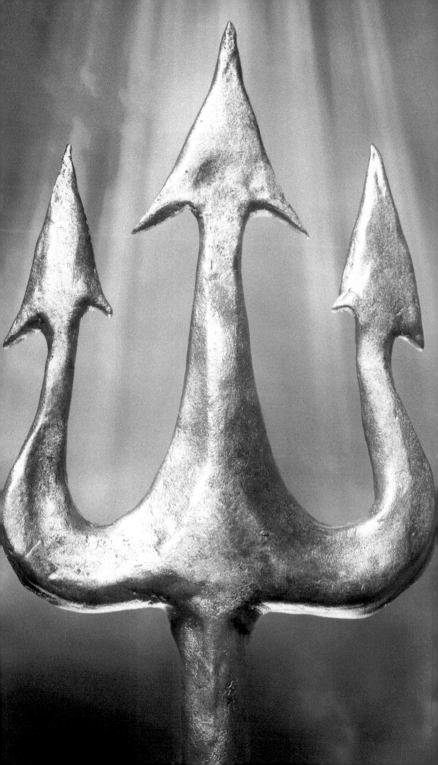

WAITING FOR HIM

Trident Security Book 3

Samantha Cole

Waiting For Him

Copyright ©2015 Samantha A. Cole
All Rights Reserved.
Suspenseful Seduction Publishing, LLC

Waiting For Him is a work of fiction. Names, characters, businesses,
organizations, places, events, and incidents either are the product of the
author's imagination or are used fictitiously. Any resemblance to actual
persons, living or dead, events, or locales is entirely coincidental.

Editing by Eve Arroyo

For my Family

ACKNOWLEDGEMENTS

As always, thanks to my Beta-readers for all you have done to help this story come to fruition—Charla, Abby, & Jessica, you're the best!

Thanks to my editor, Eve Arroyo, for all her fine tuning!

Willy, Catrina, & Randy—thanks for your unending input whenever I needed it!

Thank you, Emilia Rutigliano, for your patience and all things Russian in this book.

Thank you, Shawna, for sharing your husband's marriage proposal with me. It really helped me find the words I needed. Juan is definitely a romantic guy and a keeper.

But most of all, thanks to the fans of Trident Security Series for all your support and encouragement. I couldn't do this without you!

(If I forgot anyone, I apologize, because I cherish everyone who has had any part in helping my stories come to life!)

AUTHOR'S NOTE

The story within these pages is completely fictional but the concepts of BDSM are real. If you do choose to participate in the BDSM lifestyle, please research it carefully and take all precautions to protect yourself. Fiction is based on real life but real life is not based on fiction. Remember—Safe, Sane and Consensual!

Any information regarding persons or places has been used with creative literary license so there may be discrepancies between fiction and reality. The Navy SEALs missions and personal qualities within have been created to enhance the story and, again, may be exaggerated and not coincide with reality.

The author has full respect for the members of the United States military and the varied members of law enforcement and thanks them for their continuing service to making this country as safe and free as possible.

WHO'S WHO AND THE HISTORY OF
TRIDENT SECURITY & THE COVENANT

***While not every character is in every book, these are the ones with the most mentions throughout the series. This guide will help keep readers straight about who's who.

Trident Security (TS) is a private investigative and military agency, co-owned by Ian and Devon Sawyer. With governmental and civilian contracts, the company got its start when the brothers and a few of their teammates from SEAL Team Four retired to the private sector. The company is located on a guarded compound, which was a former import/export company cover for a drug trafficking operation in Tampa, Florida. Three warehouses on the property were converted into large apartments, the TS offices, gym, and bunkrooms.

In addition to the security business, there is a fourth warehouse that now houses an elite BDSM club, co-owned by Devon, Ian, and their cousin, Mitch Sawyer, who is the manager. A lot of time and money has gone into making The Covenant the most sought after membership in the Tampa/St. Petersburg area and beyond. Members are thoroughly vetted before being granted access to the elegant club.

There are currently over fifty Doms who have been appointed Dungeon Masters (DMs), and they rotate two or three shifts each throughout the month. At least four DMs are on duty at all times at various posts in the pit and play-rooms, with an additional one roaming around. Their job is to ensure the safety of all the submissives in the club. They step in if a sub uses their safeword and the Dom in the scene doesn't hear or heed it, and make sure the equipment used in scenes isn't harming the subs.

The Covenant's security team takes care of everything else that isn't scene-related, and provides safety for all members and are essentially the bouncers. The current total membership is just over 350. The fire marshal had approved them for 500 when the warehouse-turned-kink club first opened, but the cousins had intentionally kept that number down to maintain an elite status.

Between Trident Security and The Covenant there's plenty of romance, suspense, and steamy encounters. Come meet the Sexy Six-Pack, their friends, family, and teammates.

The Sexy Six-Pack (Alpha Team) and Their Significant Others

- Ian "Boss-man" Sawyer: Devon and Nick's brother; retired Navy SEAL; co-owner of Trident Security and The Covenant; Dom/fiancé of Angelina (Angel).
- Devon "Devil Dog" Sawyer: Ian and Nick's brother; retired Navy SEAL; co-owner of Trident Security and The Covenant; Dom/fiancé of Kristen.
- Ben "Boomer" Michaelson: retired Navy SEAL; explosives and ordnance specialist; son of Rick and Eileen.

- Jake "Reverend" Donovan: retired Navy SEAL; sniper; Dom and Whip Master at The Covenant.
- Brody "Egghead" Evans: retired Navy SEAL; computer specialist; Dom.
- Marco "Polo" DeAngelis: retired Navy SEAL; communications specialist and back up helicopter pilot; Dom.
- Nick Sawyer: Ian and Devon's brother; current Navy SEAL.
- Kristen "Ninja-girl" Anders: author of romance/suspense novels; fiancée/submissive of Devon.
- Angelina "Angie/Angel" Beckett: graphic artist; fiancée/submissive of Ian.

Extended Family, Friends, and Associates of the Sexy Six-Pack

- Mitch Sawyer: Cousin of Ian, Devon, and Nick; co-owner/manager of The Covenant, Dom.
- T. Carter: US spy and assassin; works for covert agency Deimos; Dom.
- Shelby Whitman: stay-at-home mom; two-time cancer survivor; submissive.
- Curt Bannerman: retired Navy SEAL; owner of Halo Customs, a motorcycle repair and detail shop.
- Jenn "Baby-girl" Mullins: college student; goddaughter of Ian; "niece" of Devon, Brody, Jake, Boomer, and Marco; father was a Navy SEAL; parents murdered.
- Mike Donovan: owner of the Irish pub, Donovan's; brother of Jake.

- Charlotte "Mistress China" Roth: Parole officer; Domme and Whip Master at The Covenant.
- Travis "Tiny" Daultry: former professional football player; head of security at The Covenant and Trident compound; occasional bodyguard for TS.
- Rick and Eileen Michaelson: Boomer's parents. Rick is a retired Navy SEAL.
- Charles "Chuck" and Marie Sawyer: Ian, Devon, and Nick's parents. Charles is a self-made real estate billionaire. Marie is a plastic surgeon involved with Operation Smile.
- Will Anders: Assistant Curator of the Tampa Museum of Art Kristen Anders's cousin.
- Dr. Roxanne London: pediatrician; Domme/wife (Mistress Roxy) of Kayla.
- Kayla London: social worker; submissive/wife of Roxanne.
- Chase Dixon: retired Marine Raider; owner of Blackhawk Security; associate of TS.
- Doug Henderson: retired Marine; bodyguard.
- Reggie Helm: lawyer for TS and The Covenant; Dom/boyfriend of Colleen.
- Colleen McKinley: office manager of TS; girlfriend/submissive of Reggie.
- Carl Talbot: college professor; Dom and Whip Master at The Covenant.

Members of Law Enforcement

- Larry Keon: Assistant Director of the FBI.
- Frank Stonewall: Special Agent in Charge of the Tampa FBI.
- Calvin Watts: Leader of the FBI HRT in Tampa.

The K9s of Trident

- Beau: An orphaned Lab/Pit mix, rescued by Ian. Now a trained K9 who has more than earned his spot on the Alpha Team.

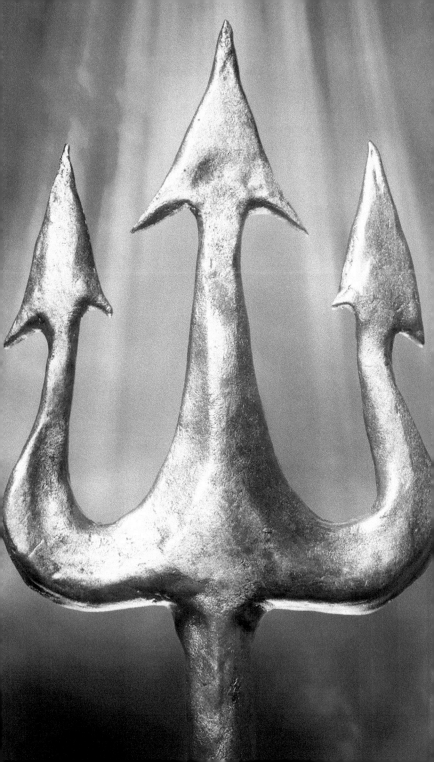

CHAPTER ONE

Boomer sat at his office desk, his eyes narrowing as he studied the paper before him. The answers should be easy, but for the life of him, he couldn't come up with the solution. He glanced at his cell phone to check the time and noted it was eighteen-twenty hours. The six-thirty appointment Colleen had scheduled for him was later than normal, but she'd told him the new client had requested the evening hour, so here he was, trying to kill a few more minutes.

Mondays and Tuesdays were the only evenings it wasn't a problem for Trident clients to come to the compound where their offices were. The rest of the week, Ian and Devon Sawyer's other venture, The Covenant, was open, and Trident clients might be a little shocked to see the BDSM club's members in varying stages of undress walking through the parking lot.

The fenced-in compound consisted of four warehouses and was off the beaten path on the outskirts of Tampa, Florida. The first building after the guarded gate was home to the club. Beyond that was another gate leading to the remaining three buildings. Trident's offices, bunk rooms, firing range, training areas, gym, and vehicle garage occupied the next two structures, and the final one had been renovated into two large apartments. The bottom one belonged to Ian and his fiancée, Angie, while Devon and his fiancée, Kristen, lived on the second floor. The rest of the building was empty space, and plans were being drawn up to construct two more apartments. One would be home to Ian's god-daughter, Jennifer Mullins when she wasn't at college. The men of Trident were her surrogate uncles, having served under her father in the teams. Ian had taken over her guardianship after her parents were killed in a home invasion the year before. The last unit would be offered to the youngest Sawyer brother, Nick, whenever he decided to opt out of the Navy. He'd made it through BUD/s, the SEALs' intensive training three years ago and was now with Team Three in Coronado, California, so the twenty-five-year-old wouldn't be joining them anytime soon.

As Boomer tapped his pen on the desk, he looked over the hints available to him and became more frustrated because he still couldn't figure it out. He glanced up as Ian walked in and sat in one of the two guest chairs on the other side of the desk. "What's a nine-letter word for vague? Starts with an 'A' and the fifth letter is a 'G.'"

"Ambiguous." Ian rolled his eyes. "And if you're going to keep asking me for help with the daily crossword puzzles, then I'm getting you a fucking thesaurus for Christmas this year instead of your bonus."

Boomer gave his boss a smirk as he filled in the blank spaces of the puzzle. "You do, Boss-man, and I'm signing you up for an anchovy-of-the-month club."

Even though he knew his friend and employee was joking, Ian got a queasy look on his face. Boomer always found it funny how, out of six retired SEALs, he was the only one who liked the oily yet salty fish, considering how much time they'd spent in and on the ocean while in the Navy. Well, maybe that *was* the reason.

"Not funny, Baby Boomer." Ian picked up the stress squeeze ball the other man kept on his desk and tossed it back and forth between both hands. "So, did you find out any information on this new client?"

Boomer threw the pen down on the newspaper and leaned back in his chair. "Nope. Colleen said the woman, a Kate Zimmerman, needed to hire Trident, but she wouldn't deal with anyone except me. I've racked my brain and can't recall ever meeting anyone by that name. I tried calling the phone number she'd left but got the standard computerized voice telling me to leave a message. It comes back to a throw-away cell."

"One-night-stand?"

He snorted but didn't take offense since all the guys on the team had participated in more one-night stands over the years than any of them cared to admit. Their time in the military and then the security business hadn't given them many opportunities for long-term relationships. Even if it did, Boomer wasn't interested. "I'd be lying if I said I remembered the first and last name of every woman I've ever slept with or scened with. But I'd like to think it would ring some sort of bell. Maybe she's a friend of a friend or something."

"Could be." They both knew a lot of their business was gained by word of mouth. "Guess we'll know in a few minutes. If she has no objections, and even if she does, I'll sit in on the meeting until we find out what she needs from us. If it's a bullshit my-husband's-cheating-on-me thing, I'll leave you to it."

"Fine with me. Are we the only two left in the office?"

Both men's phones chimed a text. The guard at the front

gate was alerting them to their new client's arrival. Murray would buzz her through the second gate and instruct her where to park. They stood, and Boomer grabbed a legal-sized yellow pad and his pen while Ian headed for the door. "Yeah. Colleen left. Polo and Egghead are on their way to New York to escort a shipment of diamonds from a dealer to the buyer here in Tampa. Jake is trying to track down one of his informants, who he's worried about—hasn't seen the guy in about two months, which he says is unusual. And my lucky brother is wedding venue shopping with Kristen and picking out pink tablecloths with matching napkins as we speak."

"Ha!" Boomer barked and shook his head. "I wouldn't fuck with him, Boss-man. You're right behind him, and karma's a bitch. Angie will be dragging your ass through the same tablecloths and napkins someday soon."

"Don't I know it. I'm trying to talk her into eloping, but I'm not having much success." The pained look on his face was mostly false since Boomer knew he'd give his woman the world if she asked for it. Well, if he didn't have to help pick out matching flowers, cummerbunds, and bridesmaids' dresses, he would. "I'll go get your client and meet you in the conference room."

"K. Just going to hit the head really quick."

WHILE BOOMER HEADED IN ONE DIRECTION FOR THE bathroom, Ian walked in the other toward the reception area. The front door could only be opened from the inside by a lock release behind Colleen's desk or by a hand scanner which unlocked the door for only those whose prints had been programmed into the system. He pulled the door open and found himself looking at a brown-haired beauty who seemed to be about Boomer's age of thirty. Wearing a pair of jeans and a short-sleeved, navy blouse, she stood about five-foot-five in her flat, off-white shoes, which matched the belt at her slim waist. Her slender build made the shirt and pants look a little big on her as if she'd recently lost some weight but had yet to find clothes to fit her new frame. In Ian's opinion, she looked too thin.

She took off her sunglasses and peered up at him with big chestnut-colored eyes. "Hi, my name's Kate Zimmerman. I'm looking for Ben Michaelson. I have an appointment with him, and the guard told me he was in this building."

When she glanced over her shoulder to where Murray was keeping watch at the front gate, Ian's eyes didn't follow hers. Instead, he looked with interest at Beau, who was sitting near the driver's door of Ms. Zimmerman's Ford Focus. The goofy-faced dog was panting, but something about his posture and the fact that he seemed to be in a "stay" position had Ian eyeballing the woman in front of him. She saw where his gaze had been, and the corners of her mouth curved upward a tad as he raised a curious eyebrow at her. Her smile didn't quite meet her anxious eyes, and when he got no answer to his unasked question, he opened the door wider. "Please come in, Ms. Zimmerman. I'm Ben's boss, Ian Sawyer. It's nice to meet you. If you don't mind, I'll be sitting in on your appointment."

Her smile faltered a little before she recovered. "Um, no. I mean, it's fine. I don't mind. It might be better that way."

Ian's curiosity was now further piqued, but he wasn't getting any bad vibes from her other than her nervousness, so he let her last comment slide for the moment. He glanced back at Beau, who was still sitting there with his tongue hanging out of his mouth and seemed to be waiting for a command. Ian tapped his leg. "Beau, *heir*."

The dog rushed over to his master, stopped, and when he received a slight hand signal, trotted past him on the way to the darkened conference room. Ian had discovered the dog when it was a young puppy. Its dying mother had dug under the compound's perimeter fence to find a human who would care for the little guy. When Beau was old enough, Ian took him to a friend who trained dogs for police departments and private security firms. Now, the silly-looking mutt was trained as an aggressive tracking dog as well as a guard dog. All his commands were given in German since it wasn't a common language in the States.

"He's beautiful. Lab and Staffordshire Terrier, correct?"

"We think so. I found him as a pup . . . well, actually, he found me." He shut the door and gestured her toward the conference room. "The vet thinks there may be something else mixed in there, maybe Great Dane, because his legs are a little longer than normal for the two breeds." He turned on the overhead lights to the room as they entered. "Please have a seat. Boomer will be here in a moment.

"Boomer?" she queried as she placed her large purse on a chair while he pulled out the one next to it for her to sit in.

Ian sat across from her, leaving his usual chair on the end empty. Although this was his company, he trusted his employee to take the lead in the unknown case. The client had requested him specifically, and Ian was willing to cede his authority for the moment, therefore giving Boomer the "head" seat at the table.

He studied the woman for a few seconds before answering her. "Sorry, I meant Ben. Boomer is his nickname from the Navy. No one uses his first name around here, but it's out of habit." He heard the man in question come down the hallway and saw him enter the room a second later. Ms. Zimmerman's back was to the door, but Ian knew the moment she realized Boomer was there without having seen him. Her body stiffened.

"Sorry to keep you waiting, Ms. Zimmerman. I . . ." Boomer walked over, peered down at the woman's face, and froze. Confusion in his eyes turned to pure shock, and Ian watched as the blood drained from his teammate's face. His normally strong voice dropped to a hoarse whisper. "Katerina?"

And with that, Benjamin Thomas "Boomer" Michaelson did something he'd never done before in his life. He fainted.

———

YES, BENNY, I WILL. I PROMISE I'LL WAIT FOR YOU FOREVER . . . forever . . . forever.

"Boomer. Boomer! Wake up, frog, that's an order!"

The words and a knuckle digging painfully into his chest finally penetrated Boomer's fog-filled mind, and his eyes blinked open. Ian was kneeling next to him with a look of concern on his face, while on his other side, Beau sat regarding him with a curious tilt of his furry head. And since Ian was kneeling and Boomer was flat on his back, it meant he was on the floor for some stupid reason. Rubbing his sore sternum, he asked, "W-what happened?"

"You okay? You fainted."

Snorting, the younger man stared at his boss like he had two heads. "Yeah, right. I've never fainted in my life. Not even when I saw the bone sticking out of my leg after the RPG attack."

It'd been a little over two years ago since the incident in Afghanistan, and the resulting injuries had almost cost him his leg. As it was, he'd needed a knee replacement after several surgeries to repair the other damage to his shinbone. After he'd recovered, his tour was just about up, so he opted out of the Navy and rejoined his former teammates here at Trident.

Ian shifted back a little as his friend sat up. "What's the last thing you remember?"

Boomer's eyes narrowed as his head finally stopped spinning. "I was dreaming . . ." Shock came over his face again, and he dragged a hand through his hair. "Ah, fuck. It wasn't a dream, was it?"

Standing, Ian offered a hand to help him up. "No. It wasn't."

"Where is she?" He looked around the room as if Katerina would suddenly reappear.

"Sitting out by Colleen's desk. I asked her to step outside so I could wake your ass up and find out what the fuck is going on. Now start talking, Ben. Who is she?"

Boomer knew his boss was not only worried but pissed because the man never used his given name unless he was in trouble, but at the moment, he didn't give a shit.

"In a minute." Striding out the door of the conference room, he went in search of a ghost.

CHAPTER TWO

Twelve Years Earlier . . .

Ben waved goodbye to the last of his friends heading to their cars parked a short distance away from the James River beach where they'd all gathered. An almost full moon was high in the sky on the warm summer night, and his going-away party had dwindled down a little after one in the morning. It was the Friday night, actually Saturday morning before he left for basic training the following weekend. He was joining the Navy and would hopefully make his way into the elite SEALs like his father before him.

Much to his wife's relief, Rick Michaelson had done his twenty years with only a few non-life-threatening injuries before getting out for good. He was now working for a friend who ran a private investigation company while also teaching history classes at the local community college. But since their only child had graduated high school and was leaving the nest, Ben's folks were talking about selling their home in Norfolk, Virginia, and moving to somewhere in Florida—maybe near his aunt in Sarasota.

He glanced around and saw Katerina sitting on a large rock near the shoreline. He'd told his best friend, Alex Maier, he'd make sure his sister got home safely. That way, Alex could hook up with Daniella Silverman, who'd been flirting with him all evening. Ben didn't mind driving Kat home since all three of them had grown up together these past seven years. Alex was six months older than Ben, who was six months older than Kat. But despite their closeness, she was a year younger than them in school because of her early December birthday.

Grabbing two colas from his cooler, he climbed up on the rock and sat beside her before handing her one of the cans. This close to his goal of a military career, he wasn't taking any chances with drinking and driving and had stopped the beer after nursing three of them in four hours. Katerina smiled at him, and he tried to ignore the twitch in his crotch, which had been happening often around her for the past few weeks, ever since she'd been his date for the prom.

He couldn't figure out why, out of the blue, he saw her as less of a buddy and more as the beautiful woman she was becoming. But there was no way he was putting the moves on his best friend's sister, no matter how attracted he was to her. The attraction would pass after he started meeting all the uniform bunnies who wanted to hook up with any man in the military. He just had to keep reminding himself of that.

"Thanks, Benny."

He rolled his eyes at her, and she giggled. She was the only person who still called him by the juvenile nickname. Everyone else had been calling him Ben, at his request, since the start of high school. "So, what're you going to do without Alex and me being around all the time to bug you and chase your boyfriends away?"

She shrugged and let out a tiny snort. "I'll be fine. It's only one more year until I get to go away to college, too. And I still have Alex for most of the summer until he leaves for Villanova." Her smile faded, and her voice dropped to a whisper. "I'm going to miss you."

Throwing his arm over her shoulder, he pulled her in for a sideways hug. "I'm going to miss you too, Kitten. But maybe I can get an assignment out of Little Creek, and then we'll be able to see each other all the time again."

They sat that way for a while, looking out over the water, with her head resting on his collarbone. When she placed her hand on his bent knee, and her thumb began to rub the bare skin his shorts didn't cover, his dick decided to betray him, noticing how good her touch felt. He tried to subtly adjust himself by shifting his hips.

Without pulling her head away, she tilted it up to look at him with those soft chestnut eyes of hers. "Are you uncomfortable? I can move."

"No, you're fine." And boy, was she. The sudden intimacy between them was making him forget all the reasons why he shouldn't be thinking of kissing her. The urge to claim her worsened when her eyelids lowered, and she stared at his mouth. He felt the soft puffs of her breath on his neck and smelled the mint gum she'd been chewing earlier, in addition to the shampoo she'd used to wash her hair. He was now painfully aware of her lush right breast crushed against his ribcage, and he thought he could feel her hardened nipple through the cotton tank she wore over her bikini top.

He tried to distract himself by counting down from one hundred in Spanish in his head, but it failed when her little pink tongue peeked out to moisten her tender lips. He stifled a groan, but when he attempted to pull away and put some distance between them, the hand on his knee tightened.

Looking back down at her sweet face, he was surprised

to see desire in her eyes, and it hit him—she was as attracted to him as he was to her. The knowledge sent every other thought from his brain, and he slowly lowered his head. When their lips were just shy of touching, he paused, wanting her to close the final gap between them. He wanted to make sure they were both on the same page, the one which would change their relationship forever. His brain tried to override his body, but it was too late. She moved the scant inch, and fireworks filled his mind as they kissed.

Fuck! She felt so incredible, tasted so incredible, he thought he'd died and gone to heaven. He shifted and eased her back until she was lying atop the flat rock with him on his side next to her. All the while, he continued to kiss her, moving his lips over hers in a sensual caress. Cautiously, he began to lick the seam of her mouth, encouraging her to open and let him in. He almost thought she wasn't going to when, all of a sudden, her lips parted and granted him entry.

Her tongue dueled shyly with his, making him even harder, which he hadn't thought was possible. Ben knew she wasn't experienced because he'd overheard a conversation she'd had with her two best friends a few weeks ago. Kat and Melanie were both shocked when their other friend, Tina, told them she'd lost her virginity to her boyfriend after the prom. When Tina had asked when they were planning on giving up their cherries, Katerina replied she was waiting for the right guy to come along, and she wasn't in any hurry.

Ben had been happy with her answer, but the way she'd said it made him think she had some guy in mind, and it annoyed the hell out of him. Then when he realized he was annoyed, it pissed him off because he wasn't supposed to be jealous of any guy she dated. He was supposed to help Alex warn the jerks off by threatening to kick their asses if they tried anything with her. He was supposed to act like her brother, wasn't he? At least he'd thought so . . . until tonight.

He was leaning on one arm while his other hand rested at her waist. He moved it up and down, closer and closer to her left breast. When she didn't stop him, he cupped it in his hand, squeezing it a few times before rubbing his thumb over her taut nipple. Her moan of pleasure spurred him on as she arched her back slightly, pushing the delectable orb further into his touch.

He was desperate to rip her shirt and bikini off to find out if her naked body was as beautiful as he'd imagined. The other morning, he'd been shocked to wake up with his hand around his morning wood while an image of her lips around his cock faded like the fantasy it had been. He hadn't been able to look her in the eye for several days afterward for fear his cheeks would heat in embarrassment, and she would know he'd jerked off in the shower after the incredible dream.

Continuing his tender assault on her mouth, he brought his hand down to the hem of her shirt, tucked his fingers under it, and began to inch his way upward again. The second his hand touched the skin of her abdomen, he groaned. It was softer than anything he'd ever felt. Unable to stand the torture anymore, he lifted his head and was pleased to see her swollen, red lips and heavy-lidded eyes. "Take off your shirt, Kat. I want to see you."

Her eyes widened as she bit her lower lip anxiously, and he thought he'd pushed her too far. Even though he was aware of her virginity, he didn't know how far she had gone with the few boyfriends she'd had. Had any of them ever seen her naked? Had she let one of them lick and nibble on her breasts? Had any guy ever gotten his hand down her underwear and touched the place that Ben was beginning to think belonged to him? All of her belonged to him, and God help him, Alex was going to kick his ass.

He was about to tell her it was okay if she wasn't ready to take the next step, but his cock leaped for joy when she reached down and grabbed the hem. It was the sexiest thing he'd ever seen when she lifted her shoulders and head off the rock and removed the tank top. He'd seen her in her bikini earlier in the day, but seeing her now in the skimpy top and her jean short-shorts, coupled with a mix of passion and uncertainty in her eyes, she blew him away. "You're so beautiful, Kitten."

Her shy blush thrilled him in a way he hadn't thought possible. She looked away from his intense stare. "You don't have to say that. I know it's not true."

Shocked, he cupped her chin and forced her to look at him. "Are you crazy? What makes you think it's not true?"

Katerina shrugged her shoulders and tried to break eye contact, but he wouldn't let her. "Answer me, Kitten, because, in my opinion, you're the most beautiful girl I've ever known."

"Oh, please." An eye roll punctuated her sarcasm. "You and Alex have dated every gorgeous girl in your class and mine. I can't even begin to compare myself to most of them. My chest is too flat, my ass is too big, my legs are too skinny, and my eyes are too far apart."

When she finished rattling off what she believed were her worst attributes, Ben wasn't sure if she was kidding or if she really thought those things about herself. It only took a few seconds before he realized she was serious, and his eyes narrowed in anger. "Kitten, there is nothing about you I would change. Your eyes are so expressive. Sometimes, I can't stop looking at them, especially when you laugh. Your chest . . ." his hand closed around her left breast again and squeezed just enough to make sure he had her attention, ". . . is the perfect size—not too small or too big—it's just right."

He moved his hand down to her denim-covered hip and squeezed again. "Your ass . . . jeez, do you have any idea how many guys check out your ass when you walk by? Especially in these sexy shorts of yours. And your legs are a mile long. Baby, men drool over legs like yours, and most women would kill for them. If I ever hear you put yourself down again, I'll spank your sweet ass. Do you hear me?"

It was obvious she thought he was joking about smacking her backside because she giggled, and he relaxed a little. Wanting to prove how desirable she was to him, he leaned down and took possession of her mouth again. This time he wasn't as gentle as before but was still cautious. He knew he had to walk a fine line here—the one between scaring her by moving too fast and making her see how good they could be together.

Her hands began pushing his T-shirt up, and he reached back, grabbed a handful of blue cotton, and stopped kissing her just long enough to yank it over his head and toss it aside. Her hand scorched his chest when she timidly touched him. As his lips found hers again, his fingers started a new exploration of her breasts through her bikini, but he knew he couldn't go much further. He wanted her first time to be special—not out here on a huge rock where anyone could drive up and interrupt them. She deserved better.

Ben was about to pull away from her mouth when his fear happened. He heard the car a moment before a bright flood light hit them, and they both jumped up into sitting positions. Damn. A cop had to pick this moment to check out the popular party spot. At least they were both still decent.

Instead of getting out of his patrol car, the lazy cop blared his air horn once. In other words—*get in your truck and drive away, jackass, because you're not getting laid here tonight.*

As they scrambled for and threw on their shirts, he gave the officer a quick wave of his hand, letting him know the message was received and understood. Taking Kat's hand, he helped her down from the rock, and they headed for his dad's pick-up, grabbing his cooler on the way. He opened the passenger door for her and lifted her into the high seat, then emptied the cooler of its leftover melted ice before stowing it in the truck's bed.

Hopping in the driver's seat, he started the engine and grinned when she broke out in a fit of giggles. "What's so funny?"

"Your shirt is on backward and inside out." She looked so cute covering her mouth as if she'd accidentally spilled the beans about something.

He glanced down, saw she was right, and laughed along with her. Before putting the truck in drive, he pulled off his shirt, flipped it around then put it on correctly. The last thing he needed was for her dad or brother to see that and put two and two together. He would need to eventually tell Alex he planned on dating Katerina, but not yet.

As he drove down the dirt road which led out to the highway, he reached across the center console and took her hand in his. He squeezed it, then set their joined hands on the armrest between them. Driving her home was the last thing he wanted to do, but if he kept her out any later, her parents, Ivan and Sylvia, would be ticked off. At seventeen, Kat still had a curfew. The only reason she'd been allowed out until two a.m. was because school was over, and she was with Alex and Ben. That and it was a special occasion since it would be a while before Ben would get a chance to come back home to visit.

Aside from the low music on the radio, a silence had fallen over the inside of the cab, and at the last second, he pulled into the elementary school lot just up the road from her house. Putting the truck in park, he turned to look at her. "I . . . I'm sorry we were interrupted back there. It took me by surprise. I never thought . . ."

She pulled her hand from his and stared out the side window. "It's okay, Benny. We'll pretend it never happened. I mean, it's not like we actually did anything."

Taking hold of her chin, he turned her head until she faced him, but her eyes remained downcast. "Kitten, look at me." He waited a moment, but she still didn't look up. "Kat, please, look at me."

His heart almost broke when he saw the unshed tears in her eyes. *Crap.* She misunderstood him, and now she was on the verge of crying. He did his best to embrace her despite the center console between them and kissed her on the top of her head. A shudder passed through her, and he hugged her tighter.

"Shhh, baby, you didn't let me finish. Just because I never thought you and I would . . . you know, get together . . . doesn't mean I'm not happy we did. I've been thinking about you and me ever since the prom when we danced those slow dances together. For the first time, I realized you're more than my friend. You're also a very beautiful woman who I suddenly found myself attracted to. I was just surprised you felt that way about me too." He froze for a second. "You do feel that way, don't you? I mean, it wasn't just an experiment for you, right?"

She pulled away so she could look up at him again. "I've felt that way for a lot longer than you have. I was so happy when you asked me to the prom even though I knew it was only because you and Mary Jo Dwyer just broke up, and everyone else was already paired up for the most part."

He at least had the decency not to deny it. That *was* the reason why he'd asked her, but he wouldn't have done it at all if he hadn't thought they'd have a good time together—which they had.

Taking a deep breath, she blurted out, "I didn't want to stop tonight."

Her face turned beet red as the implications of what she said sank into his brain. Was she telling him she would have given him her virginity tonight if the cop hadn't interrupted them? *Holy shit!* What was he supposed to say to her?

With any other girl, he would have been all over her without a second thought. He knew he could be a dog sometimes. He'd lost his own virginity two months before he turned fifteen. And like every other normal, red-blooded American male, he rarely said no when a girl offered him a roll in the sack or the bed of his truck. But he needed *her* to be sure this was what she wanted and it wasn't a spur-of-the-moment thing because he was leaving. He couldn't . . . wouldn't do that to her. Kissing her had already changed the dynamics of their relationship, but having sex with her would put them in another orbit. And he knew it wouldn't be just sex. With Katerina, it would be making love.

"Baby, do you know what you're saying?"

She nodded and then babbled nervously, "I wanted you to be my first . . . you know. I still do. I mean, I know you've been having . . . you know, sex for a long time now. I mean, everyone at school talks about who's doing who, but I haven't . . . you know . . ."

"You're still a virgin." He'd meant to say it as a question, not wanting her to know he'd overheard the conversation with her friends, but she didn't seem to notice.

"I know it's silly, but . . ."

He cupped her cheek with his hand. "It's not silly, Kat. Not at all. But as much as I want to say yes to you . . . to us, I think it would be better if we waited until I finish basic training and find out where I'm being stationed. I don't want to have one or two nights with you and then end up on a base on the opposite side of the country. It's not fair to you."

He covered her mouth with his fingers when she tried to interrupt him. "But I'll make you a deal, baby. If this is what you want . . . if you're sure, then I'm willing to tell every woman I run into from here on out that I have someone special waiting for me back home, and she's the only one I want. Will you wait for me, Kitten? Will you be my girlfriend and wait until the time is right for us?"

"Yes, Benny, I will," she whispered. "I promise. I'll wait for you . . . forever."

Alex was going to kill him.

RICK MICHAELSON STOOD BETWEEN HIS WIFE AND CHILD AT the cemetery and kept his hand on his grieving son's shoulder. His boy was on the verge of entering the military and becoming a man, but in the blink of an eye, his life had been turned upside down. They watched as the funeral director's crew unloaded scores of colorful arrangements from four matching hearses and placed them beside the caskets. The area around the grave sites was filling up with close to two hundred people who'd known one, two, or all members of the Maier family and come to pay their respects.

A somber priest made his way to the head of the graves to give the deceased their final blessing. Ivan and Sylvia would be buried side by side, just as their children, Alex and Katerina, would be in the plot next to them.

The Sunday after Ben's going-away party, the family had taken off on an hour-long afternoon drive to visit Ivan's mother and sister, but they never arrived. A fiery crash on a lonely stretch of highway snuffed out the lives of four people and left many others, like Ben, struggling to find a reason behind the terrible tragedy.

Rick knew although his son's overwhelming grief would one day become bearable, losing his best friend and the young man's family would forever change Ben's life. He just hoped when his son emerged from his grief, he came out on the right side.

CHAPTER THREE

Present Day...

Kate had known Benny would be shocked when he first saw her, but she hadn't expected him to pass out. As far as he knew, she was dead and buried in a cemetery in Norfolk, Virginia, and not living and breathing at his place of business. His boss, Ian, had asked her to have a seat out here in the reception area, but she couldn't sit. Instead, she was pacing back and forth, trying to keep her feet from running out the door and taking the rest of her body with them.

Benny would've been better off if she'd never come looking for him, but it was too late to change her mind now. The last thing she ever wanted to do was to cause him any more pain, but her life was in danger, and there was no one in the world she trusted more than him. It was sad he wouldn't be able to trust her in return. Not after what she'd put him through, even though none of it had been her fault. Her father was to blame for everything . . . her recently-deceased father. And for the first time in Kate's life, she was all alone.

The sound of footsteps caused her pacing to cease, and she turned to see Benny stalking toward her, followed by his boss and the lab mix. The look on the man's face, the man who'd once been the boy she'd fallen in love with, was now hard. Shock was giving away to anger, and it was evident by the raging inferno in his beautiful amber eyes. Eyes that still haunted her dreams after all these years.

He stopped in front of her and crossed his arms. The Navy had taken his gangly, teenage physique and made it broad, strong, and sinewy. She longed to have him pull her into his powerful arms and hold her while telling her everything would be okay. Instead, he glared at her from several feet away. "Do you want to explain how a woman I watched being buried twelve years ago is standing in front of me? Because as far as I know, reincarnation is still a myth."

"I-I'm sorry, Benny. I'm so sorry. But if we can go sit down, I'll explain everything. I promise."

Benny's clenched jaw ticked at her use of his childhood nickname and again at her vow. The last time she promised him something, she'd said she would wait for him forever. As far as he knew, that hadn't happened.

When he said nothing, Ian stepped around him and extended his open hand to her. "Ms. Zimmerman, please come back to the conference room, and we'll talk this out."

A growl from deep in Benny's throat escaped his mouth, and he ignored the warning look Ian sent him. "Her name is Maier, Katerina Maier, and you're damn right we're going to talk."

While the two of them walked back to the room, she heard him take several deep breaths before turning around and following them.

Upon re-entering the room they had moments ago vacated, Ian took the seat he'd earlier planned on giving Boomer. The meeting had taken a dramatic turn before it even began, and he needed to take control of the situation before it blew up in their faces. Boomer sat in the seat across from Kate with his arms crossed and glowered at her.

Sighing, Ian rolled his chair back a few feet to a small refrigerator in the corner, grabbed three bottles of water, and put them on the table. They were going to be here for a while. "Boom? Why don't you tell me how you two know each other, and we'll go from there."

Benny waited a moment before his harsh words came out, his eyes never leaving hers as if she would disappear again if they did. "Boss, this is Katerina Maier. She was my best friend's sister. She's also supposed to be six feet under, along with her parents and brother, in a cemetery in Norfolk, so I don't have the slightest fucking idea what she's doing here. They were *allegedly* killed in a car accident a week before I left for basic training. Tell me, Kat—are all four caskets empty or just yours?"

She winced at his accusatory tone. It also hadn't escaped her notice when he referred to her only as his best friend's sister and not his friend as well. She heard the pain under the anger in his voice but knew he'd never admit to it.

Her own voice came out a little louder than a whisper as she stared at the tabletop in front of her. "Mom and Alex are there. The car crash was real, but it wasn't an accident. We were forced off the road and rolled down a hill. My dad and I barely managed to get Alex out before the car exploded, but my mom had been killed on impact. Alex died in my arms a few minutes later. Dad and I went into hiding afterward."

She hadn't realized she was crying until Ian put a box of Kleenex in front of her, and she grabbed two tissues. When a sympathetic, warm nose poked her arm, she gave Beau a scratch behind his ear as his master spoke. "I get the feeling this is leading to Witness Protection."

Kate nodded at the man's gentle and understanding statement. "Yes. It's exactly where it leads to." Not being able to look at Benny, she instead turned her gaze to the man who didn't currently hate her. "My dad is . . . was a CPA with some questionable clients at the time. Mom, Alex, and I had no idea some of the people he dealt with weren't on the up-and-up, but he drew the line at certain . . . crimes, I guess you can say. He said the money was too good to pass up, especially when he'd been starting his own accounting business, but his conscience wouldn't allow him to let some things slide by. He tried to know as little as possible about who he was working for because he figured the less he knew, the better off he would be. It worked for him for over ten years."

"What happened?"

She drew in a trembling breath, reached for one of the water bottles, and took a few sips to quench her sudden thirst. "He found out he was doing the books for a member of a Russian organized-crime family. Dad wasn't the only one. They used several accountants and gave each the books to only a few businesses, so if one turned on them, he didn't have access to all the accounts. There was one man, in particular, Dad was dealing with. He owned a few bars in Norfolk, Newport News, and Virginia Beach, among other businesses, both legal and illegal."

Ian raised an eyebrow. "Do you know the man's name?"

Nervously nibbling on her bottom lip, she nodded. "Mm-hm. Sergei Volkov.

"Are you fucking kidding me! Sergei 'The Wolf' Volkov?" Kate flinched at Benny's sudden outburst as he jumped up and sent his chair flying back into the wall. He started pacing the room, ignoring Ian's angry glare. "Even I knew that bastard should be avoided at all fucking costs, and I was a fucking teenager!"

She looked at him with eyes that begged him to understand something she, herself, had never been able to. When her father tried to explain it to her in the days after the crash, she'd been in shock, and nothing would sink into her brain and stay there.

After the U.S. Marshals gave them new identities, and they began their new lives in hiding, her father never wanted to talk about it again. He didn't want to be reminded how his stupidity and greed had cost him his wife and son, in addition to the life he and his daughter had known.

"Dad swore he didn't know who Volkov was until it was too late, and he was in too deep. So, he did what he was paid to do and tried to stay out of trouble. But then he discovered they were selling teenage girls into white slavery. The summer and spring breaks in Virginia, the Carolinas, and Florida were the perfect times for them to kidnap a girl and make her disappear.

"Dad got a bunch of receipts and stuff he was supposed to add to the books, and he found an envelope with a list of . . . God . . . he said it was like a shopping list with the type of girls they were looking for. Specific hair color and eyes, fair skin, a certain build, that sort of stuff."

She shook her head at the thought of any girl being taken because of their appearance. "There were also a couple of photos of girls tied up. Dad recognized one of them from the newspaper. Her parents were rich and were making a lot of noise about her disappearance. He found out later most of the girls who'd been taken were the type no one would be surprised about if they took off on their own. Mostly they were teenage hookers or runaways. He said when he realized what he had in his hand, he thought about how he would feel if one of those girls had been me.

"So, he called the phone number in the paper, and the FBI came to talk to him. They wanted him to wear a wire and get them more information, but Dad refused. He was too scared for our safety. He told them that if he started asking any questions, Volkov would immediately know something was wrong because my dad only talked about the accounting when he met with him or his right-hand man."

"But they found out about the information he gave the feds, didn't they?" Boomer gritted his teeth as he sat down again and grabbed one of the bottled waters.

She nodded. "Yes, right before the accident. Apparently, the FBI thought my dad knew more than he told them, or he might lead them to Volkov. They were following us to my grandmother's that day. It was her sixty-fifth birthday, and we were going to take her and my aunt out to dinner to celebrate. The agents were using a tracking device, so they could stay further back and weren't close enough to stop a car that came out of nowhere and forced us off the road."

A shudder went through her at the memory. "All I remember is everyone yelling and screaming as the car rolled over and over down the embankment, and then silence. Dad and I got our seatbelts off and crawled out of the car. It was upside down. We managed to get Alex out through the window with the help of the two agents who'd been following us. They saw the dust and smoke and realized what happened. After we got him out and far enough away from the car, they went to get my mom. I remember wondering why they returned without her, shaking their heads, and then the car exploded. I tried to run back to get my mom, but they stopped me. I screamed and hit them, but they wouldn't let me near it. I found out later she'd died instantly from a broken neck.

"A few minutes before the ambulance and police arrived, Alex took his last breath." She swallowed hard, trying to clear the thick lump in her throat while wiping away the flood of tears rolling down her face. "I-I don't remember much of what happened over the next few days. I guess I was numb. Dad and I ended up being moved from one safe house to another until the FBI decided we could never return to Norfolk and put us in the Marshals' Witness Protection Program. We changed identities and locations three times before we settled in Portland, Oregon. We've been Joe and Kate Zimmerman for the past eight years."

At some point toward the end of telling her tragic story, Kate closed her eyes, but her tears were still falling. Her voice had become little more than a hoarse whisper, and she swallowed again, trying to regain her composure.

Slowly she raised her lids and was relieved to see some sympathy in Ben's hardened gaze. At least he knew she was telling the truth. "I wanted so badly to talk to you, to explain what happened, but they wouldn't let me. When they came to give us new identities, I told them the only way I would agree to go was if our handler kept tabs on you and let me know how you were doing. He followed your career for me as best he could since a lot of it was classified. When I heard you were in the Naval Medical Center in Maryland with a bad leg injury, the only thing that kept me from flying to see you was my father had just been diagnosed with liver cancer. It wasn't long before it spread and . . ."

Her words trailed off, and it didn't take a rocket scientist to figure out what had gone unspoken. She was surprised when Benny spoke in a gentle, sympathetic tone. "He's gone, isn't he?"

"Almost two months ago. The chemo and radiation did a number on him, but he lasted longer than the doctors expected."

There was silence in the room for a few moments as what she'd been through over the past twelve years hung in the air. Finally, Ian cleared his throat and spoke. "You told our secretary you needed to hire us. Was it just a ruse to see Boomer, or do you need our help? There's obviously a lot more to your story we're not aware of, but I would hope with your father's death, it would be safe for you to come out of hiding."

"I thought it would all be over after my father passed away," she told them with a shake of her head. "But then I noticed I was being followed, and my condo was broken into and trashed."

Benny had been looking down, but at her words, his head jerked back up. "What? When the hell was this?"

Looking back and forth between the two men, she told them the details. "All last week, I felt like I was being watched. Then Friday afternoon, I got home from work and found my condo in shambles. The police said whoever it was had picked the lock. A few things, like my laptop, camera, and jewelry, were missing, so they assumed it was just a random burglary, but I didn't think it was. Saturday, I tried to contact my handler at the Marshals but was told he was killed in a car accident two days earlier. A new handler had taken over and wanted to meet with me, but with everything that happened, I wasn't sure I could trust anyone there. So, I grabbed a few clothes and money and came to the one person I knew I could trust to help me."

Anger returned to Benny's face as his gaze flickered toward his boss. "Someone was looking for something."

Ian nodded and rubbed his chin with his index finger.

"But what? Why now, and how did they find her after all these years?"

She cringed, and whatever Benny had been about to say was lost as his eyes narrowed, focusing on her face. "How did they find you, Kat?"

"It was an accident." She sighed, knowing she had to explain a few more things. "Dad couldn't work as a CPA anymore when they changed our identity. In the beginning, we both worked odd jobs because we never knew when we'd have to change cities and names again. But after we settled down in Portland, and two years went by without any trouble, our handler helped Dad get his teaching license, and he taught high school math. When he got sick, the teachers and students held fundraisers and stuff to help me pay for whatever his insurance didn't cover. They were a big help to me. His students were always stopping by and visiting him."

A small smile appeared on her face as she recalled how his students could always lift her father's spirits. "They loved him. Anyway, when he died, I had him cremated and told everyone he would be buried back east with my mom and brother, but I didn't give them any details. I told everyone it was my dad's wish to not have a funeral, and I didn't put an obituary in the paper, even though it would be in his new name. But the students arranged a memorial at the school for him.

"At first, it was just supposed to be his students and fellow teachers at an assembly during school hours, but then it grew, and they posted it on Facebook. A local reporter saw it and ran a story about the death of a well-liked teacher. It included a picture of Dad taken at a school basketball game last year before he got too sick. I think one of his students took it, not knowing my dad avoided having his picture taken because the Marshals told us to. By the time I saw it, it was too late. It was in the print edition as well as online and on Facebook."

"Shit. Any facial recognition program could have found it." Boomer rolled his eyes and ran a frustrated hand through his hair. Sometimes technological advances can be a bitch.

Nodding his agreement, Ian leaned forward and rested his elbows on the table. "But the question remains—what are they looking for?" He studied Kate's face. "Any ideas? Did your father keep something as evidence in case he needed leverage down the road?"

She shrugged and shook her head. "Not that I know of, but he gave me this . . ." she pulled a key out of a small inside pocket of her purse, ". . . just before he died. He was kind of out of it at the end. Hospice had him on morphine, so half of what he told me didn't make sense. When he gave me this key, he told me to go home again. I asked him what he meant, and he just kept saying it was 'the key to the wells.' I couldn't get him to explain it."

Ian took the key from her and inspected it. "It looks like a safety-deposit-box key. Did he have one at his bank?"

"I checked, but they had no record of it. Maybe I should have checked another branch or another bank. But there are so many banks in Portland it would take days to check them all. Should I start calling them? Would they give me the information over the phone?"

"No, you don't need to call them. It's not in Portland." Ian and Kate both looked at Boomer in confusion. He grabbed the conference room laptop, pulled it toward him, and booted it up. "It's in Norfolk. Your dad said, 'Go home again,' so that had to be what he meant. I remember your family used Bank of America like mine did, but . . ." He paused as he tapped a few keys. "Here it is. Not far from your house is a

Wells Fargo Bank. 'The key to the wells.' That's where we start looking."

"Your house," he'd said, but the colonial was no longer hers. Some other family was living in it now. A strange girl or boy was sleeping in what was once her bedroom, and some other parents were joking with their children at the dinner table. Did they change the color of the walls? Her mother had painstakingly picked out just the right hues to go with the furniture. Was some other teenager reenacting the scene from *Risky Business*, when Tom Cruise slid across the wood floor lip-syncing to Bob Seeger's "Old Time Rock and Roll"? Alex always made her laugh when he did it.

She shook off the bittersweet memories. "So, what should I do? Just walk into the bank and ask if my dad has a box there? Will they let me open it?"

Ian tapped his fingers on the table. "Not yet. They won't let you near it without proper ID and a death certificate in your father's name . . . his real name. And even then, it might take a court order if your name isn't attached to the box's account."

He eyed Boomer. "I'll give Larry Keon a call and get what we need. The court order might take longer to get, but we'll worry about that if it turns out we need it. I'll also have him get me everything the FBI has on this Sergei Volkov."

Having the deputy director, the number two man of the FBI, on speed dial came in handy at times, and this was one of them. "In the meantime, we have to keep Kate . . . I'm sorry, but I have to ask . . . do you prefer I call you Kate or Katerina? After this is over, if it's possible, are you planning on going back to your real name?"

She gave him a wistful smile. "I hadn't given it a lot of thought. I never believed . . . I'd like to be me again, Katerina Maier. I miss her and the life she was supposed to have." A life that was supposed to include Benny Michaelson. "But you can call me Kat if you'd like. It was the one habit my father was never able to break. I was always his Kitty Kat."

He returned her smile with an optimistic one. "Then Kat it is, and we'll do everything we can to try to get your life back. But for now, we need to keep you out of the public eye. Are you sure you weren't followed from Portland?"

"Actually, I was." When she saw their surprised expressions, she quickly added, "But I got rid of them. About an hour out of the city, I started thinking about all the movies I've seen about people being followed by bad guys or cops. And then I remembered about the agents who had a tracking device on our car, and I got a little paranoid. So, I pulled into a truck stop and convinced a couple of truck drivers that I was afraid my 'abusive ex-boyfriend,'" she made finger quotes in the air with both hands, "may be using a device to stalk me. They looked under my car for me and found one by the trunk. One of the drivers was nice enough to take it with him, and it's somewhere in Southern California now."

"Smart girl." Ian dipped his head in approval of her survival instincts. "Good. Then until we get you the paperwork you need for the bank, we have to keep you hidden for now. There are bunkrooms and bathrooms upstairs here, and the compound is secure."

"She'll stay with me at my condo." The look on Boomer's face told them not to argue with him.

The corners of Ian's mouth twitched, and Kat realized he'd figured out there was more between Benny and her than just the memory of a teenage boy and his friend's sister. "Fine. But to be safe, I'm calling Tiny and having him sit outside your place."

Benny nodded his head. "Works for me." At her confused look, he added, "Tiny is one of the bodyguards we use when we need one. He'll watch our six . . . our backs." He turned back to Ian. "I'll double-check her car for trackers, then leave it here in the garage so it's out of sight."

"I can get a motel room," Kat told them. "I don't want to put anyone out."

Benny growled at her while Ian shook his head and stood. "You're not putting anyone out, Kat. The safest place for you to be is either here or with Boomer. His place is secure, and we'll have someone monitoring his condo. We're not taking any chances someone might've figured out you came to him for help."

He glanced back at his teammate. "After I call Tiny, I'll call Keon and see what he can do for us. Jake or Dev will relieve Tiny in the morning, and I'll call you with a rendezvous time so we can plan our next steps."

Nodding his agreement, Boomer stood. "Let me have your keys, Kat. You can wait here while I take care of your car."

She handed him her keychain, and then both men left her alone in the room. Well, not exactly alone. Beau was sitting next to her with a curious tilt of his head. She reached out to pet his velvety ears.

"*Braver hund.*" Good dog.

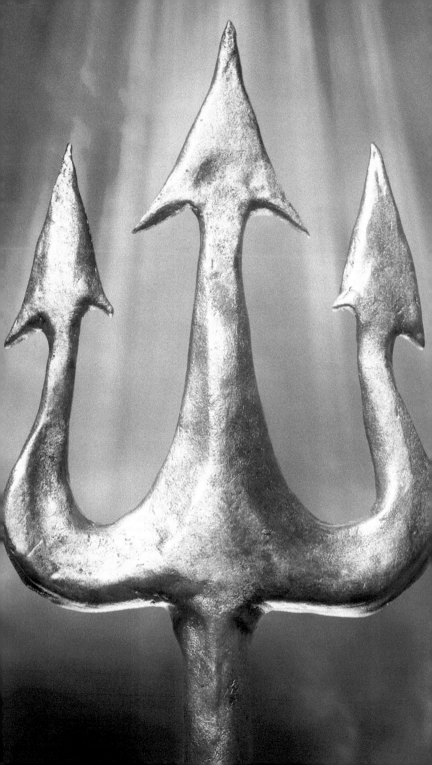

CHAPTER FOUR

K at washed her face in the bathroom of Benny's condo. After he'd taken care of her vehicle and retrieved the three duffel bags, which were full of her clothes and necessities, they had driven in silence to his place. She felt so drained after telling the two men about the horror story which her life had become, and she couldn't find any more words to say to Benny. But it bothered her that he was just as quiet. It shouldn't since the poor man had had the shock of his life tonight, having an old girlfriend . . . no, an old *friend* . . . come back from the grave. She couldn't actually classify what they were back then as boyfriend/girlfriend since they'd only kissed that one night, and he'd asked her to be his girlfriend barely thirty-six hours before she "died."

The way he'd reacted upon seeing her again, she wasn't sure if he would want to be friends with her ever again. But one step at a time. First, they needed to find out who was following her and why. Then, and only then, could she think about Katerina and Benny. For now, they were Kat and Boomer, and there were twelve years of each other's lives they knew nothing about.

She heard the doorbell ring and suddenly wondered if Benny had a girlfriend. He wasn't married, her handler would have told her, and his condo was definitely a bachelor pad, but it didn't mean he wasn't dating anyone special. When she opened the bathroom door, she heard another male voice along with Benny's, and her shoulders relaxed in relief. If he was dating someone, she couldn't handle meeting the other woman just yet.

Walking out to the living room, she was surprised to see a man who made Benny look small, which was no easy feat considering he was six-foot-one and about two hundred and fifteen pounds of solid muscle. Benny only came to the man's shoulders and was outweighed by about sixty pounds. He had soft-looking, café-au-lait skin and was shaved bald. With his mustache and goatee, he reminded her of some actor from an old TV show, but she couldn't remember who. She was wary about the man's intimidating size until he spotted her and smiled a smile that probably had women falling at his feet.

Turning, Benny gestured for her to join him. "Kat, this is my friend, Tiny. He's going to be watching the condo overnight from across the street. Tiny, this is Katerina."

The bear of a man extended one large paw toward her. "It's a pleasure to meet you, Miss Katerina."

"It's nice to meet you too, Tiny." She smiled at the diminutive nickname for such a huge man and shook his hand. "Please call me Kat. I appreciate you looking out for me."

He gave her an "aw-shucks" expression and waved his mitt of a hand as if batting away a fly. "Don't worry about it, ma'am. It's what I do. I'll keep an eye on things so you can get a good night's sleep. No offense intended, but you look like you could use it."

Tiny gave her a wink and Boomer a fist bump, then headed out the door to start his watch.

Boomer locked up behind the bodyguard and set the security system. He then turned and eyed her speculatively. "When was the last time you ate or slept?" The way she took a moment to remember wasn't lost on him. "Forget it. Come with me."

Kat followed him into his kitchen and took a seat at the table after he'd gestured to it. She watched him take bacon, eggs, spinach, and cheese from the refrigerator. "You don't have to cook for me. I can make something for myself."

He ignored her comments and continued to pull out a large frying pan, followed by the utensils he would need. Placing the pan on the stove, he turned on the gas, and a *poof* sounded as the burner lit. He then peeled off half the slices of bacon from the package and lined them up neatly in the pan. After throwing the remaining bacon back into the fridge, he pulled out a bowl and started cracking the eggs. She assumed he was making enough for both of them when the sixth and final egg made its way into the bowl.

His shoulders and arms moved with fluidity as he beat the eggs into submission. Her eyes crossed over his sinewy back from one shoulder to the other and then downward. There wasn't an ounce of fat on him as his waist narrowed. She couldn't help herself when her gaze went to his khaki-covered ass, and her mouth watered.

He was a perfect specimen of the male body. Even if he didn't have a girlfriend, she was certain he was propositioned all the time. In high school, he and Alex had been on almost every girl's "I want to kiss" list and most of the "I want to fuck" lists too. Neither one of them had ever lacked in the female companionship department, and she doubted things had changed for Benny.

The silence between them was becoming unbearable. "How are your folks? The last I heard from Chris, our handler, they lived in Sarasota."

He didn't stop making their meal, but at least he answered her. "They're fine."

Okay, the two flat words were technically an answer, but she'd hoped he would open up a little more. This reunion was just as hard on her as it was on him. Not knowing what to say next, she let the silence return.

A few minutes later, he brought two heaping plates to the table and set one in front of her and the other in front of the chair across from her. While he turned to retrieve knives and forks for them, she stared in astonishment at the full plate. Five slices of bacon, a huge three-egg omelet with spinach and provolone cheese, and two slices of multi-grain toast with butter, which she hadn't noticed him make. "There's no way I can eat all this."

He put a set of utensils next to her plate, then took one of her slices of bacon, throwing it on his own plate as if it made a huge difference in the amount of food he'd given her. "Yes, you can, and you will. Your clothes are hanging off you. Either you're wearing someone else's stuff, or you've lost weight. Now eat."

She tried to glare at him for ordering her around, but he disregarded her and pulled two glasses out of a cabinet. After filling them with orange juice from the fridge, he brought both to the table and sat down across from her. He pointed at her plate. "Eat, Katerina."

If her stomach hadn't picked that moment to growl and let him know it did indeed want to be fed, she would have tossed the food in the garbage just because of his attitude. But she admitted to herself she was starving, having realized she hadn't eaten in over twelve hours. She'd grabbed two cereal bars and a coffee from a truck stop where she'd pulled in for gas and had nothing else since.

Picking up her fork, she dug into the omelet, and a moan of ecstasy escaped her mouth when the flavors hit her taste buds. "Oh, my God, this is delicious. When did you learn how to cook?"

Clearly satisfied she would eat, he picked up his own fork. "Don't be too impressed. Omelets are pretty much the extent of my culinary expertise unless it's meat on a grill. Bachelorhood forces a guy to learn how to do things like cooking, cleaning, and doing your own laundry."

His voice lacked any emotion, and she wished she could think of a response that might make him at least smile, but nothing came to mind. She watched him take a bite of his eggs and was shocked when a question blurted from her mouth. "You never married?"

"No." The answer was short and an indication for her to drop the subject. He kept his gaze on his plate and continued to eat in silence. His demeanor had her food turning bland, and she quickly lost her appetite.

He finished his meal faster than she did. "Eat it all."

Ignoring her annoyed expression, he stood and began cleaning up the kitchen. After every item he'd used was either washed, dried, and put away or in the dishwasher, he turned around, eyeing the two pieces of bacon, a piece of toast, and a third of the omelet left on her plate. She stared at him defiantly, and he raised an eyebrow at her while crossing his arms. His eyes filled with something she couldn't name, but a shiver went through her as he lowered his voice. "I said all of it."

"Too bad because I'm full." She wasn't the child he once knew, and she refused to let him treat her like one, although she almost gave in to his sexy, deep voice.

She got up from her seat and tried to push him out of the way so she could dump the leftovers in the trash, but the solid wall of muscle wouldn't budge. "Please move."

Benny stood in her way for a few more seconds, and she expected him to start arguing with her. His eyes scanned her face, and he must have seen the exhaustion which was taking over her body because he relaxed his stance and took the plate from her hands. The commanding tone was replaced by a softer one. "I put your bags in the spare bedroom. Why don't you get some sleep? Ian should have some information for us in the morning."

Her first attempt at a response disappeared with a huge yawn, and she covered her mouth. "Sorry. I hope so." S

he began to pivot toward the doorway but stopped and looked up at him, her eyes filling with tears that didn't fall. "I know me showing up out of the blue has shocked you, but thanks for helping me. I don't have anyone else to turn to."

Benny's gaze turned into something from their youth, which she never expected, but only for a split second before becoming indifferent once more. "No problem. It's what I do," he mumbled before turning away to take care of her plate, which was still in his hand. She hesitated, hoping he would say something more, but after a few moments, she sighed and left him alone.

KATERINA HAD GONE TO BED OVER FOUR HOURS AGO, BUT Boomer was still tossing and turning in his king-sized bed. As much as his body needed sleep, his brain wasn't cooperating. Throwing off the covers, he got up for the eighth or ninth time and walked on stealth-like feet to the bedroom door across the hall from his. He had left the light on in the guest bathroom in the hallway in case she needed it in the middle of the night. Easing the bedroom door open, he was able to observe her in the dark room without the light shining directly on her. She was sound asleep facing him.

He studied her for the first time with a critical eye. Tiny had been right. She did look exhausted. And thin. Too thin. Her light brown hair had highlights he hadn't noticed before, and he wished he could see her dark brown eyes again. Those eyes had haunted him for years. Her pouty pink lips made him yearn to kiss her awake, like Prince Charming and Snow White. He shook the ridiculous thought from his brain. Time and the military had changed him, and he was no longer worthy of the young woman she once was. He doubted he was worthy of the woman she'd become either—whoever she was.

Damn. She was more beautiful than he remembered, which was saying a lot. Although they were coming less and less frequently over the years, he still had dreams about her. About the one night she'd belonged to him and how incredible it had felt to kiss and touch her. He'd often debated the adage—was it better to have loved and lost or to never have loved at all? It was an argument he'd never settled in his mind.

Closing her door again, he headed out to his kitchen. Using the soft blue glow from his digital microwave clock to see, he located a bottle of Jameson Irish Whiskey on the bottom shelf of his pantry. He thought about taking a swig straight from the bottle, but one would lead to another and then another. Despite Tiny watching his six, he knew he had to keep his wits about him in case someone figured out where Kat was. So instead, he grabbed a rocks glass from a cabinet, poured two ounces into it, and returned the bottle to its perch.

He sat in the seat he'd been in when she'd asked, "You never married?" He'd kept his eyes on his meal, but through his eyelashes, he'd watched her try to analyze his one-word response. No way would he explain to her why he would never get married. There'd been a thirty-six-hour timespan twelve years ago when she was the only woman he'd wanted to spend his life with. After she'd "died," no other woman had ever captured his heart like she had. No other woman could hold a candle to his Kitten.

Damn it! He wasn't going there with his personal pet name for her. She was "Kat" or Katerina, which was as familiar as he wanted to get with her again. He understood she had no say in the matter about leaving him, thinking she was dead, but the anger and heartbreak had long ago been embedded into his psyche. There had been many a night he'd cursed her for leaving him, the universe for taking her, and himself for loving her.

The team would figure out who was after her and why, and when she was safe, Boomer would send her on her way to wherever she wanted to go. Because there was no way he was putting his heart on the line again. He wouldn't survive it this time when she realized the man he'd become.

He brought the glass to his lips and drank the brown liquor before he had more than a split second to compare the color to Kat's eyes. The alcohol burned its way to his stomach, and he forced himself to put the glass in the dishwasher and head back to his bed. He had no idea how long he lay there until sleep finally overtook him, and he dreamed of her —his Kitten.

CHAPTER FIVE

Boomer awoke to the smell of coffee, and he glanced at the alarm clock next to his bed. Oh-eight-thirty. He sat up before the events of the prior evening assaulted him, and he groaned. It hadn't been a dream. Kat was out in his kitchen, at this very moment, making coffee. Tossing his covers off, he got up, headed to the master bath, and took care of business. Then he grabbed a clean T-shirt and sweatpants from his dresser and put them on over the boxer briefs he'd slept in.

As he strode down the hallway, he noticed her bedroom door was shut, but it didn't register in his mind before he entered the kitchen and stopped short. *Fuck!* How the hell could he have forgotten he had plans this morning? Easily. The excuse must still be asleep down the hall. Well, at least it was only his father standing in his kitchen.

He had driven up from Sarasota to go four-wheeling with Boomer today. Whoever was now keeping watch outside the condo, Jake or Devon, wouldn't have stopped Rick Michaelson from entering. The man had the same training as their entire team with a few more years of experience, and was one of the few people outside of Trident Security he could trust with Katerina's life. "Hi, Pop."

His dad turned and stepped out of the way, allowing Boomer to shuffle forward and make his own cup of coffee. "Hey, you slept in late today. I take it we're not going four-wheeling. Want to tell me what's going on and why Reverend is watching your place?"

"Noticed him, huh?"

"Almost missed if you're worried about it. Just happened to recognize his truck. Now, why is he there?"

He wasn't worried that his father spotted Jake on surveillance. Like the rest of Boomer's team, there was little his father missed. Being vigilant had been drilled into him and the others during their time as Navy SEALs. The younger Michaelson shrugged as he grabbed a mug from the cabinet above his Keurig and prepped the machine before hitting start.

He turned around and leaned against the counter while crossing his arms and ankles. "Something happened, Pop, and I have no idea how to sugarcoat it, so I'm just going to say it."

Rick's eyes narrowed, but he waited for his son, who'd paused to weigh his words, to continue. "I had an appointment with a new client scheduled for last night at the office. Boss-man was with me. Pop . . . Katerina Maier walked in the door."

As Rick paled, his eyes grew wide, and he sat down in the closest chair, almost missing it and ending up on the floor. "Holy shit. How?"

Boomer grabbed his now-brewed mug of coffee and sat opposite the older man. "Two words—Witness Protection."

He filled his dad in on the story she'd told them. He'd just finished when the lady in question came into the kitchen and stopped when she spotted the familiar face she hadn't seen in twelve years.

Rick stood with his mouth open for a moment before he recovered. "Katerina . . . wow, it really is you. I mean, I knew Ben was telling me the truth, but it's like seeing a ghost."

Boomer watched as his dad did what he, himself, had yet to do. The older man opened his arms, and Kat walked right into them, letting him hug her. He couldn't hear what Rick was saying to her in a low soothing voice, but he saw her nod her head a few times in silence. She was wearing a T-shirt and pajama pants, and both were too big on her. He would have to make sure she put back on some of the weight she must have recently lost. With everything going on, it didn't surprise him, but one of the things a good Dom did was take care of his submissive's safety and well-being.

Fuck! He had to stop thinking like a Dom and just be the operative and former SEAL he'd trained to be. She wasn't his submissive. She was a woman from his past who needed his help. Nothing more. *Yeah, jackass. Keep telling yourself that.*

The embrace between the two lasted about a minute before they both stepped back. Kat blushed as she looked over at Boomer and then back to his dad. "Hi, Mr. Michaelson. You . . . uh, look great."

Obviously, knowing the woman wasn't sure what to say to him after all these years, Rick pulled out a chair for her. "I think you're old enough to call me Rick if you want. And you're a sight for sore eyes too. Let me get you a cup of coffee."

She nodded and took the seat he offered. "Thanks, Mr. Mi—I mean, Rick. With a little milk, if Benny has some, please."

He backed up, not taking his eyes off her until his butt hit the counter, and Boomer knew how he felt. It was as if they looked away, she would disappear. Finally, he turned to the coffee machine and prepared a mug for her. "So, where do we go from here? How do we keep Kat safe?"

Boomer took a deep breath and let it out. "Well, Ian called Keon to get us ID for her along with a death certificate." The ID they could've gotten from one of their contacts who was a master forger, but the certificate was a little harder because of the raised stamp authenticating it. Besides, they were better off having documents officially forged by the FBI. "He's also getting us the file on Volkov. We should be able to head to Norfolk tonight and be at the bank early tomorrow morning." He shrugged. "Where we go from there depends on what's in the box."

Handing Katerina her coffee with milk, Rick nodded his agreement. "I'll go with you."

"No, you won't."

Boomer's dad narrowed his eyes at him. "What do you mean 'no'? You can't do this alone. You need backup."

"And I'll have it, Pop. But I don't know how long we'll be, and your birthday is Friday. Mom would kill both of us if you missed it."

Boomer wouldn't tell his dad that his mom had made special plans for his birthday. She'd gotten tickets for an intimate concert starring Rick's favorite singer, Billy Joel. There were only one hundred tickets available, and she'd won hers through a local radio station two months ago. Since the event date was the same as his birthday, she'd decided to make it a surprise.

"Ian will probably send Jake with me. We've got it covered." Not wanting his dad to think he didn't need or trust him to help out, he added, "After Friday, if this isn't settled, you can cover my six if you want, but don't get Mom pissed at me again. She's still mad that I won't go out with her friend's niece."

Rick harrumphed but then smiled. "You made the right choice there, son. I've met Diane's niece, and she gives new meaning to the word . . . uh, never mind. You're just better off and leave it at that." Boomer and Kat chuckled. It was evident Rick had forgotten she was in the room for a moment. "As for not going with you, fine. As long as someone from the team has your six. And promise me, if you need me, you'll call no matter what."

"Of course. There's no one else I'd rather have covering my ass." Boomer's cell phone rang, so he stood and grabbed it from the counter. Glancing at the screen, he hit the call button. "Hey, Boss-man . . . uh-huh . . . okay. See you in thirty."

He hung up, looking at Rick and then Kat. "Ian's got info for us, so we're heading to Trident. You have about fifteen minutes for a quick shower if you want, and we'll grab some breakfast on the way."

Rick finished the last of his coffee and set the cup in the sink as Kat left the room to go shower. He patted Boomer on the back before walking toward the front door. "I'll run to the bagel place you all like and grab breakfast for everyone. This way, you don't have to stop. I'll meet you at the compound."

As he headed toward his own shower, Boomer glanced over his shoulder. "Thanks, Pop. Grab a few extras because I'm not sure how many of us will be there. See you in a few."

As Kat lathered the shampoo into her hair, she replayed the conversation she'd had with Benny the night before.

After she'd thanked him for helping her, his response had been, "No problem. It's what I do." It was close to what Tiny had said when she'd thanked the big man earlier.

Well, what did she expect Benny to say after all this time? She'd been "dead" to him for longer than the seven years she'd been in his life. He had gone on to live without her. Now, she was just a girl he used to know who needed to hire him to keep her safe and help her escape the mess she was in. Nothing more.

Rinsing her hair, she thought about how good he looked this morning after she'd recovered from the shock of seeing his dad again. He must have rolled out of bed a few minutes before she did. His dark brown hair was a little shaggy and sticking up in several places. His eyes were tired-looking, yet still, the sexiest ones she'd ever seen. Her dreams of him over the years hadn't done the man he was now justice. He was handsome as hell, with a body that would make a nun have dirty thoughts. She may still be a virgin, but it didn't mean she was naïve about sex. In this day and age, it wasn't possible. Sex was all over the TV and the internet. It was in the movies she saw and in the books and newspapers she read daily.

The thought of Benny and sex aroused her, and she mentally calculated how much time she had before they left the condo. Taking her bottle of body gel, she squirted a small amount into the washcloth she'd found under the bathroom sink, along with a few guest towels. She washed her entire body before sliding the lathered material between her legs. She gasped as it rasped over her clit and sent waves of desire through her. Dropping the cloth, she replaced it with her fingers and began to rub in earnest. She imagined her fingers were Benny's and how he would arouse her further before replacing them with his lips and tongue. The daydream sent her over the edge faster than she expected, and she bit her bottom lip to keep from yelling out her pleasure.

After she recovered, she picked up the washcloth again and wiped away the evidence of her masturbation. She pushed her wants and needs for Benny back into the furthest corner of her mind, shutting and locking the metaphorical door behind them. Now was not the time to think about him . . . about them . . . about how good she knew they would be together. Her life was in danger, and by him helping her, so was his. Sex and fantasies were out . . . logic and reality were in.

Damn.

When they walked out the condo front door a short while later, it was within the allotted time he'd given her. Waiting outside the door was a good-looking man who Ben introduced as Jake Donovan, a.k.a. Reverend, one of his teammates at Trident and in the SEALs. He was a few inches taller and older than Benny, but otherwise, he had a similar physique—broad, hard, and sinewy. His hair color was a shade somewhere between her own light brown and Benny's dark brown, and his eyes were covered by sunglasses which only enhanced his Hollywood good looks.

He smiled and shook her outstretched hand before turning around and leading the way to the parking lot, with Benny taking the position behind her. She realized they'd placed themselves to protect her like bodyguards would.

Well, that's what they are, you idiot. That's why you came here —for protection and nothing more. At least not yet.

Benny drove her back to the Trident compound with Jake following him in his own vehicle. As she sat in the passenger seat of his Dodge Charger in silence, her stomach growled, and her cheeks burned red when he chuckled at her.

"My dad's getting us breakfast, so we can go straight to Trident."

"Okay." She turned a bit in her seat to look at him without straining her neck. "If Ian has what we need, are we going to Norfolk?"

He checked his side and rearview mirrors, then changed lanes before answering her. "Most likely. I wish I could leave you here and run up there myself, but I'm not sure what safeguards your father might have left. I may not be able to do it without you since you're his next of kin."

His words impaled her like a sword. *"I wish I could leave you here . . ."*

Whatever he'd said after that was a jumbled mess. She knew she'd been hoping for the impossible. He didn't want to be near her. He'd rather do what needed to be done and kick her out of town when it was all over. When she didn't say anything more, he glanced over. She kept her eyes downcast and took a ragged breath.

"Kat, what's wrong?" She didn't answer. "Damn it, Kat, look at me. What's wrong?" A few seconds ticked by before he cursed. "Fuck!"

She flinched but refused to look at him. He slowed down and then stopped at a red traffic light. Reaching over, he tilted her chin up until her gaze met his. "Kat, I didn't mean whatever you think I meant. When I said I wanted to go up there alone, it was from a tactical standpoint. It would be safer for you to stay at the compound. I don't know what'll be waiting for us in Norfolk, and the last thing I want is you in a position of danger. That's all."

The driver behind Jake honked his horn, and they both looked to see the light had turned green again. Taking his foot off the brake, Benny accelerated and split his attention between her and the road. "Do you understand me?"

She nodded her head and adjusted her body so she was facing forward again. There was no way she would tell him his words had her thinking he wanted to get as far away from her as possible. She'd lost so many loved ones in her life, and she'd just reconnected with the only man she'd ever been in love with. Kat couldn't give him up again. Not yet, and hopefully, not ever.

She'd made a few friends in Portland, but she never knew if she and her dad would need to move again, so it was easier to keep those friendships to a minimum. Her closest friends were her boss of over seven years and his wife. Jeremy and Eva Pierce owned the canine training facility where Kat had found a career she was good at, which also afforded her some protection.

Kat's handler, Chris, and Jeremy had served in the army together, and the latter now trained dogs for law enforcement and private firms along with his retired police officer wife. When Kat had been greeted by Ian's dog yesterday, she'd immediately recognized the dog's training. While Beau hadn't been one of J&E International K9's dogs, the training was similar for the specialized dogs worldwide, and most of the U.S. dogs were trained in the German language.

Chris had never broken his non-disclosure oath about his safeguarding Kat and her father in the Witness Protection Program, but Jeremy wasn't stupid. He knew who his friend worked for, the U.S. Marshals, and could figure things out from there. But the afternoon Jeremy had agreed to see if the young woman had it in her to be a canine trainer, he knew she had the right stuff. While she was shy around people, when it came to dogs, she showed her alpha side, and the animals respected her as one of their pack leaders. At least when this was all over, she had a life to return to if things didn't work out with Benny.

They arrived back at the compound without saying another word to each other. Boomer got out of the car after he parked and went around to open Kat's door for her. But he was too late. She was standing outside the vehicle and closing her door. His eyes narrowed, but he left it alone. *Remember, ass-hat, she's not your submissive.* His dick would like to rectify that, but his head told him, "no."

At least she let him hold the door to the office open for her, and he followed her inside along with Jake. He introduced her to Colleen, their secretary, who'd just started her work day. The two women shook hands before he led her into the conference room where his life had changed a little more than fifteen hours ago. Ian and Devon were waiting for them, and neither one looked happy.

Boomer held out a seat for Kat. "Katerina, this is Ian's brother, Devon. He's the co-owner of Trident. Dev, this is Katerina."

She held out her hand to shake Devon's before taking the offered seat. "It's nice to meet you. Please call me Kat."

Devon took the seat across from her, with Jake sitting in the one next to him. "Kat it is. And it's nice to meet you too." He glanced at Boomer. "Everything all right last night?"

Boomer sighed as he dropped into the seat next to Kat. "Yeah. Just forgot about Pop coming by this morning. He was as shocked as I was. He's stopping for breakfast for everyone and should be here in a few minutes." His gaze flicked between the Sawyer brothers. "What's the scoop?"

Ian tossed him a few papers he'd printed from an email. Some were text, others were photos. "These are from Keon. Sergei 'The Wolf' Volkov was found murdered in an empty warehouse three weeks ago. Double tap and clean." Meaning he'd taken one bullet to the head and another to the heart. No bullet casings were found. "No suspects, but the guy had lots of enemies, so it could have been anybody. But tell me what you think."

Rick walked in as Boomer was studying the pictures of the crime scene photos. He looked at them over his son's shoulder after handing a bag of egg sandwiches to Jake to distribute. Boomer suddenly zeroed in on what Ian wanted him to see. "It was someone he knew, someone close to him. The warehouse is empty. If he was killed there, and it looks like he was, he was meeting someone. He wouldn't have gone there without at least one of his bodyguards."

Ian nodded. "Exactly what I was thinking. Keon, too. The FBI has the case because he's been on their watch list for years. Everyone they've interviewed in his inner circle has denied knowing what he was doing there. So, the questions keep mounting, but the big one is . . . if Volkov is dead, who the hell is after Kat? And why?"

As Rick took the seat next to Boomer, the five men turned their attention to the bewildered woman. "I have no idea. All I know is what I've told you. My father was dying and high on morphine, so I only have his mumblings and hearsay from twelve years ago."

Boomer's mind was spinning with details, none of which added up. "What did Keon say about Mr. Maier's involvement from back then?"

Ian shook his head as he accepted the wrapped sandwich sliding across the table at him. He left it unopened. "Not much more than what Kat told us. Maier got himself in too deep to cut and run, and he ended up with information he should have never seen. Information that resulted in a price on his head."

"So, we head to the bank in Norfolk." Boomer couldn't think of anything else that would help them at this point.

"Yup. Jake, I want you to go with them and keep us updated every four hours. CC will be at the hanger at eleven-hundred to fly you all up there."

Conrad Chapman, otherwise known as CC, was a retired Air Force pilot Trident contracted to fly their jet wherever they needed to go. The small private airport they used was about twenty minutes from the compound. Ian directed his next statement to Boomer and Kat. "Keon will arrange for someone to meet you with ID and the death certificate. Kat is to stay hidden as much as possible. I don't want the chance of someone from her past recognizing her."

She frowned. "I doubt anyone would recognize me from twelve years ago, but you never know. I can get a wig or dye my hair if you want."

Before Ian answered her, Boomer spoke up. "I can grab a wig from the club."

He mentally kicked himself for mentioning The Covenant. The first building in the compound gave no indi-cation it was a BDSM club. There was a small store on the top floor, and it specialized in fetish wear and toys. Blonde wigs were popular, and they had several in stock, but he'd have to run over there without Kat. There was no way he was letting her inside the club. He'd never been ashamed of his lifestyle, but at this moment, he couldn't bring himself to tell her about it. He thought back to the shy, little virgin she'd been twelve years ago and figured she would run to the hills if she knew about his kinks. Thankfully, she didn't seem to notice his flub, and Jake sensed his predicament.

"I'll grab one before we go."

Boomer nodded his thanks, then said to the room in general, "Anything else?"

Ian and Devon looked at each other for confirmation, and both shook their heads. Ian stood and picked up his egg sandwich. "At the moment, no. Brody and Marco are due back this afternoon. I'll get Egghead on his computers to search for everything he can find on all the players in this." Brody "Egghead" Evans was their computer and tech specialist and a world-class hacker of the first degree. And Marco "Polo" DeAngelis was their communications specialist and backup helicopter pilot. He was also Brody's occasional ménage partner. "When you get to Norfolk, let me know where you're staying, so I can have Keon's man meet you with the paperwork."

After Boomer acknowledged his order, Ian left the room as the others stood. Jake pointed to Rick. "Do you mind following them back to Boomer's condo? I need to swing by my place to grab my go-to bag. It's usually in my truck, but I was cleaning it out yesterday and didn't have a chance to put it back together."

"No problem at all," the older man answered.

They all picked up their unopened egg sandwiches and headed for the door. They could eat on the way to grab their gear. As they passed Colleen's desk, the secretary handed Boomer a piece of pink paper. She had taken a phone message for him while they were in their meeting. He glanced at the message before folding the paper twice and sticking it in his back pocket. He'd take care of it later.

As they headed back to his condo, with his father following him this time, Boomer turned his head toward Kat when he noticed she was rubbing her temples. "You all right?"

She winced. "It's a headache. I've been getting them about twice a month for the last few years. I take over-the-counter migraine meds, and they help, but I ran out of them. Can we stop at a pharmacy really quick?"

"Yeah. There's one up ahead." He grabbed his phone and dialed his father's cell. Using the car's Blue-tooth feature, he told Rick their plan to stop.

Pulling into a Walgreens, he waited for his dad to park next to him, get out, and approach the Dodge's passenger door before exiting the car. Rick opened Kat's door and extended his hand to assist her from the vehicle. When they met Boomer on the walkway between the car and the building, Kat swayed. Boomer grabbed her around the waist before she could fall and eyed her in alarm. "Kat? You all right? Are you going to pass out?"

Kat rested her arms on his broad shoulders and steadied. Boomer's body reacted immediately to her close proximity, and he inwardly cursed, fighting the urge to pull her flush against him.

"Uh, no, I'm okay. Just got a little light-headed. It happens when I get a migraine."

After ensuring she had her balance again, he forced himself to step back but kept one hand at the small of her back as he escorted her into the store. Rick remained three steps behind them, his head swiveling from side to side, always on the lookout for danger. It was highly unlikely the people after Kat were lying in wait at a Florida Walgreens on the off chance she'd stop there, but one never knew.

They headed down the OTC medicine aisle, and Kat quickly found the brand she used for her headaches. Before they could reverse their direction, a pretty brunette came around the far corner of the aisle, and her face lit up as she spotted Boomer.

"Hi, M—Ben."

Boomer winced at the woman's cheerful voice and near slip of his title of Master. "Hi, Cassandra."

She approached and stopped a little too close for comfort. Normally, Boomer wouldn't have minded running into the petite submissive he'd topped a few times, but with Kat at his side, he was a little uncomfortable.

"We missed you at the club last weekend."

He scratched the top of his head. "Uh, yeah. I was working the whole weekend."

Cassandra's eyes flashed to Kat, who had taken a step closer to him and looked as if she was waiting for Boomer to introduce them. "Hi. I'm Cassandra."

Kat shook the woman's outstretched hand. "I'm Kat."

"Nice to meet you." Her eyes returned to Boomer's face. "Will you be there tomorrow night?"

Boomer gently grabbed Kat's arm and shook his head. Cassandra was a sweet submissive who waitressed at The Covenant, and he knew she wouldn't step on another woman's toes intentionally. She also wouldn't publicize what kind of club The Covenant was. "Uh, no, I don't think so. Maybe over the weekend, but I'm not sure."

Cassandra's gaze flicked to the possessive hand on the other woman's arm, and she took a step back, her eyes full of apology to Boomer. She must've realized she'd almost said too much. "Okay. If not, I'll see you some other time. Kat, it was nice to meet you. Have a nice day."

Without waiting for a response from either of them, she spun around and waved goodbye over her shoulder.

Boomer's hand gripped Kat's arm a little tighter as he turned her toward the cashiers. His father had been a few steps behind them and gave him a "you're so fucked" smile before leading the way. Boomer wasn't sure what that was all about. He and Cassandra were friends. Friends who occasionally fucked during a scene at a private BDSM club. What was wrong with that?

He glanced at Kat, who had a curious expression on her face. He knew she wanted to ask him about Cassandra. Yup, his father was right—he was so fucked.

CHAPTER SIX

They had about another half hour before they landed in a small airport outside of Norfolk, Virginia. Boomer hadn't been up this way in over a year, but his last trip had been a long weekend of catching up with people he hadn't seen in a while. Another one of his old high school friends had taken the plunge and gotten married. They were dropping like flies these past few years. His mind drifted to Alex, and he wondered, if his friend had still been alive, would he have found some woman and put a ring on her finger? He doubted it. Alex had been worse than he'd been back in the day. His friend had a new hook-up almost every weekend, going through girls as if trying to win a new Guinness world record. At least Boomer had dated several girls for a few weeks before moving on.

But all that changed after his Kitten had "died." He'd only fallen in love once in his life, and look how it'd ended. She was gone less than thirty-six hours after he professed his love. Yeah, it hadn't been her fault, but it still hurt like hell.

He glanced over to where she was curled up on the plane's couch, reading a book since her migraine had faded

Damn, she was still the prettiest woman he'd ever met despite her recent weight loss. She'd passed on the egg sandwich, letting him have it instead because she couldn't eat with the headache. He had Jake stop for a turkey and cheese sandwich for her to eat on the plane and had been happy to see her finishing it off about fifteen minutes ago.

In the recliner next to him, Jake was taking a power nap. His teammate had been up half the night trying to find his missing informant. He'd finally found the little punk in a local crack house, and Jake was pissed. The kid had been clean for six months before this setback. Jake dragged his ass out of there and into a hospital. The next stop was an agreed-upon rehab facility. Boomer had never met the informant, but if the former SEAL was putting this much work into trying to save him from the life of a homeless junkie, then there had to be something there which impressed him. Boomer hoped the kid was worth the effort.

He got up and sat down on the couch next to Kat. Against his better judgment, he grabbed her ankles and pulled her feet into his lap. She'd removed her slip-on flats earlier, and without conscious thought, he rubbed the arch of her right foot. As he dug his thumbs deep into the tissue, she closed her eyes and groaned. The sound went straight to his groin.

"God, that feels so good. Please don't stop."

His mouth twitched, and he wished he was doing other things to her, which gave him the same response. "So, tell me about Portland."

Her eyes opened just enough for her to see him through the slits. "What do you want to know?"

"I don't know. Everything? Anything? Do you have a job there? Friends?" *Boyfriends?* He was torn between wanting and not wanting to know the answer to that.

She shrugged. "Only a few close friends, but I have a great

job which I love. When we first ended up there, our handler, Chris, sent me to see an old army buddy of his. Jeremy Pierce and his wife Eva own a canine training facility for protection and law enforcement. We clicked immediately, and he taught me how to train the dogs. I've been working for him ever since. I train them in drug and explosives detection, as well as passive and aggressive tracking, depending on the dog and the agency. Passive tracking is for missing persons, and aggressive is for suspects."

"What differs?"

Groaning, she bit her lip when he dug into a particular spot in her arch. "Passive tracking, the dog will lead its handler right up to the person. When you're tracking a possibly armed suspect, you want some warning before he's suddenly right in front of you.

"There's a funny story about one of our graduates. His dog was a passive tracker and drug detector, but a few months ago, they had a suspect disappear into the woods, and they didn't have an aggressive tracker available. So, they put two officers, with their guns at the ready, on either side of the team because the handler's eyes had to be on the dog, looking for tells. This way, if the suspect suddenly appeared, they were covered.

"Anyway, they were tracking for about ten minutes when the dog suddenly sat down in the middle of nowhere. The handler tried to get him back on track, but the dog wouldn't budge. It took a few moments, but they realized the dog was sitting on a pile of leaves, and one of them spotted the heel of a sneaker. The suspect had buried himself under a pile of leaves, hoping they'd walk right by him, and the darn dog was sitting on his back." They both started laughing. "The handler kicks the guy's leg and says, 'Don't move.' The suspect answers, 'Wasn't planning on it.'"

Laughing harder, Boomer couldn't help but be impressed. It was obvious she loved her job. "Wow. That's awesome. Beau went through a training place like that in Florida. He was about six weeks old when Ian found him at the compound. His mother was a stray who'd just died, so Ian took him in."

"I noticed his training," she told him while nodding.

"Do they know where you are? Your bosses? I mean, do you still have a job after we find who's after you?" Part of him wanted her to say no, but they would both be better off if she said yes.

She glanced out the window of the plane. "Yes. Sort of. I told them I had a family emergency." At his raised eyebrow, she shrugged. "It was all I could think of at the time. Anyway, even though no one ever came out and told Jeremy I was in witness protection, he's very astute, and I'm sure he figured it out. He just told me to keep in touch and to call him if I needed anything. I should call him later to let him know I'm still alive."

"Good idea. Use your pre-paid phone since they're very hard to trace. Then we'll throw it away and get a new one. Ask him if anyone suspicious has been snooping around asking about you."

Kat nodded and tapped his hand with her left foot. It was a blatant hint to give it the same treatment he gave the other one. He chuckled and swapped them. "Better?"

"Yes, much." She groaned as he worked his thumbs deeper. "I can't remember the last time I had a foot massage. I used to get them all the time when I treated myself to pedicures, but it's been a while."

He was glad it was a professional service where she had gotten the massages and not from a boyfriend. A pang of jealousy at her dating some guy hit him in the gut, and he forced himself not to question her about other men. Who she dated was none of his business.

Glancing down at her lap, he eyed the book she'd been reading, and . . . *oh, fuck* . . . it was *Leather & Lace*, by Kristen Anders, soon-to-be Kristen Sawyer, Devon's wife. While Boomer hadn't read the whole thing, he'd flipped through and read the steamy sex scenes after Devon mentioned how hot they were. It was fucking hot porn in written format, plain and simple. It also involved BDSM, and he was shocked Kat was reading it. Did she just like reading about the lifestyle, or was she into it? And if she wasn't, would she be interested in trying it? Did she fantasize about a man doing to her the things Master Xavier did to his submissive in the book?

He shifted uncomfortably and shoved his thoughts back where they belonged—in the gutter. She was a job and an old friend, nothing more.

You might as well give up trying to convince yourself, buddy, because it's not working.

"Prepare for landing," CC announced over the intercom, and Jake's eyes flew open. That was the thing about being in special ops—you got used to catnaps and waking up completely refreshed.

Boomer swung Kat's feet to the ground so she could sit up and put her seatbelt on. He then strapped his own around his waist. They would be on the ground and in their waiting car within fifteen minutes. After he had the plane refueled, CC would get a room at the closest motel for the night, so he would be nearby if they needed him. Meanwhile, Boomer, Kat, and Jake would head into the Norfolk residential area where the two childhood friends used to live. There was a Best Western near the bank they needed. From what Boomer had been able to access online, it was the ideal motel for them. There were plenty of escape routes if things went south.

Next to him, Kat visibly shuddered.

"You okay?"

She gave him a tiny smile. "Yeah, I think so. It just hit me. I haven't been here since I was seventeen with a bright and happy future ahead of me."

Boomer reached over and squeezed her hand because he couldn't think of anything to say which didn't sound cliché. He just hoped when this was all over, she did have a happy life in her future, even if it wasn't with him.

As JAKE LET HIMSELF INTO THE ADJOINING ROOM TO THE LEFT, Kat followed Boomer into their motel room. He tossed his duffel bag on the bed closest to the door and gestured for her to take the other one. It wasn't even one in the afternoon yet, and she wanted nothing more than to crawl under the covers and take a nap.

He saw the longing look on her face before he turned to unlock the go-between door connecting the two rooms. "Take a nap if you want. Jake and I will be next door working on a few things for tomorrow."

"Okay." Kat pulled off the blonde wig she'd donned before getting off the plane and scratched her itchy scalp. Reaching to pull the bedspread down, she kicked off her shoes at the same time. "Don't let me sleep past three, please. Otherwise, I'll be up all night."

"Sure." Boomer watched as she climbed into the bed, fully clothed. She shifted a few times, trying to find a comfortable position, and finally settled on her side facing away from him. Her long brown tresses fanned across the pillow, and his hands ached to run his fingers through the soft strands. The longer he was around her, the more his old feelings for her pounded in his chest. But there were new feelings there too. Feelings he didn't know what the fuck he was going to do about.

Sighing, he walked into the other room and left the door ajar in case she needed him. Jake was exiting his bathroom and drying his hands on a towel. He raised an eyebrow at seeing Boomer alone.

"She's lying down for a while."

"Ah." They both sat down at the table for two, and Jake opened a folder with all the pertinent information they had so far. "So . . . you want to talk about work or what it's like to have an old girlfriend come back from the dead?"

Boomer knew his friend was being sympathetic despite how his words sounded. He ran a hand through his hair and glanced at the partially opened door behind him before returning his attention to Jake. "How do you know she was a girlfriend?"

"Ian keeps me around for my sniper skills and powers of observation. If she wasn't your girlfriend, there was a time you wished she was."

He leaned forward, resting his elbows on the table and keeping his voice low so she wouldn't hear him. It'd been a long time since he'd told anyone about his Kitten. "She was my best friend's sister and a year behind us in school. I never thought of her as anything more than a good friend until I took her to my senior prom. One minute she was my friend. And the next minute, I wanted something more. Hit me from out of the blue, you know?"

Jake nodded but didn't say a word.

"The night of my going-away party, a week before basic training, I found out she felt the same way. I asked her to be my girl and to wait for me. She agreed, and two days later . . . her entire family was gone."

"From what Ian told me, she didn't have a choice."

Boomer leaped from his chair in frustration and began pacing but kept his voice low. "Damn it, I know it wasn't her fault. But too much time has gone by. We don't even fucking know each other anymore. I'm not the same eighteen-year-old kid without a care in the world. I've seen and done shit she could never imagine. I've changed, and I doubt she'll like the guy I've become."

Crossing his arms, Jake narrowed his eyes at his teammate. "Close the door."

"What?"

"Close the damn door and sit the fuck down for a minute." After Boomer eased the door shut and plopped back down in his seat, the harshness ebbed from his friend's voice. "I'm a little confused here, Baby Boomer. Are you talking about the Navy and the shit we've done, or are you talking about the club and the lifestyle?

"Both, I guess," he mumbled, staring at the floor.

"Well, the SEAL shit is easy. You've served your country proud and followed orders like the good frog you are. Yes, you've killed more people than anyone will ever know about, but what it boils down to is you killed because you had to. You're not a murderer. You saved lives—civilians,' your teammates,' and your own. There's nothing wrong with anything you've done in the name of Uncle Sam and apple pie. I don't think your girl in there would have any problem with that, especially since you can't tell her most of it."

Boomer shrugged and kept his eyes downcast.

"Now, about the lifestyle. You're not the first Dom to question himself, and you won't be the last. The point is . . . which is more important to you? Can you love her without topping her? Or do you need it like the air you breathe? You said before you don't know each other anymore . . . maybe this is your chance to get to know her again. Maybe she's changed too. Maybe she wants to be topped, did you ever think about that?" He paused a moment to let the idea sink into the other man's head. "Now, stop being an ass, and let's get your girl out of trouble, all right? Think about fucking her after this is all over."

Boomer snorted, then grinned. "You're a prick, Reverend."

"Hey, I tell it like it is. You want sensitive, call Polo."

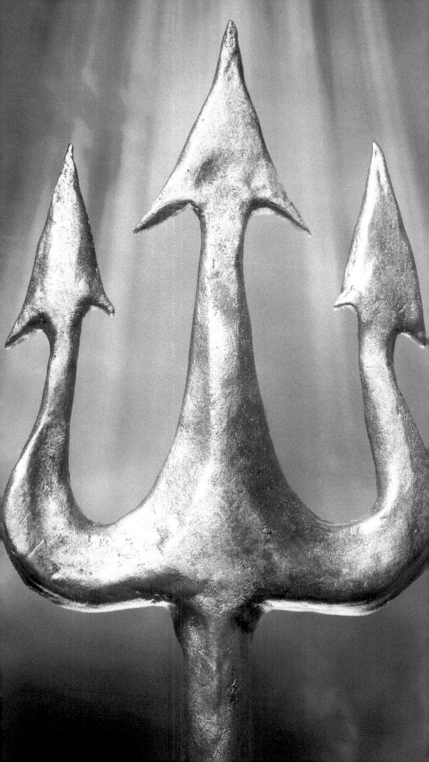

CHAPTER SEVEN

As he slipped back into his shared room, Boomer quietly shut the door behind him but kept it unlocked. Kat was still sleeping, and he didn't need to wake her yet. Jake and he had spent about thirty minutes going over what they knew and what they needed to find out. They'd called Ian to let him know where they were staying, so he could forward the information to Keon. The paperwork they needed for the bank would arrive sometime after eighteen hundred this evening.

Jake was heading out in a few minutes to scout the area around the motel and also the bank, which was three blocks away. In the meantime, Boomer was left alone to watch over Kat. He double-checked the front door locks and peeked out the window through the thin gap of the closed curtains. Nothing seemed out of the ordinary.

Spinning around one of the straight-back chairs at the table, he straddled it and sat. Kat was now lying on her other side, facing him, and his eyes roamed over her features. Her cheeks, pert nose, and soft, full lips helped form a face that could grace a magazine cover when combined with the beautiful eyes he would recognize anywhere. The sheet had shifted down to her waist, leaving her upper torso exposed. His mouth watered as he stared at the lush cleavage peeking out from under her V-neck shirt. Damn, he wanted her more now than he had as a teenager. Maybe Jake was right. Maybe the universe had sent her back to him for a reason.

Being a Dom was a major part of his life. He'd found the lifestyle he loved before he was assigned to Team Four and met Ian and the rest of his current teammates. One of his buddies from basic training had brought him to his first club after they'd been stationed together in San Diego. He spent two years there until he was accepted into the SEALs Bud/s training program. After graduating with his trident, he was assigned to Team Four, which was his father's old team in Virginia. He'd been happy to learn several of his new team-mates also participated in the lifestyle and joined the club they all frequented.

Kat stirred and moaned but stayed asleep. The sounds coming from her mouth had him growing hard, and he adjusted himself in his jeans. What would she do if he woke her by nuzzling her ear . . . her neck . . . her breasts? Would she push his hand away as he cupped her mound and flexed his fingertips into her core through her pants? Would she allow him to undress, restrain, eat, and fuck her? Would she scream when she came for him? Would she beg for more? Would she . . .

Fuck, he needed a cold shower. But that would leave her vulnerable. He'd have to find another way to tame his raging hard-on until Jake returned to keep watch. Grabbing a *Men's Fitness* magazine from his duffel, he moved to his bed and sat with a pillow between his back and the wall while crossing his ankles. He covered his erection with another pillow and flipped through the pages until he found an interesting article to read.

A few minutes later, he caught movement out of the corner of his eye and turned his head to find Kat staring at him. Her sleepy expression made him smile. "Feel better?"

She stretched her arms and back, and he bit his tongue as the actions thrust her chest toward him. "Yeah, I needed that."

Snorting, he tore his eyes away from her breasts and focused on the magazine in front of him. But he couldn't concentrate on any words at the moment "I'm sure you did. Jake went to check a few things out. Are you hungry? I'll have him pick up a pizza or something on his way back."

Throwing the sheets off her hips and legs, she stood and walked toward the bathroom. "I don't know what it is about being around you guys, but I'm hungrier now than I've been in months. Pizza sounds good, and maybe a salad?"

". . . I'm hungrier now than I've been in months."

Baby, you have no idea . . . I haven't been this hungry in years. And I'm not hungry for food.

"Yeah, sure, I'll let him know."

"I'm going to grab a quick shower to wake up."

"Mm-hmm. 'Kay."

The door closed behind her, and Boomer clutched the pillow in his lap, pumping his hips a few times in frustration. It'd taken everything in him not to reach out, pull her down on top of him, and ravage her. Now all he had to do was not think about her getting undressed and lathering her naked body.

Fuck—easier said than done.

When Jake got back and took over the watch, Boomer would jump into the shower and give himself some relief.

Picking up his phone, he typed a quick text to his teammate and then tossed it on back on the nightstand.

The bathroom door opened a few inches, and Kat stuck her head out. "Benny, I should've brought my bag in with me. Can you hand it to me, please?"

Shit, was she kidding?

If he walked over to her, there would be no way she would miss his rigid shaft bulging through his jeans. And why couldn't she come out and get it herself? A light bulb went off in his head . . . she'd started getting undressed. *Ah, hell.* Now he was hard and throbbing.

She was patiently staring at him. *Fuck!* He didn't have much choice. Biting his lip, he threw caution to the wind, along with the pillow, and stood. He grabbed her bag and strode over to the bathroom door, hoping she wouldn't look at his crotch. And, of course, the moment he had the thought, her eyes flickered downward, and her cheeks bloomed as she spotted his package.

Boomer's eyes traveled up her bare arm as she reached out for the bag. There was nothing but pure ivory skin on her shoulder, and he caught a peek of the white towel she used to cover herself. Before he could say or do anything, she shyly looked away and closed the door with a muttered thanks. Bracing his arms on the door jamb, he let his head drop forward. A few seconds passed before he realized he hadn't heard the lock engage.

Was that an invitation?

He reached for the doorknob and hesitated. If he were wrong, he'd screw up everything. He still didn't know if she had a boyfriend back in Portland, which was the first thing he needed to address. Sighing, he left the doorknob alone and ran his hand through his hair instead.

First things first, ass-hat. Get her out of danger, then you can start thinking with your dick again.

Plopping back down on his bed, he grabbed his phone again when a text message chimed. It was from Georgia Branneth.

> **GEORGIA**
>
> Hi, Master Ben. I was hoping we could negotiate a scene tonight. Please let me know. g.

Boomer stared at the message. He'd hooked up with the submissive several times over the past few months but had made it clear what they had together stayed at the club, and she was good with it. The short, raven-haired cutie was a recently divorced high-school teacher and had no desire to jump into another relationship. She was sweet, fun, and an incredible fuck. In addition to teaching, she was also a gymnastics coach and was extremely limber, which made for interesting sexual acrobatics. And less than twenty-four hours ago, he would've been fantasizing about some new positions. But now, in his brain, Kat had replaced the women in every one of his fantasies. Shit, he was a goner. And now he had to find a way back into her heart because he didn't think either one of them would settle for anything less.

> Sorry g. Out of town.

> **GEORGIA**
>
> :(K. Next time.

Boomer sighed. There might not be a next time, but he wouldn't tell the sub that in a text. And he definitely wouldn't say anything until he was sure Kat was single and on the same page as him. The room was silent, and all he could hear was the shower running. *Damn it*. He would never get rid of his erection if he kept thinking about Kat lathering herself under the spray of warm water. Grabbing the TV remote, he hit the power and then the volume buttons.

By the time Kat opened the door and exited the bathroom, he had his cock back under control, and he willed it to stay that way. She'd changed into a pair of gray sweatpants and a black T-shirt with the logo for *J&E International K9* over her left breast. Her feet were bare, and he wondered if she would be opposed to another foot massage. His cock twitched, and he shoved the thought from his brain. If Jake didn't get here soon, Boomer would have a serious case of blue balls. For fuck's sake, he couldn't even look at her feet without getting aroused. How screwed up was that?

He heard two, then three knocks on Jake's door before it swung open, and his teammate walked into the other room. Striding through the go-between door, he carried in a large pizza box and several bags. *Thank God.*

Boomer jumped up, grabbed his duffel, and headed to the bathroom. He passed a curious-looking Kat. "Start without me. I'm taking a quick shower."

"Okay. But you better hurry. Otherwise, I might eat yours."

Boomer shut the door a little harder than he should have.

"Okay . . . I might eat yours."

His mind was racing. Jesus H. Christ, ass-hat. Get your fucking mind out of the gutter. Not everything out of her mouth is an innuendo. Get in the shower, fire off your rifle, and keep it under control.

He turned on the shower and took a deep breath. *Fuck!* The room smelled of her body soap. This was getting so out of hand. Stripping fast, he climbed into the tub and grabbed the courtesy bar of soap. Tearing the paper off, he got it wet and lathered up. One hand against the wall, the other around his aching cock, he closed his eyes and groaned softly. He dragged his fist down to the root and back up to the head. Up and over, down and back up again. His hips began to pump as Boomer imagined Kat on her knees, sucking and licking him. Her lips would be soft and plump, her mouth warm and inviting. He'd grasp her hair and guide her in taking him deeper and deeper until he hit the back of her throat.

Take it, Kitten. Lick me like I'm a bowl of cream. He tightened his fist and picked up the pace. *Yeah, baby, suck it hard. I'm going to come down your throat, and you'll swallow every drop. Are you ready, Kitten?*

"Ah, fuck," he hissed as he shot his jizz into the shower spray, then yanked on his cock until there was nothing left. Light-headed, he leaned heavily on his other hand against the wall and tried to catch his breath.

Yup, he and Kat needed to have a talk because he wanted her more than ever.

KAT FLIPPED BACK AND FORTH FROM ONE SIDE TO THE OTHER, sleep eluding her for several reasons. She was in a strange room and bed, and the walls were paper-thin, so she heard every noise outside their room in the parking lot. But Benny sleeping on the other bed, and her body hyper-aware of the fact, were the main reasons she was wide awake at two a.m.

She flopped back over to her left side and stared at the beautiful man lying a few feet away. She could see him thanks to the light from the motel sign breaching the curtains' edges. Sometime in the last hour, he'd kicked his covers off. While he was wearing a pair of sweatpants, his torso was bared for her viewing pleasure. And what a plea-

75

sure it was. His shoulders, chest, and abs were sculpted to perfection, and she longed to touch each valley and peak. With her hands. With her tongue.

Moisture pooled between her legs, and she squeezed her thighs together. Over the years, she'd only had a few dates. She tried to have a normal life, but the whole time she always kept one eye looking over her shoulder, ready to run at a moment's notice. And most of those dates had never panned out. The closest she'd ever come to having a boyfriend was about two years ago.

Tim Hartman was a local police officer who'd gotten a new canine partner. He'd flirted with Kat during his training time at the facility where she worked, and she was flattered. He was a good-looking man, two years older than her, and he made her laugh, which wasn't something she did often. She had too much sorrow in her life, too much stress. They had dated for six weeks, but every time she tried to relax during intimate moments, she couldn't. He'd been understanding at first, but after several weeks of not advancing past kissing and petting, he'd gotten frustrated and then lost interest.

On the other bed, Benny took a gasping breath and began to twitch and moan. Flailing his limbs, his breathing increased as Kat sat up. What was he dreaming of? Whatever it was, it wasn't good. When he let out a pain-filled cry, she threw off her covers and leaped to his side. If she didn't wake him soon, Jake would hear him and think they were in trouble.

Kat sat down on the thin space between him and the edge of the bed, shaking his shoulders. "Benny. Ben, wake up." He groaned louder and thrashed his legs. She tried harder. "Benny, please wake up."

BOOMER LUNGED INTO A SITTING POSITION AND GRABBED HIS left leg. The sudden movement almost sent Kat flying onto the floor, and she clutched his arm to prevent it. He was panting and disoriented for a moment before the present came rushing back to him. His arm went around her waist to keep her from falling. "Holy shit, Kat, are you okay? What happened? I didn't hurt you, did I?"

"N-no, you didn't, no. Are you okay? You were moaning and stuff."

Running his other hand through his hair, he felt the dampness on his forehead. He was sweating like a pig--*damn it*. The frequency of his nightmares had been easing off these past few months, but every once in a while, they reared their ugly heads. He could still hear the roar of the RPG as it hit the truck he'd just jumped out of, the screams of the injured, and the ringing in his ears, which had taken days to disappear. The image of his shin bone sticking out of his leg still made him nauseous to think about. But he was alive . . . and still had all his limbs attached. Some of the other SEALs and Marines, who'd been there when they'd come under attack, hadn't been as lucky.

As he concentrated on getting his breathing back to normal, he downplayed the nightmare to Kat, trying to ease the worried expression on her face. "Yeah. Just some flash-backs to when I got hurt. I guess it's a good thing they only come when I'm sleeping. Some guys I served with get them while they're awake."

"Stay here a sec." She jumped up and disappeared into the bathroom. Boomer heard the water running, and then she returned with a wet washcloth. He was shocked when she sat beside him again and wiped the sweat from his face, neck, and shoulders. His muscles froze, and as cool as the cloth felt against his sizzling skin, he wished there was nothing between her hand and his flesh.

Goosebumps popped up everywhere, and his dick twitched. Swallowing hard, he watched her face as her gaze followed the cloth gliding down his arms. He couldn't stand it anymore. He had to touch her. Kiss her. Own her. He'd deal with the fallout later.

Reaching up, he cupped her chin, and she started, her eyes flashing up to his in surprise. He was in awe of her, and his voice came out as a raspy whisper. "You're still the most beautiful woman I've ever known, Kitten."

Her jaw dropped at his statement, and he took advantage of it. Rubbing his thumb across her bottom lip, he inched his head forward. He gave her time to back away. But when a small gasp escaped her, and her breathing increased, all the reasons why this was a bad idea flew from his mind. Drawing her closer, he tilted his head and replaced his thumb with his mouth.

Oh, dear God in heaven!

He'd dreamed of this moment, a moment he'd been certain would never happen again. She tasted like wine, roses, sunshine, and everything else poets compared women to.

Boomer leaned back and pulled her with him until she was draped across his bare torso. Holding her head in place, he plunged his tongue into her mouth, tasting and savoring. His other hand skimmed down the T-shirt she'd worn to bed and clutched her ass cheek through her cotton shorts. He shifted and ground his hard shaft against her mound, causing her to moan and shiver. Mouths melded, teeth clashed, and tongues dueled as she buried her hands in his hair.

Flipping her on her back, Boomer followed, never taking

his mouth from hers. His hands were everywhere at once. Her hair, breasts, waist, and hips. Skin, he needed to feel skin. Grabbing the hem of her shirt, he began to tug it upward and felt her stiffen. What the fuck? She wanted him to stop? Fuck, she did have a boyfriend, didn't she?

He ripped his mouth from hers and sat up. Trying to get his breathing and cock under control, he stood and paced the room while running his fingers through his tousled hair. "Shit, Kat. I'm sorry. I shouldn't have . . . I mean . . . you must have a boyfriend, right?"

"No."

Boomer screeched to a halt and gaped at her. "No?"

Swallowing hard, Kat shook her head. "No. I don't have a boyfriend."

No? Then why did she freeze when he tried to take things further? Because you haven't seen each other in twelve years, you ass-hat. You've only known she was still alive for about thirty-six hours, and you're ready to rip her clothes off. She deserves better than that.

"Oh." He ran a hand down his face. "Well, I'm still sorry. I shouldn't have jumped you like that. We should . . ." He cleared his suddenly dry throat. "We should get back to sleep. We've got to get up in a few hours because I want to be at the bank when they open."

KAT BIT HER LIP AND NODDED BEFORE MOVING BACK TO HER own bed. She watched as Ben quickly ran to the bathroom before returning and lying down again. His eyes avoided her, and he shifted onto his left side, facing away from her. She sighed inwardly.

Her heart was still pounding, her blood still boiling with

arousal. The dampness and tingling between her legs proved she hadn't wanted him to stop. She should have told him she'd never . . . but she hadn't been able to. He'd felt and tasted so good. His body, his touch, was what her own had craved for the past twelve years. A few more minutes. She'd wanted a few more minutes in his arms. For the first time since she'd kissed him as a teenager, she wanted more. She wanted him. All of him. A few more . . .

He was right—they needed sleep, not . . . not what they were just doing. But damn, she hadn't wanted to stop. Maybe when this was all over, if she was still alive, they could pick up where they left off. Turning on her side, she closed her eyes, but it was a long time before sleep overtook her again.

CHAPTER EIGHT

"You see anything, Reverend?" Boomer spoke into his cell phone. It was ten after eight in the morning, and Jake had been across the street for the past hour, scouting the area.

"Nothing out of the ordinary. No one lingering except a bum in the alley over this way. I checked, and he's sleeping off a bender. You're good to go."

"'Kay. I'm putting my phone on vibrate if you need me." He disconnected the call and scanned the bank's parking lot one more time before getting out of the rental they were using. On full alert, his head swiveled as he walked around to the passenger door and opened it for Kat. He hurried her across the lot and into the large brick building which housed the Wells Fargo Bank. There were a few occupants, but no one paid them any attention as they strode past the tellers and approached the only desk of three which didn't have a rep already assisting a customer.

The man stood and gestured for them to take the seats across the desk from him. "Good morning, my name is Brad. How may I help you today?"

"My friend's father passed away, and we found out afterward that he had a deposit box here," Boomer told him as they all sat down. It was a small lie since they weren't positive this was where Mr. Maier had opened the account. "The number on the key is 522, and we have his death certificate."

"Okay, I'll need a proper form of ID, and then I'll look up the account to see if there are any restrictions on it."

Kat handed the man the certificate and Florida ID, which an FBI agent had dropped off last night. It was the first time in twelve years she had a driver's license in her birth name. The picture was one Ian had snapped two nights ago at the office and then emailed to his contact in the federal agency. Since she hadn't been wearing her wig in the photo, they'd left it in the car. Boomer had been nervous about it, but they didn't want to make anyone in the bank suspicious.

Her knee began to bounce as the banker studied the document, then began tapping away on his computer. Boomer reached over and placed his hand on her thigh, stilling her nervous movement. The contact sent tingles and heat up his arm, and a quick glance at her face told him she also felt the electricity between them. Giving his brain a mental shake, he focused on Brad across the desk from them.

The banker stopped typing and frowned. Kat's muscles clenched under his hand as Boomer asked, "Is there a problem?"

"Uh, no, sir. I was just surprised to see the box hasn't been accessed in over twelve years. But it was paid in full for twenty, so there's no problem. The joint box-holders included Ms. Maier here, as well as Alexei Maier and Sylvia Maier."

Kat's eyes filled up. "Alex was my brother, and Sylvia was my mom. They're both deceased as well."

An expression of sympathy crossed the man's face. "I'm sorry for your loss, Ms. Maier."

"Thank you."

He stood and skirted the desk. "If you give me a moment, I have to retrieve the bank's access key from my superior."

"Sure," Boomer replied. "No problem." He watched as the banker walked toward a closed door labeled "Branch Manager" and knocked.

"So, we lucked out, right?"

He couldn't see into the now open door from this angle but kept it in his peripheral as he turned back to Kat. "Huh?"

"No court order needed."

"Right." He gave her a tentative smile, scanning the faces of the bank occupants as the two of them waited. The hair on the back of his neck raised in caution. His inner alert system was telling him something was wrong, but he couldn't see anyone or anything out of place. Pulling out his phone, he shot off a brief text to Jake. However, the "all clear" response did nothing to ease his sudden anxiety.

About two minutes later, Brad returned with a large keyring. "Sorry for the wait. If you'll follow me, it's right this way. I'll retrieve the box, and you can examine the contents privately."

Leading them into the security box vault, the banker quickly located the long-ignored box, number 522, and placed his key in one of the two slots. He then stepped back to allow Kat to do the same. After it was unlocked, he slid it from the wall and handed it to her. "You can use the room on the right outside the vault. I'll wait here until you're done."

"Thank you." Despite her calm outward demeanor, Boomer knew Kat's insides must be a bowl of Jell-O. Whatever her father had hidden here in the bank, it was something people wanted to kill for. He followed her into the room and shut the door behind them. The space was the size of a closet, and there was nothing in it except a shelf and an overhead light. Her hands shook as she set the box down.

The tension rolling off her did nothing to calm his thoughts that something wasn't right. "Do you want me to open it?"

Kat bit her bottom lip and shook her head. "No. I've got it." After taking a deep breath, she lifted the lid and stared at the contents in confusion and disappointment.

"That's it?" he asked over her shoulder. It couldn't be it.

"I don't understand. My father had a security box all these years for a . . . a picture?" She picked up the old, three-by-five color photo and studied it. "This is my dad when he was a kid. He's what, about four or five years old here?"

Boomer checked the box for anything more and found it completely empty. He took the photo from Kat and turned it over, but the back was blank. No name, date, or message. Strange. Flipping it over again, he examined it. "Looks like it. Any idea where it was taken? Is that his childhood home he's standing in front of?"

"I'm not sure. If I remember correctly, they moved twice before settling in Murfreesboro, North Carolina, when my dad was eleven or twelve. But I don't know where they lived before that." Her eyes flashed to Boomer's face as a thought must have occurred to her. "My aunt would know. Last I heard, she was still alive. Chris told me that about . . . I don't remember. A year ago, I think."

"Where does she live?" he asked as he replaced the lid and picked up the box.

She tucked the photo into her purse. "In Murfreesboro. She still lives in my grandparent's old house. It's just over an hour from here. It's where we were going when . . ."

Not needing her to finish her statement about the tragic

day so long ago, he took her hand and headed for the door. "Let's get out of here."

"It's Glen Patterson from Wells Fargo. You told me to call when anyone accessed the Maier deposit box . . . A guy and a girl . . . I don't know his name, but her ID says she's Katrina, uh, I mean, Katerina Maier . . . They're in there now, but I'm sure they won't be for long . . . A license plate? Yeah, I can probably get it . . . My office window faces the parking lot . . . After this, we're through, right? I don't owe you anything anymore . . . Good . . . I'll text you the plate and car info."

The bank manager disconnected the call, relieved that the last of an old debt was paid off. He'd sworn off gambling several years ago after his wife threatened to leave him and take the kids. It'd taken a while, but he'd finally repaid all his monetary debts. This last "information" debt was the only thing he still owed. Now all he needed to do was one more thing . . . he parted the window blinds and waited for the couple he'd seen follow Brad into the vault.

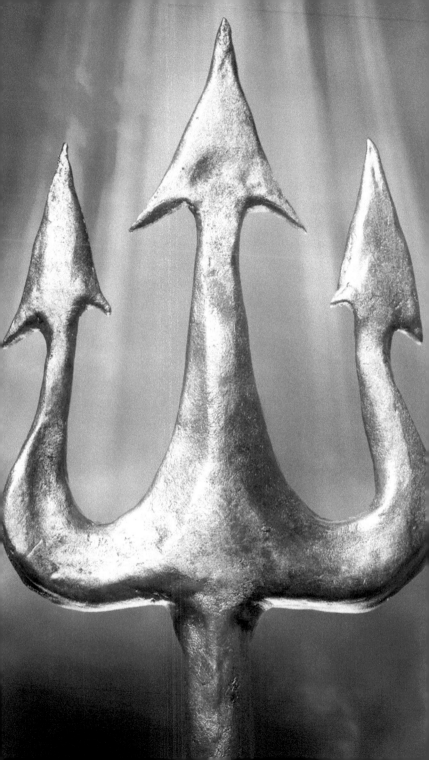

CHAPTER NINE

Fifteen minutes later, they were back in their motel rooms and packing their things. The plan was to head to Murfreesboro to talk to Kat's aunt. And wasn't that going to be a jaw-dropper for the older woman? As far as she knew, her brother and niece had died twelve years ago, and she had no other family left. Kat's grandfather had died when she was seven, and her grandmother passed away four years ago, never knowing the true fate of her son and his daughter.

While Jake was next door, collecting his stuff and the FBI files, Kat came out of the bathroom with her toiletries. Boomer winced at her pale, pinched face framed by the wig she was once again wearing. "You okay?"

She tossed her things into her duffel and sighed. "Yeah. I'm just wondering where this is all going. I mean, what if we don't figure it out? And on top of everything, I'm about to shock the shit out of my Aunt Irina. What am I supposed to do, knock on her door and yell 'surprise'? Look how well it turned out when I did it to you. You fainted, so the poor woman will probably have a heart attack."

Her rant was stopped when Boomer grasped her arm and

pulled her into a comforting embrace. "Shhh. It'll be fine. She'll be shocked, but then I think she'll be ecstatic to know you're alive. Yes, I fainted . . ." He grabbed her chin and forced her gaze upward. On his face was a teasing frown. "And don't ever repeat that to anyone else. Ian is already blackmailing me with shit assignments for the next year." She smiled as he intended. "But now I'm past my shock, and I'm thrilled you're alive, Kitten."

It hadn't been his intention when he first pulled her into his arms, but he couldn't resist her. Bending forward, his lips caught hers, and his cock sprung to life. He teased the seam of her mouth with his tongue and rejoiced when she opened, granting him access. Last night, he'd been spouting poetry at the taste of her, but now, she must've just brushed her teeth again because she was minty fresh and delicious. Poetry was the last thing on his mind.

One of his hands went to the nape of her neck, and his fingers spread out to hold her head in place. His other hand clutched her hip, pulling her flush against him and his bulging erection. They moaned almost simultaneously when he shifted his head, and the new angle allowed him to plunge his tongue deeper. Her tongue tangled with his as her hands slid up his shoulders and into his hair.

"Ah, shit. Sorry, but we need to get on the road."

They jumped apart. Kat's face turned red before she spun around and began throwing the last of her stuff into her bag. Shit, Boomer thought. What the hell was he doing? If it weren't for Jake's interruption, he would have forgotten the danger Kat was in and thrown her on the bed for a hard, fast, and sweaty rutting.

Adjusting himself, he acknowledged his teammate over his shoulder. "Yeah. Give us a minute. We'll be right out."

"No prob."

A few seconds later, he heard the door to Jake's room open and close again. He'd be getting the car started for their trip, and Boomer hurried to grab the last of his stuff. He glanced around the room, making sure they weren't forgetting anything, before taking Kat's bags for her. Pinning her with an intense stare, he told her, "We're not done, Kitten. Not by a long shot. Just wanted to let you know. Once you're out of danger, we're picking up where we left off, and there will be no interruptions. Understood?"

She bit her lip and nodded, but her gaze lowered from his face to his chest. Convinced she knew he meant to have her in his bed soon, naked and sated, he turned and headed for the door. Because his hands were filled with their bags, Kat hurried around him and opened the door.

"I can carry my stuff if you want."

"Not," he snorted. She may be used to doing things on her own after all these years, but that was about to change. It went beyond wanting to be her Dom. His parents had raised him to be a gentleman, and Kat deserved to be treated like a lady.

Jake was standing by the open trunk while the sedan was running. "Radio says there's an accident on the highway, and traffic is backed up for miles. We'll have to GPS around it."

"'Kay." As Boomer tossed the bags into the trunk, an SUV came squealing into the lot, and both men's heads turned.

Drawing their weapons, they backed up to use their rental car as cover and stood in front of Kat, protecting her. Four large men climbed out of the Escalade, and each had a semi-automatic in hand but didn't point them at the trio. It was the only reason Boomer and Jake didn't open fire.

"Give us girl, and you can valk avay."

What the fuck? From the accent, it was obvious the Russians had found Kat, but how the hell had they known where she was? Jake would have spotted anyone casing the bank, so the info had to have come from someone inside. Brad, maybe? It really didn't matter how they'd been found, the point being it was four guns against two, with one unarmed woman. And since the guns weren't blazing, Boomer knew they wanted Kat alive . . . for now.

He eyed the man who'd spoken. The cocky bastard was the smallest of the group, but that wasn't saying much since he was about six-three and built like a brick wall.

"Not going to happen. Why don't you take me instead?" Boomer heard Kat's surprised gasp behind him but ignored her. His mind was too busy assessing the threat and figuring out how to eliminate it without getting Kat, Jake, or himself killed in the process. Both of their motel room doors were now closed and locked, and even if they weren't, the three of them would've been trapped inside with a small window as their only hope for escape.

Their rooms had been at the far end of the motel, so around the side of the building was their closest large cover. An unoccupied minivan parked next to their rental would also provide an obstacle to hide behind. They had to avoid a public shootout unless it was absolutely necessary. Boomer didn't want to risk a hail of bullets flying around the motel, possibly hitting an innocent bystander, although, at the moment, they were the only seven people in sight.

He reached back and grabbed Kat's arm, never taking his eyes off the foursome. They would only get one shot at this, and he needed to be ready.

The lead Russian narrowed his eyes at them. "Vhy don't I shoot you dead like dog, and take vhat I vant?"

It was time to bluff. "Because if you shoot me, you'll never get what you're looking for."

"Vhat you mean?"

Boomer took a small step to his left, keeping Kat behind him and the rental car between the threat and them. He was confident Jake knew his intentions and would be right behind them. But first, he needed to get the focus off Kat. "It means Ivan left a series of clues, and I'm the only one who knows what he was talking about. I'm the only one who knows how to find the treasure."

At the mention of "treasure," recognition gleamed on the Russian's face. *Bingo!* If they thought Kat was useless to them, it would be easier to protect her.

"Then you and girl come vith us and ve let friend live."

Shit! Boomer opened his mouth to respond, but sirens sounded nearby, and the Russians' attention flashed to the parking lot entrance. The cops might be on their way. However, they were still too far to help. But it was the break Boomer had been waiting for.

Without a moment's hesitation, he took off to his left, pushing Kat in front of him, knowing Jake had his six. Shouts, followed by gunfire, filled the air. He blocked Kat's body from the threat of flying bullets as best he could as they rounded the building at full speed.

As they cleared the corner, Jake was on their heels and returning fire. "Fuck! Goddamn it!"

Boomer didn't slow but checked over his shoulder. The sirens were getting closer, and the gunfire came to an abrupt halt. Shouts in Russian reached his ears, but he had no idea what was being said. "What?"

"Nothing, keep going!"

Skirting the back of the motel, Kat stumbled. If Boomer's hand hadn't been around her arm, she would've face-planted. A screech of tires came from the front of the building as he plastered her between his body and the rear wall. Jake stopped beside them, breathing heavily, and peered around the corner. "Sounds like they're taking off. I think we're good."

There was something in the other man's voice that caught Boomer's attention. When he glanced over, what he saw had his heart rate surging again. Blood was pouring from a wound on the left side of Jake's pale face. "What the fuck!"

He watched in horror as Jake slid to the ground, and Kat's scream pierced the air.

CHAPTER TEN

Boomer stepped outside the emergency room with Kat and scanned the area for any danger. Keeping her hidden in an alcove, he pulled out his phone and called Ian. When his boss picked up, he gave him the rundown of what had happened.

"So, Reverend's going to be okay?"

A car drove by, and Boomer eyed it before answering. "Yeah. A bullet hit the wall as he came around the corner, kicking out a nice-sized chunk of brick. Struck him near the eye and scratched the cornea, but the doc says it's not as bad as it looks. He's got some stitches for a laceration right above the eye. The fucker bled like a bitch and scared the crap out of us. He needs an eye patch and some eyedrops for a week or so. Then he's got to follow up with an ophthalmologist. They had to give him something for the pain. The fact that he took it tells you he's hurting."

Ian snorted, clearly relieved the injury wasn't worse. "Yup. The fucker even hates taking Tylenol. So, what's the plan from here?"

"I'm going to call CC, have him pick up Jake when he's released, and then fly him home. We told the cops it was an attempted carjacking. Whether they believed us or not is another story. One of the detectives is an old friend of my dad's, so I think he gave us some leeway. It also helps the only witness was the motel clerk, who hid behind his desk while calling 9-1-1. I'm just glad we still have carry permits in Virginia. Otherwise, we'd still be in interrogation."

His gaze met Kat's. "We're heading to Murfreesboro in North Carolina. It's about an hour or so from here, and Kat's aunt lives there. We're hoping she can tell us about the photo from the safety deposit box."

"All right. But watch your six. When CC lands with Jake, I'll send Dev and Marco up to meet you. Depending on how much sleep CC's had, they may not be there before tomorrow morning. I want you to check in every two hours until your backup arrives. And I've activated your tracker, so don't lose your phone."

"Anything else, Mom?"

"Cut the sarcasm, frog. I don't like knowing these guys are gunning for Kat, and you're in their way. From what you told me, they want her alive, which means you and anyone else can end up as collateral damage. Watch your ass and call me the second you see trouble. Worse comes to worst, I'll call Little Creek and send some of Team Four to help you. They're training stateside at the moment."

"Yeah, I doubt Uncle Sam would like that, Boss-man, but I hear you. I'll be careful and keep you posted."

"Every two hours, or I start calling people."

Before Boomer could respond, his boss disconnected the call. Beside him, Kat was still pale, but at least she'd stopped shaking. She'd been great at the scene, administering first aid to Jake while Boomer had made sure their assailants had indeed taken off moments before the cops arrived. It wasn't until after the EMTs took over that the shock of being shot at finally hit her. Now, he pulled her in for a hug. "You okay?"

In his arms, she began to shake again. "I'm so sorry, this is all my fault. Jake or you could've been killed. What if he loses his sight in that eye?"

He hugged her tighter and ran his hands over her back. "Shhh. Calm down. None of this is your fault. And you heard the doc, Jake is going to be fine. Please, for a Navy SEAL, this is the equivalent of a hangnail."

Kat huffed. "How can you joke about this?"

Pulling back so she could see him, he cupped her chin. "It's one thing you learn in the military, Kitten. Joking is a way of dealing with things. The alternative is going nuts. And I'm serious. Jake and I have been in far worse situations than today. I was only freaking out about you being in the middle of it all. If something happened to you, I don't know what I would've done. I just got you back, and I'll be damned if I lose you again."

He dipped his head, and her breath hitched a split second before he claimed her mouth. This wasn't the time or place for a make-out session, but he needed to give her something else to think about. And since he constantly thought about the two of them having sex, why should he be the only one? He kissed her hard and fast, plunging his tongue into her mouth and taking a quick taste of her. When he ended the brief kiss, he was pleased to see she was flushed, glassy-eyed, and out of breath. Soon. He had to make her his soon. But first, he had to keep her safe and find out what the fuck was going on.

"Come on, let me fill Jake in, and then we're getting on

the road. I want to put as much distance as possible between us and the bad guys."

It was now after four p.m. Between the police interviews and waiting for an eye specialist, the rest of the morning and afternoon flew by. With rush-hour traffic, it would be closer to six by the time they hit Murfreesboro, if not later.

———

As it turned out, with an unplanned stop and the traffic worse than they expected, it was twenty-five after seven when they pulled into Irina Maier's empty driveway. They both climbed out of the car, and Boomer looked around. He'd been confident they hadn't been followed.

Before they left Jake, he'd told them to return to the car rental place and switch cars, just in case one of the goons had tagged it. Boomer could've kicked himself for not thinking of it first. They'd even gone one better and returned the car to one rental place before walking across the street to get a new car from another one. And this time, he used an alias credit card and ID, which he was pissed he hadn't done with the first rental. They hadn't thought the Russians would know they were in Virginia less than twenty-four hours after they'd arrived. It was too late to change things now, so he had to pray the goons hadn't memorized their license plate and traced it.

After driving a mile down the road, he'd pulled over and disabled the GPS tracker most agencies used nowadays to track their vehicles. Once he was sure they didn't have a tail, he'd gotten on the freeway heading southwest. While sitting in traffic, they'd taken advantage of a truck stop and grabbed dinner to go. It wasn't great, but it'd been some much-needed nourishment since they'd missed lunch.

Ivan Maier's childhood home was a one-story ranch on approximately two acres of land. Trees dotted the property, and it was obvious Irina Maier liked to garden or, at least, hired someone to do it. Fall flowers were in bloom, and their beds were strategically placed around the property, so wherever one looked, there was an array of colors—pinks, reds, yellows, and blues. The brick home was well taken care of, and it looked like the white shutters had recently received a fresh coat of paint.

Taking Kat's hand, Boomer approached the front door and rang the bell. He could hear the chime go off, but there was no other sound from within. Knocking was met with the same result. Peering in the front window, he saw nothing amiss, but just to make sure, they circled the house.

"Maybe she's out to dinner with friends."

Boomer hoped Kat was right, and there wasn't a more nefarious reason for her aunt not being home. They had no idea if Volkov's people would come here looking for answers to whatever questions they had for Kat. "Come on. Let's find a room for the night. We can come back in a little while and see if she's home."

She sighed. "Okay. I guess we don't have a choice."

He opened the passenger door for her and closed it after she swung her legs inside. Skirting the hood, he glanced toward the end of the driveway and noticed a man in his late sixties getting mail at a row of boxes.

Holding up a finger to Kat for her to wait a minute, he jogged down the drive. "Excuse me? Sir?"

The man was eyeing him suspiciously, so he stopped several feet away and lifted his palms to indicate he was no threat. "I'm sorry, sir. My girlfriend is a . . . a distant relative of Ms. Maier. We were passing through and thought we'd stop in and say hi. You don't happen to know where she might be, do you?"

He didn't know what Irina's neighbors knew about her brother's family, so he didn't want to mention Kat was her niece.

The man's gaze shifted beyond Boomer, so he glanced back and saw Kat was out of the car and walking toward them.

"Damn!"

Boomer's head whipped around again to face the old man. "What's wrong?"

The neighbor seemed to realize he'd alarmed him. "Oh, nothing to worry about, boy. Any thoughts I had about you snowballing me with your bullshit story went out the window when I saw your girlfriend there. She looks exactly like Irina . . . well, younger, of course. What did you say your name was?"

"I didn't, sir, but it's Ben Michaelson. And this is Kate Zimmerman."

Again, he didn't want to tip the man off about Kat's lineage. He held out his hand, and the man shook it.

"Name's Harry Bernhard. I live across the street. What branch of the military are you, son?"

Boomer's eyebrows raised in surprise. "Navy, sir. Retired SEAL, to be exact. How'd you know?"

"Retired from the Marines about twenty years ago. Major. Can always spot someone who has seen combat. It's the way they carry themselves. Iraq? No, don't answer. Sometimes I forget you black-ops boys can't answer that question."

Boomer's mouth ticked upwards. "No, sir, I can't. Let's just say I've been around the block a few times."

"I hear you. Now, about Irina. She expecting you?"

From his side, Kat answered before Boomer had a chance. "No, she's not. As a matter of fact, she's going to be very surprised to see me. I-I haven't seen her in a very long time." Boomer gave her a subtle look. Realizing she'd said too much, she tried to cover her ass. "I've lived on the West Coast for over ten years and just moved back East. I was hoping to surprise her."

"Well, I hope you're not in a hurry because she and a few members of her women's group took an overnight road trip to Roanoke Rapids. They go every other month to see a show and play some slot machines at the Royal Palace out there." At Kat's expression of dismay, Harry added, "Don't fret, missy. She'll be back tomorrow by noon."

Smiling, Boomer put his arm around Kat's shoulders and squeezed. She got the picture and put on a happy face while he spoke. "That'd be fine, sir. We just got into town and came straight here, so can you recommend a motel nearby?"

Harry scratched his head. "Well, you're a little out of luck there because Murfreesboro doesn't have any motels. Nearest one is about twenty miles away in Franklin. But we do have a nice bed and breakfast in town. Always clean and not too expensive. And it's right across the street from a good place to eat."

"That'd be great. What's the name of the B&B?"

"Carmichael's. Drive straight back into town, and it's on your left after the first traffic light. Can't miss it."

Extending his hand again, Boomer thanked the man. "And I'd appreciate it, sir, if you see Irina before we do, please don't spoil the surprise."

"No problem, son. And call me Harry. I might see you both tomorrow anyway. Irina always brings me back a blueberry pie from this great bakery they have out there. Good night, now."

"Good night."

As they returned to the car, Boomer peeked over his shoulder and caught the old man doing the same. He might be friendly toward them, but he was protective of Irina, and it showed. "I think your aunt has a boyfriend."

"Huh? What are you talking about?"

He jerked his thumb toward the end of the drive. "Harry. I wouldn't be surprised if he's got a thing for her."

Kat glanced over her shoulder at the older man before climbing into the car. "Really? Well, good for them. She's a sweet woman, and I always wondered why she never married."

After shutting her door again, Boomer rounded the car and settled in the driver's seat. "Maybe she never met the right guy until now."

"Maybe."

KAT WAS QUIET AS BENNY DROVE BACK INTO TOWN. NOW THAT the stress from this morning was leaving her body, her mind was filled with everything that had happened in the past twenty-four hours. Unfortunately, one irrelevant thing kept popping up. It was what she'd found on the bathroom floor this morning. The pink piece of paper from a memo pad must've fallen out of Benny's pocket by accident. She knew it was his because it said "Ben" in his secretary's neat handwriting. Apparently, Kat wasn't the only one who didn't use his nickname.

The message scrawled on the paper was what was bothering her as she replayed the words in her mind.

Tanya would like to play with you at club tonight. Please call. 813-555-9438.

Kat had never asked him if he had a girlfriend, and she hadn't heard anyone mention one, but it didn't mean he wasn't dating. And what did Tanya mean by "play with you"? Play what? Darts? Pool? And what club? Night club? Country club?

There were too many variables, but her mind kept flashing to the book she was currently reading—*Leather & Lace*. It was a romance novel, but the sex was not "vanilla," which was a term used by book websites when the sex in the story was tame. By comparison, Leather & Lace was what they called erotica, and the sex involved BDSM—Bondage, Discipline, Sadism, and Masochism. Kat loved to read, and while she didn't fully understand "the lifestyle," as it was called, the fictional books about the subject were fun. And hot. Holy shit, were they hot. Her vibrator tended to go through quite a few batteries when she was reading one of those novels.

It was the word "play" which was bugging her. It was used a lot in BDSM books, and those stories were usually set in clubs. Sex clubs. Didn't the woman they'd met at the pharmacy yesterday mention a club? Could Benny be into something like that? And how did she feel about it? Kat didn't know what to feel or think at this point. And she was too embarrassed to ask him about it. What if she was wrong? Oh God, what if she was right?

"Kat."

She jumped at the sound of his deep sexy voice. "Wh-what?"

Pointing at the large house they were parked next to, he said, "We're here. You okay?"

"Um, yeah. Sorry." She blushed. "My mind was elsewhere."

"Yeah, it's been a long day. Come on. Let's get a room and climb into bed."

Oh boy.

CHAPTER ELEVEN

While Benny was in the bathroom, Kat stood in their bedroom and stared at the king-sized bed. Due to some local couple getting married over the weekend, there was only one room available at the B&B. It was a large room with a sitting area as well, and Benny had offered to sleep on the couch. But by the look in his eye when he said it, Kat knew the couch was not where he wanted to be. He wanted to be in the big bed . . . with her. Together. Naked. And if she was honest with herself, she wanted all that and more.

She thought back to the kiss they'd shared in the motel before Jake had interrupted them. Kat hadn't known which end was up or whether she had been coming or going. All she knew was she'd been lost and didn't want to be found. Lost in Ben's arms was where she always wanted to be, and, Lord help her, she wanted more. She'd longed to rip off his shirt and explore the hard chest her breasts had been crushed against. His cock had been stiff against her abdomen, and she'd wanted to climb his body and wrap her legs around his hips so he'd have been lined up with her pussy.

Recalling the delicious moment had her wet with desire

She might be inexperienced, but there were things the human body knew instinctively. And her body wanted to mate. Here. Now. With the one man she'd been waiting for all these years.

The toilet flushed, and she jumped. Hurrying, she pulled the covers back and climbed into the bed. She'd only brought one of her duffel bags with them, so she was wearing the T-shirt and shorts she'd worn to bed last night. They weren't exactly sexy, but hopefully, she wouldn't be wearing them long. Losing her virginity while people were trying to kidnap her was not how she wanted it to happen. But she did want it to happen with this man. The man she'd been waiting for since she was seventeen.

Taking a deep breath, Kat pulled back the covers on the other side of the bed in a blatant invitation for Benny to join her. And waited. God, she was so nervous. What if he turned her down? What if she did something wrong? He would know instantly she wasn't experienced, wouldn't he? Would it turn him off?

The bathroom door swung open, and Kat's eyes flashed to Benny's as he strode into the room. She knew the moment the pulled-back covers registered in his brain because he froze and raised his eyebrow at her. She gushed, "There's no, uh . . . no reason for you to sleep on the couch . . . I mean, we're adults, right? And, I . . ."

Her words trailed off, and Benny smiled at her nervousness. She was sitting on the side of the bed closest to him, and he stalked over and then sat down beside her, crowding her a little. Her heart began to pound in her chest as her eyes dropped from his intense stare. "If I share this bed with you, Kitten, sleep will be the last thing on my mind. I want you. I want to be on top of you, under you, behind you, and *in* you. If it's not what you want, too, then say the word, and I'll sleep on the couch." He glanced over at the offensive piece of furniture. "No matter how much it pains me to do so."

Wetness coated Kat's panties, and she was close to coming from his sexy voice alone. Her hands twisted together in her lap. "I want . . . I want you to sleep with me . . . I mean, not sleep-sleep, but . . ."

———

BOOMER CHUCKLED AND COVERED HER TREMBLING LIPS WITH his fingers. "I know what you meant, Kitten. Damn, you're beautiful when you blush. Just like back in high school."

He moved his hand to cup her cheek yet continued to brush her lips with his thumb. He'd thought she'd be too tired and stressed for intimacy tonight, but sex was a great stress reliever. His dick had hardened when he saw all the signs of her arousal—rapid pulse, increased breathing, swallowing hard, and nipples pebbling under her thin shirt. When her eyes had dropped to her lap, the natural reaction of a submissive excited him.

Fuck, her plump bottom lip was made for him to nibble on. He couldn't wait any longer and leaned forward, replacing his thumb with his lips, teeth, and tongue. Groaning at her taste, he plunged his hand into her hair and held her in place while his mouth and tongue did wicked things to hers. His other hand found her breast and massaged the lush flesh.

When her hands went around his neck, he pulled away, and she whimpered at the loss of contact. "Wh-what's wrong? Did I do something wrong?"

A rumble came from his chest. "Are you kidding? No, you didn't do anything wrong. It's just . . ."

He sighed heavily. There were things he had to tell her.

"Kitten, when it comes to sex, I've changed, and I'm not sure what your response will be."

His cock was yelling at him to shut the fuck up and get on with it, but his brain and heart were telling him this was important. He couldn't go any further without telling her about his wants and needs. Her submitting to him was something he craved, and he didn't think he could live without it.

"What is it?"

The wariness in her voice was killing him. "When I'm with a woman . . . in bed . . . I need to be in charge . . . of everything. I like to . . . shit, this is the first time I've ever been nervous about telling a woman this. I'm a Dominant, Kat. Do you know what that means?"

Her eyes widened in surprise, but for some reason, she didn't seem as shocked as he'd expected her to be. "Um, it means you're into . . . um . . . tying women up and spanking and stuff. The opposite of 'vanilla' sex, right?"

He wasn't sure why he was stunned by her answer. After all, she'd been reading Kristen's book about BDSM. "Yeah. That's part of it, but it's so much more. It's about a power exchange. While a Dom may seem to be in charge of the scene, the submissive has all the power."

Kat's eyes narrowed in confusion. "I don't understand. I mean, I've read books on the subject, but it's hard to separate fact from fiction sometimes."

"Yeah, well, a lot of books out there give false impressions of the lifestyle. You see, when a Dom and sub are scening, or playing as it's also referred to, then a sub sets all the limits and boundaries. We use lists at the club that cover every form of play—what a sub enjoys, wants to try, or absolutely will not do under any circumstances. A good Dom will honor that list. He'll push the sub's limits, but if the sub says her safeword, all play stops. So, you see? A sub has all the power."

She bit her bottom lip again, and he used his thumb to rescue the abused flesh. "What are you thinking about, Kitten?"

"I guess I don't understand what people get out of it. I mean, if a sub has all the power, like you said, then what does a Dom get out of it?"

Getting uncomfortable in his current position, Boomer stood and circled the bed. He lay on his side facing her and propped his head up with his hand, then rested his other hand atop hers over her abdomen. His thumb rubbed her wrist in small, sensual motions as little goose bumps appeared on her skin. "A Dom gets satisfaction in knowing he has his submissive's trust that he'll take care of her. Her submissiveness is his greatest pleasure, and in return, his greatest desire is to give *her* pleasure beyond her wildest dreams. Her mind, body, and orgasms belong to him, and he treats each as the most precious gift in the world because they are."

Kat's pulse sped up again as he spoke. He could see she was struggling with something but waited it out. He couldn't rush this—it was too important.

"Can I ask you something?"

From her tone, he wasn't sure it was something he wanted to hear. "Of course, baby. You can ask me anything you want."

"You . . . um . . . you dropped a note in the bathroom this morning. From Tanya."

Shit. He didn't even realize his secretary's call-back note was missing. He'd forgotten all about it. "And you want to know about her and the club."

She nodded, and he sighed. "Yes, I belong to a private

club. Ian and Devon own The Covenant, and it's in the first building at the Trident compound, but you'd never know it from the outside. Tanya is a friend, nothing more. We've played in the past, but there is nothing between us relationship-wise. I don't have a girlfriend if you're worried about that. I would never cheat on a woman I was in a relationship with."

"I didn't think you would."

He interlocked their fingers and squeezed. "Well, honesty is a big part of my lifestyle, so I just wanted it on the record. And the lifestyle is a big part of my life." He took a deep breath and forged ahead. "I want you to be part of my life too. We can start off slow. I'm not going to handcuff you and do wicked things to you . . . well, at least not yet. But I'd like to introduce you to my lifestyle and show you how good things can be between us. Can you give me . . . us a chance?"

Her hesitation was killing him. He prayed her answer wasn't no. Holding his tongue, he noticed Kat shift nervously. "There's, um . . . something I need to tell you. Something important."

Oh, God help him. This was over before it'd begun. His wariness crept into his voice. "Okay. You can tell me anything, Kitten. Whatever it is, we'll deal with it."

"I, um . . . I mean, I've never . . . shit, this was easier in my head . . . I've never had sex before." The last five words came out in a rush, and she stared at their twined hands, not daring to look at him.

Boomer froze. *Huh? What the fuck!* Was Kat saying she was still a virgin? She was twenty-nine years old! How the fuck had she made it to twenty-nine and never had . . . never done . . . *holy shit!*

Clearing his throat, he tried to remain calm and not freak her out. "Uh, wow, um . . . damn, didn't see that coming. How

. . . I mean, why . . . shit, help me out here, Kat. I'm not mad or disappointed . . . just shocked you never . . . that you're still a virgin."

Yeah, well, you could've said that a lot better, idiot.

He reached up and touched her chin, turning her head so she was looking at him. She was mortified—that was evident. But she had nothing to be ashamed about. In fact, he was thrilled no other man had ever taken her. "Don't be embarrassed. Talk to me, baby. You said earlier you wanted to have sex with me. If you want to do this, we need some communication here. I need to know things to make it good for you. The first time can be uncomfortable if I don't do things right."

"If you're talking about breaking my . . . you know . . . I did it years ago with . . ."

His eyes narrowed, and he growled. "With who? You just said you were a virgin."

"I am! But just because I've never been with a man doesn't mean I didn't have urges and needs. So, I took care of it myself, with—"

"A vibrator," he finished for her.

Kat nodded, her cheeks getting redder by the second.

"Damn, that's hot. The thought of you . . . shit!" Boomer hadn't thought he could get any harder than he already was, but the images bombarding his brain sent his hormones into overdrive. He was wishing he'd changed into a pair of sweatpants because he was going to have zipper marks on his cock from his jeans. He needed to keep his inner beast in check, or he'd scare the shit out of her.

"I have to ask, baby, why haven't you ever had sex? Don't tell me there was never an opportunity. You're gorgeous and must be beating them off with a baseball bat. I know you were in hiding and all, but after starting a new life in

Portland, there had to have been guys who tried to get you into their beds. Otherwise, it doesn't say much for the male population in Oregon."

She snorted. "Please, I know I'm not ugly, but I'm far from gorgeous. I'm a plain Jane, nothing special."

Was she kidding him? Growling again, Boomer snatched her hip and tugged until she was on her side, then sent a stinging slap to her left butt cheek.

"Ow! What was that for?" Her eyes were wide with shock . . . and something else . . . arousal.

"Rule number one of my world, Kitten, is you never . . . *ever* . . . put yourself down. It's one of the fastest ways for you to earn a punishment. There is no way you're a 'plain Jane.' I still remember the night of my party, and I told you how beautiful you were. But it doesn't even come close to how beautiful you are today. You're the woman who enters a room, and men instantly want you in their beds. But then you speak, and they want to fall down on their knees and worship you. You're sexy as sin, both inside and out, and I want to prove it to you. But you still haven't answered my question. Why haven't you had sex before now?"

He knew it was ridiculous to hope she'd been waiting for him. Waiting for a time when she could be with him again. But that's what he was dying to hear from her lips.

"I don't know. I mean, I dated a few guys, but it never felt right. It felt like something was missing. And now, I think I know what it was."

Boomer held his breath.

"It was you, Benny. None of those other guys were you. My heart and body always knew they wanted you and no one else."

His heart felt like it was going to burst from his ribcage.

Hauling her against his hard chest, he grasped her hair. "Jesus, that's the sexiest thing I've ever heard."

Rolling on his back, he pulled her with him and claimed her mouth again. Tasting . . . savoring . . . marking her as his. His other hand slid down her back until it reached her ass, and he gripped her cheek.

A thought popped into his frazzled brain, and he tugged on her hair to break their lip-lock. Breathless, he said, "Kitten, I need you to tell me this is what you want. I'll make it good for you, I promise. We'll keep things 'vanilla' for now, but I'm going to give you a safeword anyway. If I do anything that scares or hurts you, say the word 'red.' I'll stop immediately, and we'll talk about what's wrong, okay?"

Kat tried to nod, but his hand was still holding her hair. "Yes. This is what I want. And if anything doesn't feel right, I'll say 'red.'"

"It's important, baby. I'm not a mind-reader. You have to tell me if you don't like something or if it hurts. Don't let me keep doing something because you think it's what I want. The only thing I want is to give you pleasure and a hell of a lot of orgasms." Her eyes widened. "Oh, yes, Kitten. I'm going to give you plenty of those. Now sit up for a second and take your shirt off."

He wanted to rip it off her, along with her shorts, but he had to take baby steps for her first time. And a few harmless orders would get her used to him issuing them. As he watched her intently, Kat pushed off his chest and knelt beside him. Blushing, she reached for the hem of her T-shirt and lowered her eyes.

"Uh-uh, Kitten. Eyes on mine. You'll be able to see how beautiful I think you are."

KAT LIFTED HER EYES AT THE SAME TIME SHE LIFTED HER SHIRT. Her vision was blocked momentarily while she pulled it over her head, but when her gaze met his again, she saw heat. Desire swirled in the amber irises and made her think of molten lava. She felt a rush of juices between her legs and bit her lip.

"You're going to leave teeth marks on your bottom lip, and I'd prefer any marks to be made by me." His gaze swept her body as she blushed. "You're gorgeous, Kitten, and don't even think of correcting me. I love what I see, but I want more. I want to watch you play with your tits like you do when you're alone, and no one is watching."

"Holy shit!" Kat clasped her hand over her mouth, mortified the words had escaped her. "I mean . . . you want me to do that in front of you? It's embarrassing."

Boomer chuckled. "Oh, this is going to be so much fun. Your innocence is the biggest fucking turn-on I've ever had. And there's nothing to be embarrassed about, sweetheart. Things are going to get a lot more intimate than this. I'm not asking you to do anything billions of women haven't done for thousands of years."

He sat up and pulled his own T-shirt over his head. "But I'll tell you what . . ." To her amazement, he grasped the garment in two hands, ripping off a long strip of the fabric. "Let's make this more about feeling instead of seeing."

Kneeling before her, he put the strip over her eyes and tied it behind her head. When it was secure, she felt him lay back down. "Okay, let's try this again. Lift your hands and cover your tits, Kitten." Her hands moved slowly, unsure, but she followed his commands. "Mmm, good girl. Now squeeze and massage them. Push them up and in . . . damn, that's hot."

Kat couldn't believe she was doing this. But Benny's voice was low and commanding, and she couldn't help but want to do his bidding. As she followed his orders, she felt herself relaxing into the moment. She pushed down her embarrassment and nervousness and let his voice rumble through her veins.

"Take your thumbs and index fingers and pinch your nipples for me, baby. Roll them and pull them."

She felt the bed shift again but couldn't see what he was doing, and the unknown made her shudder in anticipation. Playing with her nipples, she moaned at the sensations that raced through them and straight to her pussy. Her thighs clenched involuntarily as her clit throbbed with need.

"Cup your breasts again, Kitten. Up and in."

She brought her hands down a little, then lifted. The bed dipped again, and she cried out as his mouth closed around one nipple. Her clit went into overdrive as he sucked, licked, and—*holy crap*—nibbled on the taut peak.

"Oh, oh, Benny! Oh my God!"

He didn't say a word. Instead, he switched to the other nipple and gave it the same attention. Her thighs began to quiver, and just when she thought they'd give out on her, he wrapped his arms around her and eased her down to the mattress. His mouth never left her breasts as he continued to ravage them. Every hum, slurp, and pop seemed to echo throughout the room.

Part of her wanted to watch him, but another part craved the suspense of not knowing what he would do next. She could feel he was straddling her hips, and the bed shifted back and forth as he moved downward. Soft kisses rained on her ribs and abdomen until he reached the top of her shorts. Grasping the sides, he slid them down and kissed every newly-exposed inch of skin.

Kat gasped as his tongue licked the crease between her hip and thigh, and more cream seeped from her core. Before she knew it, she was completely naked and wondering what he was thinking as he stared down at her. She wasn't sure how she knew what he was doing, but she could sense it. His hands slid up and down her outer thighs, from her hips to her knees, and she wished he would do the same to the inside.

"I've dreamed about this since my senior prom, Kitten. Even when I thought you were gone, you invaded my dreams. For the longest time, I prayed it'd all been a nightmare that never happened, but then I'd wake up and . . . I'd grieve again. And the worst part was, while I grieved for the loss of my best friend, I grieved more for the loss of the woman I loved. I've never loved another woman and never will. To have you in my arms and bed is a miracle I'll never take for granted."

During his speech, he'd kissed his way back up her body until he claimed her mouth again. Her heart filled with love for this man, and she wrapped her arms around him. She was drowning in his passion and moaned when his bare hips came in contact with hers. His hard erection pressed into her lower abdomen, and she had a fleeting thought—when had he removed his jeans? Oh, who the fuck cares? She was just glad he did. As he nuzzled her neck, she panted, "I want . . . I want to see you."

"Hmm, you will, baby. But for now, I want you to use your other senses—feel, hear, smell, and . . ." He licked her lips. "Taste. Well, I'll be the one tasting for a little while. Spread your legs for me, Kitten. Wide."

The bed dipped back and forth until she felt him settle between her thighs. His hands spread her a little wider, and she had a sudden urge to beg him . . . for what she didn't know. She felt a puff of air a second before his tongue licked the length of her slit, and her hips surged upwards. "Oh, my God! Holy shit!"

GRINNING AT HER RESPONSE, BOOMER LICKED HER AGAIN, BUT this time he held her hips in place. He groaned as the flavor of her juices saturated his taste buds. It was the sweetest cream he'd ever tasted, and he lapped at her relentlessly. She was trimmed, not bare, but it was fine with him. All he cared about was he finally had her in his bed, and he would make this a night neither one of them would ever forget. He wanted to ruin her for any other man. His Kitten would know him, and only him. She squirmed, moaned, cried out, and begged as he took her higher and higher. Her hands clutched the sheets . . . his hair . . . her own hair . . . everything within reach as if looking for a lifeline to hold on to. His thumb strummed her clit like a guitar string as he impaled her with his stiff tongue.

He replaced his thumb with his mouth, sucking on her little pearl. Two fingers plunged into her quivering pussy, which was soaked for him. Damn, she was on fire for him, her heat scorching his fingers as he thrust them in and out of her tight channel. He shoved them all the way in and searched . . . she gasped . . . there it was, the spot he was looking for. As he rubbed it, her pleas became frantic. "Come for me, Kitten. Let go and come." He sucked her clit hard.

Kat threw her arm over her mouth to muffle her screams of release as she came in waves of ecstasy. But Boomer didn't stop, and as one orgasm ebbed, another built right behind it. As pleasure crashed over her again, he licked and stroked, prolonging it as long as he could. When she came down from the second one, he eased up. Pulling his fingers from her pussy, he gave her clit and slit a few last licks.

Sated, she lay there panting, her skin glowing with a sheen of perspiration. Reaching up, he removed her partially dislodged blindfold and waited for her eyes to meet his. When they did, he slowly licked the last of her juices from his fingers. Her eyes widened slightly, but they got as big as saucers when her gaze slid down his body to his rigid shaft, standing impressively proud.

"It's all for you, Kitten. And don't worry, it'll fit."

Nodding, she reached out tentatively, and his hips jerked forward when her fingertips brushed against him. Taking her hand, he wrapped it around his cock. "Tighter, baby." He showed her how to give him a hand job, from root to tip. His head tipped back on his shoulders, his eyes closing as he groaned loudly. "That's it. Cup my balls, but be gentle. Not too hard with the family jewels."

He grinned when he heard her giggle. "Yeah, right like that. Roll them in your hand."

Her touch was the sweetest of tortures, but he wanted to give her the opportunity to explore a little. When the bed shifted, he opened his eyes just enough to see what she was doing. Kat was on her elbows and knees, and he realized what she was up to a second before her mouth closed around him. "Fuck!"

She recoiled, releasing him. "Sorry!"

Grabbing her hair, he guided her down again. "Don't be sorry, Kitten. It felt incredible, and I want you to do it again. Just watch the teeth, and you'll do fine. Taste me, baby. Lick me."

He hissed when she did as she was told. Her mouth was pure sin. Hot, wet, and wild. She was shy at first but started to get into it quickly. Her tongue swirled around his shaft as her head bobbed up and down. Boomer held back the urge to thrust his hips forward until his cock hit the back of her throat. Soon, but not tonight. He had other plans for tonight, and there was only one place his cock wanted to be right now . . . deep in her pussy.

Tightening the grip on her hair, he pulled her off him. "That felt amazing, but lay back down. Tonight isn't about me."

As she scurried into position, he reached across the bed and grabbed his wallet from the nightstand. Finding the condom he had in there, he swiftly opened it and rolled it onto his aching cock. Spreading her legs wide, he used two fingers to make sure she was still wet enough . . . well, that was an understatement because she was drenched. She watched as he lined himself up with her entrance. "You're tight, baby, so I'll take this slow. It may feel a little uncomfortable until you stretch more, but it shouldn't hurt, okay?"

"Please, I want you. I know you'll make it good."

Her faith in him tugged at his heartstrings and humbled him. She was panting again, the anticipation showing in her gaze. He eased the tip in, and her hips tilted for more. He slowly pumped in and out, using short strokes and going deeper each time. "Fuck, you're so tight. Am I hurting you?"

"N-no, more, ooohhhh, pppleassse mmmmmore. Oh God, it feels so good, so good. Benny, pleasssssse!"

His fingers found her clit and rubbed it in circles as her body greedily took him inside. When he was finally all the way in, her hips began to undulate. Her legs wrapped around his hips, and her feet dug into his ass. He couldn't hold back anymore. Rising above her on his elbows, he started to fuck her faster and harder, urged on by her erotic cries for more. The feel of her tight walls around him was heaven.

Dipping his head down, he sucked on one nipple and

toyed with the other. She was getting close, and he fought to hold his own release back until she came again. Shifting to his knees, he grabbed her hip with one hand and pinched her clit with the other. As she began to fly off the cliff, he clutched her hips hard, probably leaving fingerprints, but he'd worry about that later. All that mattered now was his need to come, to be one with her. His balls drew up tight, and after three or four more thrusts, he followed her into the deep chasm, grunting as he came inside her. Black spots appeared before his eyes, and he knew right then he'd found his forever home.

Collapsing, he used his arms to keep most of his weight off her. His lungs heaving, he buried his face in the crook of her neck. "Are you okay, Kitten?"

"Better than okay."

He chuckled at her mumbled response. Groaning, he reached down to secure the condom and pulled out of her. He kissed her nose. "Don't move. I'll be right back."

"Mm-hmm."

Boomer hurried into the bathroom as fast as his shaking legs could carry him. He disposed of the condom and grabbed two washcloths, wetting them both. Walking back to the bed, he quickly swiped one over his deflated cock and balls, then dropped it on the floor atop his torn shirt. When he placed the other warm cloth between her legs, Kat's eyes flew open, and her thighs clenched together. Well, as much as they could with his hand and arm sandwiched between them.

"W-what are you doing?" Her startled words came out as a squeak.

"Taking care of you. Now, open up, so I can clean you."

"I can do it."

He grabbed the hand she was reaching down with and pinned it to the bed. Growling softly, he said, "It's my job to take care of you, baby. This is one of those things a Dom does, and it pleases me. Now, open your legs for me."

SHYLY, KAT EASED HER LEGS WIDER AND CLOSED HER EYES AS Benny washed away the evidence of their lovemaking. None of the orgasms she'd ever given herself had been so intense, and she savored the last sensations coursing through her body. Part of her was embarrassed by what he was doing, but the other part felt . . . adored and . . . loved? He'd said earlier he'd loved her . . . past tense. But how did he feel about her now? She opened her eyes until she could just see through the slits and watched him as he bathed her. When he was done, he dipped his head down and kissed her hip, making her smile.

He saw her amusement and shrugged. "Couldn't resist."

Standing, he tugged the covers from underneath her and placed them on top of her. He then shut off the light and climbed in behind her. Spooning her, his arms held her tight. "Sleep, Kitten."

And she did.

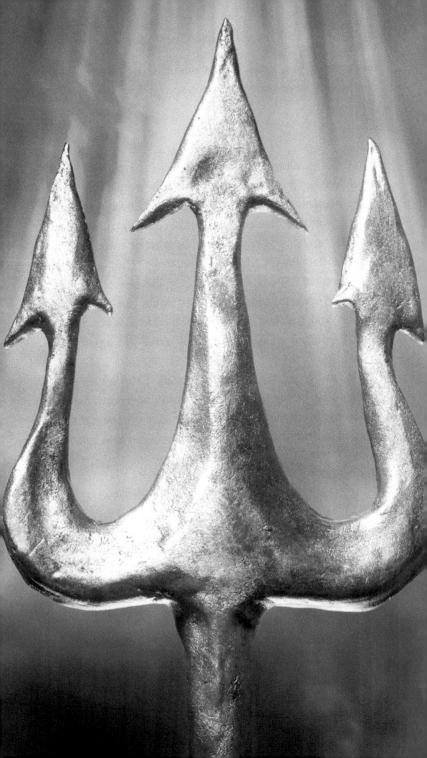

CHAPTER TWELVE

Sitting across from Kat in the little coffee shop, Boomer was happy to see her digging into her breakfast. After their morning round of love-making, she'd told him that she was starving from burning off all those calories. If that was all it took to get her to eat and put some meat back on her thin bones, then who was he to complain?

He popped the last of his toast in his mouth, chewed, and washed it down with a sip of strong coffee. "You ready to see your aunt again?"

She swallowed a mouthful of French toast and syrup. "Yes, but I'm not as nervous as I was last night. I'm excited now. I only hope she doesn't faint."

Her eyes glistened, and he knew she was teasing him. Shit, he was never going to live that down. "Keep it up, Kitten, and next time I get you naked, I'll give you so many orgasms, *you'll* be the one fainting."

He chuckled at her blush. Damn, she was adorable. He eyed her plate and saw she was almost done, so he signaled the waitress for their check. Glancing up at the wall clock b the exit, he noted it was just after 11:30. They'd slept in since Harry had said Kat's aunt would be home around noon.

Boomer had checked in with Ian before breakfast and learned Jake was back at the compound, irritable but resting. The Trident women—Kristen, Angie, and Jenn—were fussing over him and driving him bat-shit crazy. CC was flying Marco and Devon to an airport about thirty minutes from Murfreesboro, and they would rendezvous with them around thirteen-hundred hours. Hopefully, by then, they would know where they were headed next.

Tossing enough money on the table to cover the check and tip, he stood and helped her out of the booth. He didn't let go of her hand but instead linked their fingers together, smiling to himself at how right it felt. This morning while he'd been lying in bed watching her sleep, he realized he was in love with her. Some might call him insane since she'd only walked back into his life less than three days ago, but the truth was, he'd never stopped loving her. And now they had a chance at the future they'd been denied so long ago.

He held the car door open for her, scanning the little town for any threats, but nothing seemed out of the ordinary. Yeah, a few people were eyeing them, but this was a town where everyone knew everyone, and the two of them were strangers. He smiled and said hello to an older couple on his way to the driver's side, then climbed in and started the engine. There wasn't much else to do but hope Irina and her friends had made it back early, so he did a U-turn and steered the car toward her house.

Glancing at Kat, he noticed she was getting nervous again and squeezed her hand. "Everything will be fine, Kitten."

"Oh, I know everything will be okay with my aunt, but I'm scared she won't know anything to help us find out why those men are after me."

"If she doesn't, we'll find another way to figure it out. Brody is still hitting the computer, trying to find what we're missing. Maybe by the time Marco and Dev get here, we'll have some more info."

Pulling into the driveway, they saw a tan Toyota Camry, and Boomer sighed in relief. Despite what she'd said at breakfast, he knew Kat was stressing over the first few minutes of this upcoming reunion, and he was grateful she didn't have to wait any longer. Parking behind the other vehicle, he climbed out and walked around to her door. As he helped her out, the front door to the house opened, and Boomer wasn't too surprised to see Harry walk out.

The older man met them halfway. "I kept my word and haven't said anything to her, but I thought it'd be best for me to be here. It's not every day a woman's niece comes back from the dead."

His words startled them, but Boomer was the first to recover. "How'd you know?"

Harry grinned. "I ain't stupid, son. I've known what happened to Irina's brother and family for years, or at least I thought I did. Their pictures are all over the place in there. It wasn't hard to put two and two together. Although, I'm sure I'm missing a few pieces of the puzzle, along with Irina.

"So, how do you want to do this? She's in the kitchen making coffee and heating up my pie."

Boomer looked at Kat, who shrugged, then back at Harry. "You know her better than we do now, so we'll follow your lead."

The other man nodded. "Okay. Why don't you wait out here then and give me a few minutes?"

The couple agreed and watched as Harry disappeared back into the house. It was four, maybe five minutes before the door flew open, and a shorter, older version of Kat came barreling out to the front yard. She gasped and cried out but never slowed down, running straight to her niece with open arms. Tears fell from both women as they embraced. Irina kept pulling back, staring at Kat, and then hugging her fiercely again. "Katerina, Katerina! Oh, my Lord! I don't understand, but I've never been so happy in my life. My Katerina is back!"

Boomer joined Harry on the front steps, giving the two women a few minutes alone.

"I take it this is going to be a long story, isn't it, son?"

"Yes, sir."

Harry raised an eyebrow at him. "If you'd like, I can come back later. I just wanted to make sure Irina didn't need me."

He thought about it a moment and decided Harry might come in handy. Once they left, they'd need someone to keep an eye on Irina just in case anyone came here looking for them. He'd also call Ian and see if Trident had some contacts they could use to protect the older woman. Kat would be devastated if anything happened to her aunt. "If it's all right with you, sir, I think it would be better if you heard everything."

Harry tilted his head in acknowledgment and continued to watch the tearful reunion.

Twenty minutes later, the four sat around Irina's dining room table, sipping coffee. The pie in front of each of them went untouched, except for Harry's. While listening to Kat tell the older couple what had happened twelve years ago to the present, Boomer regarded the quaint little home. Pictures of Katerina, Alex, and their parents were strategically placed throughout the rooms, and it was apparent how much Irina loved and missed her family.

Sadness filled his chest as he spotted a picture from Alex and Boomer's graduation ceremony. He remembered the photo of the Maier family well because he'd been the one to take it with Kat's camera at her request. The four of them looked so happy, their futures bright with promise. But all the happiness had been destroyed by greed and evil.

He shook his head to clear the anger building up inside him and returned to the present.

Kat's story was interrupted by the occasional "Oh, dear," and "You poor child," from Irina. She hadn't let go of her niece's hand since they'd come into the house, and Boomer knew the feeling of needing to be connected to the long-lost woman.

When Kat took a breath after telling them how she ended up at Trident, Boomer took over. "We're doing everything we can to keep Kat safe, Irina, but we need your help. Ivan gave her a key to a safety deposit box in Norfolk. Only a photograph was inside it, and we hoped you could tell us where it was taken."

As Kat took the picture out of her purse and handed it to Irina, Boomer gave the retired Major a military hand signal to indicate more had happened in Norfolk and that he'd fill the man in later. Kat had agreed with him when he'd suggested they not tell her aunt about the attempted kidnapping the day before. It would only worry her.

"Oh, my, this brings back memories. This is your dad when he was about five or six years old. So, I was about seven then. That's my mother's prized rose bush at the corner of the house. It was beautiful. This is the house we lived in first before we moved to Durham. We moved to Murfreesboro when I was twelve, almost thirteen. That's when Daddy took over the pharmacy here. Before then, he worked for other pharmacists."

Normally, Boomer wouldn't have minded the woman reminiscing the past, but she'd skipped over some important information. "Irina, do you remember the name of the town the first house was in, the one in the picture?"

"Oh, of course. That's what you need to know, isn't it? This was our house in Mint Hill, about a half-hour east of Charlotte."

Boomer nodded. "I've heard of it. My bosses grew up in Charlotte, and their folks still live there. You wouldn't happen to remember the address in Mint Hill, would you?"

"Of course, dear. It was 58 Sycamore Road, but it's not there anymore."

Everyone stared at the woman in confusion as Kat asked, "What do you mean, Aunt Irina?"

"Didn't your father ever tell you? Well, obviously, he didn't. Our home in Mint Hill burned down—there's nothing left."

"What? How come I never heard of this?"

While Kat was shocked, Boomer held back a groan. He'd thought the old house was where they had to go next, but now he wasn't so sure.

Irina patted Kat's hand. "It was no secret, Katerina. I guess you just don't remember ever hearing the story. The house was struck by lightning one night and went up in flames. Luckily, we all got out unharmed, but the house was a total loss. The only things left were a pile of rubble and the chimney. That's when my father took a job at a pharmacy in Durham. The pay was better there, and my grandmother had just passed away, so we were able to stay in her house for a while."

Irina stood, went to the bookshelf, and retrieved an old photo album that looked like it was from the 1970s. She brought it back to the table and handed it to Kat. "This has all our pictures from back then. We still have them because my mother had brought them to her sister's house one day and accidentally left them there."

Kat fingered the flower-covered album. "I remember this. Mom kept it with all our other albums."

"I have them all, Katerina." She pointed to the shelf, and Kat's eyes followed. They filled up when she saw the stack of albums her mother had kept in the family room. "When I had to sell your house after . . . after the accident, I kept everything with sentimental value. Some of it's up in the attic, but I liked flipping through these at night when I was missing you all so terribly. I always wondered what would happen to everything after I was gone, but now . . . now it all belongs to you, my beautiful Katerina."

Kat stood and hugged her aunt, and the flood of tears started again. Harry caught Boomer's eye and jerked his thumb toward the front door. Happy to get away from the crying—he never knew what to do or say around women in tears—Boomer followed the older man to the front steps. Harry gave a fake, exaggerated shudder and shook his head. "Damn, I hate when women cry. Gives me the fucking willies."

Boomer barked out a laugh. "Same goes for me."

"Glad they waited until I was done with my pie. Now, why don't you tell me what you don't want Irina to know."

He filled the man in on the abduction attempt. "I'm going to call my boss before we leave and have him send someone to keep an eye on Irina, just in case."

Pulling out his cell phone, Harry replied, "No need. We may be a small town, but our sheriff is former special ops himself. Makes sure his deputies aren't slackers. He also happens to be my younger brother. If it's all right with you, I can have him come by, and you can fill him in. If you hadn't noticed, strangers kind of stick out around here, especially city slickers."

Boomer knew the man was right but would reserve judgment of the locals' ability to protect Irina until he met the sheriff. "Okay. Why don't you call him while I check on the status of my team? My backup should've landed by now."

As if summoning them, Boomer's phone rang, and Marco's nickname of "Polo" appeared on the screen. Answering it, he gave his teammate an update and Irina's address for their GPS. Confirming they were about thirty minutes away, he hung up and waited for Harry to finish his own call. With everything under control at the moment, the only thing bugging him was they had no idea where to go from there.

When the two men reentered the house, they were relieved to see the waterworks had been turned off again. The women were sitting at the table going through the old photo album as the men sat down again. Kat flipped a page, and Boomer immediately noticed something . . . actually, several somethings. "Kat, let me have the album a second, please."

At his excited tone, she glanced at him and shrugged. "Sure, what's wrong?"

He quickly scanned the pages before and after the one she'd been on. There were six photos on every page, each neatly lined up with the others. But on the left side of the current page, a picture was missing, probably the one from the deposit box, and the picture next to the empty space was turned upside down.

Boomer gently peeled back the plastic sheet protecting the photos and removed the inverted one. It was another picture of Ivan standing at the corner of the old house, but

Irina was also in this one. The seven-year-old was grinning and showing off her missing front tooth.

Boomer flipped it over and found what he hoped was their next clue.

"That's my dad's handwriting."

Kat hadn't needed to tell him. After all these years, he still recognized Ivan Maier's precise penmanship.

"What's it say, son?" Harry asked.

He read off what appeared to be some sort of code. "NW-X-17D-24A."

"Does anyone know what it means?"

They all looked at each other with confused faces. Kat asked what they were all thinking, "Now what?"

Boomer sighed. "I'll call Brody. Maybe he can figure out what your father was trying to tell us. Kat, while I'm doing that, can you check the backs of all the other pictures in there? Irina, is it okay if we take this album along with the others? There might be something else in them we're missing."

"Of course, Benny. They belong to Katerina anyway."

Boomer tried to hide his wince at her calling him "Benny." She obviously picked it up fast from Kat's use of it.

He strode to the front door and took out his phone again. When he was done filling in Egghead, a patrol car pulled up to the mailboxes next to the road. Harry must've heard it because he came outside at the same time the sheriff exited the vehicle.

Harry introduced the two men, and they shook hands. "Pleased to meet you, Sheriff Bernhard."

"Same here, Ben. But call me Marty. Harry tells me we might have a problem here."

"I hope not, Marty." Boomer filled the other man in, and

just as he was wrapping things up, a rental sedan pulled into the drive. "Here's my backup."

More introductions were done as Devon and Marco joined the group. Devon clapped his teammate on the back. "So, what's next, Baby Boomer?"

Boomer growled but didn't take the teasing bait. The guys only added the "Baby" to his nickname to get a rise out of him or ease tensions. Instead of getting snarky, he told them about the note on the back of the photo. "I think our next stop is Mint Hill. There's gotta be some reason why Ivan used those two pictures as clues."

"I agree. It'll take about four and a half hours to get there, so it'll be too late to look around tonight. We can stay at my folks' place. They're out in San Diego visiting my brother while his team's INCONUS." Nick, the youngest of the Sawyer family, had followed in his brothers' footsteps and was a Navy SEAL on Team Three. It'd been a few months since he'd been on U.S. soil.

Boomer looked at his boss in confusion. "Why can't we make a puddle jump in the jet? We can be there in under an hour."

"CC's daughter went into labor about two hours ago with his first grandchild. He was refueling and heading right back down to Tampa. I'll call Ian and have him get ahold of Chase. He can send one of his jets to Charlotte for us."

Chase Dixon owned Blackhawk Security and supplied Trident and other companies with additional trained personnel or transports if needed.

"All right. Then we better get on the road. Let me get Kat." He rolled his eyes. "Get ready for more tears as she and her aunt say goodbye."

Almost as one, the other men all shuddered.

CHAPTER THIRTEEN

It was just after six p.m. when they all walked into a pub not too far from the Sawyer family home. Kat couldn't help but notice the drooling stares from most women toward the three handsome men who surrounded her. The guys were impressive by height and physiques alone, but add in their good-looking faces, and she could just imagine how many of the women wished they were her at the moment. She was sure they might change their minds when they found out people were trying to kidnap and possibly kill her.

After they sat at a table, a pretty waitress with fake tits openly flirted with Benny, Devon, and Marco, but only the latter flirted back. From what Kat had been told, Devon was happily engaged, while Marco was single. As for Benny, he only seemed to have eyes for her, which made her body tingle when she saw the heat in his gaze. She hoped it meant he wanted her as much as she wanted him. Not knowing how many bedrooms there were in Devon's parents' house, she didn't know the sleeping arrangements for the night. Kat prayed she and Benny would be sharing a room.

"So, Kat, what was Baby Boomer like as a kid?"

She glanced at Devon in amusement. "I know his nickname is Boomer because he's trained in explosives, but why do you call him Baby Boomer?"

"Two reasons. One, because he's the youngest guy on the team. And two, because he hates it."

Kat giggled as Benny rolled his eyes. "So, of course, the more he hates it, the more everyone uses it."

A grin spread across Devon's face. "Pretty much, yeah. A lot of nicknames received in the military are not ones we would've picked for ourselves. Mine's 'Devil Dog,' and while it's a long story, let's just say it involved my foot locker and a month's supply of Drake's Devil Dogs."

She laughed. "I love those! Mom always used to stock up on those and Yodels." She looked at Benny's other teammate. "So, Marco, what's your nickname, or don't you have one."

"I got lucky with mine—no embarrassing story behind it. They gave me 'Polo' as in Marco Polo."

"Oh, how cute!"

The other men chuckled, and Marco pretended to be insulted. "First time someone's called my name cute."

The waitress returned with their drinks, and Kat thought the woman would melt when Marco winked at her. But as soon as the giggling blonde walked away, he turned his attention back to Kat. "So, tell us about when Baby Boomer was a juvenile delinquent. Give us some good dirt we can use against him."

They spent the next hour eating and telling tales. She told them about Benny, Alex, and her antics back in high school, and they told her what they could from their military and Trident days. She quickly found out teasing and practical jokes were a large part of the teammates' relationships.

When they'd finished dinner, she realized she felt more relaxed than she had in years.

From the pub, it didn't take them long to reach the Sawyer home. As Benny followed the other rental car up the long driveway, Kat couldn't help but gawk at the . . . estate, she guessed she could call it. "Holy cow! This is where Devon and Ian grew up?"

The large home sat on several acres of land, but despite its size, it wasn't ostentatious. The lawn was beautifully manicured, and trees, shrubs, and flower beds dotted the landscape, similar to her aunt's place but on a grander scale. Four columns were spaced evenly across the front of the brick and stucco house, and both vehicles parked in the circular drive surrounding a water fountain.

"Actually, no. Mr. and Doc Sawyer bought this the year after Dev enlisted. I'm not sure if you've ever heard of their dad out on the West Coast. His name is Charles, but those close to him call him Chuck. He made a fortune in real estate when his boys were younger, and now they've got houses all over the place. Doc Sawyer is a plastic surgeon, and they both do a lot of charity work, so they travel a lot."

"Wow. The name doesn't sound familiar, but I'm not big on reading about people I don't personally know."

"They visit Tampa a few times a year, and we visit them when we can. They've kind of adopted the rest of the team as their own. You'll get along with them great. Nicest people in the world. Laid-back. Despite the nice houses and cars, you'd never know they were loaded. They remember what it's like to be a struggling middle-class family."

Benny grabbed their duffel bags before they followed Devon and Marco into the house. After shutting the door, Devon reactivated the security system. "Polo, you can crash in Ian's room. Boomer, you and Kat can take the two guest rooms at the end of the upstairs hallway."

"We only need one room."

Devon raised an eyebrow but didn't question the statement. "Okay. Why don't you show her to a room, and I'll check in with the office? I'll see if Egghead made sense of those letters and numbers."

Kat followed him up the elegant staircase and down the hall to one of the guest rooms. He shut the door behind them, dropped their bags, then drew her into his arms, kissing her senseless. She lost track of time before he pulled away and then stared at her with lust-filled eyes. "I've wanted to do that all day."

Giggling, she admitted, "*I've* wanted *you* to do that all day. Well, and a few other things."

He pinched her ass, and she squeaked. "Little tease. I have to go back down and find out if Brody has any information for us. Why don't you relax or take a shower? I'll be back up in a bit."

Placing a swift kiss on his lips, she turned and sashayed to the bathroom, swinging her hips seductively. "Don't be long."

———

WHILE KAT WAS SHOWERING AND GETTING READY FOR BED, Boomer joined his teammates in the entertainment room, but not before taming the hard-on she'd given him. A glass of Jack Daniels awaited him, and he thanked Devon for his foresight. "Anything from Egghead?"

"No, but he's running the sequence through every code-breaking program he has. And a few you don't even want to know he has access to." The geek was one of the most talented hackers in the business, and if the FBI, CIA, and NSA couldn't have him as one of their own, they were just grateful he was on their side of the law.

Marco was occupying one of the recliners and had the TV

tuned to a baseball game with the volume on low. As the other two took seats on both couches, Boomer's phone rang. He pulled it from his pocket and checked the screen.

CALLER UNKNOWN

That wasn't unusual. "Michaelson."

"Boom-Boom. What's going on?"

"Hey, Carter, what's up?" Boomer was a little surprised to hear from the black-ops agent. It'd been over two months since he'd seen him at The Covenant, enjoying an evening of play. T. Carter had become close friends with the men of Trident after running into them on numerous missions over the years. Each of them owed him for being in the right place at the right time on several occasions. If it hadn't been for him, one or more of the team could've been killed by a sniper at the Trident compound almost a year earlier. Boomer had no idea which one of the U.S. alphabet agencies the man actually worked for, but from experience and the stories he'd heard over the years, he was glad Carter was on their side. You could sum the man up in one word: deadly.

"Spoke to Ian and then Keon this morning, and they told me what you've been up to the past few days. I did some digging and found some intel for you."

"Shit—you're the best. Hang on. Polo and Dev are with me. Let me put you on speaker." He punched the correct button and set the phone on the coffee table, so they could all hear the information. "All right, go."

The man's deep voice rumbled from the speaker. "Rumor has it Sergei Volkov's own people put a hit out on him. It was suspected he was making deals under the table and not telling those above him on the food chain. He was getting greedy, and it was pissing some people off. Again, rumor has it his second-in-command did the dirty deed and then

135

replaced him. Name's Viktor "The Bull" Dryagin, a mean mother-fucker. Not a guy you want to be fucking with. Word is he immediately began looking for buried treasure."

"'Buried treasure'... what the fuck does that mean?"

"Apparently, many years ago, an accountant of theirs was killed along with his family in a car accident . . . sound familiar?"

"Yeah," Boomer replied cautiously. He didn't like where this was going.

"Yeah, well, three days *after* this accountant was allegedly killed, a large sum of money disappeared from several accounts this guy had access to. Transferred off-shore and then to parts unknown."

"Fuck!" he spat out. "How much money are we talking about here, Carter?"

"Fifteen mil."

"What? Holy shit!" Boomer shoved his hands into his hair and almost pulled a few chunks out in frustration and disbelief. "Aw, fuck me. Ivan stole fifteen million dollars from the Russian mafia. Was he fucking crazy?"

"My guess . . . it was his form of revenge, Boom."

Marco nodded in agreement while Devon spoke. "Sounds like it. From what I understand, Ivan was a simple family man. Looks like he exacted his revenge where he could hurt them the most—in the purse strings."

Still trying to wrap his head around this new development, Boomer stared at the ceiling. "I don't get it. From what Kat told us, they both worked and lived middle-class lives. Nothing to indicate that kind of money. So, what the hell did he do with it?"

"That's the big question. Carter, any ideas?" Devon asked.

"Sorry, Devil Dog. All I know is Volkov had been looking for the money for years, even though the higher-ups wrote it off as a loss. If I get wind of anything else, I'll give you a buzz."

"Thanks, man."

The call disconnected, and after going over a few more things with his teammates, Boomer headed upstairs to the bedroom he was sharing with Kat. He wasn't sure if he should hit her with this news tonight or wait until morning. He had to tell her soon because there were questions he needed answers to.

Opening the door, he froze at the sight before him. Damn, she was so fucking beautiful that she took his breath away.

Kat was sitting on the queen-sized bed wearing nothing but a soft, green towel. Her bare arms and legs glistened with newly applied lotion, and the tropical scent of coconuts hung in the air. It must be from Doc Sawyer's guest stash because it differed from what Kat had used earlier at the bed and breakfast. She was brushing her towel-dried hair, struggling to get a few knots out.

Boomer shut the door and strode purposely toward her, holding out his hand. "Let me do it for you."

Surprise popped into her eyes, but she handed over the brush, then turned so her back was to him. Sitting behind her, he took a section of her long locks and glided the bristles through them. When he hit a snag, he made sure he wasn't hurting her as he began to work the light brown strands free. Wordlessly, he continued, section by section, until the brush flowed easily with each pass.

"There. All done."

When she peered at him over her shoulder, there was no mistaking the heat in her gaze. Her voice was low and husky when she asked, "How did you do that?"

His eyes narrowed in confusion. "Do what?"

"You turned something I do every day into an erotic gesture. I thought only guys in romance novels did things like that."

Boomer smirked and leaned forward to lick her ear. "You ain't seen nothing yet, Kitten."

Encouraged by the shiver that coursed through her, he moved her damp hair to the side, and she tilted her head to give him better access to her neck. He kissed, licked, and nibbled the sensitive skin there as he reached around and tugged the towel free from her body. Bringing one hand to her breast, he plucked and rolled the hard little peak until she squirmed and begged him for more.

"Do you trust me, Kitten?" he whispered in her ear while his hands continued to push her arousal higher and higher.

She was panting as her back arched in pleasure. "Oh, God, yes. Yes, I trust you."

He growled and kissed her bare shoulder. Scanning the room, Boomer spotted what he needed. He hurried over to the French doors leading to a small balcony and removed one of the tasseled ropes holding the heavy curtains back. It was perfect for what he wanted to do to her.

Returning to her, he chuckled at the doe-eyed expression on her face. "I promise you, baby, you're going to love this. Put your hands behind your back." He was pleased when she only hesitated a split second before doing as he requested. With practiced ease, he secured her wrists together, then checked to ensure the rope wasn't too tight. The material used to create the crimson braid was soft and silky, so he didn't have to worry about it chafing her tender skin.

He caressed her cheek. "Your safeword is 'red.' If you get scared or something doesn't feel right, just say 'red,' and I'll untie you right away. Okay?" He kept it simple for now, like an on-off switch. As things progressed between them, he would introduce the "yellow" safeword, which she would use to slow things down before continuing.

"Okay."

"Mmm. That was rule number two. Rule number one was no putting yourself down. Now, rule number three is, when we are playing like this, I want you to call me Sir or Master. Can you do that for me, Kitten?"

"Yes. Yes, Master."

He leaned down and brushed his lips to hers. "Damn, it sounds so nice coming from your mouth. Say it again."

Her tongue peeked out to moisten her lips. "Yes, Master."

Boomer snarled like a beast that sensed its mate was in heat. He crushed his mouth to hers, holding her in place by grasping her hair. Lips melded, teeth clashed, and tongues dueled as he reveled in her taste. His cock was thick and hard in his jeans, but he wasn't ready to take her . . . yet. He had some dirty, delicious plans for her first.

Abruptly, he broke them apart. There was another set of lips he wanted to claim. Pulling his wallet from his back pocket, he placed it with his gun on the nightstand. He then spotted the box of condoms they'd grabbed earlier while gassing up at a truck stop. Snagging one, he grinned when he realized she'd opened the box for him—*such a naughty girl.*

Stripping quickly, he laid across the bed, picked her up, and positioned her until she sat on his face. Her legs were next to his ears, and her core was just inches above his mouth. Her scent drove him crazy, but before he began his feast, he told her, "Rule number four, Kitten, is no coming without permission. Concentrate hard, and you'll be able to do it. The longer you hold out, the more pleased I'll be. And the more pleased you make me, the harder you'll come when I let you."

Kat whimpered with need, and her pussy wept with it. "Y-yes, Master."

"You can make some noise if you need to. The guys are on the other side of the house." He chuckled and rubbed his chin stubble against her inner thigh. "Just don't scream too loud. Otherwise, they may think we're in trouble down here."

"O-okay. Please."

"Mmmm. I like that word. Please, what, baby? Tell me what you want, and maybe I'll be nice and give it to you."

Her entire body blushed, and her thighs quivered in anticipation. "Oh, God. Please . . . um . . . please lick me."

"Lick you where?" he teased.

"T-there. Between my legs."

"Uh-uh, Kitten. You can do better than that. We need to work on your dirty bedroom talk. Ask me to eat your sweet pussy." His hands moved from her hips to her ass cheeks, and he squeezed and massaged them. "Think about all those naughty books you read. Tell your Master what he wants to hear."

She closed her eyes and swallowed hard, but he wouldn't make another move without her verbal request. "Please, Benny . . . I mean, Master. Please eat my . . . my sweet pussy."

"With pleasure, baby. With pleasure."

BENNY TUGGED HER DOWN, AND SHE CRIED OUT THE MOMENT she felt his mouth kiss her pussy lips. Alternating, he suckled on each one, then licked and nibbled them. His tongue lapped at her slit while his nose bumped against her clit. Kat suddenly realized why he'd restrained her hands. She was at his mercy and could only, literally, sit there and take it. He teased, tantalized, and tortured her. His strong hands held her in place as she tried to squirm and grind her mound into his mouth.

"More, oh please, more. Don't stop, please don't stop." Her own words sounded incoherent to her, and she hoped she was making sense to him. Behind her, her hands found the skin of his chest and scratched it. Sensations bombarded her as years of sexual frustration boiled to the surface. His tongue did more for her than her vibrator had ever done. If it weren't for his hands holding her, she would've fallen flat on her face into the mattress. Higher and higher, he took her. Oh God, she was so close!

His tongue impaled her, and she shattered into a million pieces. Her body shook with the impact. Up was down, down was up. Nothing made sense as wave after wave tumbled over her. White lights and black dots filled her vision, and she thought she would pass out. She soared to the heavens and back again. How had she lived her entire life without knowing what it was like to fly?

Oh, shit! That wasn't supposed to happen, was it?

He'd told her not to come without permission. "I'm s-sorry," she sobbed and heaved, her body still reeling.

Boomer shifted her until she was sitting on his chest. His mouth and chin were coated with her juices, and he licked off what he could reach. "Shh. It's okay, baby. We can work on it."

He chuckled. "After all, practice makes perfect. And I plan on practicing with you over and over again. But next time, Kitten, you will be punished if you disobey me. And your punishments will consist of my hand spanking your bare ass until you beg me to fuck you."

His words almost made her come again. The thought of him draping her over his lap was something she'd been thinking of ever since he'd slapped her ass the night before.

She saw him grab the condom he'd tossed on the bed, and her sex quivered. Never had she known such lust and desire. He reached around her and covered himself before his hands grasped her hips and positioned her over his hard shaft. Kat rose up on her knees to give him room and moaned as he rubbed the tip along her slit. Her body yielded to him as he inched into her tight channel. The drag of his cock against her walls was pure heaven.

Benny lowered her slowly until she was fully seated on him, then held her there. "Oh, fuck, woman! You're burning me alive. I won't be able to take this slow for long, sweetheart."

Every nerve inside Kat was alive. Each slide and twitch of his cock was sweet torture. Her walls clenched, and she loved how it made him moan. "Don't want slow," she panted. "Fast . . . please . . . fast."

"Thank fuck!"

Tightening the grip on her hips, he began to raise and lower her in time to his thrusts. The position felt so different from last night, and she quickly felt her orgasm building. With her hands still behind her, her chest was shoved forward, and her tits bounced with every movement. He pulled her down across his torso and took one of the orbs into his mouth. The dual assault on her pussy and nipple had her begging. "Oh, shit! Oh, Benny . . . Master . . . more, please. Oh my God, I'm going to . . . oh, please . . . I need . . . oh, help me . . . I need . . . please . . ."

She felt one of his hands slide between them, and as his fingers found her clit, he stopped sucking on her nipple only long enough to command, "Come, Kitten. Come for me."

He pinched her clit while his teeth bit down on her taut peak, and she began to fall. "Oh . . . oh . . . oh, shhhhhiiiii-itttttt!"

BOOMER WATCHED AS SHE SPIRALED INTO OBLIVION WHILE HE continued to pound into her from underneath. Her pussy was his home, and there was nowhere else he wanted to be. His balls drew up tight as his lower spine tingled. A few more thrusts and he was there.

"Fuck, baby, yeah . . . oh, fucking yeah . . . *aaaaahhhhhhhh*, shit!" His body went rigid as his seed filled the thin barrier between them. Her walls were milking every last drop from him, and she melted on top of him. He slowed their rhythm to a stop, gasping for breath. Sweating, panting, tingling, quivering—he swore it would take hours to recover.

Boomer reached around and untied her wrists. His hands massaged her arms up to her shoulders, making sure her circulation hadn't been cut off. "You okay, baby?"

"Mm-hmm."

Chuckling, he reached between them and squeezed the rim of the condom before pulling out of her. She moaned in protest as he rolled her off him onto her side. Leaning toward her, he kissed her pert little nose. "I'll be right back."

"Mm-hmm."

He was back moments later with a washcloth. "Spread your legs for me, Kitten."

"Mm-hmm."

Snorting his amusement, he began to clean her. "Mm-hmm? Is that all you can say?"

"Mmm," she mumbled. "You knocked the dictionary out of my head. Can't think."

He grinned and tossed the cloth back into the bathroom, where it landed on the tiled floor. Pulling back the covers, he picked her up and settled her sated body on her side of the bed and nestled in behind her. Her ass cheeks cradled his softened cock as he squeezed her hip. Once this craziness was behind them, he planned on preparing her ass to be taken. He hoped like hell it wouldn't be on her hard-limit list.

Shit! How the hell were they supposed to make plans for the future with a fifteen-million-dollar price tag hanging over her head? Not wanting to spoil her contentment, he decided to wait until the morning to tell her about the money. Although, she hadn't given him much choice as he realized her breathing had turned shallow and she was asleep. Holding her close, he cupped one breast and closed his eyes.

CHAPTER FOURTEEN

K at awoke in a sweat, and it took her a moment to comprehend it was Benny's body heat which had her ripping off her covers. When he didn't move or say anything, she realized he was still asleep as he spooned her from behind, his arm anchored around her waist. The morning sun was peeking through the sheers covering the French door's clear panes, and she suddenly needed to use the toilet. When she tried to ease out of the bed, his arm tightened around her and his hand found her breast and squeezed. She bit her lip and tried again. This time when she shifted, the hand went south to her pelvis and his hips thrust forward. His morning wood was now nestled between her lower cheeks, and he pumped a few more times, groaning, but still in slumber.

Shit! It felt so good, so naughty, but if she didn't get up soon her bladder was going to stage a protest. "Benny?" She shook his arm. Of course, all that did was make him grind his erection into her flesh again. She raised her voice a little louder and tried again. "Benny, I have to get up."

"Why?" he mumbled.

"I have to use the bathroom."

Slowly, he released her, and she crawled out of the bed. She was halfway to the door when he asked, "What time is it?"

Kat glanced at the bedside clock. "Seven-fifteen," she told him before entering the bathroom.

GROANING, BOOMER SHIFTED ONTO HIS BACK AND WATCHED her ass disappear into the bathroom. He grabbed his stiff cock and gave it a few rubs, then scratched his balls. Behind the now-closed door, the toilet flushed and then he heard the sound of the shower coming on.

He lay there for a minute, letting the morning fog clear from his brain when a thought occurred to him. This time he didn't have to worry about what she would think if he joined her. Throwing the covers off, he strode across the room and was happy to find the door unlocked. Deciding to have a little fun, he used his stealth training and slowly cracked open the door. Steam had filled the room, but through the mirror, he could still make out her naked form stepping into the shower. It was an open walk-in stall behind thick glass blocks with no door or curtain to shut.

Kat's back was to him as he slipped into the room and shut the door behind him. Silently, he eased over to the shower opening, stepped inside, and leaned against the tiled wall. He watched as she tilted her head back, and with closed eyes let the water sluice down her face, neck, shoulders, and lower. His eyes followed the writhing streams of liquid as her hands pushed her wet hair off her forehead. A rivulet flowed down her spine and disappeared into the crack of her ass. And still, her back remained toward him.

Boomer's pulse raced as his eyelids and balls grew heavy. Gripping his hard, thick cock, he slowly stroked it while he watched her grab a pink loofah and a bottle of body wash. The scent of coconuts filled the air, and it made him even harder, reminding him of how good she smelled last night. The loofah was now lathered, and soap bubbles began to coat her skin. He tugged on his cock, and pre-cum oozed as his gaze followed the pink bundle as it passed over every inch of her skin. She spread her legs and moaned loudly as she soaped up her pussy. Boomer bit his lip, trying to stay silent.

"Are you going to stand there all day, watching me and playing with yourself?"

A grin spread across his face. "How did you know I was here, you little tease?"

Turning, she gave him a saucy smile. "I felt the cooler air when the door opened. And I also have great peripheral vision." She continued to run the loofah over her body as she watched his hand pump up and down.

"Are you sore this morning? Be honest because you rode me pretty hard last night."

A blush spread over her cheeks as she nodded.

"It's okay, Kitten. I can just take care of this," his chin dipped toward his groin, "while you finish showering over there."

Kat bit her bottom lip, then her tongue caressed her upper one. "Or, I could . . . you know . . ."

Boomer snorted in amusement. "We're going to have to work on your naughty vocabulary. Does 'you know' mean you're offering to blow me?"

Her gaze stayed on his hand as it slowly worked his cock —up, over, back, and down, in a mesmerizing rhythm. "The other night was the first time I ever did . . . you know, but I've read lots of books, so I was just doing what they said."

"Well, you did a fine job. I loved fucking your mouth, but this time I want to come down your throat. Do you think you can handle it?"

"I-I don't know, but I want to try . . . Master."

Boomer growled. "Fuck, I love hearing that from your lips. Sit down on the bench, baby, and let me rinse off really quick. Then, I'm going to fuck your sweet mouth."

The built-in tiled bench was in two separate sections, one higher than the other. The lower one would be the perfect height for her to sit on while she gave him a blow-job. He took the pink loofah from her hand and lathered up his body, taking extra time to clean his cock and balls for her. After rinsing the suds off, he stepped toward her. She licked her lips, and he groaned as he guided his aching cock to her waiting mouth. "Lick it, baby. Like a lollipop."

KAT'S TONGUE GLIDED UP THE THICK VEIN ON THE UNDERSIDE, and Benny hissed. "Oh, yeah. Do it again."

Encouraged, Kat began licking in earnest. Gripping him by the root and cupping his sac, she remembered how he told her he liked it. A drop of pre-cum appeared at the tip, and she ran her tongue over it. It was salty, but that's all that registered to her taste buds.

His hand grasped her wet hair and pulled her closer to his groin. "Open wide. Take me in as far as you can."

Her mouth formed an "O," and she wrapped her lips around his hard flesh. Being careful not to hurt him with her teeth, she sucked him like a straw in a thick milkshake.

Groaning, he thrust his hips, forcing her to take a little more of him each time. He was so wide, she wasn't sure if she could get all of him in her mouth, but she wanted to try.

Swirling her tongue around him made him tighten his grip on her hair, and the pain from her scalp went straight to her clit, making it throb with need. She didn't care if she was sore and brought one hand to her mound.

"Uh-uh, Kitten. I didn't say you could play with yourself. You save that for me. I'll take care of you after I come in your mouth."

She whimpered around his cock. She needed to touch herself, but she wanted to please him more. Her mind had become focused on her clit, and she lost track of what she was doing. Kat gagged and coughed when his tip hit the back of her throat. Reflexively, her jaw closed a little, and he jerked his hips. "Shit, baby, watch those teeth!"

Releasing him, her eyes filled with apology. "Sorry! I didn't mean . . ."

"Shhh. It's ok. This is something you have to practice. I'll hold back a little so you don't choke. Okay?"

Kat nodded and tried again. This time she kept her mind on what she was doing because she didn't want to bite him. His hand guided her, and she followed his lead. Slow at first, his thrusts gradually became faster and shorter.

"I'm going to come, baby. Swallow what you can."

"Mm-hm."

BOOMER'S BALLS DREW UP TIGHT, AND BLACK SPOTS APPEARED before his eyes. "Oh, fuck! Damn, you feel so good. Swallow, baby."

Boomer shot his load into her mouth, and Kat immediately began to choke.

"Shit!" He quickly pulled out, and the rest of his cum hit her in the face and neck. What had made it into her mouth came right back out as she spit on the shower floor. Coughing and hacking, she looked at him in horror as he knelt before her.

He used his hands to wipe her face clean, using water still flowing from the showerhead. "Shhhhh. Baby, it's okay. Shhh. Breathe, Kitten, breathe through your nose."

"I . . ." Her voice was barely audible as she tried to catch her breath. Watery, red eyes tried to focus on him and failed. She coughed a few more times and then finally cleared her throat. "I'm s-sorry."

Boomer pulled her into his arms and rested her head on his shoulder. His hands rubbed up and down her back. "There's no reason to be sorry, baby. No reason at all. Most women do the same thing the first time. I should have warned you. Sex gets sloppy sometimes . . . most times. And swallowing cum isn't for everyone. But I'm proud of you for trying. Are you okay?"

She took a ragged breath. "I-I think so?"

Pulling back, he looked at her and grinned. "I gather it wasn't what you expected."

"Not at all." She giggled and wiped the last of her tears away. "I'm sorry, but in books, they always write how sweet and delicious it is, and it's not." She winced. "Sorry, I didn't mean to insult you."

Boomer stood and helped her up as well. "C'mere. Let's get you cleaned up again. And I'm not insulted. That's one thing about those romance books . . . everything is perfect in them. In reality, some people find cum bitter and salty, while others enjoy the taste."

As they washed each other, Kat's embarrassment over the incident seemed to ebb from her body. Wanting to return the pleasure he'd received, he put his hand between her legs, but she hissed and grabbed his wrist. "No. Don't."

"Sore?"

"Yeah, sorry."

His hand gripped her chin, and he made sure her eyes were on him. "Stop saying you're sorry, Kitten. Everything you're feeling is normal. Stop living in those fantasy worlds for a minute. Sex is dirty, messy, and, yes, sometimes a little painful. But I'm looking forward to showing you how the pain can be turned into pleasure. I know you're reading Kristen's book, and from what I've read, she does a pretty good job of getting her sex scenes true to reality. If you have questions when we get home, she'll be a good person to talk to."

"Kristen? You mean, you know Kristen Anders? You've read her books?"

He almost smirked at the hint of jealousy in her voice. "I've only skimmed through the sex scenes, and yeah, I know her. Except she'll be Kristen Sawyer soon. She's Devon's fiancée and submissive."

Wide eyes stared back at him. "Oh, my God! I didn't know that. Why didn't you tell me?" She playfully smacked his chest and then shut off the water. They'd be prunes if they stayed in any longer.

Boomer took one of the guest towels from the rack outside the stall and wrapped it around her before taking another for himself. "Sorry, I kind of had other things on my mind."

"Like people shooting at us and stuff." Her voice had grown quieter as if the reality of the past few days had come back to her in a rush.

Grimacing, he followed her into the bedroom to get dressed. "Yeah, stuff like that."

Ten minutes later, they joined Devon and Marco in the large, eat-in kitchen. The two of them eyed Boomer, and he shook his head—no, he hadn't told her yet. When they were settled with coffee and bagels at the table, he squeezed her hand. "Kat, we found out some information last night and have a few questions for you."

Warily, she put down the coffee cup she'd just picked up. "Okay. Shoot."

"What happened in the few days following the accident?"

The color seeped from her face, and he squeezed her hand again. Taking a deep breath, she took a moment to think back to that terrible time. "Um . . . the FBI brought us to a hospital for treatment, then arranged for us to be pronounced . . ." She swallowed hard. "Um . . . pronounced dead. They snuck us out of there and took us to a safe house. We changed safe houses after twenty-four and forty-eight hours. I was so numb and upset, I don't even know where we were."

"It's okay, baby. Do you remember if your dad had access to a computer?"

She shook her head. "I don't . . . I don't remember. I'm sorry. I remember they took our cell phones, and we could watch TV, but I don't think we had a computer. One of the agents may have had one, though. It was so long ago, I honestly don't remember. Why? What did my father do?"

The tears in her eyes were killing him. "We think your dad stole money from the accounts he was in charge of for the Russians a few days after the accident. Did he give you any indication he'd come into a large sum of money over the years?"

"OH. MY. GOD. NO . . . NO . . . NO!" ANGER BOILED WITHIN Kat as she shook her head. How could her father have done this to her? It had to be why those men were after her. "We had a joint account at the bank. The only money there was what the marshals had given us to start over with, and our paychecks were directly deposited. As far as I know, it was the only account he had. How much . . . how much money did he take?"

When Benny didn't answer her immediately, she looked at Marco and Devon. "How. Much?"

"Fifteen million dollars," Devon told her quietly.

Whatever color had returned to her face drained again. She jumped from her seat and began to pace the kitchen, her hands raised in disbelief. "Fifteen . . . fifteen million. Holy shit! Holy! Fucking! Shit! Daddy, what the fuck did you do? Fifteen million dollars! Where . . . where . . ."

Devon interrupted her rant with his soothing voice. "That's what we have to figure out, Kat. From what our contact told us, Sergei Volkov was killed by his own people. A man name Viktor Dryagin has taken over, and we think he's the one who wants to find you and the money."

"But I don't know where it is!"

Benny stood and embraced her. His strong arms and body heat instantly calmed her. "They don't know that, Kat. But your dad left us clues which will hopefully tell us where the money is."

"And if we don't find it, what then?" she cried into his shoulder.

"One step at a time, baby. We'll find a way out of this. One step at a time."

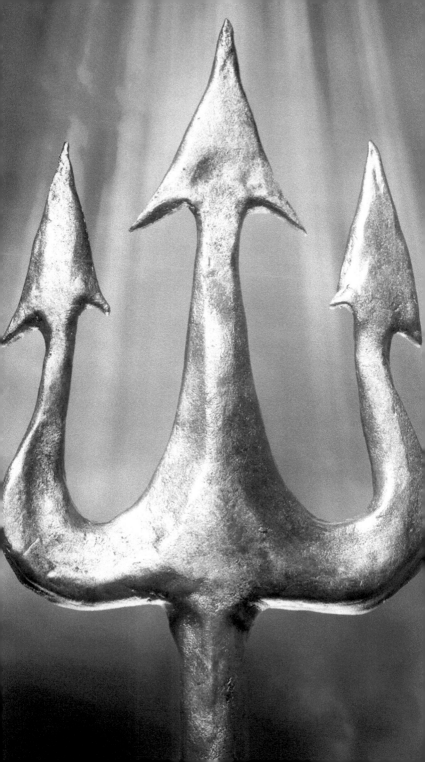

CHAPTER FIFTEEN

"Viktor? It's Ruslan."

"Vhat you have for me?"

"Ve traced rental to business in Tampa. Trident Security. Former military. Place vell-guarded. Paranoid group."

"*Blyat*! Any sign of girl?"

"Nyet."

"Keep looking. I vant that money. Kill anyone who gets in vay."

"*Horosho*."

Viktor the Bull hung up the phone and tossed it on his desk. He was this close to getting the money the fucking accountant had stolen from Sergei years ago. The higher-ups had written it off long ago, despite it being a lot of money, because they had plenty to burn. But thanks to a talented computer geek, fifteen million dollars was finally within Viktor's reach. When he'd gotten the okay to off Volkov, he'd renewed his efforts to find Ivan Maier. With a bit of money thrown in the right direction twelve years ago, they'd learned the accountant and his daughter had survived the ___ident." Unfortunately, the trail went cold after a few sightings. Now with the latest facial-recognition program, he was on the hunt again. And this time, he would succeed.

THE TWO RENTAL VEHICLES PULLED UP TO THE FORGOTTEN piece of land. It, along with surrounding properties, had been abandoned long ago. A few dilapidated barns and houses, built over seven decades ago, dotted the area. Brody had hacked into the local government computers and gotten the coordinates of Ivan Maier's childhood home or what was left of it. Irina had been right. All that remained from the old house was the foundation, charred pieces of wood, and a brick chimney. The weeds and a few animals in the area had made their home in the ruins.

All four of them exited the vehicles and stared in dismay at the sight before them. A breeze blew Kat's hair in several directions, and she quickly put it up into a ponytail with a band she pulled from her pocket. "So, now what? What are we looking for?"

Boomer held out his hand to her. "Watch your step. There's lots of old debris around, and you can't see it well with these damn weeds."

As Boomer led her closer to the foundation, Marco jumped down into what had been the basement. It looked like the area was a hangout for juveniles with nothing better to do. Empty beer bottles, soda cans, garbage, and the occasional used condom littered the area. Devon circled the area around the foundation and inspected the chimney before joining his teammate in the hole. Instead of jumping, he pushed aside a useless metal door and took a set of cement stairs that once lead to the backyard.

From the former front steps, Boomer and Kat scanned the area below. "Anything?"

"Aside from all this crap, Boom, I'm not seeing anything out of place," Marco told him while kicking some rubbish out of the way. "It's either long gone or well hidden. Did Kat's aunt say anything about an underground shelter or a well on the property?"

Kat pulled out her cell phone. "No, she didn't, but I can call her."

Boomer nodded his agreement. "It's a possibility, but there were other pictures from this property in the album. He picked the ones in front of the house for a reason."

They spent the next twenty minutes searching above and below ground, and Kat made several calls to her aunt whenever they had questions. Frustrated but unwilling to give up, Boomer jumped into the basement.

Devon walked over to where his teammate landed and held out his hand. "Let me see the photo again."

"Here." He gave his boss the picture, and they examined it together. Young Ivan was standing at the corner of the house, where the front and chimney sides met. Nothing stood out, and Devon turned it over to the writing on the back.

"Fuck." Boomer threw his hands up in irritation and spun around in a circle. "Ivan couldn't fucking say 'X' marks the spot?"

The others mumbled in agreement as he faced what was left of the fireplace on the first floor. There had to be something they were missing. He tilted his head back and stared at the sky as if it held the answers. The morning sun was still over his right shoulder.

Son of a bitch!

He quickly checked the compass on his military watch and then stared up at the chimney again.

"Holy shit! I think I've got it." Praying his epiphany was right, he scrambled up the stairs to the backyard and jogged around the foundation to the right.

"What?" Devon was on his heels, with Marco not much further behind. "What is it?"

The three stopped and gazed at the partially damaged brickwork, but only Boomer understood what he was looking at. "This side of the house is facing northwest." He took the photo back from Devon. "It says 'NW dash X.' Northwest. And look at the upper left corner before the chimney narrows . . . there's an 'X' on that brick. It's like a crossword puzzle, I think. I remember Ivan doing them all the time . . . in ink! '17D dash 24A' Seventeen down and twenty-four across."

As Marco stepped up to the bricks and began counting down and across, Devon smacked Boomer on the back. "I'll tell Ian not to bother with the crossword dictionary as your Christmas present."

He snorted, then yelled for Kat to join them. She was skirting the foundation when Marco pulled out his Leatherman knife. With her phone to her ear, she gaped at the trio clustered close to the brick wall. "Aunt Irina, I'll call you back." She disconnected the call. "What is it? Did you find something?"

"Nice code-breaking, Baby Boomer. The brick here is loose." Marco slid the blade into the mortar cracks and wiggled it a few times. When the brick was out far enough, he used his fingers to pry it the rest of the way and stepped aside. "You solved it, you get to put your hand in there."

The opening went further than the brick had, and Boomer shivered as he thought about all of the creepy crawlers that might be in the dark crevice—spiders were not one of his favorite things. Peering into the small space, he announced, "I think there's something in there."

Reaching in, his hand found a small shelf inside, and sitting on it was a long, round piece of plastic. He pulled the object out and glanced at the others. An old Pepsi bottle with a piece of paper rolled up and tucked inside was apparently their next clue. "Why do I suddenly get the urge to sing 'Message in a Bottle' by The Police?"

Kat took it from him and, with a turn, unscrewed the cap. Using her pinkie, she slid the note out and then unrolled it, with Boomer watching over her shoulder. Ivan Maier's handwriting appeared. "Is he kidding me? Really, Dad? Another bunch of numbers? God, even in death, the man can be infuriating! He's lucky I still love him."

Taking the paper from her, Boomer handed it to Marco and said, "Looks like routing and account numbers. Think Egghead can find it?"

"Is whiskey wet?" the man retorted, pulling his phone from his pocket and bringing up the number he needed.

"Don't tell him I asked, he'll go on an hour-long tangent."

"Try a five-hour tangent. Egghead? Got a job for you."

Twenty minutes later, they were all headed back to Charlotte, with Devon driving the lead car. In Benny's passenger seat, Kat stared out the window, still in disbelief. Brody, whoever he was, had been able to trace the numbers to a bank and an account in the Cayman Islands without any trouble. From what he could figure out, Ivan Maier had opened the secret account three years before the hit was put out on him and his family. The initial deposit had been a mere one thousand dollars with no other activity until the day fifteen million dollars was transferred from a bank in Switzerland. Since then, the money had just sat there collecting interest, to a grand total of twenty-three million dollars and change.

It was apparent her father had planned his revenge ahead of time in case he ever needed to go through with it. While he never touched a cent of the money, two years after he and Kat had settled in Portland, he'd contacted the bank and named her as a joint account holder. Kat was a millionaire on paper, but the money was tainted with the blood of her mother, brother, and anyone else those bastards had killed or hurt in the name of greed. And she wanted no part of it.

"Now what do we do? I don't want to hand the money back to criminals, but I'll do it if it means I get my life back."

"First things first. We'll head back to the Sawyers' and get the rest of the team on a conference call with our FBI contact. We'll figure this out, I promise you, baby." He brought her hand, which he'd been holding, to his mouth and kissed her knuckles. "I promise. Then you and I will get to know each other all over again." Leering at her, he licked her fingers. "Over and over and over again."

Kat groaned, then giggled. "We have people trying to kidnap me, with probably no qualms about killing you and your team if you stand in their way. I have over twenty-three million dollars in ill-gotten gains in a bank in the Cayman Islands, and you're thinking of sex."

"Kitten, when it comes to you, I'm always thinking of sex." Benny froze, then moaned and smacked the back of his head on the seat's headrest. "Shit!"

"What's wrong?"

"I forgot my dad's birthday was yesterday. I never called him. Shit."

She squeezed his hand. "I'm sure he'll understand. Weren't they going to the Billy Joel special last night?"

"Yeah. We're almost at the Sawyers'. I'll call him when we get there."

"Will you tell him happy birthday from me too?"

Benny glanced at her before his eyes returned to the road. "Of course, baby. But I'm sure he'd love to hear it directly from you. My folks have always loved you."

And she had always loved them. After returning to Sarasota Wednesday evening, Rick had told his wife about Kat's miraculous return, and she'd called Benny's cell phone right after their pizza dinner in the motel. Kat and Eileen Michaelson had laughed and cried over the phone for about twenty minutes before promising to see each other as soon as possible.

Kat's smile grew wider as he pulled into the long drive, waiting behind Devon for the electronic gate to open. They had reached their temporary home. "I've always loved them too. I still remember the barbeques at your house when your dad's team returned home from wherever they'd been. Those are some of my favorite memories from back then."

Snorting, he put the car in park. "You were just hot for the guys on my dad's team. So were my cousins, Jessica and Vicki."

"Oh, my God, I forgot all about them. How're they doing?"

"Jess is in California working for some big-shot Hollywood producer, and Vicki is married to a cop in New York and is a pediatric nurse."

"Wow." They climbed out of the car at the same time. "That's great. I'm happy for them. Do you see them at all?"

He shrugged and pulled out his phone. "Not as much as

we'd like. The last time we were all together was about a year and a half ago at Vicki's wedding."

Before making the call, Benny escorted Kat inside. While a fence surrounded the entire property, she knew he felt better if she was out of sight.

Following her up to their bedroom to pack up once more, he hit the speed dial for his dad's cell. "Hey, Pop. Happy belated birthday. Sorry I didn't get a chance to call you."

Rick Michaelson's deep voice came over the line. "No problem, son. How is everything going? You all right?"

Boomer filled him in on what had happened since they last spoke two days ago and assured him that despite Jake being injured, everything else seemed to be falling into place. Now they had to figure out what to do with the money and how to get the Russians' target off Kat's back for good.

"You need me?"

Sighing, he sat on the bed while Kat gathered her things from the bathroom. "Not up here, Pop. We have one of Chase's pilots heading up to Charlotte to bring us home. We'll have a team pow-wow in the morning if you want to drive up, but it's up to you."

"Margaret wants to take us out for breakfast for my birthday in the morning, so I'll head up after we eat. Figure I'll get to you around fourteen hundred. Sound good?"

"That's cool. Tell Aunt Margaret I said hello. Ian is getting in touch with Keon, and Carter has been hitting up his contacts, so maybe we'll have a plan by then." Kat walked back into the room, looking lost and confused over everything that had transpired. A thought occurred to Boomer.

"Why don't you bring Mom with you, so she can see Kat? They can visit with Angie, Jenn, and Kristen."

Her mouth turned upward, and she nodded enthusiastically while his father agreed it was an excellent idea. He let Kat say a quick "Happy birthday" before she handed the phone back to him and began to fold her clothes into her duffel bag.

After Rick said his goodbyes, Boomer hung up and hooked his finger into a belt loop on her jeans. Pulling her in between his legs, his eyes met hers. "You okay? You know I won't let anything happen to you, right?"

This time when she nodded, it wasn't in delight. Her gaze shifted to the side, and he knew something was bothering her. "Kitten, listen to me." He waited until she was looking at him again. "I know with everything going on, the last thing you want to hear from me is a bunch of D/s rules. But one thing I will insist on from now on is honesty. I need you to be honest and tell me what you think and feel."

"About what?"

He shrugged and then pulled her closer. "About anything and everything. I want to know when and why you're happy, sad, scared, excited . . . horny." She giggled while he smirked and waggled his eyebrows at her. "There's the smile I was looking for. But I mean it, baby, talk to me. Tell me what's going on in your pretty little head."

Biting her bottom lip, she pushed on his shoulders until he lay on the bed with his feet still on the floor. She climbed on top of him and straddled his hips with her knees. Boomer sensed, despite their position, she needed to say something important, and he rested his hands on her waist.

"I'm scared."

The words came out in a whisper, and he almost didn't

hear them. "About what, baby? I told you, the boys and I are not letting those bastards anywhere near you. I'd die first."

Kat's eyes widened and filled with tears. He could have kicked himself in the ass at that very moment.

"Shit, Kitten. That's not what I meant. I mean, it is what I meant, but nothing will happen to me. I promise. Ian, Devon, and the rest of the team? We're damn good at what we do. We're not going to let anything happen to you." He rubbed his knuckles up and down her sides. "I just got you back, and I'll be damned if someone comes between us ever again."

Tell her, his mind yelled at him, *tell her you love her!* But he couldn't. Not yet. She wasn't ready for that yet. But soon. Soon she was going to know she belonged to him. And he belonged to her. She was the only woman who would ever hold his heart in her hands.

She was staring at her hands where they touched his chest. "I'm just scared someone else will get hurt because of me. Jake could have lost his eye."

"And he could've been killed a thousand times on any of our missions. He could be hit by a bus walking across a street tomorrow. It's how life is, baby. You should know it better than anyone. But we will protect you, and whether you agree with it or not, your life comes before the team's. Every one of them will tell you that. It's who we are and who we trained to be. And when this is all over, you and I . . . I want a future with you, Kat. The future I never thought I'd have."

"I want that, too, but I can't bear the thought of losing you. So, if you get hurt," she clenched her fists, taking his T-shirt with them, "I'm going to kick your ass, you hear me?"

"Damn, you're fucking sexy as sin."

She rolled her eyes. "I'm serious, Benny."

Before she realized what was happening, he sat up and pushed her down to the side until she was halfway across his lap and face-first into the comforter. Lifting his palm, he let it slap down on her ass cheek. Not too hard, but enough to make it sting.

"Ouch! That hurt!" She reached back with her hands to cover her backside. Since this was new to her, and they weren't actually playing, he let her. But when she eyed him over her shoulder, he saw heat in her gaze, and his cock stirred.

"It was supposed to hurt, Kitten. The next rule is . . . no rolling your eyes at your Dom. That and sarcasm are the fastest ways to get a spanking." He helped her to stand. "And the only thing saving you from a proper spanking is we have to head to the airport soon, so finish packing while I grab my stuff." He got to his feet as well and patted her ass. "But soon, my hand and your butt will get very well acquainted, and you'll beg me to let you come. Trust me."

Ignoring her gaping mouth, he gathered his things, chuckling to himself. Oh yeah, teaching her was going to be fun.

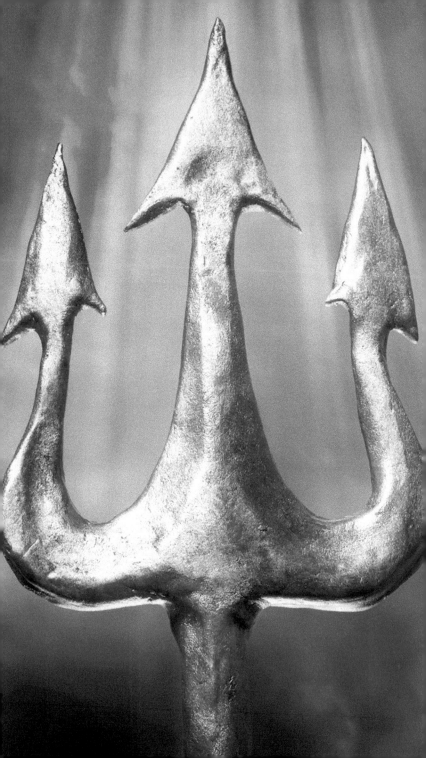

CHAPTER SIXTEEN

Kat was trying to concentrate on reading *Leather & Lace* but was finding it very hard not to replace Master Xavier with Benny in her mind. Master X was paddling Rebecca for lying by omission. She hadn't told him she'd been getting death threats, and he'd found out when someone tried to run her off the road.

Kat imagined she was the book's female lead, draped over a spanking bench and tied down with her bare ass in the air. Master X/Benny paused after several strikes to caress her red-hot cheeks. The fictional heat and pain were going straight to Kat's pussy and making it throb. Oh, she knew Rebecca was crying and not enjoying her punishment, but Kat was remembering how the sting of Benny's quick smacks had startled her both times. And then they'd made her wet. Wet and wanting more.

She squirmed a little in her first-class-style seat on the private jet taking them back to Tampa. They'd had time to kill before the plane landed in Charlotte to retrieve them, so Devon had taken them to one of his favorite places for lunch. It was a sports bar, which she hadn't minded, having grown up watching almost every sports game her brother and Benny had played in high school. It'd been football in the fall, followed by hockey during the winter months. Then springtime and baseball came, and Alex pitched while Benny played third base. Kat had always been on the sidelines, cheering and giggling with her girlfriends over how hot the guys all looked in their uniforms. But unlike some of her friends, Kat had paid attention to the games and learned enough to hold her own when discussing sports with men.

Devon had introduced her to the main reason he picked that particular restaurant—the hamburgers. Kat almost ordered a house salad, but the men had all insisted she get a burger, telling her they were the best ones she would ever have in her life. When she gave in, Benny smiled and squeezed her knee under the table. She knew he was worried about her weight loss, which was still noticeable, but she had to admit, it felt nice knowing he wanted to take care of her.

Devon and Marco had filled her in on some more funny stories about Benny while he'd rolled his eyes and tried to put a different spin on things. It was obvious he was very close to these men, respected them, and valued their friendship.

A pang of loss hit her again, and she wondered if Alex and Benny would still be best friends if things had turned out differently for everyone. She liked to think so and then wondered how the boyfriend/girlfriend thing would have worked out between her and Benny.

"What are you thinking so hard about, Kitten? You almost have steam coming out your ears."

Benny sat beside her and took her hand in his. She shrugged, then remembered what he'd said about honesty. "Just a bunch of what-ifs. I was wondering how our lives would have turned out if my father had never gotten mixed up with Volkov. Yours, mine, and Alex's. Would you and I still have been together?"

His thumb rubbed the back of her hand in soothing circles. A sad smile appeared on his handsome face. "I want to say 'yes,' but honestly, I don't know. I'd like to think so, but we've both changed so much in twelve years that it's hard to tell. My parents' marriage is in the minority when it comes to SEAL team members. Many of them don't make it."

Kat turned in her seat to face him better, and he lifted her legs so her calves crossed his lap. "Don't get me wrong, there were times my mother wanted to throw him out on his ass. Like most of the guys, he'd come back from a mission and be in a deep funk for a while until his mind caught up to the fact that his body was back in the States. Sometimes, the things we've seen and done are hard to shake. And since SEALs aren't allowed to discuss most of our missions outside the team, it strained my parents' relationship. I'm just grateful they stayed together through the rough spots. My mother is a strong woman, stronger than most." His smile changed and now lit up his handsome face. "And now that I think of it, so are you. So, yeah, I think we'd still be together."

"I'd like to think that too. Do you think we'd have kids? As close as we used to be, there are so many things I don't know about you now. I don't even know if you want kids."

He grabbed her around the waist and pulled her into his lap. "Kids with you? Hell, yeah." He nuzzled her neck. She was glad his teammates couldn't see them from where they sat toward the back of the plane as he cupped her breast, squeezing and massaging it. "As many as we can have. Don't think of me as a caveman . . . well, in some ways I can be . . . but the thought of you 'barefoot and pregnant' with my children is a big, fucking turn-on. And just think of all the fun we'd have trying."

His hand left her breast and worked its way between her thighs. He rubbed her sex through her sweatpants, and she knew he could feel the heat and moisture emanating from her. Kat moaned lowly and separated her legs to give him a little more room to work with. She completely forgot they weren't exactly alone. All she knew was the pleasure he was giving her. She squirmed on his lap, trying to get closer to him, and felt his rigid cock against her hip.

Benny lowered the tone of his voice. "Sit still, Kitten. Put your arms around me and your face against my neck. Try to stay quiet."

Desire flooded her. She did as she was told as he loosened the tie to her sweatpants and put his hand inside them. His fingers brushed over her clit and went lower to her wet pussy. Her breathing increased as her lips touched his neck.

Putting one finger inside her, he stroked her gently at first. "You like this, don't you, Kitten? You like how I'm playing with you, knowing Marco or Dev could walk up here at any moment and see my hand down your pants. They could see how flushed and aroused you are." He added a second finger, maintaining the same slow, torturous pace. "Answer me, Kitten. Do you like this, knowing you could get caught being so naughty? Do you want to come?"

"Yes," she moaned into his neck. "Please. More. Faster."

She let out a low, disappointed cry. Instead of doing as she wanted him to, he removed his hand from her pants and brought it to his mouth. Pulling back to watch him, her eyes widened as he licked her juices from his fingers.

"Mmm. So sweet and delicious." His hand went back down her pants, and this time he began to play with her clit. His eyes were on her face, watching her reactions. "I wish I could throw you on one of the couches and bury my face between your legs. I could eat you for hours, making you come over and over again until I've had my fill. And then I'd put you on your hands and knees and take you from behind. Fucking you. Claiming you. Owning you. You're mine, Kitten. Mine."

His last word had come out on a growl, and she moaned with need and want. He'd spoken the truth. She was his. She always had been and always would be. He owned her heart, mind, and soul. No other man could make her feel the way Benny did. She loved him. Still. Now. Forever.

Her heart rate and breathing increased as her eyes closed. With his other hand, he grabbed her hair and pulled her mouth to his. She instantly opened her lips and let his tongue into duel with hers. He increased the pace and pressure of his fingers against her clit, but it wasn't enough to send her over. And, holy shit, she wanted to. She wanted to fall into an orgasmic abyss.

His teeth came out to nibble on her bottom lip and then along her jaw. Lowering his hand, he put two fingers back inside her as his thumb took over the assault on her clit. Sucking on her neck, he marked her as his fingers pumped harder and faster. "Come for me, baby. Fly for me."

Her orgasm hit her hard. Pussy walls squeezed and throbbed around his fingers as a rush of fluid escaped her. He'd retaken her mouth, muffling her sounds of release, and waves of pleasure assailed her. His fingers slowed while she floated back to him. He smiled at her flushed face and sated expression. "Liked that, didn't you?" Pulling his hand from her pants, he licked his fingers as she cuddled closer.

"Mmm-hmm." Her cheeks flushed, but this time it wasn't from arousal. "Do you think they heard?"

Chuckling, he gave her a quick kiss. "If they did, it's nothing they haven't heard before in the club." He lifted her and placed her back in the seat next to him. "Stay here while I get a towel to clean you up."

A few moments later, he returned with two paper towels, one damp and the other dry. "This was all they had on board."

She sat blushing while he quickly cleaned between her legs and retied the strings of her sweatpants. He left her briefly again to dispose of the paper towels, then adjusted himself before sitting beside her. "Next time, we'll have to officially induct you into the mile-high club with my cock deep inside you."

She giggled and snuggled against his chest as he wrapped his arm around her shoulders. "You're incorrigible."

BOOMER LOVED THE FEEL OF HER IN HIS ARMS. SHE FIT LIKE she'd been created just for him. And if he had his way, he'd never let her go. His fingers brushed against the mark he'd left on her neck. He needed the world to see he'd staked his claim until he could get a collar around her throat.

Shifting slightly, he adjusted himself again. He was harder than granite but would have to wait until later to take care of it. This had been all about Kat. About pleasing her and showing her she belonged to him. "What's the first thing you want to do when this is all over? I can get some time off, and we can travel a bit. Maybe go down to the Caribbean for a few days. Find ourselves a deserted island where we can walk around naked and fuck like rabbits."

"Is sex all you think about?" she teased.

"When it comes to you, yup. I have a very long list of wicked things I want to do to you, and all of them end with my cock deep inside your body. But I'm sure we can find time to do other things, like eat and sleep."

As she shook her head in amusement, her hand settled on his cotton-covered six-pack. He squelched the urge to push it lower, not wanting to start something they couldn't finish. "You know what I want to do the most?"

He placed a chaste kiss on her forehead. "Name it, and we'll do it."

"I want to go bowling."

"Ha! What?" Boomer couldn't stop the bubbly laughter that escaped him if he tried. "Bowling? Are you serious? I'm offering you a trip to the Caribbean, filled with incredible monkey sex, and you want to go bowling?"

A wide grin and playful eyes lit up her face. "Yes. Bowling. And stop laughing at me."

"I can't help it, Kitten. You say the funniest things. You've always been able to make me laugh." She pinched his side, and he grabbed her wrist to stop her. "Okay. Okay. I'm not laughing *at* you. But why bowling?"

Her head returned to rest on his strong upper body. "Because we always had the best times when we were bowling. You, me, and Alex. Especially on the Retro Disco Nights we used to go to."

She lifted a shoulder and let it drop again. "I don't know, it just seemed like that's when we all let loose and didn't care about anything but enjoying ourselves. I remember our last Halloween when the two of you had everyone lined up in the alleys dancing 'The Hustle.' You were dressed like John Travolta in *Saturday Night Fever*, and Alex was the *Grease* version of Travolta. I don't think I've ever laughed so hard in my entire life."

Boomer roared at the memory. "Oh, my God! I forgot all about that. My mom taught us the steps. It took Alex two weeks to get it right because he had no sense of direction. He'd go left while everyone else was going right. So we had him face everyone, like a dance instructor, and it worked out."

"It was the best night ever, and it's why I want to go bowling." Her laughter died, and she picked at an invisible piece of lint on his shirt. "I haven't bowled since . . . since my world fell apart."

Tightening his hold on her, he lifted her chin with his other hand. "I can't change the past, baby. But I will do everything I can to make sure you spend the rest of your life laughing and living it to the fullest." His lips met hers. It wasn't a seductive kiss but one filled with promise. "I love you, Kitten."

Kat froze, then pulled back to see his entire face and stared at him in disbelief.

"Do you want me to say it again?" She nodded slowly, and he grinned. "I. Love. You. Katerina. Maier. I've loved you for a very long time. And I plan on spending the rest of my life showing you how much you mean to me. You're the only woman I will ever say those words to."

Her eyes filled with tears at his declaration. His pounding heart tried to escape its confinement as Kat's words came out in a whisper. "I love you too. Always. And I'll never say those words to another man."

"Good. Now that we've gotten the mushy stuff out of the way—kiss me."

And she did.

"THEY JUST ARRIVED AT COMPOUND. GIRL, THREE MEN. TOO many people. Vill have to vait until alone."

Listening to his minion report in, Viktor paced back and forth in the bar's office. It had once belonged to Volkov, but Viktor had taken ownership within days of killing the greedy bastard. The main difference between the two men was Volkov had been stupid and sloppy, whereas Viktor had common sense. He knew to ensure anyone privy to his secrets was eliminated as soon as they outgrew their usefulness. Sometimes even before then.

Growing up an orphan in the USSR, Viktor had come to rely on no one but himself. Making his first kill at fourteen had been a blessing in disguise. The perverted bastard had tried to molest him in an alleyway after catching the teen stealing food from a sidewalk vendor. While struggling on the ground, Viktor had managed to grab hold of a broken bottle and shoved it into the creep's neck, slicing the artery. Instead of running, he stood there and watched the man's life end in a puddle of blood. What he hadn't known was someone else had been standing in the shadows as the whole incident unfolded. A man known only as Dmitry *Sishnik*—the Scavenger.

The trained assassin had taken Viktor under his guidance and taught him everything he knew. At first, the teenager thought Dmitry was another deviant, using his offer of food, shelter, protection, and education to extract sexual favors. But he soon learned that wasn't the case. The older man had merely wanted a protégé to pass his craft on to. He'd been trained by one of the best in the same manner, and it had been his way of paying it forward and passing on his legacy.

After learning everything he could from his mentor, Viktor's final act before leaving his birth country was to kill him quickly and painlessly. It was the least he could do for the man who had changed his life for the better and was dying of cancer. As a frail Dmitry struggled to get out of bed one morning, Viktor could see the pain and humiliation in his eyes. He couldn't stand to see his suffering anymore, and without a word, he swiftly broke the man's neck. Viktor knew the Scavenger was grateful to his apprentice, for he would've never been able to bring himself to commit suicide, and a slow, agonizing death would have been worse.

Since coming to America, Viktor had been working for a Russian network of criminals as an enforcer/assassin. But he was getting older and wanted to start enjoying the good life like his bosses were. Now, there was only one thing standing in his way. It pissed him off the Maier woman was being well protected, but he'd be damned if they couldn't find a way around it. He wanted the money, and she was the last known connection to it. He'd figured out how to hide the funds from his bosses, funneling it into his recently acquired businesses. It would also help him advance further in the association. Knowing he couldn't take the chance of his men screwing up, he made a decision. "I'll be on next flight to Tampa. Find way to get girl, but do nothing until I get there."

CHAPTER SEVENTEEN

While Jenn, Angie, and Kristen entertained Eileen Michaelson and Kat near the koi pond, Boomer, his dad, and five teammates sat around the unlit fire pit. A few months earlier, for Ian's birthday, everyone had helped Angie surprise him by transforming the area between the last two buildings in the compound into *Ian's Oasis*. They'd ripped up the asphalt and laid down sod before adding an outdoor kitchen, a TV, seating areas, and shrubbery. The backyard, as it was often referred to, had quickly become a place to hang out and relax. At the moment, country music played in the background, and a misting system kept the area cool despite the elevated Floridian temperatures.

Ian handed Boomer and Rick their new beers, then sat back down and opened his own. He continued to fill the older man in on what they'd discussed earlier with the FBI's Assistant Director. "So Keon will be talking things over with his boss and the head of the task force who's been leading the investigations into the Russian mob in Norfolk. Obviously, they have no desire to hand the money back over to them. But as it stands now, even though the money is part of a criminal investigation, he thinks any statutes governing it may have expired. So, it means the money might belong to Kat, whether she wants it or not. I have Reggie checking into things on his end."

Reggie Helm was one of Trident's lawyers and a Dom at the club. They consulted with him and his three partners on everything from criminal to civil to contract laws.

Boomer popped the cap off his beer and took a swig. "Kat said she wants nothing to do with it. As far as she's concerned, it's tainted money. I wouldn't be surprised if she donated all of it when this is over, but we'll deal with that once she's out of danger.

Rick nodded at his son and then turned back toward Ian. "Has Carter turned up anything new?"

"Of course I have. I'm not a fucking slouch like this bunch of pansies."

The men looked up in surprise as the black-ops agent strolled onto the grass from the parking lot. Usually, at least one of them was alerted when someone entered the compound unannounced, but the guards were under orders to allow Carter entry at any time. The team hadn't known he was in town, but that was nothing new. The man was a ghost, coming and going as he pleased.

From where he'd been sleeping by the women, Beau ran to greet the man, who took a moment to roughhouse with the dog before grabbing a beer from the outdoor refrigerator. He downed half of it, then shook hands or fist-bumped each of the men with a few more insults mixed in. Taking a seat next to Jake, he smirked. "Finally got a scar on that Hollywood face of yours, huh? The whole pirate thing you've got going on is pretty fucking hot. You know, blow the man down . . . or up . . . or whatever you're into. Too bad you're not my type."

While the others roared with laughter, Jake snorted and gave his friend the finger. "Fuck you, jackass. This damn patch is driving me crazy, but not as much as the women are." He hitched a thumb toward the far end of the backyard. "You'd think I was paralyzed from my eyebrows down the way they're trying to do everything for me. I'm just glad the mother hens have Kat to fuss over now."

The men agreed. With the exception of Boomer's dad, they were all Doms and preferred to take care of their subs, not the other way around. And in Jake's case, a gay man with no sisters, having a bunch of women worrying over him was a little unsettling. He loved the Trident women dearly but wasn't used to all the attention.

"So, Boom-Boom. You going to introduce me to the pretty brunette over there?" Carter did his best imitation of Groucho Marx's eyebrow wiggle while studying the group of women. The man loved the ladies, all types, and could be the biggest flirt at times.

Boomer growled. "Hands off, jackass. Don't even think about it."

"Oh, well, a man can dream, can't he? She's a sexy little thing—you know, in case you're ever looking for a third." Ignoring his friend's scowl, he took another drink and sighed while settling into the Adirondack chair. "Damn, that tastes good. Anyway, back to the current problem. I've done a little research on Viktor Dryagin. He's been in the U.S. for about twenty years, but before that, he trained under one of the best assassins in the USSR at the time."

"Shit." Boomer dragged his hand down his face in frustration. A trained assassin was not someone he wanted anywhere in the same hemisphere as Kat.

"Yeah, I know. But it seems he's been backing off on his enforcer role in the mob and using Volkov's death as a way to move up in the organization. From what I hear, the mob wrote the money off years ago. So, my best guess is, Dryagin will be hiding it from his bosses if he ever gets his hands on it."

Leaning forward, Ian scratched Beau's ears after the goofy-faced dog sat at his feet. "So, there's a good chance very few people know Kat has access to the money. And if she does give it away, then we can eliminate the threat altogether."

Boomer shook his head. "I don't like it. What if he doesn't believe she gave it away? And we have to wait on the legalities to make sure she *can* give it away. This guy wants the money, and Kat is the only link."

"Which is why I want you two to stay here at the compound. Lord knows it won't be the first time we've been under attack, and I'm sure it won't be the last. I'll call Chase and post a few more guards."

"What about the club?" Devon asked his brother. "Tomorrow and Tuesday, we're closed, but what do you want to do about tonight?"

Ian thought about it for a few moments. "I don't think we have to close at this point. With a few extra guards at the gate and in the compound, we should be good. And with Egghead's increased perimeter security system, no one will get anywhere close to the compound without being noticed. You and I will sit down with Tiny and Mitch tonight and go over all the precautions."

Devon nodded his acknowledgment. In addition to being a bodyguard, Tiny was head of the club's security, and Mitch Sawyer was their cousin and The Covenant's manager. While Ian and Devon had gone into the Navy, Mitch had gone to college and gotten his MBA. As a result, he'd been the obvious choice to run the club the three of them co-owned.

Brody stood and smacked Boomer on the shoulder. "I'll grab one of those medical alert bracelets I used on Angie. Kat can wear it until she's out of danger, so we can track her if necessary."

"Thanks, that'd be great." Boomer and the others knew firsthand how well the geek's little toy worked. Angie and Jenn had been taken hostage a few months ago, and while organizing the rescue, the team had been able to gain vital information via a one-way microphone hidden in the GPS bracelet.

As his buddy jogged to the office to get the device, Boomer glanced over and saw Kat walking toward him, her pale face bothering him. He reached up, took her hand, and pulled her into his lap. "You doing okay, Kitten?"

She cuddled against his chest. "Yeah, just getting a little tired, and I think I might be getting a migraine, so I want to take my meds as a precaution. Is there a place I can lay down for a bit?"

"Sure. We have some bunk rooms above the offices. We'll be staying there tonight anyway." He helped her to her feet and then stood as well. "I'll grab our bags and take you up there."

"I can read you a bedtime story if you want. Women tell me I'm quite entertaining in bed."

KAT GAPED AT THE STRANGER GRINNING AT HER, AMUSEMENT swirling in his deep blue eyes. He'd been talking to Jake when she first walked over, but now that his attention was on her, she wondered how she hadn't noticed what a hunk he was. His dark blond hair must fall right below his shoulders because he had it tied back in a small ponytail. A snug T-shirt covered his upper torso, and his jean-clad legs were long and lean. From how he had them stretched out in front of him, she guessed he was a few inches taller than Benny. And like the men of Trident, he had the physique of a warrior, sculpted from hard work and training. No health club or steroid needle could produce such a perfect male specimen. Holy crap, the man was gorgeous in a dangerous, bad-boy sort of way. "Um . . ."

"Stop being an asshole, man." Benny snarled, putting his arm around her and drawing her into his side. It was a blatantly possessive gesture and made her shiver in delight.

The hunk feigned being insulted, his large hand spread across his broad chest. "Who? Me? I'm a jackass. Egghead's the asshole."

"I heard that!"

As Brody plopped back down in his chair, the other man chuckled. "You were supposed to hear it, asshole." He turned his attention back to Kat, and his gaze softened. "Sorry, little one. The name is Carter, and your boyfriend here should know by now that I'm just joking, although his obvious jealousy tells me you're something special to him. If he treats you wrong, just let me know, and I'll kick his scrawny ass for you. Okay?"

When he winked at her playfully, Kat couldn't help the smile spreading across her face. It was hard not to like the man instantly. "Nice to meet you, Carter. I'm Kat. And thanks for the offer, but he treats me just fine. He knows I swing a mean baseball bat if he doesn't."

"Ha! You've got claws. I like you already, Miss Kitty-Kat. It's my absolute pleasure to meet you."

Her heart clenched at the nickname her father used for her as Carter's eyes flickered toward Benny. "She's a keeper, man. Don't let her get away."

"Yes, she is." Lowering his head, he gave her a quick kiss. "And I don't plan on losing her again."

A FEW MINUTES LATER, KAT WAS STRIPPED DOWN TO HER underwear and in bed as Boomer pulled the covers up to her chin. Some of the six spare bedrooms had bunks, but this was one of two with a queen-sized mattress. An attached bath meant she didn't have to go out into the hallway for any reason.

He placed the bracelet Brody had given him around her left wrist. "This has a tracking device in it, Kitten. If something happens to you, which we'll do everything we can to avoid, it will help us find you. It's just a precaution." He brushed her hair away from her cheek. "Are you sure you don't want me to stay with you?"

She nodded, her eyelids growing heavy. "I'm good. Your parents aren't staying much longer, so go sit with them. I'll be asleep in no time."

Kissing her on the forehead, he saw she was right. By the time he shut off the light and opened the door, she was already going under. When he returned to the backyard, he noticed a few people had left. Jenn had gone to work, having switched shifts with another waitress at the pub owned by Jake's brother. Marco and Brody were also gone, and Devon mentioned they were in the office working on an embezzlement case. Kristen and Angie were over by the outdoor kitchen, preparing a dinner of grilled chicken, salads, corn, and potatoes, while Ian turned on the giant gas grill.

Boomer sat beside his mom, who'd joined his dad by the fire pit. Eileen smiled at him. "I'm still having a hard time wrapping my mind around the fact she's back, but I have to say, I haven't seen you this happy since high school. And I'm thrilled for you too. For both of you. Back then, I could see how good you two were together, even if you didn't."

Blushing wasn't something he did often, but he never talked about women with his mom. He knew she wanted grandchildren one day but wasn't one of those mothers who nagged their sons to get married. "She's the one, Mom. She always was, and I've said it several times within the past few days, I'm never letting her go."

Eileen reached over and squeezed his hand. "I know you won't, Ben. Just keep both of you safe."

"I will."

"Fuck!" Boomer's dad leaped from his chair, holding his shoulder. "God-fucking damn it! I just got stung by a bee. Leaned back on the fucker."

His wife and son jumped up and began pulling on Rick's shirt, trying to get a look at the site. The last time he'd gotten stung, his foot had blown up like a balloon, and they knew if a bee got him again, the reaction could be worse. Eileen now carried an Epi-pen and Benadryl capsules in her purse, just in case.

Boomer saw the large welt forming at the back of his shoulder. "The stinger's out. Any trouble breathing, Pop?"

"No. But look, I'm already getting fucking hives. Eil, just give me the Benadryl. I'll take the pills first, and if it gets worse, I can use the pen."

She dug them out of her purse as Kristen approached with a water bottle. Rick quickly popped the pills into his mouth and washed them down with the cool liquid. "Fuck. How the hell could something so damn tiny hurt like such a bitch? 'Scuse my language, ladies."

The women all chuckled at him, having heard a lot worse from their men. Angie had made an impromptu icepack with a zip-lock baggie and handed it to Boomer. After ordering his father to sit back down, he stuck it between the affected shoulder and chair. "Mom will have to drive home. The Benadryl knocked you on your ass the last time you got stung, old man."

Rick grumbled and cursed the dead bee some more.

"You don't have to drive home tonight," Kristen informed them. "You know you can always crash in one of our spare bedrooms."

Smiling at the younger woman, Eileen shook her head. "Thanks for the offer, Kristen. But I have an early dentist appointment in the morning. It'll be better if we go home. I just want to wait a while to make sure Rick's reaction doesn't get worse."

About a half hour later, Rick's hives were gone, but he was having difficulty keeping his eyes open and barely touched his dinner. Boomer helped him to their car while the women packed up some food for Eileen to take home. Opening the driver's door for his mother, Boomer kissed her on the cheek before she climbed in. "Text or call me when you get home so I know everything is okay."

"We'll be fine, but I'll text you anyway." She glanced at her husband, who was trying to stay awake but failing. "He'll be asleep before we hit the highway. Love you, Ben. And tell Katerina we said goodbye. Try and come visit us next weekend, please."

"If this is all over, we will, Mom."

He shut her door and watched his parents drive away. For the first time since he was a teenager, Boomer saw his future and loved it. He was going to make Kat his wife, and they would give his parents grandchildren to spoil rotten. Maybe he could convince them to move closer than Sarasota.

Smiling, he went to fix Kat a dinner plate, looking forward to feeding her in bed . . . among other things.

"Following car with same last name as boyfriend. Must be parents."

Viktor smiled as he walked down the hallway leading to his plane. His men had taken down the license plates of vehicles driving toward the Trident compound. It was the only property off that road, so it was easy to assume someone using it could be a possible target. Thanks to his contacts in law enforcement, they'd been able to run the plates and find out who they belonged to. If they couldn't get into the compound to get the girl, they'd have to make the girl come to them.

"Don't lose them. I'm on vay." Disconnecting the call, he winked at the pretty stewardess as he boarded the plane. Things were looking up.

CHAPTER EIGHTEEN

Kat tried to pull the short skirt lower, but it wouldn't go any further. After taking a nap and eating the dinner Benny had literally fed her in bed, she felt confident she'd nipped her migraine in the bud. She'd been surprised and then excited when he'd asked if she wanted a tour of The Covenant. Apparently, Sunday nights tended to be their slowest, but it didn't mean there wouldn't be plenty to see. He'd provided privacy papers she had to sign and a limit list and protocols she needed to adhere to. Most of them were easy enough to remember, and Benny had assured her everyone would help her if she accidentally did something wrong. She hadn't been cleared to play since she needed a mandatory background check and blood work, so he told her they would fill out the limit list together at another time. Tonight, she was only allowed to observe and learn what BDSM was about.

When Angie and Kristen discovered she would be joining them, they'd been thrilled and offered to lend her something to wear. They'd taken her to the huge apartment Ian and Angie shared on the first floor of the compound's last building. Kristen and Devon had the unit above theirs, which was just as spacious.

Since her stress-induced weight loss, Kat had dropped to a size six from her normal size ten, but Angie had a few items they'd been able to adjust to her smaller frame.

The black skirt she now wore was a wrap-around that tied at the back of her narrow waist. It had a slight A-line cut and covered her ass as long as she didn't spin around, making it flare outward. On top, she sported a teal-blue camisole with lace trim. While her assets were covered, barely, she was still self-conscious of the fact she had no underwear on. Benny had insisted, and she had to admit doing so made her feel naughty and sensual. But that didn't mean she wanted to be flashing anyone other than him.

Glancing at Kristen and Angie as they walked across the compound to the club, she realized she was the least scantily dressed. Angie wore a snug pink teddy that stopped at the middle of her thighs. The stretchy lace material was just sheer enough to see through, but the woman acted as if it was no big deal her nipples could be seen. Kat could also see she wore a matching thong and was almost jealous of the woman's toned yet curvy body. Angie had told her Ian had a thing for lingerie. He loved to browse through some of the nicest and naughtiest intimate catalogs looking for new things for her to wear.

Kristen's outfit fell somewhere between the other two. She wore a matching black bra and panty set with a sheer black overlay. While it was sexy, it wasn't any less than what some women wore poolside or at the beach.

As they walked through the gate separating the club from the rest of the Trident compound, flip-flops slapped against their heels, almost in sync. The girls had told her the club floors were carpeted, except inside the scene areas, so most submissives went barefoot. No glass was allowed in what they called "the pit," so they didn't have to worry about anything that might cut their feet. The scene areas were polished wood and constantly wiped clean by the staff to eliminate any "ick" factors.

Walking up the stairs to the second-floor entrance, the butterflies in Kat's stomach took full flight. Her nervousness must have shown on her face because Angie gave her an encouraging smile while holding the door open for her. "Relax. You'll be fine. Boomer will give you a collar to wear, so no one else will be allowed to touch you. If you have any questions, just ask one of us. We've all been in your shoes before . . . well, actually, your flip-flops."

Kat walked through the door, and her eyes immediately found Benny's. He was waiting for her in the club's lobby along with Devon and Ian. And holy hell, did they all look like they just stepped out of a *Playgirl* magazine photo shoot.

Ian and Devon both wore leather pants, but the styles were slightly different. Ian's had a zippered front, and he paired the black pants with a snug gray T-shirt. Devon's crotch was laced up, and he wore a matching black leather vest sans shirt. But it was Benny who she thought was the sexiest, and she hoped she wasn't drooling. Under his open brown leather vest, he was shirtless with his rock-hard chest and abs showcased in skin bronzed by the sun. His faded jeans fit like a glove, and the bulge behind his zipper made her mouth water. A brown leather belt went through the loops at his waist, and was a close match to the well-worn boots on his feet.

He held his hand out to her, grinning broadly as she took it. "Damn, baby. Just when I think you can't get any sexier, you prove me wrong. I think I'm going to start calling you my little sex-kitten."

Pulling out a simple, black leather collar, he indicated for her to turn around and lift her hair. His fingers brushed against her skin as he placed it around her neck, connecting the hook and eye clasp in the back. Fingering the thin strand, she faced him again. "Okay?"

"For now. I'll have to start thinking about a permanent one for you like Angie and Kristen have. I want to design it myself."

Kat was thrilled he wanted to show everyone she belonged to him. She'd noticed the other women's collars earlier. Kristen's was a platinum choker with evenly spaced diamonds along its entire length. She'd shown Kat the removable sapphire pendant, which she occasionally wore with it. The custom-designed collar matched the engagement ring Devon had also given her, which had tiny blue stones surrounding the large teardrop diamond.

Angie was wearing one of two collars Ian had gotten for her. Her everyday one was a yellow-gold, Byzantine-styled chain with a padlock pendant, which she'd been wearing earlier. The one she had on now was a two-inch wide, white-gold necklace with a diamond heart in the center. It was stunning and must have cost a fortune. But Kat didn't care what collar she wore, as long as it was Benny's.

He reached for her hand again and placed a yellow "no-play" band on her wrist. "Are you ready to go in?"

A nervous giggle escaped her, and she took a deep breath. "Oh, what the hell. You only live once or, in my case, twice. Let's do this before I lose my courage."

The group laughed with her as she followed Benny to the large wooden doors leading into the main club. Tiny was standing guard and pulled open one of the doors for them. It didn't escape Kat's notice he was wearing a holstered gun on his hip. She'd been told they'd increased security at the compound until she was out of danger. The huge man smiled at all three women as they were escorted past him. "Hello, Miss Katerina. Hello, ladies. Looking beautiful as always. Have a nice evening."

Kat thanked him as she crossed over the threshold on Benny's arm. Her jaw dropped as the club's sights, sounds, and smells assailed her senses. She tried to look everywhere at once, but it was physically impossible, so she took in one section at a time. The second floor was basically a horseshoe that overlooked the floor below. To their left, at the base of the "U," was a curved, dark-wood bar with intricate carvings. A shirtless bartender was serving drinks to the members. She'd been told his red bowtie and black pants were the submissive male employee's uniform. A female server was waiting for her round of drinks, dressed in a short black skirt, red bra, and bowtie.

But it was the patrons who had her agape. While some were dressed in clothing suitable for any club in the city, others were practically, if not completely, naked. Chatting at the bar were two women dressed in fashionable outfits, but kneeling at their feet was a guy wearing only a thong and a black collar attached to a leash. Other people were walking around in various stages of dress, and Kat was grateful for what little she was wearing. At least her tits and ass were covered.

Scanning the area, Kat loved how the gray carpet and burgundy walls gave the club a warm atmosphere. Lighting consisted of wrought iron chandeliers and sconces, and there were numerous seating areas with couches, chaise lounges, winged-back chairs, and dark wood tables. Across from the bar was a grand staircase to the floor below. Brass railings ran down the side of the steps and around the balcony. More seating, in the form of pub tables and stools, allowed members to sit and observe the activities in the pit from above.

Two men, one of whom looked eerily similar to Ian and Devon, approached the group, and she guessed this was their cousin Mitch. He was a little shorter than the brothers, and his blue eyes weren't as striking, but his hair and facial features were definitely from Sawyer DNA. Wearing black dress pants and a snug black T-shirt, he carried himself confidently.

The other man was slender and, with his salt and pepper hair and goatee, she assumed he was in his fifties. With his black leather pants and dress shirt, an image of Dracula popped into her mind. All he was missing was a cape and some fangs. The way he looked her up and down made her shiver and step closer to Benny. Studying the two men, the first word that came to mind was dominant, and Kat realized she could categorize the club patrons by their dress and/or manner.

Next to her, Benny put his arm around her shoulders and gestured to the two newcomers. "Kat, this is Master Mitch, co-owner and manager of the club. And this is Master Carl, who better be nice if he wants to remain standing."

Master Carl ignored Benny's warning as he took Kat's hand and kissed her knuckles. "So, this is the little kitten Master Carter was talking about. He didn't lie when he said you were one mighty fine-looking feline. Me-ow. You're welcome to use my scratching post anytime you want, my little pussy . . . cat."

While Benny growled and plucked her hand from the other man's grasp, Kat blushed awkwardly. The group laughed, and Ian tugged on Master Carl's arm, forcing him to step back out of her personal space. "You'll have to forgive Master Carl, Kat. We've been trying to housetrain him for a while now. One of these days, he's going to piss in the wrong sandbox. Aside from being a sadist, he's harmless."

"Um . . . okay." Kat wasn't sure what else to say to that.

Kristen put her hand on Kat's arm. "Don't worry. He comes off as a shark, but he's actually a big teddy bear. But if he offers to show you his bullwhip, run in the other direction."

Master Carl tried to frown but wasn't successful. "Everyone ruins all my fun. However, it is a pleasure to meet you, little one, and I welcome you to our club."

Before anyone could say more, Tiny rushed over and addressed Ian. "The front gate has three unknown males in a vehicle demanding entry to the club. The guards have them at gunpoint."

As Tiny and Devon took off for the door, Ian turned to his cousin. "The women don't leave your sight, and no one goes out to the parking lot until we clear this."

"Got it. I'll post extra security at the doors." Mitch waved over two men in red button-down shirts and began to bark out orders.

Meanwhile, Benny pointed at the manager, but his eyes were on Kat. "You stay with Mitch, no matter what, and do exactly what he says. I'll be right back."

Kat felt the blood drain from her face, but she managed to nod. "O-okay. But be careful."

She wasn't sure if he'd heard her because he and Ian were already running out the double doors to the lobby. Angie put her arm around Kat's shoulder as Kristen stepped in front of her, drawing her attention. "It's going to be fine, Kat. This is what they do, and they're the best-trained men out there."

Neither one wanted to tell her how they both knew that firsthand. Last year, Kristen had almost been collateral damage when a hitman was after Devon, Ian, Jake, and

Brody. And five months ago, Angie and Jenn had been held hostage by dirty DEA agents after Angie's best friend's undercover operation was blown. Unfortunately, her friend, Jimmy, had been killed during the successful rescue of the women, and Angie was still grieving and having nightmares over the incident.

Mitch rejoined them and suggested they take Kat to one of the empty seating areas. "She's very pale, and I don't want her to faint." As the women sat, he signaled one of the waitresses to bring over some water bottles. Taking one, he opened it and placed it in Kat's hand. "Drink, Kat."

She had no memory of how the water bottle had gotten into her hand—she'd been concentrating on the doors leading to the lobby. At Mitch's words, she glanced at her hand, then up at the pretty brunette waitress smiling at her.

"Hi, do you remember me? We met at the store the other day. I'm Cassandra. It's nice to see you again."

Recognition dawned. Now Kat had two things running through her mind. One, was Benny okay outside? And two, had he had sex with the petite woman standing before her? She tried to be polite despite the waves of jealousy coursing through her. "Oh, yes. Hello. It's nice to see you too."

Cassandra handed water bottles to Kristen and Angie, who thanked her. She turned back to Kat. "I had a feeling I'd see you here soon. It looks like Master Ben is off the market, and I'm happy for you both. He's a great guy and deserves someone special. Anyway, if you need anything else, just let me know."

Watching the friendly waitress walk away, Kat felt Angie's hand on her arm. "I know what you're thinking, Kat. You have to get past the fact that Boomer had a life while he thought you were gone. The point is, he's with you now, and

I can tell by how he looks at you that he doesn't want anyone else."

Kat nodded, then took a sip of water, knowing the other woman was right. Sitting near the koi pond earlier in the day, the subject of her walking back into Benny's life and right into his arms was the main topic of conversation. Angie and Kristen hadn't talked much about the club in front of Jenn and Eileen Michaelson, but they had while finding something for Kat to wear. They explained how some of BDSM interactions were just physical, without the emotional entanglements and drama which came with traditional relationships. And whether she liked it or not, there were women at the club who Benny had played with.

She knew they were trying to put her mind at ease. It wasn't as if she'd expected him to be a celibate monk for twelve years when he thought she was dead. But the few men she had dated over the years had never given her a reason to be jealous, so it was a new emotion for her. One she would have to get past if she wanted this to work between them—and she wanted that more than anything else in the world.

It was a good ten minutes before the men came back into the club, and Mitch visibly relaxed. Kat could tell by the way they were joking and laughing that nothing serious had happened. The three women began to stand as their men approached, and Ian waved for them to sit back down. "Nothing to worry about. Just a few barely-legal, drunken jack-asses looking for some slap and tickle. Somehow, they heard about the club and thought it was a combination strip-show and whorehouse. The idiotic driver pulled out a knife when the guards wouldn't let them in, then wet his pants when faced with a full arsenal. The cops arrived and are taking care of them."

The group broke out into chuckles and comments about

stupidity as Benny took Kat's hand and pulled her up into his arms. "You okay? I'm sorry we had to scare you."

She melted into him. "It wasn't your fault. I'm just glad no one got hurt. I wouldn't be able to live with myself if they did."

"Hey." His hand went under her chin and tilted her head back so she could see his face. "I keep telling you, none of this is your fault, Kitten. I know it's hard for you to believe, but the bad guys and your dad are to blame. Although I doubt he realized he was putting you in danger by taking the money, but he should have."

Leaning down, he lowered his voice, his lips touching her ear. "Now, since the excitement is over, how about I give you a tour and get you excited in another way? A way that will get you wet and begging me to do wicked things to you."

Blushing at his suggestion, Kat shivered and let him lead her to the grand staircase. He handed a club card to one of the security guards, who scanned it through a hand-held computer. It showed Benny had two or fewer alcoholic beverages served to him, and they were allowed to enter the pit. Kat's yellow wristband indicated she wasn't allowed to play as a guest, so they didn't need to know if she'd had anything to drink.

Descending into the pit, Kat's butterflies were back, and she shuddered. Benny must've felt her reaction because he stopped and pulled her to the side of the stairs out of traffic. "Are you okay? Are you sure you want to do this? If you don't, we can leave now, Kitten. This is a part of my life, but I want you in my life more than anything. I can give it up if I have to."

She knew he meant it by the look in his eyes. He loved her and wouldn't let anything stand in the way of them being together. Not even something he'd enjoyed for years without her. "No, I don't want to leave yet. I don't know if I can do this, but we won't know until I try, right? Can we just take it slow?"

With a tender touch that melted her heart, Benny cupped her cheek. "Absolutely. I'll tell you what—we'll walk around for a bit and observe a few relatively tame scenes. Then we'll go back to our room and discuss what you liked and didn't like, okay? We can't play here tonight anyway. If something bothers you, tell me, and we'll move on. You mean more to me than the lifestyle, Kitten, and every good relationship has a compromise between both parties. We just have to find ours."

TAKING THE LEAD AND HER HAND AGAIN, BOOMER WEAVED HIS way through the crowd. He bypassed Mistress China whipping a male submissive, a wax-play scene, and another where the female sub's nipples and clit were in clamps. They came upon a spanking bench where a submissive named Shelby was strapped down and getting her ass reddened by Carter. The real-life blonde was known for wearing different colored wigs to match her skimpy outfits, and tonight was no exception. Her straight purple hair complemented her polka-dotted bra and mini-skirt currently pulled up around her waist.

Boomer glanced at Kat and smiled at her shocked yet interested expression. She wasn't looking away, and he took it as a good sign. Stepping behind her, he grabbed her hips and let her feel his erection against her ass. He was pleased when she gave him a little wiggle in acknowledgment.

Shelby's position let everyone see her bare ass and shaved sex. Her cheeks were red with Carter's handprints, and her pussy wept. The Dom stood to the side of the bench and leaned down to say something to the sub while his hand squeezed her tender flesh. Whatever was said had her nodding her purple-coifed head. Grinning, he took two steps toward a black duffel bag sitting on a side table and rummaged through it.

Boomer felt Kat hold her breath while waiting to see what Carter would pull from his toy bag. The Dom selected a small, new package and broke the seal. A black item fell into his hand, and before returning to his sub, he also retrieved a lubricant tube.

Boomer moved Kat's hair off her shoulder to whisper in her ear. "This is what I want to do to you someday soon. He's going to plug Shelby's ass, and it'll stimulate all the nerves until she begs him to let her come."

KAT COULDN'T TAKE HER EYES OFF THE SCENE IN FRONT OF her. It was the most erotic thing she'd ever seen in her life, and even though a part of her was embarrassed for watching, she found it arousing and couldn't shy away. While Benny's words tickled her ear, Kat eyed the handsome Dom, who was definitely enjoying himself. His cock was bulging behind the zipper of his brown leather pants, and she couldn't help but think, good Lord, he was huge. A snug, short-sleeved Henley showed off his sculpted torso, and she would have to be dead not to appreciate his physique. At the V-neck, she could see a hint of his bare chest, and his chin had a dusting of evening stubble. As her eyes traveled further upward, she realized he'd caught her staring at him. Kat blushed when he gave her a playful wink before returning his attention to his restrained submissive.

She couldn't take her eyes off Carter's hands as he prepped the anal plug and then used his lubed fingers to prepare Shelby to take it. Music filled the air, and, to the beat, he pumped one, then two fingers in and out of her back hole.

The submissive obviously loved it because she was begging for more. "Faster. Harder. Please, Sir." But the Dom just chuckled and took his time stretching her, getting her ready to take the large plug.

Kat was shocked to realize her pussy was clenching to the beat as well. Benny rubbed his erection between her ass cheeks, and she moaned and tilted her hips, wanting him to do it again. And he didn't disappoint her. From behind, he reached between her legs, and she gasped when he plunged a finger into her own dripping pussy. She clenched her legs together. Glancing down and then around, she made sure her skirt still covered her in the front and no one was watching them. No one was, and Benny stroked her sensually, following Carter's tempo.

His sultry voice whispered in her ear. "My Kitten is nice and wet. I hope Carter makes this scene quick. Otherwise, I'm going to say to hell with the rules. I'll bend you over the back of a couch and fuck you right here in front of everyone."

One of his other fingers brushed across her clit, and Kat's legs started to shake as more moisture flowed from her pussy. The desire running through her body had her embarrassment quickly taking a back seat to her need for more pleasure. "I-I thought we could . . . couldn't play."

She almost cried in disappointment when his fingers retreated and he lowered the back of her skirt down again. Turning her head toward him, she watched in awe as he licked her juices from his finger.

"You're right. But I couldn't help myself. I'll be good, I promise. Very, very good."

The wicked amusement in his voice told her he was speaking innuendos, and she wished they were allowed to play. She wanted nothing more than to bend over and feel him deep inside her, pounding into her from behind. Raw need flooded her. She licked her lips as she stared at his. "Would you be disappointed if I said I wanted to go back to our room right now and play?"

A satisfied smirk crossed his face, and Kat knew the one thing he didn't feel was disappointment.

CHAPTER NINETEEN

Eileen Michaelson rolled over and studied her fifty-eight-year-old but still handsome husband. It was two-thirty in the morning, and she couldn't sleep while Rick snored off the remaining effects of the Benadryl. Thank God he hadn't needed the Epi-pen, but he'd dozed the entire ride home, then barely made it through the evening news before climbing into bed. An over-the-counter medication did what many terrorists and bad guys had tried but failed to do over the years—knock her big, bad Navy SEAL on his cute ass.

At times, she couldn't believe they'd been married for almost thirty-five years. Their anniversary was six months away, and she loved Rick more than ever. They had a rough first few years with him being out of the country for weeks or months at a time, and phone calls had been sporadic depending on the team's mission. But it was moments like this when she was grateful she'd weathered the storms and stuck by him.

After they'd been married five years and suffered two miscarriages, she had been losing hope of giving Rick the child she knew they both wanted so desperately. Then one day, while he was deployed God-knew-where on the other side of the world, she brought home a pregnancy test after missing her period for the second time in as many months. She'd been terrified to hope it was positive and that she could carry the baby to term if she was.

It had been another three weeks before she was able to tell Rick he would be a father. She had just passed into her second trimester, and the only two people who knew were her mother and his. The two grandmothers-in-waiting had noticed the subtle changes in Eileen's body and had been sworn to secrecy until Rick could be told. He'd been on cloud nine after she'd given him the news over the phone, but five more weeks passed before they were again in each other's arms. And, somehow, he'd been stateside several months later when she'd given birth to their son.

Over the years, they'd had their ups and downs but managed to keep their marriage afloat despite Rick's long absences for missions he couldn't tell her about. Now they were enjoying their semi-retirements in Florida. She worked as a part-time tutor for children with learning disabilities and volunteered at a local animal shelter.

Rick picked up an occasional assignment for Trident or filled in when a fishing buddy needed an extra mate for his charter business. But despite their happiness, something was missing. Eileen hoped Katerina's return meant their son would settle down and give them the grandchildren they looked forward to spoiling. If any two people deserved a happily-ever-after, it was Kat and Ben.

Lightening flashed outside their bedroom window, and a crack of thunder followed. Fast storms typical in Florida, and it would probably clear within thirty minutes or so. Unable to go back to sleep, Eileen decided to make herself a little tea and maybe read for a while.

Using a hint of the light coming through the blinds from the street lamp out front, she grabbed her lightweight bathrobe and crept out into the hallway, closing the bedroom door behind her. She flipped the light switch, but nothing happened. Trying again, she assumed the storm had knocked out the power and used her hands along the wall as a guide. It wasn't until she stepped into the kitchen that a thought occurred to her. The street lamp wouldn't have been lit if the neighborhood had lost power. She realized she wasn't alone a second before a strong hand covered her mouth, blocking her scream.

"Be quiet or I vill cut throat."

BOOMER'S ARM WAS AROUND KAT'S NAKED WAIST, AND HIS hand found her breast. He knew he should let her sleep after the sexual gymnastics they'd performed earlier, but his cock was hard, and he wanted her again. He'd seen the exchange between Kat and Carter earlier, and while a part of him was jealous, another part wondered if she would be interested in letting the other Dom join them someday. It was all about pleasing her in every way possible. He'd taken part in several ménages over the years, including a few with the black-ops agent. Carter would never poach another man's woman, but the guy loved the female population and any way he could please them sexually was fine with him.

Massaging the lush breast, Boomer kissed Kat's bare shoulder and ground his erection against her ass. She stirred in his arms and rolled toward him, letting him replace his hand with his mouth. He teased the nipple, sucking and licking until her back arched. A moan escaped her, and his eyes lifted to see she was fully awake. And there was just enough moonlight coming through the blinds for him to see she was very much aroused.

Giving the taut nipple another swipe of his tongue, he grinned at her. "Sorry I woke you."

She shoved her hands into his hair and tugged downward until his mouth closed around her breast again. "No, you're not, and neither am I. Don't stop, it feels so good."

Legs, hips, shoulders, and arms shifted, and soon his torso was cradled between her thighs. One hand plucked her other nipple as he continued to suck on the first. Her sighs and gasps were making him harder. "Hands above your head, Kitten. Hold onto the headboard, and don't let go. I heard Carter crash next door about ten minutes ago, so you might want to keep those sounds of yours on the low side. Although I doubt he'd mind hearing you."

Her hips bucked against him, and he pinched her nipple, making her cry out. "Oh, oh, shit!"

Boomer swapped tits, latching his mouth onto the one he'd just pinched. He sucked the stiff peak into his mouth and shifted his body to the side so his hand could slide down to her pussy. With one finger, he circled her clit once, then twice before going lower to her engorged lips. She was ready for him, but he wasn't ready to take her yet. He wanted to tease her until she begged him like she'd done earlier when he'd eaten her through three powerful orgasms.

He cautiously eased a finger into her hot channel, hoping she wasn't sore. When she opened her legs wider, giving him better access, he added another finger and began to flick her clit with his thumb. One of her hands left the headboard and grasped his hair. He let her breast go with a pop. "Uh-uh, Kitten. What did I tell you? I've been waiting for an excuse to spank you tonight, and you just earned it."

Kat squeaked. "W-what? Are you serious? I'm ready to come, and you want to spank me?"

"Damn straight. C'mere." Sitting up, he grabbed her hips and flipped her onto her stomach, ignoring her gasp and squeal. He lifted and then settled her across his lap. Her naked ass taunted him, and he caressed the pale cheeks as she squirmed. Another idea came to mind, and he reached over to the nightstand where he'd placed a new tube of lubricant earlier. He couldn't take her virgin hole yet, but he could give her a little taste of what would come.

Boomer parted her ass cheeks, and Kat instinctively reached back with her hands to cover herself. "What are you doing?"

He grabbed her wrists with one hand and held them at the small of her back. "Shh. Easy, Kitten. I won't do anything I don't think you'll enjoy. Give it a chance. That's all I'm asking. Okay?"

Her tense body relaxed a little, and he let go of her wrists. Caressing her back, ass, and legs, he felt her melt into him even more. His thoughts strayed to what he'd been thinking of before she woke. Figuring he would never know unless he asked her, he decided to go for it. "What do you think of Carter?"

"What do you mean? He seems like a nice guy."

"Are you attracted to him?"

Kat looked at him over her shoulder, her brows furrowed in confusion. "I think most women would say he's good-looking." She didn't add, "as long as they weren't dead," but he was sure the words were on the tip of her wet little tongue.

"That's not what I was asking, Kitten, and you know it." He squeezed her ass, then slid his fingers to her wet pussy, teasing her as she wriggled in his lap. "Now that you're no longer a virgin, if you and I weren't together, and Carter hit on you, would you sleep with him?"

She gaped at him. "Are you mad at me? There's nothing for you to be jealous about. I'm with you, not Carter. Just because I think another guy is good-looking doesn't mean I want to sleep with him."

He flicked her clit and smiled when she shifted her hips, trying to get closer and top from the bottom. Raising his other hand, he slapped her ass hard and then plunged his finger back inside her, stroking her higher, but not high enough.

"Ow! Ohhhhh, shit!"

"Like that, hmm? Put your hands under your cheek and keep them there. Pain can be very pleasurable, Kitten. I plan to show you just how much." He slowed his teasing pace. "Now, back to my question. I'll admit I had a moment of jealousy earlier, but I know Carter well enough that it's not an issue. What I'm trying to find out is how you would feel if I asked him to join us . . . in here . . . right now."

Kat tried to flip over to stare at him, but he held her firm. "You—you mean like a ménage? A threesome? Seriously?"

"Seriously. And if you say no, then it's fine. We haven't gone through your limit list yet, so I figured I'd ask."

Pushing up on her hands, she twisted her upper torso. "Can you stop so I can turn over a sec, please? So we can talk about this first. I can't think when you're doing that. I'm not saying no, but I'm not saying yes either."

Pulling his finger out of her pussy, he turned her over and sat her on his lap, his rigid cock pressed against her hip. Whether her answer was yes or no, he would still give her a few orgasms before finding his own release. He'd been involved in a few first-time ménages, but this was Kat, and *all* of this was new to her.

Reaching over, he turned on the bedside lamp so they could see each other better. "Let me explain a few things first before you answer me. One of the things about a ménage is trust. You have to trust me to make sure the third, whether it's Carter or someone else, doesn't do anything you don't like or anything that would hurt you. Everything he does will be cleared by me first, and I won't allow anything you're uncomfortable with. The third in a scene is there to enhance the woman's pleasure. Imagine I have four hands instead of two, touching you and pleasing you. Maybe while my mouth is eating your pussy, his will be sucking these luscious tits of yours."

He closed his hand around one and began to tease her. Moaning, she wiggled in his lap and thrust her chest out, inviting him to do more. "While I'm fucking your sweet cunt, he'll be fucking your mouth. But don't worry, he won't come in your mouth . . . he'll come all over your chest at the last second. Then I'll make you come before I do. So, tell me, Kitten. Do you want to experience two men doing nothing but pleasing you, making you shatter into a million pieces over and over again?"

"Yesssss." Her answer came out as a hiss, all but begging him to do whatever he wanted.

He stopped his sensual assault on her breast and grabbed her hair, holding her so she looked directly at him. "Say it again, Kitten. I need to know that you won't have any reservations after we start. Is this what you want? You, me, and Carter?"

Her hand came up to cup his jaw, his stubble rough against her soft palm. "Yes, as long as you're the one in control, then yes, I want this. I want to try new things with you, but only if you want them too."

"I love you, Kitten. I promise this will be good. If something scares you or doesn't feel right, use your 'red' safeword, okay?" Leaning down, he took possession of her mouth, tasting, teasing, and savoring before pulling away again. "Okay?"

"Okay. And I love you, too."

"One other thing. While we're playing, don't forget I want to hear 'Master' from your pretty mouth and call Carter 'Sir.'"

She licked her lips. "Yes, Master."

Raising his hand above the headboard, Boomer knocked on the wall between their room and Carter's. He wasn't too surprised when the door opened a second later and the man walked in wearing only a pair of sweatpants. The gray cotton was doing nothing to hide his prominent hard-on. His hair was still damp from a shower and slicked back, down from its earlier ponytail.

"Jeez, it took you fucking long enough. I thought I would have to start whacking off in there." At Kat's astonished expression, he added, "Hello, little one. Yes, the walls in here are thin enough to hear through. We need to have Ian fix that. But if you'd said 'no,' I wouldn't have told you I heard anything because I wouldn't want to embarrass you."

He stopped next to the queen-sized bed, regarding her appreciatively. "Damn, you're even prettier naked."

Kat had been so shocked at his sudden appearance, then his bare torso had snagged her attention, and she'd forgotten she was nude. She was about to raise her hands to cover herself, but Benny stopped her.

"Uh-uh, Kitten. There's no need to hide. Let him look at how beautiful you are." He turned her in his lap so her legs fell to either side of his and his erection nestled against her ass and lower back. Taking her wrists, he brought her hands up behind his neck while her head rested against his shoulder.

She shuddered at the heat in Carter's eyes as they traveled over her body, lingering on her breasts and exposed pussy. His intense gaze made her wetter, and she blushed more deeply.

While Benny's hands closed around her breasts, Carter cupped her cheek. "I love seeing women blush, little one, but don't be embarrassed. You have a gorgeous body, and it's a privilege to see it. But I need to hear you say you want me here one more time. I'm not going to do anything Boomer doesn't approve. He knows what you like and what you don't. Do you want me to be a third in your bed, fucking you and pleasing you? I need a verbal answer, sweetheart."

Kat was so turned on by his words and how Benny had been playing with her nipples that she didn't hesitate. "Yes . . . Sir. I do."

She still couldn't believe that she'd agree to this, but she didn't want to take it back. She'd read many books about ménage relationships and had several fantasies about it happening to her. But only if Benny was with her.

"Thank you, and I'm truly honored. I promise you'll enjoy every minute of it, starting now. Boom, I do believe you mentioned a spanking, hmm?"

Kat's eyes went wide, and a little squeak escaped her. "What? I'm supposed to enjoy that? Seriously?"

"Ha!" Benny barked and chuckled. "As I told you before, Kitten, yes, seriously. I've been itching to spank your sweet ass, and, yes, done right, you'll enjoy it. Now, would you like to continue or say your safeword?"

Both men patiently waited as Kat worked her way through this in her mind. She couldn't deny the idea of being spanked turned her on, but would it hurt too much? He'd said they wouldn't hurt her, and there was some pain which was gratifying. She also had her safeword, which she knew undoubtedly would be heeded if she said it. The few spanks Benny had given her so far had aroused her, but she was still nervous. "Is this a punishment spanking or a pleasure spanking, Master?"

"Since you used my title so nicely, it will be a pleasure spanking, Kitten. Let us show you how a little pain can take you higher than you've ever been."

Without saying a word, Carter held out his hand to her. Making her decision, she took it and let him help her stand. Smiling down at her, he addressed Benny. "Why don't we up the heat factor for her? She can sit on my face while you redden her ass."

Kat's mouth dropped open as Benny climbed off the bed, apparently not embarrassed he was naked in front of the other man. "Excellent idea, my friend. Before I forget, when Kat blows you later, she's not a fan of swallowing yet, so that's a hard limit for her right now."

Her entire body blushed in embarrassment, but neither man seemed fazed.

"Understood." Carter lay on the bed with his head at the edge closest to them. "Climb up, Kitty-Kat, and let me taste your sweet pussy."

Kat's legs shook as Benny helped her back onto the bed so she was straddling the other man's head, facing his bare feet at the opposite side. Carter pulled her knees a little wider apart, so she was closer to his mouth, but didn't start tasting her yet.

When she was positioned right, Benny pushed on her back until she lowered her upper body onto Carter's, her head resting on his rock-hard abs. Rolling her eyes upward, she saw his stiff cock bulging in his sweats and wondered what he looked like. Would he be bigger or smaller than Benny? Would they taste similar or completely different? She didn't know but was curious to find out. Feeling Carter's breath against her wet sex, she shivered in anticipation. *What was he waiting for?*

"Are you comfortable, Kitten?" Benny caressed her back and ass as goose bumps popped up all over her porcelain skin.

"Yes, Master."

"Good. Go for it, man."

Carter wasted no more time before feasting on her. His tongue and mouth attacked her, and she cried out how good it felt. He licked her entire slit from end to end, then back again, over and over, like she was an ice cream cone, as his fingers found her clit. The pressure on her little nub was light, only enough to tease, but nothing more . . . and she wanted more. Oh fuck, how she wanted more! He nibbled on her pussy lips, and she felt her juices flow. Moaning, she ran her tongue along the right side of the muscular "V" which disappeared into his sweats. His hips flinched, and his dick twitched in response. Kat smiled wickedly, feeling empowered she could evoke a reaction like that from a noticeably experienced man.

Just as he impaled her with his stiffened tongue, a hand landed hard on her right ass cheek, and she jumped, but Carter held her hips so she didn't get far. Pain, then heat, then pure desire shot through her.

Another slap sounded a split second before she felt the same on her other cheek, and the pain barely registered in her mind. All she could concentrate on was the euphoric high she was climbing. Benny massaged the flesh he'd struck this time, and the sensations he evoked made her juices flow into Carter's mouth. The man groaned and lapped up every drop.

Kat didn't know what to react to or how. The dual assault on her buttocks and pussy had her head spinning, and all she could do was moan, pant, and enjoy. Her hands clenched Carter's thighs through his sweatpants as she tried to grind her pelvis into his face. He speared her with his tongue again. "Oh, shit. Holy fucking shit, it feels so good. Oh, God!"

———

BOOMER'S COCK GREW HARDER AT THE WORDS AND SOUNDS coming from Kat, and he spanked her ass a few more times, spacing them out until his handprints covered her cheeks and the sit-spots at the top of her thighs. The mix of white, pink, and red was so enticing. Pressing his hands against her flesh, he held the heat in and let the pleasure-pain combine with whatever Carter was doing to her. Boomer knew it wouldn't take much more for her to go over the edge. Earlier in the night, she'd been able to hold off and orgasm twice on command, so he decided to give her a break this time. "Come whenever you need to, Kitten."

"Y-yes, M-Master. Thank you. Oh, shit! Don't stop, S-Sir, please! Holy hell . . ."

Carter must have done something she really liked because her words became mumbled amid her keening as she buried her face into his abdomen. Boomer found the tube of lubricant near the pillows and grabbed it. Squirting it on his fingers, he instructed his friend, "Spread her cheeks for me, man. It's time to introduce her to a little anal."

Not stopping his assault on her pussy, Carter reached back and squeezed her tender ass cheeks, separating them. Her puckered virgin hole winked at Boomer, and he coated it with lube. Gasping, she clenched, and he heard Carter's muffled chuckle.

"Whatever you just did, do it again. It made her gush. Damn, she's fucking delicious."

"And I didn't even push in yet, but that's next. Relax your ass, Kitten. You'll feel some pressure, but I'm only using my finger, so it won't be too uncomfortable. Once you relax, you'll feel it in your pussy."

"Y-yes, Master. I'll t-try."

"Good girl." Boomer rimmed her entrance, ensuring there was plenty of lube, then eased his index finger into the center. Using an in-and-out motion, he advanced a little further with each pass. "Relax, Kitten. Let me in, and I swear you'll come hard when I get there."

"OH FUCK! I'M READY TO COME NOW. JUST A LITTLE MORE, please . . . more!" She had no idea what "more" she was begging for, and it didn't matter as long as they continued what they were doing. Between their four hands, Kat couldn't move her pelvis. She was at their mercy, and there was no place else she wanted to be. Without realizing it, she dug her nails into Carter's thighs until his solid muscles tightened further, and he grunted.

Her fingers flew open. "S-sorry."

His mouth left her pussy long enough for him to say, "Don't be sorry, Kitty-Kat. I like being clawed. Just don't draw blood, and we're good."

"Oh shit!" Kat cried out. Benny had used her distraction to plunge past her sphincter, and the nerves in her ass lit up like the Fourth of July. He'd been right—all the nerves seem to be directly connected to her clit, which was pulsating relentlessly. If only someone would . . . "Pleeeassseeee . . . I need to . . . Oh, fuck . . ."

Carter sucked on her clit, and that was all it took for her to come, her orgasm sending her spiraling into an abyss. She was flying and falling simultaneously, not knowing which way was up. Her body shook as wave after wave of ecstasy rippled through her. Screams of pleasure assailed her ears, and it took her a moment to realize they were coming from her. Twisting the sheets in her hands, she bucked her hips, trying to get away . . . trying to get closer. Carter's mouth and tongue continued their onslaught as Benny fucked her ass with his finger, and the combination had her on a steep climb once again. "No . . . yes . . . oh shit, yesssss . . ."

A slap landed on her right butt cheek, then her left. It was all too much, and she went over again, quivering and shouting. Spots appeared before her eyes as she spun out of control. Never in her life could she have imagined an orgasm this good . . . this intense. She'd always thought women claiming they'd had one like this had been exaggerating. Now she knew they did exist, and she was capable of having them . . . more than once.

The men eased off, then stopped as Kat collapsed on Carter's body. Her lungs heaved for oxygen, and Benny picked her up and laid her on the bed. "Okay, Kitten?"

While she nodded, trying to catch her breath, Carter stood, wiped his glistening face with his hand, and then removed his sweatpants. Holy shit, the man was perfection. His impressive cock was standing proud as he gave it a few strokes.

The two men stared down at her as she eyed them both. Damn, they were hot. She thought of all the women who'd pay a million dollars to be in her position or any other position Benny and Carter wanted to put her in.

Tough cookies, ladies, I'm not trading places with anyone. I'm playing catch-up with the rest of the female population.

"Ready for more, Kitty-Kat?" Carter knelt on the bed while Benny grabbed a condom from the box on the nightstand. He would have to get more if they kept going at this rate. It was the third one he'd used tonight.

"Hell, yeah!" She covered her mouth as they chuckled at her. Her brain-to-mouth filter had to be broken when it came to sex. "I mean . . . oh, whatever . . . hell, yeah!"

"Boomer's going to fuck your sweet pussy while you suck my cock. Don't worry, I'll pull out and come all over those pretty tits of yours instead of in your mouth. Okay?"

She nodded in agreement.

Carter grabbed her chin. "Uh-uh, Kitty. The answer is 'yes, Sir.' Before was all about you. But now, you be a good girl, do as we say, and we'll let you come again before we do."

He'd transformed before her eyes. His face was stern, and he'd dropped the tone of his voice. Gone was the teasing playmate, and in his place was a commanding Dominant—sexy and sinful. She glanced at Benny and saw the same intense expression. Holy hell, she'd do or say whatever they wanted her to, as long as they kept looking at her like she was the sexiest thing they'd ever seen. Her pussy clenched as she turned back to Carter. "Yes, Sir."

"Boom, how do you want to do this?"

Climbing on the bed, Boomer grabbed Kat's hips. "On all fours, Kitten. I'm going to fuck you from behind while you suck him off. When he's ready, I'll pull you upright so he can come on you."

Following orders, Kat got on her hands and knees, facing

the foot of the bed. Carter knelt in front of her as Boomer settled in behind her. He quickly donned the condom and lined his aching cock with her slit. Watching his friend guide Kat to take him into her mouth was so fucking hot that he wasn't sure he'd last long. But they'd make it good for her again before that happened.

Carter hissed as her mouth closed around him, and he firmly grasped her hair, showing her the pace he wanted. Boomer rubbed his tip along her pussy lips and found she was still soaking wet. Clutching her hips, he thrust forward and was rewarded with a sexy moan from her as he buried himself inside her to the hilt.

Carter cursed. "Shit, her mouth is a fucking deadly sin. Make her moan again."

"No problem." He was gliding in and out of her channel, reveling in the feel of her tight walls. He dreamed of the day he could take her without any barrier. Flesh on flesh. Reaching around, his fingers found her clit, and soon she was moaning repeatedly.

On either end, both men set the same pace. In and out. Slow, at first. Each stared down where their cocks disappeared into her body, filling her. Hisses, moans, groans, slurps, and slaps filled the air as all three took their pleasure and gave it back in return.

Carter reached down and moved her hair which had fallen around her face again. "Can you take me a little deeper? Breathe through your nose."

"She's got a strong gag reflex." Boomer's hands rubbed her bare back, sides, and hips as he continued to pump into her tight, hot pussy.

Carter wrapped his fingers around his thick shaft about three-quarters of the way down. "I won't go too far, Kitty. Just a little further."

Kat nodded and took a deep breath through her nose without releasing him. Carter's hand pulled not-so-gently on her hair while his other one found one of her tits and rolled the perky nipple between his fingers. Simultaneously, Benny reached around her hip and pinched her clit. Her muffled scream of pleasure made both men smirk, knowing it wouldn't take much more for her to explode.

Her moaning, breathing, and heart rate increased as both cocks fucking her picked up their pace. All the signs pointed to her impending orgasm, and Carter addressed his friend. "She's getting close, man, and so am I. Get ready to lift her up."

Clutching her hips, Boomer adjusted his knees. He leaned forward, put his arms under her armpits, and grabbed her shoulders. The new position allowed him to impale her harder and faster on his cock, driving deeper. He felt her inner walls begin to pulsate around him but waited for the other man to tell him it was time to pull her up.

Carter's grip on her hair intensified as he murmured words about how good she was. A growl escaped him. "Now!"

Boomer drew her upright, and she had no choice but to release the cock from her mouth. The new position made her sink further onto the shaft in her pussy. Carter's fingers pinched her nipple and sent her over the edge as he squirted his hot cum on her breasts and abdomen. Dual cries and curses of release were joined by a third as Boomer shot his own load deep inside her.

No words were spoken for a few moments as all three regained their breath. Kat groaned as Boomer eased from her body and turned her onto her back. He quickly disposed of his condom in a nearby garbage pail. Carter stood on shaky legs and went to the bathroom to retrieve damp and dry towels. He handed both to Boomer, who cleaned her.

Carter leaned down to kiss Kat's forehead. "Thank you, Kitty-Kat. You were amazing. I'm going to leave you in your Dom's care. Sleep well."

"You too," she murmured, fading fast into slumber.

Carter chuckled as he grabbed his sweatpants and pulled them on. "Thanks, man. As I said before, she's a keeper."

Finishing with Kat's torso, Boomer found a clean section of the damp towel and started wiping between her legs. "I know. You going to be around in the morning?"

Opening the door, Carter looked back at his friend. "Unless I get called away on something, I figured I'd stick around in case you need me for anything until she's safe. You guys . . ." He jutted his chin toward Kat. ". . . and your ladies are the closest thing I have to family, and I'll do anything I can to keep you all around. Later."

Boomer's hand slowed to a stop as he stared at the now-closed door. The black-ops spy had been there many times when they'd needed him, but he wasn't known for sticking around long. And saying the team and their women were family to the loner was something Boomer had never expected to hear. They knew very little about their friend's life, even less about his past, and he was sure they knew him better than most. Hell, Carter had always been a nice guy, patient with the submissives, and certainly loyal, but how could a man with hands so deadly hide such a loving heart?

Turning his attention back to Kat, who was almost asleep, Boomer picked her up and put her head on the pillow. He tossed the towels on the floor and reached over to shut off the light. Lying beside her, he drew the sheet over their bodies and soon fell victim to gratified exhaustion.

CHAPTER TWENTY

K at woke up wrapped in Benny's arms and hotter than a pig on a spit. She wasn't used to sleeping with someone, and while she loved being near him all night, she sometimes wished his body temperature was twenty degrees lower.

Easing away from him, she threw the sheet off and sat up. According to the bedside clock, it was a little after ten, and she didn't know why she was surprised she'd slept so late. After all, she'd been up half the night having incredibly naughty sex and loving every minute.

Stretching, she stood and headed toward the bathroom. A humming reached her ears, and she realized it was coming from the pile of clothes they'd practically ripped off each other the night before. Searching through the shirts, pants, and skirt, she found his cell phone, still on vibrate from being in the club. Noting the name and number, she decided to let him know he had a call.

"Benny?" No answer. Kat walked back to the bed and shook his shoulder. "Benny? Wake up. Your mom's calling."

"*Mmm*," he mumbled into his pillow. "Ooo's ih?"

"Your mom."

"-All -ack -ater."

Kat grinned as he went right back to sleep like a little kid. She placed his phone on the nightstand and headed for the bathroom again.

Fifteen minutes later, after a nice relaxing shower, she strode out to the common area of the second floor where the kitchenette and living area were. Her wet hair, combed back, dampened her clean T-shirt. She'd been staring down, past her baggy sweatpants to her bare toes, noticing they desperately needed a pedicure, when she realized someone else was in the room. Blushing at Carter's presence, she made her way over to the coffee machine.

He grinned as she brushed past him, then sat at the table. Never taking his amused eyes off her, he sipped his coffee. "Good morning, Kitty-Kat."

"Um, good morning." Concentrating on the Keurig as if it was the most complicated piece of machinery she'd ever used, Kat busied herself. She wasn't sure what to say to the man who'd been a third in her and Benny's sexual escapades. Was she supposed to thank him? That might be weird. Maybe she should just act like nothing happened. While she was embarrassed seeing him this morning, she didn't regret what they'd done. She may have only recently lost her virginity, but like most women, she'd had her fantasies—although she'd never dreamed that particular fantasy would happen to her. And, oh boy, had the reality been a hundred times better than anything she'd ever thought up.

Running out of things to do at the counter, she hoped he would leave the room, saving her from making a fool of herself. However, after her coffee was ready, she had no choice but to turn around and face him.

Using his foot, he pushed out the chair across from him

and indicated with his chiseled chin for her to sit. It would be more awkward if she refused, so she sat with her coffee in hand, her eyes downcast. She was startled after a moment of silence when he let out an exaggerated sigh and stood. Kat watched as he began to pull out a Cheerios box, a bowl, and milk from the cabinets and refrigerator before setting them down in front of her. He grabbed a knife and spoon from a drawer, and a banana from the counter, adding them to the other items. A napkin was the last thing he placed in front of her.

Sitting back down, he pointed to her and then the food. "Eat, little one. Your clothes are hanging off you. You've obviously lost weight recently, and I doubt it was intentional."

Kat snorted as she poured some cereal into the bowl. "Are all Doms this bossy? You all keep ordering me to eat."

"Yes, when it comes to a submissive's health and safety, we're very bossy." He regarded her momentarily as she prepared her breakfast, adding milk and sliced banana. After he seemed satisfied with how much food she'd filled the bowl with, he said, "Now, while you're eating, there are a few other things we need to discuss."

When her hand stopped the loaded spoon halfway to her mouth as she gaped at him, he reached over with his fingers and started it again. "I said, 'while you're eating.'"

She put the spoon into her mouth and then pulled it out empty. He smiled at her. "Good girl. Now, what happened last night, or early this morning as it were, is between you, Boomer, and me—no one else. If you choose to have some girl talk with the others, that's one thing, but I will not let anyone know what happened between us. I don't kiss and tell about things that happen behind closed doors. Understood?"

Kat nodded and swallowed. "I mean, yes, Sir."

"You can drop the 'Sir' this morning, Kat. Only when we're playing or in the club is the formality necessary. Now, I don't want you reading too much into what happened and being all embarrassed around me. There's no need for it. Boomer is a good friend, and as I said before, it was an honor to play with you. If it was a one-time thing, that's fine." He shrugged. "If it happens again, that's fine, too. But think of it as . . . I don't know . . . as we all went out bowling and had a fun time. Nothing embarrassing about bowling, right?"

Surprised he'd used the same activity she'd been talking to Benny about on the plane, Kat laughed, the tension she'd felt disappearing. "Um, no, I guess not. Unless it's naked bowling."

"Now there's a sport that won't be on TV anytime soon." He sat forward and took another sip of his coffee. "You're a beautiful, sensual woman, Kat. Never be embarrassed about that. Just because you enjoyed something outside the norms of society doesn't mean it was wrong. You were just brave enough to try something millions of women want but don't have the courage to experience for themselves."

"I never thought of it that way."

"And that's what's wrong with society nowadays." Having overheard some of their conversation, Benny walked into the room, fresh from his own shower. He stopped next to the table, eyeing her breakfast, and was apparently satisfied with what he saw. "Everyone is too scared to try something they've only dreamed about. And it's nice to see you eating. You two okay?"

The question was addressed to them both, but it was apparent the only person he was worried about was Kat. She glanced at Carter, who nodded at her, then grinned back at Benny. "Yup. We're good." After tossing his cell phone on the table, Benny kissed the top of her head and made a beeline to the coffee machine. "Did you call your mom back?"

"Not yet. Need caffeine first. She's probably already planning for us to visit for a few days. But before we do that, we have to figure out how to get the target off your back."

Kat peered down at the phone which had landed next to her. For some reason, the screen had lit up, and what she saw had her brow furrowing. "Um, Benny. It says you have twenty-seven missed calls."

SPINNING AROUND, BOOMER SNATCHED IT FROM THE TABLE and stared at the screen. "What the fuck? Shit, they're all from my mom. Fuck, something must have happened to Pop."

He hit the speed dial for his mother's phone, pacing impatiently until she picked up. An evil chill ran down his spine. When it connected, his words rushed out. "Mom? It's me. What's wrong? My phone was off."

"B-Ben? Y-You have to come h-home quickly and bring K-Katerina. T-they're going to k-kill your father if you don't."

He froze at the terror he heard in his mother's voice. "What? Who? Mom, are you there? Who's going to kill Pop?"

An astute Carter immediately pulled out his phone and called Ian. "If you're not already in the office, get there. They've got Boom's parents." He hung up on the other man's loud curses.

"Mom! Fuck! Hello?" At first, Boomer thought they'd been disconnected, but then he heard his mother cry out in the background as someone else took the phone. "Who the fuck is this?"

"This is man who vill kill parents if you don't bring vhat ve vant. You have two hours, or I start playing vith knife. I vill kill if see police. Bring girl and money."

"You son of a fucking bitch! I'm going to kill you if you hurt one hair on them! You hear me, you piece of shit! Hello? Hello? Fuck!" He threw the phone across the room and didn't even care it broke into a million pieces. They had plenty of backup phones downstairs, and Brody could switch Boomer's phone number over to one.

"The team's alerted. Ian will be downstairs in a minute." Carter was almost to the hallway when he turned around. "I'm grabbing my stuff. We'll get them, Boom. We'll get your folks out of this, and Kat too."

Boomer nodded his thanks and looked at Kat crying, her mouth opening and closing without any sound. Pulling her out of her seat and into his arms, he hugged her tight. "It's all right, baby. He's right . . . we'll get my folks out of this."

"H-how? You have to take me with you, and—and the money too. T-trade me for your parents."

"No! Fucking! Way!" He grabbed her shoulders and gave her two short shakes until he had her full attention. His angry eyes flared at her. "No fucking way am I doing that, Kitten. Not happening. This is what we do. We rescue people. These assholes have messed with the wrong team. And there's no fucking way I'm trading you for my parents, much less bringing you with us. You're staying right here in the compound."

"You can't leave me here! What if . . . what if they see I'm not there and kill your parents, Benny? I can't let that happen! You have to take me with you! We'll give them the money! Please!"

She was becoming hysterical, and there was no time for it. He shook her shoulders again, talking over her rambling, putting his best Dominant tone into his voice. "No, Kat. No! Listen to me, dammit! You're not going anywhere near these fuckers. You're staying right here, and unless you don't want to sit for the next year, you'll do exactly what I say. Your safety is my number one priority, and I can't do my job if I'm worrying about you *and* my folks. Now, we don't have time to argue, so are you going to obey me, or am I going to have to tie you to a fucking chair?"

Carter jogged past them, heading for the stairs with his gear. "Time's a-wasting, dude."

"Kat? Answer me!"

She was shaking and sobbing, but somehow his words penetrated her scrambled brain. "Um, o-okay."

"Good girl." Snatching her hand, he led her toward the stairs. Now that he didn't have to worry about her, his mind was free to worry about his folks.

KAT WATCHED AS THE COMMAND VAN SPED OUT OF THE compound, followed by two black SUVs. Beside her, Jake put his arm around her shoulders. "Everything is going to be fine, Kat. Come on. Let's go inside. It'll be an hour or so before they get there, and we'll hear everything when they do."

She'd been adamant about listening in on the rescue along with Jake. It'd been decided he would stay behind to watch Kat, along with Murray, the compound's daytime guard, and one of Chase Dixon's men. The other two contract agents had gone with the rest of the Trident team and Carter. Since the patch still covered Jake's dominant eye, the black-ops spy was taking his place as team sniper. Jake wasn't pleased about missing the rescue, but he knew he might be a hindrance, and Kat needed guarding, too.

Thankfully, Kristen, Angie, and Jenn were on their way to a book promotion at a Barnes & Noble in Spring Hill, about an hour north of Tampa. Since Angie had designed the book cover for *Leather & Lace*, Kristen's publisher had thought it would be a great idea for her to appear with the author. They'd invited Jenn to be their paid gofer for the day, and she'd switched shifts at the pub so she could join them. The three women had left an hour before Boomer had gotten the call from his mother, so they had no idea what was going down. Ian and Devon preferred it that way—no point worrying them if it wasn't necessary. Hopefully, the excitement would all be over before they returned later in the afternoon.

Beau trotted after Kat as she followed Jake into the offices. The team had opted to leave the trained canine behind as extra security for Kat. The only other person in the compound, besides the two guards, was Trident's secretary, Colleen, who looked up as the other two approached her desk. "Don't worry, Kat. These guys know their stuff, and they're the best."

"I know." She gave the younger woman a small smile. "I just won't be able to relax until I hear from Benny that everyone's okay."

"Can I get you something? Tea, maybe?"

Kat shook her head. "No, thanks. My stomach's a mess, and that'll just make it worse."

"Why don't you lie down for a bit upstairs?" Jake asked her. "You're pale, and I don't want you getting sick on me." She was about to object, but he held up his hand, stopping her. "I promise I'll come get you when they get there. There's nothing any of us can do until then. Please, Kat? Don't make me get my bullwhip."

While Kat gaped at him, Colleen snorted, which earned her a stern look from the Dom. She just grinned at him, knowing he'd been teasing the other woman. "He's just messing with you, Kat. Just threaten to mother him until his patch is removed, and he'll run in the other direction. Women scare him."

"Keep it up, little one, and I'll be on the phone to your Dom. Reggie will be more than happy to tan your hide tonight."

The secretary giggled. They both knew she loved to get spanked by her Master. "Yes, Sir."

Turning back to Kat, Jake pointed to the stairs. "All kidding aside, please lie down for a bit, Kat. Take Beau with you. As soon as I hear them nearing the house, I'll come get you."

She grumbled but headed for the staircase, her eyes heavy from the stress. "Bossy Doms. *Hier*, Beau."

As the canine followed Kat, Jake turned to Colleen. "Did you get a hold of Tiny yet? I want him here as an extra precaution."

"I spoke to him, and he said he'd be here as soon as possible, but it'll be about two hours. He had to take his mom for an MRI of her knee to see if she needs surgery. He'll be on his way as soon as he drops her off."

The phone rang, but she continued as she reached for it. "And don't forget I'm leaving in about a half hour. I have to take the firearms training course Ian scheduled me for, but I can cancel if you need me to." Not waiting for an answer, she brought the phone to her ear. "Hello, Trident Security. How can I help you?"

Happy it would leave him with one less person at the compound to worry about, Jake gave her a quick wave indicating she should leave for her course and then headed for the war-room. He'd promised Brody he wouldn't touch anything except the camera feeds and communications equipment. The geek was very anal about who was allowed in his technological lair. There was also a spare company laptop that Brody had set up for him, refusing to give him access to the mainframe computer, or as Egghead called it, his baby.

Gripping the desk chair, Jake made sure it was under him before sitting. His perception was off because of the eye patch, but he'd gotten used to it after the first two days. Still, he didn't always get it on the first try when he went to grab things.

Waking the laptop from sleep mode, he checked the time. About fifty more minutes before they got there. Nothing to do but wait . . .

CHAPTER TWENTY-ONE

"Can't you drive any fucking faster?"

"Relax, Boomer." Ian waited for an oncoming car to pass, then drove around the little old lady behind the wheel of her seven-year-old Ford Taurus, cruising at ten miles under the speed limit. The communications van driven by Marco followed suit, as well as Devon in the other SUV. "We're loaded to the gills with weapons and ammo, so I have no desire to get pulled over. They said two hours, and we only used an hour and ten of it. Five more minutes and we're there. Now chill, or I'm leaving you in the com-van."

"Like fucking hell!"

Ignoring his youngest employee, Ian continued to the Michaelson's house in a quiet neighborhood on the outskirts of the city. He parked a few hundred feet down from the driveway, out of view of anyone looking out the windows. The other vehicles pulled up behind him and the occupants got out, scanning the area. In this part of Sarasota, the property lots were larger, so houses were more spread out.

Rick and Eileen Michaelson had fallen in love with their semi-retirement home after house-hunting for days with a realtor eleven years ago. It was secluded enough for quiet and privacy, yet close enough to others, so they could become friends with their neighbors. A six-minute drive was all it took to reach the more populated residential and commercial areas.

While it sucked their neighbors had been too far away to hear screams for help, if there'd been any, it was to the team's advantage. Once they blended into the tree line, they wouldn't have to worry much about someone calling the police regarding a small army of men with guns running around. While Boomer got out, joining the rest of the team, Ian tapped on the microphone of his headset. "Reverend, you there?"

A burst of static came through then cleared. "Yeah, Boss-man. What's your status?"

"Just pulled up. How are things there?"

"Five by five." The military code meant all is well. "Just going to go get Kat. Stay safe, brothers."

"Amen." Ian exited the vehicle and met the rest of the team by the side of the comm van where weapons and equipment were being double-checked and strapped on. The men were dressed in camouflage and armed to the teeth. "Carter, find yourself a sniper position. My guess is they're in the family room. It's the largest and has the most windows to see if anyone is coming. Rear of the house, northwest corner. Scan the front and side windows for tangos on your way." Without a word, the spy disappeared into the trees with his trusted MK-11 sniper rifle. "Polo, Dev, take one of the SUVs, drive past the house and park up the road—approach by foot from that direction. Work your way around and stand by to breach the kitchen door. Check the windows on your way, too. Egghead, I want to know where the heat signatures are and how many, then use the side door to the garage. Wait a count of three after we breach—I don't want you getting in the way of any crossfire." He turned to Chase's two men. "Burke, Dusty, you're with the geek."

Brody reached into the van and pulled out a handheld heat-detecting device, then took off after his two temporary teammates with all of them using the tree line as cover.

"Boom, you're with me at the front door." Ian waited for a reply, but Boomer was staring in the direction of his parent's home.

"Hey! Boomer!" He got in the younger man's face. "This is just like every other mission, frog. I need your head in the game."

Knowing his boss was right, Boomer took a deep breath and went into battle mode. Anything else could result in one of his teammates getting hurt or killed, and he'd be damned if he was the cause of that happening. "I'm good. Let's just do this."

Ian waited a moment until he was clearly satisfied his friend was in the right mindset. Then readying his assault rifle, he took point, leading the way to the edge of the property. The house sat back from the road, and, thankfully, Boomer's mom loved to landscape with trees, shrubs, and flowers. There wasn't too much to use as cover, but enough, so it was better than nothing.

Going about twenty feet into the trees parallel to the property, they stopped and waited for the team to check in with intel. Carter was first. "Blinds are all pulled shut. No signs of movement."

"Fuck!"

Ian glared at Boomer but didn't say anything about his low-volume outburst. He'd do the same if the situation was reversed. "Heat signatures?"

It was a few moments before Brody's reply came over the

airwaves. "Nothing at the front end of the house. Going around the east side. Blinds are shut here, too."

The waiting was killing Boomer, but he knew it was necessary. The more intel, the better their chance of ending this without getting his parents killed—if they weren't dead already.

Pushing the ugly thought from his head, he listened for his teammate's next report.

"No heat, east side."

"Take it around back," Ian replied before heading for the front door. Staying low and watching for anything out of place, Boomer followed him. After using two trees to stop and scan the area, they reached the porch and silently flanked both sides of the front door, waiting for another update. Devon and Marco alerted they were ready for the breach command at the rear kitchen door.

"Two positives, full heat, ninety-nine and ninety-eight degrees. Both on the floor of the family room."

"Just two? What the fuck? Take it around the west side, Egg. Make sure there are no surprises. Dev, Burke, make sure there are no boobytraps on your entrances . . . I don't like this."

Boomer didn't either as he began to inspect the door frame. The only good thing was, if it was his parents lying on the floor, they were still alive, otherwise their heat signatures would be cooler. Unless they'd been killed, and the tangos left only moments before the team arrived. But why would they have done that without Kat and the money?

On Ian's side, there was a thin row of paned windows down the length of the door. He took a quick peek and then shook his head. "Nothing that I can see."

Brody rounded the house, jogging up to them. "No one else in the house, Boss-man."

Grimacing, Ian acknowledged him with a nod. Something was wrong . . . seriously wrong. But the only way to find out was to enter the house . . . very carefully. "Burke, Egghead's with us, so it's just you two. Since you can't see inside, I don't want to take a chance the door is rigged, so wait for us to let you in. Dev, how's the back look?"

"Clean."

"All right. Pick the lock instead of knocking it down. Let me know when you're ready."

Boomer was working on the deadbolt, and once it clicked, he turned his attention to the lock on the knob. In less than two minutes, they were ready to go. Ian got the "ready" from Devon as Boomer stood with his hand on the doorknob, waiting for the signal.

"On three. One . . . Two . . . Three."

The front and back doors opened simultaneously, and the five teammates stormed in. Since he didn't have a shot from the trees, Carter had shouldered his rifle and hoofed it to the back door, two steps behind Marco, with his Sig Sauer pistol in hand. Weapons at the ready position, they moved systematically through the house, clearing each room, closet, and hiding place along their way to the family room. Brody stopped at the door leading to the garage and, after checking for boobytraps, opened it for the others.

Nothing could have prepared Boomer for what awaited them in his parent's family room. His mother was frantically trying to get out of the duct tape which was wrapped around her bare legs from ankles to knees. Her arms were also taped behind her in a similar fashion. The bastards had even put it over her eyes and mouth. All the poor woman could do was squirm futilely.

But it was his dad who held Boomer's shocked attention. Lying in a pool of blood, the man was ashen. Like his wife,

Rick had been trussed up, but it appeared the Russians didn't see a need to cover his face as well.

Boomer's feet were nailed to the ground as the others pushed past him, cursing and dropping to their knees to help the couple.

Next to him, Ian was barking into the phone, demanding 9-1-1 send an ambulance to their location for a home invasion gunshot victim. That broke Boomer from his shock, and he dove to help Devon and Brody free his father.

Now that he was closer, he began assessing Rick's injuries. In addition to a gunshot wound to the abdomen, he'd been beaten . . . viciously. His face and torso showed bruises, swelling, and split skin, which had to have occurred over several hours.

Brody began handing them items from an emergency medical pack, ripping open the packages as he went. Pressure dressings were applied as Devon worked to start an IV. Rick's breathing was labored, but, thank fuck, he was alive.

Behind Boomer, Marco and Carter cut through Eileen's bindings and began to peel the tape from her face, very slowly. They'd wait until they got her to the hospital and let the doctors use an anti-adhesive to remove the rest. Duct tape could be like glue against the skin and was more painful to remove the longer it was on. As it was, they couldn't help but peel off a layer of skin from her lips and parts of her eyebrows. But it didn't bother her because when they freed her mouth, she started screaming for her husband, desperately trying to get to his side as they held her back.

Knowing he needed to calm his mother, Boomer switched places with Marco, who took over holding the pressure bandage to staunch the flow of blood from Rick's abdomen.

"He's alive, Mom. Pop's a fighter. We got this. We're gonna get him to the hospital, and he's going to be all right."

Sitting on the floor, Boomer had his arms wrapped around his crying mother, rocking and assuring her everything was going to be okay. He released her only for a moment when Burke and Dusty began collecting everyone's weapons to hide them in a concealed compartment in the van before the cops showed up. Since none of them had been fired, the guns weren't needed as evidence and would only cause trouble with the locals. The camouflage clothing could be explained by saying they'd been on their way to play paintball or something stupid like that.

Ian squatted down next to Boomer and his mom. Taking her hand, he squeezed until he got her attention. "Eileen, we're doing everything we can for Rick, but I need you to tell us what happened before the cops arrive."

When she didn't answer immediately, Boomer knew her adrenaline was wearing off, and shock was setting in. He gave her a shake and tugged her chin so she was facing him. "Mom, help us out. You gotta tell us what happened. Where'd they go? When did they leave? How many of them were here?"

"I . . . uh . . . oh, God, Ben!" Her body began to tremble.

"It's going to be all right, Mom. But we need to know. When did they leave? How long ago?"

Eileen shook her head, trying to clear her mind. She probably had no concept of how long she'd laid there, struggling to free herself or reach Rick after she'd heard the gunshot. "It was . . . it was a few minutes after you called. They . . . there were three of them . . . they said that was all they needed us for, then they covered my eyes and mouth. They were being . . . being rough with me, and Rick yelled for them to leave me alone. That's when I heard the gunshot.

They had beaten him a few times while . . . while we were trying to get a hold of you."

Boomer swallowed the guilt swarming through him. He'd been getting laid while his parents were being brutalized.

"I don't know how long it's been. They left right after that. Rick was able to talk for a while, but then he started fading. When he stopped talking, I thought he was . . ." She choked on the last words.

"He's not, Mom. Pop's alive, and he's going to stay that way." When she began crying harder again, he pulled her back into his arms and looked up at Ian, who now stood next to Carter. "They're going after Kat. This was all a ruse to get most of us away from her."

The two men nodded in grim agreement. Boomer reached for his headset only to find it'd fallen from his ear sometime in the last few minutes. "Tell Reverend to get her to the panic room."

Ian glanced at Carter and jutted his chin toward Eileen. The spy knelt and took her from Boomer so he could stand to talk with his boss. Ian grabbed his arm and pulled him into the kitchen. It was far enough away for Eileen not to overhear them, yet Boomer could still see what was happening in the other room. "We can't get a hold of him. He's not answering the com or his cell. There's also no answer at the office or front gate."

"Fuck!" His words were hissed low but urgent and desperate. "They're already there! We've got . . . shit!" He looked at his watch. "If they left right after the call . . . an hour drive . . . fuck, they would've gotten there almost thirty minutes ago. How are we going to get back there? It's probably too late! Shit!"

At the beginning of Boomer's panicked rant, Ian had hit a speed dial number on his cell. He held out a hand to shut him up as the connection was made. The younger man glared at him, then turned to watch his teammates work on his dad. Fear like he'd never known punched him in his gut—fear for his father and fear for the woman he loved more than life itself.

Sirens penetrated his brain. Help was on the way, and it was getting closer by the second. Help for his father, but what about Kat . . . and Jake and the others?

PLACING HIS HAND ON HIS TEAMMATE'S SHOULDER IN sympathy and solidarity, Ian waited impatiently for his call to be answered.

"Can this wait, Ian? I'm walking into a meeting with POTUS."

He didn't give a crap that the deputy director of the FBI was entering the Oval Office. Not when Kat, Jake, and the others were in danger. "No, it can't."

Larry Keon sighed heavily over the phone and then said something to someone else before coming back on the line. "You've got two minutes."

After filling the man in, Ian told him what they needed. "How fast can you get me a chopper back to the compound? And as much as I hate to ask, can you send Stonewall's SWAT? Things may go to shit by the time we get there if they haven't already."

The Tampa FBI Special Agent in Charge, Frank Stonewall, and the men of Trident weren't the best of friends after a few past incidents. The man hated Carter even more, with the feeling being mutual. The order coming from the SAC's superior would ensure there were no arguments or delays in the SWAT team's response.

"I'll call you back in a minute. Text me the coordinates of their house. And tell Carter to stay out of trouble. I'm going to need him by the time my meeting is over, and I don't want to have to bail him out."

"Will do." He hung up just as a slew of police officers and paramedics filled the house. Burke and Dusty had met the cops outside and told them the suspects were long gone, so no weapons were drawn. Brody, Marco, and Devon moved out of the way for the emergency personnel to take over but stayed close to assist if needed. Carter stood by Eileen, holding her hand as a female EMT began to assess her for injuries.

Next to Ian, Boomer's brow was scrunched in confusion. "Why didn't they kill both of them? I mean, I'm thanking the good Lord they didn't . . . but why? These guys don't give me the impression they have any ethics, so why let them live?"

Ian gestured to the organized chaos with his hand. "For this. This is to hold us up even further. It's giving them more time to get to Kat and force her to give them the money. If we walked in, and there was nothing more we could do here, we would've already been on our way back to the compound." He was about to say more, but his phone rang. "Keon, what've you got?"

"State Police chopper will be landing in the schoolyard up the street from the Michaelsons' within the next ten minutes. SWAT is on the way to the compound. Give me the officer in charge at the scene, and I'll clear you out of there." Waving over a sergeant, Ian explained who the other man on the line was and then handed him the phone, ignoring the supervisor's astonished expression.

———

BOOMER WAS BEING TORN IN HALF. HE WANTED TO STAY WITH his folks, but Kat needed him. As the paramedics placed his father on a gurney, he approached his mother as she sat on the couch with Carter. Boomer knelt in front of her, taking her attention away from Rick. The pale complexion of her face made the tape's sting glaringly obvious, and he winced, knowing it had to be painful. "Mom . . ."

Eileen cut him off. "Katerina's in danger, isn't she?"

"Yeah, she is. We have a chopper coming to take us back to the compound. I want to stay with you and Pop, but I—"

"No. You go get her and bring her back with you. Your dad will be okay, and I'm fine." She cupped his cheek, and he leaned into her touch. "She's your future, Benjamin. Go save her."

Boomer swallowed the thick lump in his throat. Standing, he helped her up and hugged her tight. "I'll be back soon—with Kat. Call my cell . . . shit . . . I broke mine and didn't have time to replace it. My calls are being forwarded to Ian's. I'll call Aunt Margaret to meet you at the hospital. Okay?"

"I'll contact Margaret. You just do what you have to. I love you. Stay safe and bring her home."

"I will. Love you, too, Mom."

With the help of the female EMT, Boomer escorted his mother to the waiting ambulance. The medics said his father was stabilized, but he was still unconscious. As they loaded his parents into the back of the rig, in the distance, he heard the *thump, thump, thump* of the approaching helicopter.

Ian sidled up next to him. "Our ride is almost here. Keon cleared us to take off and file the police reports later. Burke and Dusty are taking one of the SUVs and following your folks to the E.R. I want them guarded until this is over."

The ambulance doors slammed shut, and the vehicle

started down the driveway. "Thanks, Boss-man. I appreciate it."

Ian clapped his teammate on the back as they started jogging toward his SUV. It was faster to drive the quarter mile to where the helicopter was landing on an empty baseball field. The rest of the team was already on their way in the communications van. "It's what family does, Baby Boomer. Now, let's go get your girl."

CHAPTER TWENTY-TWO

For about fifteen minutes, Kat tried to get comfortable on the couch in the recreation room above the offices, but her mind wouldn't settle down to let her. This was all her fault. If she hadn't brought her problems to Benny, then his parents would have been safe. Now, she had to pray the team got to them in time to save them. The wait was killing her. Finally giving up on getting some rest, she stood and headed for the stairs with Beau at her heels.

Instead of going toward the offices, she went out the front door to get some air. She smiled when Beau made a beeline for a hard rubber ball and returned to drop it at her feet.

"So, you want to play, huh?" The goofy-faced dog seemed to grin at her before answering her with a low woof. "Fine, we'll play fetch for a few minutes. Maybe it'll make the time go faster."

Beau gave her another woof and then took off after the ball she threw across the compound. As she waited for the dog to return, she glanced to her left and saw Murray standing guard at the front gate. In the opposite direction the man from Blackhawk Security, who had been introduced to her as Jason "Tuff" Tanner, was walking toward the back of the compound, keeping watch for anything out of the ordinary. Both men were armed and Kat felt safer knowing they were there.

Beau ran up to her and dropped the ball which was now covered in dog drool, but she didn't mind since she was often slobbered on by the dogs she trained. Throwing the ball again, she heard the office door open behind her and turned to see Colleen walk out, carrying her purse. "Are you leaving?"

The younger blonde woman stopped next to her. "Yes. The team has been training me to shoot, but I still have to take a course to obtain my firearms permit before I can carry a gun. Ian and Reggie want me to get it because of all the guns on the premises. With the bad guys they deal with here, they wanted to be sure I could use one if I had to. I have to admit though, it makes me feel like some bad-ass chick when they take me shooting."

Kat laughed as Colleen giggled and posed like one of the stars of a popular TV show from the 1970s with her fingers forming a pretend weapon. "Oh, that's awesome. I love the *Charlie's Angels* reruns. Maybe Kristen, Angie, and I should join you. I think the original three were two brunettes and one blonde, and then another blonde replaced the first, so we'd be perfect. And I love those retro clothes."

"Oh! Maybe we can talk the Doms into having a seventies theme night at the club. That would be so funky."

Laughing harder, Kat reached back and grabbed her ass cheeks. "A spanking to disco music? Now that sounds really kinky."

"Shelby would love it! She loves theme nights. I'll run it by her and see what she thinks." Checking her watch,

Colleen added, "Shit. I'm going to be late if I don't leave. I'll see you later. Jake promised to text me and let me know everything is okay with Ben's parents."

Kat waved goodbye as the secretary ran to her Toyota Prius and drove away. Checking her cell phone, she saw she still had a least another fifteen minutes or so before the team reached Sarasota. Not ready to go back inside, she began to wander around the compound while continuing to play fetch with Beau.

Finding herself in the club parking area, she ambled over to the guard gate to see if Murray needed water or anything. She was just about to speak when the guard's head turned toward the road at the sound of an approaching vehicle. A black Cadillac Escalade with tinted windows pulled up to the closed gate and stopped. The guard eyed the vehicle warily and placed his hand on his sidearm, ready to draw the 9mm handgun if necessary.

Everything seemed to move in slow motion as Kat watched the driver's window roll down and Murray pull his weapon from the holster at his hip. But it was too late as the driver fired his own silenced pistol, and she gaped in horror as the burly guard's body jerked with the impact of the bullet hitting his upper right chest. Stunned, Kat was frozen in place, staring at the man as he fell to the ground, blood starting to saturate his shirt and the weapon dropping from his hand.

Three doors to the SUV opened, and two large men exited from the front, armed with black handguns. The driver was a little taller and leaner than his counterpart, who Kat thought resembled a pig with his flat nose and pock-marked skin. Another man climbed out of the backseat, and she gasped. It was one of the Russians who'd tried to kidnap her from the motel in Norfolk, dragging a terrified Colleen out of the vehicle and holding a gun to her head. Next to Kat, Beau growled and barked, sensing his humans were in danger but unable to get through the closed gate.

"Call off dog and toss cell phone on ground. Come vith us or I kill friends. Now!"

Keeping her gaze on the wide-eyed secretary trying to hold it together, Kat placed a shaky hand on the security scanner until the gate began to slide open. "Beau, *platz*." The canine continued to growl with the hair on his back raised but laid down as ordered. "Let her go, and I'll come with you. If you hurt her, I'll never tell you how to get the money."

The big man smirked, and Kat shivered, knowing he would gladly torture her for the information. Pig-face from the front passenger seat had his gun trained on her while the driver aimed his at Murray, who was, thankfully, still alive. The injured guard looked more pissed than anything, but with his gun lying near his feet and being outnumbered, there wasn't much he could do.

Pulling her phone out of her pocket, Kat placed it on the ground and stepped forward, her hands in the air. The sunlight hit the gold medical alert bracelet on her wrist, and she remembered Benny telling her about the GPS unit in it. If she went with these men, he still had a way to track her. She had to do it, refusing to let anyone else get hurt because of her. "Please, let them go. I won't fight you. I'll show you where the money is."

The man holding Colleen's arm was obviously in charge as neither of the other men spoke. Shoving the woman viciously to the ground next to the guard, who struggled to put his body in front of hers for protection, the Russian indicated for Kat to get into the vehicle. "Come. Now. Or ve kill them."

Kat hurried over to the rear driver's side door as the man

stepped back and let her scramble into the vehicle. He slid in beside her, forcing her to move to the other side. Before he shut his door, he instructed the driver, "Kill them."

Horrified, Kat dove for the door handle next to her, but the bastard grabbed her hair, preventing her escape. Pain shot through her scalp.

"*Packen*," she shouted through the open driver's door and was relieved to see Beau respond to the command, lunging toward the man with his weapon aimed at the two people on the ground. The driver brought his arm up to block the vicious attack, and his gun went off into the air, the slug striking a nearby tree. Twisting wildly, the man screamed in pain as the dog's razor-sharp teeth tore through his flesh, down to the bones in his forearm.

The chaos allowed Murray to snatch and fire his own weapon, dropping the driver with a bullet to the head. With what should have been an easy kill from across the hood, a distant shout caused Pig-face to turn his head and botch his own shot, missing Murray by inches when he rolled to protect Colleen.

Through the windshield, Kat saw Jake and Tanner running toward the front gate, weapons in hand. The combination of reinforcements arriving, and Beau releasing the driver and turning his attention to the second threat, had Pig-face diving into the front seat and slamming the door shut. He climbed over the console, threw the vehicle in reverse, and floored the accelerator as Beau made a futile attempt to find access on the passenger side.

None of Kat's would-be rescuers could risk taking a shot with her in the line of fire. A quick turn of the steering wheel spun the car around, and they took off toward the highway at a high rate of speed. At the end of the road, before they turned left to take the northbound lanes, Kat spotted Colleen's vehicle on the shoulder with its driver's door wide open. The Russians must have ambushed her and forced her from the car.

"Where are we going?"

Neither man answered her. She urged herself to remain calm and look for a way to escape, but she couldn't stop trembling.

Not knowing what else to do, Kat prayed.

LEAVING THE HEAD AND WALKING BACK TOWARD THE WAR-room, Jake continued to listen to the banter of his team members on the overhead speakers he'd turned on and cursed because he was missing the action. He knew Carter was the perfect person to take his place, but it was still irritating he was out of commission until his eye healed.

Just as he entered the room, Ian's voice came over the air. "Reverend, you there?"

Stepping up to the microphone, Jake pressed the transmit button. "Yeah, Boss-man. What's your status?"

"Just pulled up. How are things there?"

"Five by five," he answered. "Just going to go get Kat. Stay safe, brothers."

"Amen."

Turning around, Jake headed past the reception area to the stairs, taking them two at a time. He hoped Kat had gotten some rest because she needed it. When this was all over, he wouldn't be surprised if Boomer planned on taking her somewhere quiet to recuperate. The kid could use a vacation after this, as well.

Striding into the rec room, he glanced around and found it empty. Figuring she was in the bedroom she and Boomer had used last night, he went down the hallway and knocked on the only closed door. Not receiving an answer, he knocked again and, instead of waiting, turned the knob and opened the door. Empty. "Kat?"

Still no answer. He raised his voice. "Kat? You up here?"

A quick check of the rest of the rooms told Jake she wasn't on this floor. He hurried back down the stairs and into the war-room again to scan the live camera feeds and figure out where she was. As he'd headed to the bathroom earlier, Colleen had been collecting her purse to leave for class.

Now, on one monitor, he could see her car was gone, and Tanner was on the north side of the property, walking the perimeter behind the buildings. His gaze shifted to the other feeds, looking for Kat. His blood ran cold when he saw the view of the front gate. A black SUV was idling at the entrance, Murray was on the ground, three men were holding weapons with one pointed at Colleen's head, and Kat was opening the gate.

"Fuck!" Pressing the button for the frequency Tanner and Murray's headsets were on, Jake barked into the microphone, "Tangos front gate, man down, man down!"

Seeing on the monitor that Tanner had heard him and was running from the far end of the property toward the gate, Jake unholstered his Sig Sauer P226 and took off like the hounds of Hell were on his heels. He hit the front door running as Tanner rounded the building at full speed.

Tearing across the compound, they heard Kat scream the German command for Beau to attack one of the men before Murray retrieved his weapon and fired a shot. The driver was dead by the time he hit the ground. But the gorilla on the other side of the SUV aimed his gun at Murray, and Jake brought his own sidearm up, yelling at the top of his lungs, "Drop your weapon!"

He was still too far away to make an accurate shot, and he couldn't risk hitting either woman or Murray. His command had the bastard missing his kill shot, thank God, but unfortunately, the guy dove through the passenger door and threw the car in reverse. Beau took off after the retreating vehicle, barking ferociously.

"Fucking-A! Get your truck, Tuff!"

As the operative reversed directions, Jake ran to the gate where Colleen was ripping open Murray's shirt to expose his wound. The guard groaned and turned his head toward Jake. "They've got Kat. Two tangos left. Both with 9mms—didn't see any other weapons."

Hearing Tanner revving his Ford F-150's engine, Jake glanced at Murray's shoulder wound, which was now visible. "How bad? Can you get to the war-room? I need someone on the radio."

"Yeah, it's a through and through. I'll live. Help me up."

The phone in the guard shack rang, but everyone ignored it. With Jake's and Colleen's assistance, the guard stood while letting out a roar of pain. "Fuck, that fucking hurts. 'Scuse my language, Colleen."

Holding his good arm, the still-pale secretary rallied and took charge of the situation, aiming the big man toward the Trident building. If the situation weren't so serious, Jake would've smiled at how far the once timid secretary had come out of her shell these last few weeks. Her training on how to respond to different emergency scenarios was paying off. "Like I haven't heard Ian curse fifty times a day. Let's get you inside. Jake, I'll call 9-1-1, but what else do you need?"

Tanner screeched to a halt next to them, and Jake threw

open the passenger door. As he jumped in, he ordered, "Murray knows the tracking system. Bring up Kat's GPS location. Give it to us on the compound's frequency. Then get on the team's frequency and let them know what's going down."

He slammed the door, confident the secretary and guard, a retired Army sergeant, would do what needed to be done. Tanner floored the accelerator and swerved around the dead body outside the gate.

As they approached the intersection of the highway, Tanner demanded, "Which way?"

The vehicle slowed, and Jake frantically searched in both directions. "Left! Holy shit, I owe that fucking dog a steak. Slow down, so I can grab him."

Beau was about fifty yards north of the intersection, running on the shoulder of the road, still trying to chase after the long-gone vehicle, but at least he pointed them in the right direction. As Tanner slowed the truck, Jake opened his door. "Beau! *Hier!*"

The lab-mix ran back to the truck and took a flying leap onto Jake's lap. He pushed the dog into the back seat and slammed the door. Punching the accelerator again as soon as Beau cleared the doorway, Tanner was already speeding back up. Jake reached up to tap his headset before remembering he never had one on—he'd been listening in through the speakers in the war-room.

"Let me have your headset." The operative ripped the device from his ear and tossed it to Jake, who hooked it to his own ear. "Murray, you there?"

Static came over the earpiece and then the guard's pain-filled voice. "Yeah, I'm here. Bringing up the GPS. Give me a sec. Colleen's on the phone with 9-1-1. What direction are you heading?"

"North. Beau was heading that way, but we haven't caught up to them yet. Have you gotten a hold of Ian yet?"

"I will as soon as I get Kat's location for you. Here it is. Looks like they're still on the highway in front of you. I'm bringing up the GPS in your phone . . . they're about a mile ahead of you. I'll let you know if they change direction."

Motioning with his hand, Jake confirmed they were heading in the right direction, and Tanner sped up even more as they both scanned the vehicles in front of them. "Good enough. As soon as we spot them, I'll try to get a plate for you. Black Escalade, right?"

"Affirm."

Tanner glanced at Jake. "What do you want to do? Follow to see where they're going until we get backup and a roadblock?"

Lifting his hand to adjust his eye patch, Jake had to agree. They couldn't risk Kat's life by running them off the road. "Yeah. Get them in sight and hold back."

Just as they spotted the Cadillac up ahead, Murray's voice came over the headset. "Hey, Jake? I've got Ian on the other channel. Get this. They're just boarding a state police chopper en route back to the compound. And they have FBI SWAT responding here. They figured out it was a ruse to get most of them away from here."

"A little late to the party, but better than nothing. The team is still too far out." He pulled his cell phone from the side pocket of his cargo pants. "Get me a phone number for someone on SWAT instead of playing telephone tag with you."

"Stand by."

Trying to formulate a plan, Jake prayed Boomer wasn't going to lose his woman again . . . and permanently this time.

BOOMER COULDN'T BELIEVE WHAT MURRAY HAD JUST TOLD them over their headsets . . . ah, fuck, yes, he could. They'd all fallen for the deceptive ploy, and it'd worked. While he knew they would've still rescued his parents, in hindsight, they should've put Kat and the others into the compound's panic room until they had more information about what was happening. But it was too late for that. Now, Kat was in the hands of men who had no trouble killing anyone who got in their way, and once they had their money, she was expendable. Damn it, he couldn't lose her again—he wouldn't survive the loss this time.

The helicopter's rotors were thumping in time to his pounding heart rate. The only chatter at the moment was from the pilot and co-pilot. The team and Carter were waiting for updates from Murray about what was going on. The pilots were pushing the bird as fast as they could, but Boomer was afraid they wouldn't get there in time to save Kat. Even at full throttle, it would still take them about twenty minutes from Sarasota to Tampa. He'd have to trust Jake and Tanner to do what they could until their backup arrived. It was just frustrating to sit and wait for info without being able to do anything.

From what Murray had said, one of the tangos was dead next to the compound's gate. That meant there were only two more they were aware of. With Egghead's medical alert tracking bracelet, they would at least know where Kat was. The FBI's SWAT team was now in direct contact with Jake and rerouting to intercept the getaway vehicle. There were too many variables, and Boomer didn't like the odds.

Brody shifted in his seat. "You know, Ian, this is why we need our own fucking bird."

Nodding, their boss crossed his arms. "Not that it helps us now, but it's being delivered in two weeks. We're storing it at the airport with the jet until the helipad is built. That starts next week, by the way, along with the obstacle course Devil Dog planned out."

As his teammates and Carter added more mindless chatter through the chopper's headsets, the ground below them came and went rapidly. Boomer just hoped it was fast enough.

He glanced at his dive watch—seven minutes down, about thirteen minutes to go. "Fuck."

CHAPTER TWENTY-THREE

Shivering, Kat tried to sit as far away from the man she now recognized as Viktor "The Bull" Dryagin, Volkov's right-hand man and self-appointed heir to the dead man's criminal empire. Ian had shown her pictures of the man who Benny and Jake had confirmed was the leader of the group who'd tried to kidnap her from the motel in Norfolk.

Dryagin and Pig-face hadn't spoken to her since they'd fled the compound about ten minutes ago, speaking to each other in Russian, which only enhanced her fear and anxiety.

What were they planning on doing to her to get the money? She'd gladly give it to them if she could only be certain she would still be alive once they had it in their greedy little hands. The only thing she wanted was the chance to have the life she craved . . . the life she deserved with Benny.

She didn't even know if Rick and Eileen were alive and doubted the Russians would tell her. All she could do was pray Jake and Tanner were tracking her and creating a rescue plan. Benny had assured her that was what his team specialized in, and she trusted them to get her out of this damn mess.

"*Blyat!*"

Kat didn't know what Pig-face had said in Russian, but by the way he spat it out, she guessed it was a curse word. A split second after he said it, he slammed on the brakes, sending her flying forward, her head smashing against the headrest of the seat in front of her. Black spots and white stars filled her vision as a myriad of sounds assaulted her ears. Loud screeching, yelling, whaps, pops, and the rush of air escaping surrounded her. It took her a moment to realize both her head and the car were spinning as Pig-face tried to control it on four shredded tires. The bare rims were grinding against the asphalt as the vehicle rapidly slowed. What the hell was happening?

Somehow, he managed to keep them from flipping over, and the vehicle finally came to an abrupt halt in the middle of the highway. Before Kat could think about escaping, Dryagin snatched her by the hair and hauled her to his side, his weapon pressed against her temple. Tears filled her eyes as she tried to ease the pressure on her scalp. Outside the SUV, smoke from the blown tires began to settle, and all was quiet except the three occupants' heavy breathing and Pig-face's cursing in both languages.

"*Yobaniyi ment!* Fucking cops blew tires. Vhat now?"

Hope flared in Kat's chest as she heard sirens approaching. She just prayed these two men didn't do anything stupid that would get them all killed. The sirens switched off one by one as several vehicles came to a screeching halt, surrounding them at a distance.

Kat tried to glimpse what was going on, but the only direction Dryagin's grasp allowed her to see was through the window next to him. She realized they were turned sideways on the highway, facing the southbound lanes. Further past the line of idling patrol cars with their flashing lights and unmarked SUVs, she saw the signs of traffic beginning to build beyond the roadblock which had been quickly put in place. Police officers—some in uniform, others dressed in all black—used their vehicles as cover and pointed handguns, shotguns, and rifles at the getaway vehicle. If Kat thought she was scared earlier, she was now beyond terrified.

Please, God, don't let them decide to go down in a hail of bullets.

Several minutes passed before two men behind one of the police cars caught Kat's attention, and she gasped when she focused on Jake. His arms gesturing wildly, Boomer's team-mate was arguing with a red-faced man in an ill-fitting suit. It was obvious the man wanted Jake away from the scene, but he wouldn't budge.

A sudden voice over a loudspeaker interrupted the Russians' rapid conversation in their native language. "Throw out your weapons and come out with your hands in the air."

Pig-face rolled his window down halfway and yelled, "Fuck you."

Okay, Kat thought, *that command didn't go over well. Now what?*

"Please let me go. We're surrounded. If you cooperate, I'm sure the judge will go easier on you." Actually, she wasn't sure of it at all, but it sounded good, right?

"Shut up." Dryagin's head swiveled as he eyed what was going on around them. "Ruslan, demand new car or ve kill girl."

Well, shit, that didn't sound comforting, but at least the bastard had let go of his grip on her hair, and she could sit up a little better. Before she could move away from him, the big man grabbed her upper arm, pulled her across his lap, and switched their positions in the backseat, putting her between him and most of the police officers. He held her close, still pointing the deadly end of his pistol at her head.

She listened as Ruslan, aka Pig-face, shouted their demand out the window, and the hostage negotiator on the megaphone responded. Kat got the feeling she was in for a very long and stressful afternoon.

STANDING ABOUT TWENTY-FIVE YARDS FROM THE DISABLED Escalade, Jake gritted his teeth as SAC Frank Stonewall got in his face, demanding he and Tanner leave the area. "You're fucking civilians, and this situation is now under the jurisdiction of the FBI. Get back in your fucking truck, and get the hell out of here, so we can do our jobs."

Keeping his voice low and threatening, Jake towered over the shorter man and leaned in so he wasn't overheard by anyone else. "Listen, you fucktard. The only reason you were called in was because we were short-handed, and Ian couldn't get a hold of us. You know damn fucking well Keon will ream you a new asshole with one quick phone call. Now, we're willing to step back and let the SWAT commander take over, but I'll be fucking damned if I let that woman out of my sight again, so take your attitude and shove it up your ass."

The SAC looked ready to explode but held his tongue when a tall, dark-haired man dressed all in black and carrying a megaphone approached them. "Jake? I hear this mess started at Trident. Fill me in so I know what we're dealing with. You'll have to tell me what's up with the eye patch later."

Jake shook Calvin Watts's extended hand. The agent was

the lead negotiator in charge of the Tampa area FBI SWAT team. Having mutual friends, they played basketball against each other almost every Tuesday night at the local YMCA, and Jake was relieved the man was there. He'd seen Watts's team in action before and was confident they could get Kat out of this in one piece.

"Hey, Cal. I appreciate the fast response. Thank God Ian had you en route, and TPD had cars nearby with the spike strips available. The tangos kidnapped Boomer's woman from the compound. They shot our guard in the shoulder, but he was able to drop the original driver, so now it's just two of them in there, plus Kat. Tangos are Russian mobsters from Virginia. Kat's father appropriated a large sum of money from their boss about twelve years ago, and they want it back."

Ignoring the SAC who stood by, still seething, Watts, who was officially in charge of the incident, gestured then started walking toward the newly arrived SWAT command van, and Jake followed. "Okay, how much money are we talking about here? I doubt they'd be taking such a big risk for a few thousand."

"Try fifteen million, plus twelve years' interest, sitting in the Cayman Islands." Cal whistled his amazement as he opened the back door of the large truck and climbed in after Jake. "Yeah, I know, far from chump change. From what I understand, Kat's dad was an accountant for the mob but didn't realize who he was really dealing with until he was too far in. After keeping his nose clean for a few years, he discovered evidence of white slavery and gave it to the FBI. A few days later, Kat's family was run off the road. The crash killed her mother and brother and sent her and her dad into the Witness Protection Program. Kat didn't know it until her father died recently, but the old man transferred money out of the mob's accounts a few days after the accident and sent it to a dummy account. Revenge, I guess. A string of unrelated events put these bastards back on her trail, leading us here."

Watts shook his head. "Damn, you boys don't like anything simple, do you? All right, let's get this rescue underway. They're demanding another car and a free pass, or they'll kill her. The usual shit these idiots think we'll cave for. Any idea what their names are, so we can start developing a profile?"

A tech typing away on a nearby computer keyboard looked up at Jake, waiting for his answer. "No ID on the driver, but the guy in the back seat with Kat is Viktor Dryagin, a trained assassin who took his boss's place in the organization after he got the okay to off the guy. From what I hear, he won't go down easy."

"Guys like him never do. Anyone else here from Trident?"

"One of our contract guys, Tanner, is over by his truck, staying out of the way and keeping our dog from staging his own rescue. The rest are on their way. When Brody gets here, he can listen in on a microphone Kat's wearing. It's one of his toys we've used before."

Picking up two headsets, Watts tossed one to Jake. "Okay. Stick around and stay out of Stonewall's face. I'm not in the mood for his fucking blubbering. And ears only. Keep your microphone off—you're here out of professional courtesy, and I trust your input, but I won't have you interfering with the negotiations."

Understanding the man was making a huge concession by allowing him to stay, Jake replaced the Trident headset over his left ear with the new one, pocketing the former which was only on the compound's frequency. Murray was now in an ambulance on his way to the hospital with Colleen in tow, so there wasn't anyone back at the war-room for him to talk to. "Thanks, and no worries. I trust you to do your thing."

"Sir?" Both men looked at the second tech monitoring several radio frequencies, among other things. "We've got a State PD chopper requesting permission to land nearby. Says they have the rest of the Trident team with them."

Cal raised an eyebrow at Jake, who shrugged. "Friends in high places, what can I say?"

The negotiator barked out a laugh. "Yeah, okay, Smitty. Since the highway is shut down in both directions, tell TPD on the ground to clear a landing zone in the southbound lanes south of us and ask the state boys to stick around. We might be able to use them."

"Yes, sir."

"Hey, Cal?" The agent followed when Jake took a few steps backward, away from the techs, acknowledging whatever Jake was going to tell him was for his ears only. "We've got an extra man with the team. Black-ops with federal clearances up the ass, and don't ask for any other information because I can't tell you. Just know he's got Moran, Keon, and POTUS on speed dial, and the same in reverse."

The agent's surprise was evident at the mention of the director and assistant director of the FBI, along with the President of the United States, but he let Jake finish. "The man is one of the best snipers I know, and he's got my spare rifle on board the bird. Not stepping on your toes here, just know I trust him with my own mother's life."

"That's saying a lot coming from a SEAL sniper." Jake waited while Cal mulled things over, knowing he would have to accept his response either way. "All right, I hope we don't need him, but here's what we'll do."

UNDER THE WATCHFUL EYES OF HIS TEAMMATES, BOOMER paced back and forth behind the line of law enforcement vehicles and personnel. The only reason he was back there and not leading a full-out assault on the Cadillac Escalade in the middle of the highway, some forty yards away, was Ian had threatened to handcuff him to Tanner's truck. "This is taking too fucking long."

Since they all knew how this had to play out, no one answered him, letting him vent his frustrations verbally. Hostage negotiations were a psychological game for the lead negotiator. There were five steps to the technique of communicating with the hostage takers—active listening, empathy, rapport, influence, and behavioral change. An ideal situation would have the bad guys releasing the hostage and surrendering without escalating things. Unfortunately, very few hostage situations were ideal.

For a trained team of former Navy SEALs, such as Trident, it was difficult to sit back and let another team take over. But they all knew Calvin Watts's SWAT was one of the best nationwide, with a long history of successful missions to their credit. If they had to relinquish the rescue to a law enforcement agency, they were lucky it was his team.

It'd been over an hour since the police spike strip had been thrown on the highway, blowing all four tires on the Russians' SUV. Kat must be going out of her mind with fear, and Boomer knew exactly what it felt like. At least the team had an inside man. Jake was still in the communications van and using Marco's borrowed earpiece to pass on information to them. Occasionally he would ask a question to give the hostage negotiator some intel, which Ian or Boomer hopefully had the answer to.

Also in the comm van was Egghead, who was using a program on his tablet to listen in on the conversation taking place between the two Russians, thanks to the microphone in Kat's GPS bracelet. The men spoke mostly in their native language, but the geek had a TPD officer also plugged in, translating for him. Unfortunately, they weren't learning anything from the exchange which could help them end the incident peacefully.

"Ian?" Jake's voice came over the team's earpieces.

"Go."

"These guys are getting antsy. They insist on taking the State PD chopper, or they'll start cutting her up with a knife. With Dryagin's background, Cal thinks we're running out of time."

Boomer's eyes widened in horror, but a glare from his boss had him keeping his mouth shut. There had to be a reason for Jake telling them this, knowing he was listening. "We have an idea, but we need your input to see if it'll work. Cal wants you and Boomer in the comm van."

Both men headed to the FBI command center after being waved under the yellow Do-Not-Cross tape spanning the width of the highway. They ignored a dirty look from SAC Stonewall as they passed him and a few other agents along the way. Now wasn't the time for a pissing match with the Special Ass-hat in Charge.

Ian opened the door and allowed Boomer to climb in ahead of him. Both men shook hands with Cal Watts before the negotiator laid out the plan Jake and he had devised. Ian stated he thought it was a good strategy since they were down to the wire with Dryagin's threats, but Boomer was terrified something would go wrong. "What if she doesn't get it or even fucking see it? She's probably petrified. What if she doesn't understand what we want her to do?"

Crossing his arms, Ian addressed Jake. "You've seen Kat in action twice now. Once at the motel and again at the compound. Do you think she can focus on what we're telling her? If she doesn't, this shit will get ugly real fast because we can't let the chopper take off with her in it."

Even though it seemed Boomer was playing the pessimist, that's what the team did—examined a situation from every angle before giving it a go. Jake took a deep breath and let it out. "At the motel, she didn't hesitate, and from what I heard afterward, she jumped in to make sure I was okay. The injury didn't bother her. Same goes for what just happened at the gate. Yeah, she was probably scared shitless, but both she and Colleen made us proud. Kat was able to think fast enough to give Beau the command to attack. And from what I saw really quick on the monitor, she also didn't hesitate to open the gate and do what she had to do to save the others. I'm positive, as long as we get her attention on the way to the chopper, this will work."

All eyes turned to Boomer. They were out of options, and he knew it. "It's gotta be me. Out of all the voices, it'll be mine she'll be listening for and focus in on."

Cal nodded. "Agreed. But just in case, I want Ian with you, and you'll be flanked by two of my men." He pointed his finger at Boomer. "You know how this goes, man. Don't do anything stupid out there and fuck up my operation."

A lesser man would have been insulted, but Boomer knew the negotiator was right. The SWAT team trained day in and day out with each other and knew exactly what each other was thinking and how they would react. Bringing in an unknown, such as himself, no matter how well trained, could throw someone's timing off, and that's when things became a cluster-fuck. "Let's do this."

KAT COULDN'T HAVE HEARD RIGHT. THE MAN ON THE megaphone said the Russians could take the police chopper wherever they wanted to go if they released her. When the response was she was going with them, the jackass agreed.

What the fuck?

Maybe they would continue to track her through her GPS and stage a rescue somewhere else. Or maybe they had something up their sleeve.

A trick. That had to be it. Right?

God, she hoped she was right. At least Dryagin had put away the sharp knife he was threatening to use to cut off her fingers. But then again, the gun was pointed at her head again, so she was still in deep shit.

Down the road, the helicopter's rotors sped up, and they all watched as the craft hovered a few feet off the ground, moving north in the southbound lanes until it was directly across the median from the disabled Escalade. The pilot positioned the chopper so the tail was facing them but turned slightly so they could see the open door on the left side, then set it back down on the ground. From what she could tell, no one was inside except for the solo pilot.

Kat decided to try one last futile attempt at getting the Russians to leave her behind. "Please, let me go. You have the helicopter to escape in, and I'll write down the account number and password for the bank account the money is in. Please."

"Shut up!" Dryagin tightened his grip on her arm and eyed the activity surrounding them. "Open door and get out. Be stupid and you regret it."

"I have a feeling I'll regret it either way," she mumbled, pulling on the handle and easing the door open. She climbed out slowly, still in his tight grasp, as he got out behind her. Once she was blocking the officers' line of fire, Pig-face also exited the vehicle, his own gun pointed toward her as well. As a unit, they made their way over the grassy median with Kat held close to both of them.

"Kitten!"

Her head swiveled at the sound of Benny's voice as Dryagin forced her down a slight incline toward a low guardrail. It took her a moment to spot him in the southbound lanes standing next to Ian and two men dressed in black holding very large weapons. Kat's eyes filled with tears as she climbed over the thigh-high railing. Would this be the last time she ever saw him?

"Kitten, I love you! Remember, a sub always listens to her Dom!"

What? Was he fucking kidding her? Okay, the "I love you" was great, but why bring up subs and Doms?

Behind her, Dryagin growled, "Faster. Move." He urged her up the small incline.

"Kitten! Remember!"

Kat focused on Benny again. He and Ian were waving at her.

No! Wait!

They weren't waving. They were signaling her. One. Two. Three fingers. And then their right arms, palms down, making the sweep out in front of them from their waists up over their heads—the K9 sign language for "down." Holy shit, on the count of three, they wanted her to hit the dirt and stay down!

She copied the silent command, hoping the Russians thought she was waving. "I love you too!"

Keeping her eyes on Benny and the chopper in her peripheral vision, she waited for the signal and prayed she understood them correctly. Two steps before she would need to duck for the slow-moving rotor, he raised his hand in a fist and one by one, uncurled his fingers.

One.

Two.

Three.

Kat let her knees buckle, and she dropped to the ground so fast that Dryagin had no chance of stopping her. She felt his hand release her arm, unable to hold onto her sudden dead weight. The man shouted something foreign in surprise, then roared his anger. As she covered her head, two simultaneous shots sounded, followed by shouts and running feet.

She didn't dare look up until she heard Benny's voice again. This time he was right next to her. "Kat, are you okay? Please, tell me you're okay!"

His words came out rushed as his hands quickly roamed her body. She rolled onto her side, thrilled to see his handsome face. "I'm okay, I'm okay. What happened?"

He hauled her to her feet and wrapped his strong arms around her, coming close to crushing her. "Oh, thank God, you're all right! I was so fucking scared. Are you sure you're okay?"

Leaning back, he searched her face for confirmation. She nodded as her body began to tremble in the aftermath of the crisis. Glancing over her shoulder, she saw both Russians dead on the ground a few feet away, surrounded by men in black. Dryagin was missing half of his head, while Pig-face had been shot in the chest, leaving a bloody gaping wound. Kat quickly turned back around, her stomach threatening to revolt. Benny wisely moved them several yards away from the dead bodies.

Ian approached and ran a hand down the back of her

head as if reassuring himself she was indeed okay. "Well, Kat, I'm sorry this happened, but you can add yourself to a growing list of people who owe Master Carter their lives."

It was then she noticed Carter and a man dressed in black on the far side of the southbound lanes, handing their rifles to a uniformed officer. "What happened?"

"Carter and another sniper were in the woods over there, and as soon as you dropped, the Russians aimed their guns at the cops. The snipers took them out. These two weren't going to let themselves be taken alive."

Kat shuddered, knowing it was true, and she could have also been dead.

Jake appeared next to Ian, shaking his head and jerking a thumb toward the spy and two feds. "Damn, I know they have to take my rifle for a while until the required investigation is complete, but I'm tired of going through all the paperwork to get them back. This is the second time in less than five months."

He gently pulled Kat from Benny's grasp and into his own embrace. "You are one kick-ass lady, you know that? Giving Beau the attack command was quick thinking. You kept your head together and helped save not only your own life but Murray's and Colleen's, as well."

Her eyes widened when she realized she'd forgotten about them. "Oh, my God! How are they? Murray was shot. Is Colleen okay?"

Releasing her back into Benny's arms, Jake nodded. "Murray's as tough as leather—he'll be back to work in no time. The bullet went straight through and didn't hit anything vital. It's also not the first time he's taken one, although it's the first time with us. Colleen only has a few scrapes, but she's fine, and Ian told her to take a few days off. Reggie is with them at the hospital. Once we're done here, I'll check on them. Then I'm getting Beau the biggest fucking steak I can find. Thanks to him, we were able to figure out what direction they took you in and catch up pretty quickly."

"In that case, I owe him a steak, too. And you too. All of you." Jake just grinned and waved her off. Facing Benny again, she saw the worry still in his eyes. "Are your parents okay?"

He paled, and her heart clenched. "Mom will be okay, but Pop was shot in the stomach." She gasped and brought her hand to her mouth. "He's in surgery, and we have to get back down there. I want the paramedics to look at you really quick while I see if we can hitch a ride back down on the chopper."

Kat shook her head. "I'm fine. Let's just go. We have to be there for your mom."

Ian stepped aside to let a female medic into their little group. "I'll get us clearance, but I'm sure we have a few minutes before we can take off anyway, so let this nice lady check you over."

Although she was just as anxious as Benny to get going, she knew it would be pointless to argue with a group of Doms. She was quickly learning that when it came to someone under their care, they were extremely protective. A few minutes later, she was medically cleared. Aside from a hematoma on her forehead, where she'd hit the headrest, and bruising on her arm from Dryagin's grip, the only other thing which hurt was her scalp from having her hair pulled.

After thanking the medic for the quick examination, Kat turned toward where Benny was talking to Ian, Carter, and Marco. The rest of the team had split up, with Devon and Brody heading to the hospital to check on Murray and Colleen. Jake was returning to the compound with Tanner and Beau, followed by several federal agents. There was still a dead body at the gate that needed to be hauled to the morgue and a crime scene to be processed.

She walked over to the group of four men and straight up to Carter, throwing her arms around him. "Thank you for not missing."

The black-op spy barked out a little laugh and hugged her back. "You're welcome, Kitty-Kat. And there was no way I was missing. I've grown quite fond of you. Besides, Boom-Boom would've never forgiven me if I let anything happen to you."

He kissed the top of her head and then released her. Kat stepped back, and Benny extended his hand toward Carter. "Thanks again, man. My list of IOUs keeps growing. I hope someday I'll be able to repay you."

Taking the younger man's hand, Carter pulled him in for a man-hug and slapped him on the back. "No offense, but I hope I never need you to repay me. I'm catching a ride back to the compound, and then I have to head out. Duty calls. But I'll be in touch to check on Rick. Kiss your mom for me."

"Will do."

As their friend walked off to hitch a ride with one of the many officers and agents still on the scene, Benny took Kat's elbow and steered her toward the helicopter behind Ian and Marco. It was time for her to start praying for one more miracle.

CHAPTER TWENTY-FOUR

K at held her breath as the helicopter descended to land at a heliport near Sarasota Memorial Hospital, where Rick had been transported. Benny had contacted his mom before they lifted off from the Tampa highway and had been told his father was still in surgery. Ian and Marco planned on waiting with Kat, Benny, and Eileen until Rick was out of surgery. The two teammates would then retrieve the other two vehicles still parked near the Michaelson house, driving the comm van back to Tampa and leaving the SUV for them. The rest of the team would take care of the cleanup at the compound, the reports which needed to be filed with both the FBI and local law enforcement, and anything else that needed to be done.

From information Ian received from the FBI, it seemed as though Dryagin had not shared the knowledge that he'd found Kat with the rest of the Russian mob. They had no idea she was the only living link to the money, so the feds and Trident didn't think anyone else would come looking for her. She planned to give the money to charity, so hopefully soon, it wouldn't matter if anyone else made the connection. But it would have to wait for now.

A Florida State Police car was waiting for them at the heliport to drive them to the hospital. As soon as they landed, and it was safe to do so, they disembarked and piled into the vehicle, with Ian taking the front passenger seat. Kat was sandwiched between the other two men in the backseat, and Benny hadn't said a word to her since he told her to let the medic examine her. She understood he was worried about his dad, so she remained quiet as well and took his hand in hers in silent reassurance that she was there for him. He gave her hand a quick squeeze and an even quicker smile, which didn't quite reach his eyes, before turning back to stare out the window.

When they reached the hospital, the four stopped at the reception desk to find out what floor the surgery waiting room was on, then took the elevators to the third floor. Dusty and Burke were standing guard in the hallway, and Ian told them the threat was over, allowing the contract agents to head back to Tampa. Eileen and Rick's sister, Margaret, sat in the warmly decorated room with other patients' family members as they waited for word on their loved ones.

Eileen stood as soon as she spotted Benny, and he went right to her, hugging her tightly. When he let her go and greeted his aunt, Eileen embraced Kat. "Thank God, you're okay. I was so worried until Ben called me to say you were safe."

The day's stress finally hit Kat as a huge sob escaped her. "I'm so sorry. This is all my fault."

"Hush, now." Benny's mom pulled away just enough so they could see each other's faces. The worry was evident in both women's eyes, but sympathy also showed in Eileen's gaze. "This is not your fault, Kat. And Rick will be fine—I know it. He's a fighter, and I know he'll come through this. We just have to pray until it happens."

Despite everyone telling her it wasn't her fault, Kat couldn't convince herself it was true. Stepping back, she gave Ian and Marco a chance to give their words of comfort to the older woman. Kat had no idea how Eileen was able to stay so calm. Her face and arms still showed the redness where the emergency room staff had removed the duct tape. A pair of scrubs they'd given her to wear covered the same marks on her legs. If their roles were reversed, Kat was certain she'd be hysterical by now. As it was, she was close to it. Not wanting to upset anyone, she took a deep breath and sat in one of the empty chairs, trying to get comfortable for what was most likely going to be a long wait.

BOOMER PACED THE HALLWAY OUTSIDE THE WAITING ROOM, needing to move instead of just sit. Three and a half hours had passed since his father had been wheeled into the surgery suite, and they still had no word on how he was. From what his mom knew from the ER doctors, Rick had needed a transfusion to replace the blood he'd lost, and he didn't regain consciousness while they worked on him.

What if his dad died? His mother was a strong woman, but losing her husband of almost thirty-five years would devastate her. And what about Kat? He knew she was blaming herself for everything that happened, no matter how often they told her it wasn't her fault. If his dad didn't make it, how would they convince her that sometimes bad shit happened to good people, and there was no use playing the "what if" game?

At the end of the hall, a set of automatic doors swung

open, and a gray-haired man wearing blue scrubs appeared, walking toward the waiting room. Hoping this was the news they'd been waiting for, Boomer hurried back in time to hear the doctor ask for Rick Michaelson's family.

The group of six huddled around as Dr. Finkelstein explained what happened. "The bullet nicked the large intestines, but we were able to repair it. The bullet also bounced around and damaged some blood vessels before ending up in the spleen, which we had to remove to stop the bleeding. He was very lucky to have gotten here when he did. Another half hour and he wouldn't have had a chance which, as it stands now, is fifty-fifty. I wish I could say it was better odds, but you need to prepare yourselves for the possibility. He's heading to the recovery room now, and we're giving him another transfusion to get his blood volume back up. We also have him in a medically-induced coma for now. Once his blood results stabilize, we'll see about easing him out of it."

"When will we know if he's going to make it?" Boomer couldn't help the grief and worry in his raspy voice. Even though he'd thought about it earlier, it wasn't until the doctor verbalized that Rick could die, did Boomer truly believe his mother may become a widow.

"It'll be at least ten to twelve hours before I expect to see any significant improvement to the point he's out of danger."

"Can my mom and I see him, please?"

Dr. Finkelstein nodded his head. "Sure. I'll have one of the nurses come out once they have him settled in Recovery. You'll only be able to see him for a few minutes. He's got a lot of tubes going in and out, plus he's intubated and on a respirator, while we have him in the coma, so just prepare yourself for that. I'll be back in about an hour or so to check on him and send him up to the ICU."

Boomer shook the man's hand. "Thanks, Doc."

Five minutes later, a heavy-set female nurse, with a gentle smile, escorted his mother and him into the Recovery Room. The usual hospital antiseptic smell grew even stronger as they approached the gurney where Rick was resting on his back. The doctor was right. There were tubes everywhere— an intubation tube in his mouth, IVs in both arms, transfusion tubing, and wires from a monitor hooked up to the middle finger of his left hand. A bloody drainage bag and a urine bag hung low on one side of the stretcher. The *beep-beep-beep* indicating his heartbeat did little to reassure Boomer his father would make it. In Afghanistan, he'd lost two friends who he'd been certain would survive their combat injuries, only to have their hearts stop beating due to excessive internal bleeding.

He touched his father's arm as his mother kissed Rick's brow, murmuring words of love and encouragement. The man was so pale that he almost blended with the white bedsheets. Glancing at the monitor above the stretcher, Boomer noticed the blood pressure reading—82/40. It was way too low. Hopefully, the blood being forced into his veins would increase the numbers soon.

Leaning down, he kissed his father's cheek, then straightened and wiped the tears which began to spill from his watery eyes. "Love you, Pop. You keep fighting, you hear me? We still have a lot of fishing and shit to do. I plan on giving you some grandkids one day, and you better be here to spoil them rotten."

They stayed there in silence, willing Rick to heal and return to them until the nurse kindly told them they had to leave. She would let them know when he was transferred to the ICU. As they left Recovery, Boomer noticed his mother trembling. He took hold of her elbow in support while anger began to overtake his worry. Anger at himself and the team for not foreseeing the possibility of his parents being in danger. Anger at Kat's father for starting this whole mess. Anger at the Russians who dared to hurt the people Boomer loved. And on top of it all was the frustration of not knowing if his father would live or die.

His jaw clenched, and he could feel the vein in his temple ticking away with every beat of his heart. His free hand was balled into a fist, and he forced himself not to punch the nearby wall.

With a white hospital blanket wrapped around her upper body, Kat stood with Ian in the hallway outside the family waiting room. Unable to control his emotions at the moment, he held up his hand to stop her from approaching him. He needed a few minutes to himself to settle down. Otherwise, he would start throwing things, and he didn't think the hospital staff would appreciate it.

Handing his mother off to Ian in silence, Boomer kept walking to the end of the hallway and slammed the down button for the elevator. A brisk walk outside the huge hospital would help him clear his mind. There had to be a deli nearby where he could get everyone something to eat. He didn't want to leave the hospital until his dad was awake, and he doubted his mother did either. Some sandwiches would hold them over for a few hours.

The last thing he saw as he boarded the elevator and the door closed was his beautiful Kitten watching him. At least he knew she was safe and back in his arms for good.

KAT STOOD WITH IAN IN THE HALLWAY, HER GAZE FIXED ON the double doors which Benny and Eileen had disappeared through a few minutes ago. She shivered, wondering why it always seemed so cold in hospitals. Her T-shirt and Bermuda shorts, which had felt stifling during her time with the Russians, now seemed inadequate to keep her warm. Every time her father had gone for treatment or had been admitted for one reason or another during his illness, Kat always made sure she brought an extra sweater with her, even in the summer.

Ian must have noticed her shiver because he walked over to a door marked "Linens" and returned a moment later with a knit blanket he'd taken from one of the shelves. Wrapping it around her shoulders, he stated, "It always seems cold in hospitals, plus your adrenaline from earlier has worn off, and post-shock has kicked in. This will keep you warm for now. Marco and I will retrieve my truck and the comm van after Boomer and Eileen return. I'll grab a sweatshirt I keep in the trunk for you."

She gave him a weak smile. "Thanks. I think you're right. I'm suddenly very tired. Once they move him to ICU, I'll try to nap in a chair for a bit."

As he nodded his agreement, the doors to the Recovery Room swung open, and Benny and his mother walked toward them. Eileen was paler than before as she wiped her eyes and nose with tissues. But it was the look on Benny's face which had Kat's stomach clenching. He looked so livid she half expected him to start yelling and punching things. She'd never in her life seen him so angry, and it scared her.

She stepped forward to hug and comfort him, but he held up his hand, stopping her in her tracks. Her heart squeezed as tight as her stomach had, and she held back a sob of grief. He blamed her. He blamed her for everything. She should never have brought this to his doorstep. She should have found a way to get out of the mess herself, and then, if she was still alive, she could've come to him without danger dogging her heels.

Benny didn't say a word to anyone as he gave his mother's arm to Ian and then continued down the hallway to the elevator. She watched him punch the down button harder than necessary. When the car arrived, he stepped inside, and her happy future disappeared behind the closing doors.

CHAPTER TWENTY-FIVE

"Hey, Kat. Wait up."

Damn it! Twenty feet away from avoiding the obnoxious asshole!

She'd thought she could slip away without being hit on for the eighth or ninth time in four days, but apparently, she wasn't that lucky. If she could get rid of him now, she wouldn't have to see him again until Tuesday. The Friday training ended at twelve-thirty today, so the officers with long commutes heading home for the Fourth of July weekend could beat rush hour traffic.

Pasting a not-too-friendly smile on her face, she turned around to face Officer Rob DaSilva of the Eugene Police Department as he stopped in front of her. He was just under six feet tall and good-looking, but he thought he was God's gift to women and was sexist. The worst part was the man couldn't seem to take "no, thank you" for an answer.

"Yes, Officer DaSilva. Did you have a question about today's training?"

"Uh, no. Look, I know you playing hard-to-get is just an

act in front of the other guys, so now that we're alone, do us both a favor and agree to go out with me."

His leering grin and the way he talked to her chest had her temperature at a near boil. The only reason she wasn't telling him where to shove his egotistical attitude was she tried very hard to be seen as a professional, aggressive-K9 trainer in a predominantly male-oriented career. But it didn't mean he was allowed to harass her.

He must have placed his German Sheperd in his department-issued, air-conditioned vehicle since the beautiful animal was nowhere to be seen. She felt sorry for the dog, being partnered with an arrogant ass.

Glancing around, she saw the rest of the trainers and trainees had either left, were still out on the practice field, or heading toward the kennels. At least fifty yards away, no one was close enough to be used as a diversion. She'd been heading toward her little cabin on the large ranch, a mere twenty feet away.

After returning to Portland two weeks ago, she'd sat down with her bosses and explained everything. They had been wonderful and offered her the use of the empty cabin instead of returning to her apartment, where she no longer felt safe. Jeremy had also hooked her up with his attorney, who was starting the process for her to be "Katerina 'Kat' Maier" again now that she no longer had to hide from anyone.

She'd been shocked when the deputy director of the FBI had called her, at Ian's request, to tell her the money in the Cayman Islands was hers to do with as she pleased. Any statutes which may have covered the money had expired, and since there was no one left alive who would fight her for it in a court of law, she was now a reluctant millionaire. Kat wanted no part of it. After she got over the shock and her name changed, she would look into charities that could benefit from the ill-gotten gains.

"Look, Officer DaSilva—"

"Rob."

God, she hated his smirk. Gritting her teeth, she crossed her arms, ensuring they covered her breasts instead of thrusting them upward. He didn't need any more encouragement, just the opposite, in fact. What he did need was a two-by-four cracked over his thick skull. "Officer DaSilva, I'm here to train you, not date you. I'd prefer if you would please keep things professional."

Taking a step toward her, it was obvious he wasn't deterred. "C'mon, babe. I'll show you a really good time." She saw something click in his eyes like a light bulb went off in his dense brain, and he tilted his head. "Oh, wait a minute . . . I get it. I saw you chatting it up before with the dike from Salem P.D. You play for the other team, don't you? Well, it's all right. With one good fuck, I can fix that. Why don't you let me show you what a real man can do for you that other chicks can't?"

"Oh, don't worry. She knows what a real man can do. Don't you, Kitty-Kat?"

At first, she'd gaped at Officer Obnoxious, but now she stared opened-mouthed at Carter sauntering toward them.

Where the hell had he come from?

His expression was deadly, matching the tone of his voice, and she was so glad it wasn't boring into her. Instead, it was aimed at the cop, who suddenly didn't look too sure of himself.

Carter had a good four or five inches on the other man and was twice as broad in the shoulders. He looked like he could take DaSilva down with *both* hands tied behind his back and not even break a sweat. Wearing faded jeans, which fit like a glove, black leather boots, and a snug gray T-shirt from Jenn's University of Tampa, the man was sex on two long legs. Add in his surfer-boy good looks, hair pulled back into a small ponytail, and chiseled body, she was certain he left soaking wet panties, broken hearts, and satisfied women everywhere he went.

The hunky spy walked up to her, pulled her into his arms, and . . . *holy shit* . . . dipped her! His lips locked on hers as he kissed the ever-living shit out of her. Kat was so stunned all she could do was hold on for dear life.

Ending the kiss, he winked at her before setting her upright as she stared at him in utter shock. The corners of his mouth ticked upward as if he was trying to hold back his laughter while his gaze never left hers. "Now, if you'll excuse us, we have better things to do. Come along, beautiful."

He took her arm and turned her toward the cabin before glancing back at DaSilva. Like a coiled deadly cobra, Carter glared at the other man as if he were prey. "Oh, and by the way, if I ever hear you disrespect a woman like you just did, especially this one, they'll never find your body. Understood?"

Kat's blood chilled at the unveiled threat, but apparently, Officer Obnoxious was too stupid to know not to poke the viper, who was more than ready to strike. DaSilva blustered, his face flushed blood red in his attempt at bravado. "You can't threaten me! I'm a cop! I can have your ass arrested so fucking fast you won't know what hit you."

Releasing her arm, Carter pivoted toward the other man. He took two deliberate steps forward and, faster than she could blink, grabbed DaSilva by the throat, leaning in so only the cop could hear him. She longed to know what Carter had whispered because the formerly arrogant man flinched and paled before being freed and taking a step backward.

Without another word, he turned tail and scurried away like the weasel she thought he was.

"Let's go inside, Kitty-Kat. We have things to talk about." Carter gestured toward the door, waiting for her to lead the way.

As her shock faded, Kat's pissed-off attitude returned. She crossed her arms again and stomped her foot while glaring at him. "What the fuck was that all about? I had it under control. What did you say to him? And who do you think you are, walking up and kissing me like that?"

A smirk appeared on his handsome face, and she couldn't help but think it looked so much better on him than it did on Officer Obnoxious. The cocky bastard mirrored her stance but left out the foot stomp. "Like what? I didn't give you any tongue . . . well, not a lot of tongue. Just pretend we're bowling partners again . . . who just happen to kiss when we want to get rid of pricks like him. The other option was to beat the shit out of him, but I doubt your boss would've appreciated it. And I know you had control, but mine was better."

He lifted a shoulder and let it drop again. "It's a Dom thing, so you might as well get used to it. As for what I said to him, sorry Kitty-Kat, you're better off not knowing— gives you plausible deniability if I ever have to follow through with it. And before you ask, Boomer doesn't know I'm here. Now, we can have this conversation out here, or we can go inside and eat the lunch I've been keeping warm in your oven. Hope you like Italian, I was in the mood for pasta."

Kat was blinking, twitching, and gaping at the man who strolled past her and held open her door. Furious, she didn't even know where to begin. "You were in my cabin? How did you get in there? Wait . . . how the hell did you find me in the first place? And what do you mean, 'it's a Dom thing . . . get used to it'?"

An exaggerated sigh escaped him as he rolled his eyes. "So many questions. Uh, let's see." He ticked off the fingers of one hand. "The answers are—yes, I was; I picked the lock; and please, finding you was like finding a cat in a fishbowl— pun intended. We'll discuss the 'Dom thing' after we eat. Now, either get your pretty ass inside, or I'll spank it out here where anyone can see."

Her eyes narrowed, and she scoffed in disbelief. "You wouldn't dare."

He mimicked her stare, and she shivered as a chill went up her spine, knowing his countenance looked more lethal than hers. "Oh, yes, I would, little Kitty. One thing I don't do is issue idle threats. Would you like me to prove it to you? I can guarantee you'll regret it."

Holy shit! He really would do it. Refusing to lower her gaze, like the good submissives she'd been reading about, she held her head high and stomped into her cabin. The aroma of garlic, tomatoes, and oregano assailed her sense of smell as the door closed behind her. Her mouth watered, but she swallowed, not wanting him to know it smelled delicious.

Brushing past her, Carter strode into her kitchen as if he belonged there. Plates, utensils, glasses, and napkins for two were set on her dinette table. She stared daggers into his back as he busied himself at the oven. Using her mitts which she kept in the bottom drawer, he removed several aluminum containers and a foil-wrapped loaf of bread.

"Make yourself at home, why don't you?"

Transferring the food to the table, he gave her an impish grin which caught her off guard. "Thanks, but I already did. You can help by getting us something to drink. I brought beer and soda since I didn't know what you preferred or had already."

Kat snorted and headed to the refrigerator. "What? That wasn't in your investigation of how to find me and break into my home?"

"Watch your tone, Kitty-Kat. You're in enough trouble with me at the moment, but again, we'll discuss that after we eat. I'll take a beer, please. Then sit because I'm starving, and I'm sure you are too. You've had a long day."

"How do you know?"

He shrugged his shoulders and then tossed the mitts on the counter. "Because I've been watching you all morning. The last thing you ate was a granola bar at six-thirty unless you snuck something in while I ran for our meal, which I doubt. You still haven't regained the weight you lost, and from what I can tell, you've lost more. You can't go that long without fueling your body, little one. And despite what advertising executives believe, most men like some meat on their women—gives us something soft to hold on to. Now, sit . . . please."

Gaping at him again, she put two beers on the table and sat in the chair he held out for her. She was so confused about why he was there as she watched him fill her plate and then his own. Once he seemed satisfied all was in order, he took the seat across from her.

"Dig in."

Like she'd noticed Benny had done every time they ate together, he waited until she picked up her fork and took the first bite of her lasagna. Her eyes rolled back into her head as the flavors hit her taste buds. "Oh my God, this is heaven. Where did you get this?" She didn't wait for his answer before shoving another forkful in her mouth.

Carter chuckled and then started on his own meal. "Glad

you like it. I found a little Italian deli about five miles from here called The Red Pepper."

"Wait a minute. I've eaten there before, and it's never been this good." Putting down her fork, she reached for a piece of garlic bread, offering him one, which he thanked her for.

"The sign said, 'Under New Management,' so maybe they have a new chef."

They ate in comfortable silence for a few minutes until Kat started feeling full, and her curiosity started getting the best of her. "Okay, so tell me why you're here."

Picking up his napkin, he wiped his mouth and then took a sip of his beer. "That was going to be my question to you. What the fuck are you doing here, Kat, when the love of your life is moping around Tampa, driving everyone bat-shit crazy?"

Her gaze fell to the table. "I'm not the love of his life. Benny hates me. I almost got his parents killed. And Jake and Colleen and Murray and . . . and . . ."

She didn't realize she was crying until he reached over and brushed away the tears on her cheek. Leaving the last of his meal, he stood and pushed her chair back from the table. Before she knew what he was doing, he'd picked her up in his arms and carried her to the couch.

Sitting again, he settled her on his lap and gently guided her head to rest on his shoulder. The tender Dom held her while she sobbed until she slowly regained control. "He doesn't hate you, little one, and I don't know why you would think that. I've known Boomer for many years, and this is the first time I've ever seen him depressed. He wasn't this bad when he was laid up in the hospital, and they weren't sure if he'd lose his leg. Now, why are you here instead of with him? I know it's not because you don't love him. Anyone can see how much he means to you. So, talk to Master Carter, and we'll see how to fix this. And Rick is fine, by the way. He was discharged from the hospital the other day."

"I know. I called the hospital every day. Before I left, I told the desk clerk I was his niece so I could check on him." She took a shuddering breath. "I can't face him and Eileen. And I sure as hell can't face Benny. This was all my fault. I should never have gone to him for help."

He let out a low growl. "It was not your fault. You weren't the one working for the Russian mob and stealing money from them. And you sure as hell didn't tell those bastards to go after Boomer's folks. So, try again. *Why* are you here when you're still wearing his collar?"

Her hand flew to her throat. She hadn't been able to remove the simple collar Benny had placed around her neck. No matter what, her heart knew she would never love any man as much as she loved him. The collar was her last connection to him.

Instead of giving another lame explanation, she concentrated on Carter's question this time, trying to find the real answer. "I guess . . . he was so angry at the hospital, I was afraid he'd tell me to leave. So, instead of giving him the chance, I left. Deep down, I was hoping he would come after me, but . . . but he didn't."

"Oh, Kitty-Kat. I am so going to make sure he spanks your ass for that. Do you know the reason why he didn't come after you? The reason he's been getting drunk almost every night at the club? Or why he's turned down every sub who's offered to help him forget you?"

Feeling more miserable by the second, her gaze fell to her lap, and she shook her head.

"Because the first time you left him, it wasn't your choice or fault. But this time, Kat, you *chose* to leave. You walked out on him when he needed you the most. He wasn't angry with you . . . he was frustrated at the situation. And I'm sorry you misinterpreted his frustration as anger. He loves you. But he's hurting, thinking you don't love him enough to stay with him."

Her tears started again, and she tried to wipe them away as fast as they rolled down her cheek. "Oh, God, w-what've I done? I do l-love him, and I'd never hurt him on purpose. I was j-just scared. Everyone I've ever loved is gone and . . . and the one person who's still here, I pushed away. C-Carter, w-what am I going to do?"

Holding her head in his big, calloused hands, he forced her to look him in the eye. "What you're going to do is go dry your eyes while I clean up, and then we have a plane to board in . . ." He glanced at his black military watch. "In a little over an hour."

Her mind spun in five different directions. "What! What are you talking about? I can't just get on a plane and leave. I have to work and . . . and . . ."

He lifted her from his lap until she stood on her own two feet and then rose from the couch. Grabbing her shoulders, he turned her toward her bedroom. "I spoke to your boss. I told him you were leaving and to consider this your resignation."

Kat put on the brakes so quickly that he almost tripped over her. "When was this? And, holy shit, you can't just tell my boss I quit. What if I didn't want to go with you?"

"Oh, you're going with me, Kitty-Kat. It was never a question. I explained the situation to Jeremy and Eva, and they're happy for you. They also said if it doesn't work out, you will always have a job here. But the choice is yours. You either check the bags I packed for you to see if I missed anything important, or I tan your hide and carry you out of here. I suggest you don't take option number two, because it's a long flight, and you'll want to be comfortable. Now, go wash up."

He gave her a gentle shove toward the door, ignoring her sputtering and shock. She tried to glare at him over her shoulder, but he was already heading to her kitchen. Her mind racing, she hurried to her bedroom, and sure enough, there were her three duffel bags all packed.

Undoing the zippers, she searched through them and found he'd pretty much thought of everything she would need for now, including her migraine medication. One bag had all her toiletries, while another was full of shirts, pants, shorts, and two pairs of her favorite shoes. The last bag . . . *oh, fuck a duck* . . . had her intimates—panties, bras, pajamas . . . and, *what the heck?* Pulling out the lacy garment, she blushed while holding it up.

"I figured you would need something for the club tonight, so I found a little boutique near the deli. The cute, blonde sales clerk was all too happy to help me pick something out."

His appearance in her doorway had startled her for a moment before she recovered and gave him an unladylike snort. "I'll just bet she was. She probably offered to model it for you, too."

As he leaned against the doorjamb, the corners of his mouth ticked upward. Kat examined the black lacy teddy, which left nothing to the imagination. "Um . . . where's the rest of it? I can't walk around in just this."

"Why not?" Kat gaped at him while he grinned like the devil himself. "Don't panic, love, the bra and panties that go with it are in there too. That's just the coverup."

Snorting again, she shoved the lingerie back into the bag. "You and I have different definitions of a coverup."

Carter stepped over to the bed and grabbed all three bags by their handles. "Did I forget anything? I cleaned out your fridge earlier, so nothing would spoil, and I just took out the garbage. I told your boss you'd be back in a week or so to say goodbye and pack up the rest of your stuff."

She ran to the bathroom, wet a washcloth, and wiped her face as fast as possible. Finding him waiting at her front door, she glanced around for anything else she needed. Her purse and the book she was currently reading were on her coffee table, and she snatched them up. A quick check assured her that her phone was still on her hip. "I think we have everything I need for now. You're so sure Benny and I will work this all out, aren't you? What if the damage is done and he doesn't forgive me?"

"Then I kick his ass and keep you for myself."

He held open the door for her, and she turned the lock on the inside knob before passing him. With one hand, he gestured for her to walk around to the back of her cabin, where a rental car sat. After opening the passenger door for her, he popped the trunk for her bags and then climbed into the driver's seat.

"I think we'd kill each other if you kept me for yourself, not that I'd let myself be kept. You're quite infuriating at times, you know?"

"Ha! I've been told that a time or two, Kitty-Kat." He started the car and put it in Drive. "Shit. I keep forgetting to ask. I was talking to Eileen when I checked on Rick, and I called you 'Kitty-Kat' to her. She said it was your father's nickname for you. I didn't know, Kat, and if it bothers you, I can stop. Does it?"

Kat shook her head and turned to face him after putting her seatbelt on. "No, it doesn't. The first time you said it, it threw me a little. But then I realized how much I missed hearing it. Just like when Benny calls me Kitten—no one else but him ever called me that. As long as it's said with the affection I know you mean, then I like it, and you can keep using it. It makes me feel special."

"Then I'm honored." He pulled out of the long driveway onto the road leading to the highway. "You are special, little one, and don't you ever forget it. Now, let's get you and your Dom back together, shall we? Before Ian finally breaks down and kicks his ass."

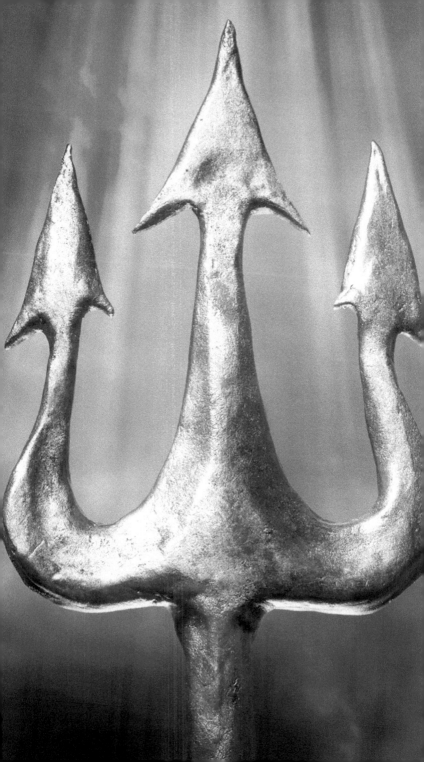

CHAPTER TWENTY-SIX

A little after midnight, Boomer handed over his car keys before Tiny would open the club door for him. How sad was it the big bouncer knew he was here to get drunk . . . again? Aside from Monday and Tuesday, when The Covenant was closed, and he'd gone to Donovan's, he'd been here every night since his dad had been released from the hospital. He'd offered to stay at his parents' house until Rick was more mobile, but his mother had insisted she could handle things and he should go after Kat. Instead, Boomer returned to Tampa and began drowning his sorrows.

The other Doms had taken pity on him and put up with his morose drinking, making sure someone drove him home every night. Then, after popping Tylenol for his resulting hangovers, he'd take a taxi back to work the next day or catch a ride with one of his teammates.

Ian had wanted him to crash in one of the rooms above the offices, but it would only bring back painful memories of the night he and Kat slept there—well after they had done other things, of course. At least at his condo, she'd only slept in the guest room. And damn, her scent was still there—he knew because he went in there all the time just to sniff her pillow like a heartbroken ass.

There was no way he was chasing after Kat. She'd ripped his heart out and stomped on it on her way out of the hospital to return to Oregon. When he'd returned, much calmer, with a sack of sandwiches and sodas, he'd discovered Kat missing. Ian and Marco had left to retrieve the vehicles. Leaving the food with his mother and aunt, he searched the entire hospital, starting with the cafeteria, thinking she might have gone for coffee.

After not finding her in any of the public places in the building, he'd asked the security guard at the main entrance and found out Kat had left, taking a cab to God knew where. He couldn't call her to find out where she was going because her phone was still back at the compound, and she had given the medical alert bracelet back to Brody, so the GPS was out as well.

An hour of worrying later, Jake called to say Kat had arrived at the compound and packed her duffel bags in her car, which had still been parked in the garage behind the offices. After speaking to SAC Stonewall, she drove away. Jake hadn't been able to stop her since, in all the confusion, he hadn't known she was there until it was too late. He had to check the security videos to see what she'd done.

Boomer had told her he loved her, and although she'd said the words back to him, she'd obviously not meant them. Or maybe she had, but his job and the violence involved were too much for her to handle. While he hadn't been the one to kill any of the Russians, a fact which still pissed him off, Kat had seen up close and personal how dangerous his job was. Maybe she couldn't deal with it. Either way, the ball was in her court. He'd be damned if he would beg her to come back to him.

He said hello to a few people on the way to the bar and almost winced when he saw the bartender, Master Dennis, grab a bottle of Jack Daniels to start making his drink. Had he become so predictable in less than two weeks? Maybe he should fuck with the guy and switch to Southern Comfort. The thought left his brain as fast as it'd come. He wasn't in the mood to joke around. Instead, he sat his sad-sack ass on an empty stool and nodded his thanks when the drink, mixed with a dash of Coke, was placed in front of him on a cocktail napkin.

He'd spent most of the day and half the night following some fucktard around who was cheating on his wife of six years. The guy was in deep shit because his suspicious spouse had the purse strings, and their prenup was clear—cheat, and he doesn't get a cent. And Boomer had the pictures which would make the bastard drop to his knees and cry buckets.

Mulling over his boring yet successful day in solitude, it wasn't long before clinking ice was the only thing remaining in the glass, and he caught the bartender's eye for another one.

"Scratch that, Dennis. Master Ben will be playing tonight."

Boomer glared at Carter as the Dom smacked him on the shoulder, then leaned against the bar with an annoying grin on his face.

"I'm not fucking playing tonight, Dennis. Fill it up."

Picking up the empty glass, Carter handed it to the amused bartender while shaking his head. "Nope. You're playing, so no more booze. Two waters, please, Den."

Turning back to Boomer, he ignored the dirty, pissed-off stare he was getting. "I've got a lovely new submissive who wants a little action, and I think she's just what you need to get out of this fucking funk you're in. Your other option is

SAMANTHA COLE

the one Ian and Devil Dog came up with, but I think you'll choose door number one after you hear what's behind door number two."

His eyes narrowed. He wasn't in the mood for this shit, but apparently, everyone was done with his pity party except him. "What's their option?"

"A session with Mistress China, who I must say is head-over-her-pretty-ass about the idea. You know how much she loves to whip pathetic guys back into shape." Carter paused to take a drink from one of the water bottles that'd been placed in front of them. "So, what's it going to be, Boom-Boom? Some hot sex with an even hotter sub or China's bullwhip?"

Astonished, Boomer grunted. "You've got to be fucking kidding me?"

"No, he's not."

He sighed heavily and spun around on the barstool to face Boss-man and found the rest of his team in attendance.

Shit.

Just what he fucking needed—an intervention.

All five wor their best Dom faces, daring him to give them shit. Add in the super-spy, and there was no way he was getting out of this. His choices were clear—a lashing from the sadistic Whip Mistress or fucking a willing submissive who might let him forget about Kat for a little while.

The problem was . . . he didn't want to forget about her. He wanted her by his side and in his bed for the rest of his life. Fucking another woman would never change that. Instead, it would make him feel like he was cheating on the only woman who would ever own his heart. And that right there was his answer. "If I lay off the booze and get my head on straight, can I pick door number three?"

Ian cocked one eyebrow. "Door number three?"

"I need some time off. I've got to go after her . . . to Portland." He swallowed hard, refusing to break down in front of the men who were brothers to him. "She's my life. I don't care if I have to get on my knees and beg or tie her ass up and kidnap her, but damn it, I'm not letting her get away this time. I love her, and I've got to get her back."

"Thank fuck! Now we can put an end to this fucking pity party of yours. I was about to start watering down the Jack." Ian took a step toward him. "But she's not in Oregon, Boom."

His eyes narrowed as he slid off the stool and stood. Panic assailed him. If she wasn't in Portland, where the hell was she? "What do you mean? She's somewhere else? Where? Her aunt's?"

He might have asked Ian the questions, but Carter answered. "Downstairs in room four, waiting patiently and presenting herself for her Dom. Don't fuck it up. And don't freak out when she tells you I kissed her."

Running toward the grand staircase, he barely heard the other Dom's last words and the chorus of snorts and chuckles from his teammates. All he could think about was Kat was waiting for him on the other side of the building. Ian or Devon must have waved at the bouncer at the top of the stairs because he let Boomer pass without checking his membership card for alcohol consumption.

Tamping down the urge to push people out of his way, he made his way through the crowd as fast as possible, dodging bodies and cursing along the way. On the other side of the cavernous room, two sets of hallways led to twelve private rooms, six in each. An on-duty Dungeon Master, stationed between the entrances to both hallways, nodded at him as he ran past. Grinding to a halt outside room four, he paused to catch his breath and calm himself down. Carter had said she was presenting herself for her

Dom, so her Dom is what he needed to be when he walked into the room.

He didn't know who had taught her how to present, but he had a strong feeling it was Angie and Kristen. Since their Masters knew about Kat being here, it was pretty much a given for them to know as well. And he was positive those two match-makers couldn't pass up an opportunity to help create a happy-ever-after.

Wait . . . what the fuck? Did the fucking spy say something about kissing Kat? Damn, he'd kick the guy's ass later if he didn't have a fucking good excuse for it—and maybe even if he did.

Inhaling deeply, he turned the knob and opened the door. His breath caught at the sight of her and got stuck in his chest. She was kneeling on a red satin pillow in the center of the room, knees shoulder-width apart, back straight, head bowed, and upturned hands resting on her thighs—presenting perfectly. Dressed in a black bra and panties with a sheer lace teddy over them, she was the most beautiful thing his eyes had ever seen in his life, and his cock agreed. He noticed a shiver go through her body, and it thrilled him. When he remembered to breathe again, he entered the room, closed the door behind him, and stepped over to stand in front of her.

For a few moments, he remained silent, letting her anticipation build while he took in her beauty. His hands were shaking, itching to touch her. He was about to speak when he noticed papers spread out on the bed behind her. Skirting around her, he picked them up and was surprised to see her completed limit list and a note from one of the doctors on staff clearing her for play after an earlier examination. There was also a note from Ian saying Brody had done Kat's background check.

Holy shit. Obviously, several people had a hand in expediting her clearance for the club. He'd have to remember to thank everyone.

Scanning her limit list quickly, he grinned when he saw a checkmark in the green column of several activities he wanted to do with her tonight. Stepping back in front of her, he spread his legs and crossed his arms while wiping the smile from his face. She had some punishments coming to her before they talked and then had some fun. He lowered his voice. "Stand, Kitten, and strip for me. As pretty as your outfit is, I want to see you naked."

He was pleased when she didn't hesitate and impressed at her gracefulness as she rose up on her feet in one fluid movement. One by one, she removed the three garments and handed them to him, all the while keeping her gaze on his feet.

Damn, she was gorgeous. Her hair was pulled back into a simple ponytail, and he couldn't wait to wrap the silky strands around his wrist. Tiny goose bumps popped up on her soft skin, and he knew it was from desire and anticipation instead of cold. The rooms were kept at a comfortable seventy degrees for that reason. A blush spread across her chest, but it wasn't as pink as her nipples which were already puckered and distended, waiting for him to feast on them. His gaze traveled south, and when it reached the junction of her hips and legs, his cock hardened painfully, and his knees almost buckled. She was waxed bare, and since the skin wasn't red, he knew she had to have done it before today. Tossing the lingerie on the bed behind her, he asked, "What's your safeword?"

She spoke for the first time since he entered the room. "Red, Sir." Her voice was husky and seductive, and he held back a reactive groan.

"Good girl. Look at me, Kitten." When her head tilted up, he was floored by the various emotions he saw flash through her eyes—anticipation, fear, and hope. He prayed the fear was only because she was worried he was mad at her. Well, part of him still was, but it was fast being pushed aside by relief over her being here. For now, a little fear in her was good. A jolt of awareness passed through him when he noticed his collar around her slender neck.

Holy fuck! He was about to throw out his man card and break down crying in front of her from the sheer pleasure of seeing the leather band still in place. He swallowed the lump in his throat. "When did you wax your pretty pussy, and why?"

When her eyes shifted away from his in evident embarrassment, he added, "Uh-uh, Kitten. Eyes on mine. If you look away again before I permit it, you'll just add to your punishments."

Her gaze met his again, but this time her eyes were wide in surprise . . . and there it was—unadulterated lust. God, he loved her. "Yes, baby. You have some punishments headed your way, but I'll explain that in a minute. Answer my question. When and why did you wax? I'm not complaining . . . quite the opposite, really."

"The other day, Master." His pounding heartbeat sped up further, threatening to burst from his chest at her use of his title, but he stayed quiet, letting her finish. "I was reading everything I could about the lifestyle, and there were a lot of mentions of how both Doms and subs liked it because it made a woman more sensitive."

Boomer hadn't thought he could be more stunned or pleased than he already was. Her punishment would have to wait—they definitely needed to talk first. "You've been researching BDSM? Why?"

Her cheeks turned tomato red, but to her credit, her eyes remained focused on his. "Because it means so much to you, and I . . . I hoped . . ."

"You hoped what?" This time her gaze fell, and he used his fingers to tilt her head back up, waiting for her to meet his stare again. His heart squeezed when her eyes filled with tears, but he didn't let them sway him. She couldn't be allowed to top from the bottom, whether it was intended or not. He needed to be firm with her if this would work between them. "That's five more spanks on top of the ones you already deserve. Now, you hoped what, Kitten?"

Kat swallowed hard. "I hoped you would change your mind and come after me. I wanted to please you by learning as much as I could about being your submissive. I know I haven't learned everything yet, but I was hoping you'd teach me the rest."

A bullet to the gut wouldn't have hurt as much as her first statement did. His brow furrowed in confusion. "What do you mean you hoped I would change my mind, baby? I never wanted you to leave in the first place. I came back to the waiting room, and you were gone. I figured you had just gone to clear your head and get a cup of coffee or something. Next thing I know, Jake's calling to say you showed up at the compound in a taxi. You collected your things and drove away in your car. Stonewall said you went to the office, gave your statement, and left."

Much to his embarrassment, his voice cracked with emotion. "I needed you, and you were gone. But this time, you chose to leave. I was never more hurt in my life, Kat."

Her tears were now streaking down her face, but neither one moved to wipe them away. "I—I know I hurt you . . . I mean. I know now. Carter t-told me when he showed up in Portland to bring me back. I never meant . . . meant to hurt you. But you were so angry at the hospital and didn't want to talk to me, s-so I thought you were blaming me for your dad being shot. And . . . and for your mom, Jake, and the others being hurt and almost killed. I thought you hated me for putting everyone in danger. I've lost everyone I ever loved, and d-didn't want to wait for you to push me away. I'm so sorry."

She finally stopped talking and took a deep, ragged breath. Boomer couldn't handle it anymore and pulled her into his arms, holding her tightly while stroking her hair and bare back. "Shh . . . it's okay, Kitten. I wasn't mad at you. I was just mad, in general, over things I couldn't control. I was mad at myself for not thinking my parents might be targeted, and then I was pissed we fell for the ruse, and you could've been killed because not enough people stayed behind. At the hospital, my adrenaline crash, combined with the doctors telling me it would be hours before we knew if my dad would make it, sent me into a tailspin. I walked away from you because I didn't want to take it all out on you inadvertently. You didn't deserve it, and I was afraid I'd hurt you. Not physically, of course, but I just needed a few minutes to get myself back under control."

He loosened his embrace so he could see her face. "I love you, baby. I would never push you away. But I thought you didn't want to be part of my life because of the potential for violence. My job can be dangerous at times. I thought you realized that and didn't want to be a part of it."

"And I thought you were mad at me. Guess I should have asked you."

A wry smile appeared on her red, wet face. Cupping her chin with both hands, he used his thumbs and then his lips to wipe away her salty tears. "Yes, you should have, but I'm as much to blame as you. I should have explained why I was walking away from you. We'll have to work on our communication, but we have the rest of our lives to do that. Right now, I want to pick a few things off your limit list and have some fun. Because of our mutual misunderstandings, I'm going to clear the slate for everything up until I walked into this room, which means you'll only be getting those five spanks you've earned. I can't very well punish you for something that was also my fault. After that, we're going to start fresh. Okay?"

"Okay, Sir."

His thumb brushed over her plump, pink lips, and he imagined how they would look circled around his aching cock. But first things first. "I liked it better before when you called me 'Master.'"

For the first time since he walked in the door, Kat truly smiled at him, and it was as if the sun had come out. It brightened the room as much as his heart. He hadn't lost her, and as soon as he could get a permanent collar designed for her, they would have a ceremony so everyone would know who she belonged to. "Yes, Master."

Glancing around the room, he quickly categorized which one they were in. Each of the private rooms was designed differently, and some of the play equipment varied. Several rooms were like this, with a few pieces of equipment and assorted chains, hooks, and restraints hanging from the walls and ceiling. Other rooms were theme rooms, such as an office, classroom, doctor's examination room, police station lock-up/interrogation room, and a harem/stripper pole room.

Due to the popularity of the rooms, Devon, Ian, and Mitch were discussing putting an addition on this end of the warehouse for more rooms. This room, however, was perfect for the scene he had in his mind.

Taking Kat's hand, he led her to a spanking bench sitting in one corner. "Hop on up, Kitten. Let's get your punishment over with so we can get to the fun stuff. We'll talk more later, but I'm so fucking hard for you, I can't wait much longer." It was the truth—his cock felt like it had an impression of his zipper on it.

Boomer was thrilled when she didn't hesitate to kneel on the bench and place her torso on the upper flat portion. It was then he got his first look at her bare ass, and what he saw had him dropping to his knees behind her.

Holy fuck! She had an anal plug in her!

Caressing her soft butt cheeks reverently, he couldn't resist the urge to lean forward and lick her exposed, dripping pussy. Her moan shot straight to his dick, and he had to open the button and zipper of his pants to relieve the painful pressure. "When . . . holy shit, Kat . . . when did you start using an anal plug? Damn, that's a beautiful sight."

Without waiting for an answer, his tongue attacked her hairless pussy again. Her honey was the sweetest thing, and he ate her like a man who had been without for eons—licking, nibbling, and suckling on the swollen lips between her legs. The more juices he lapped up, the more her body produced for him. Shit, he could do this all fucking night.

"Oh, oh, Benny! Oh my God, please don't stop!"

Her breathy demand told him she was getting close, and, unfortunately for her, he did stop. Punishment before pleasure. Squeezing her cheeks a few times to get the blood flowing to them, he rose to his feet again. "Answer my question, Kitten. Tell me about this plug in your ass. And I hope you did it on your own. Otherwise, I may have to kill someone."

In between gulps of air, she responded, "Y-yes, I did it myself. L-last week, I found a shop in Portland that sells them. The woman there helped me pick out a beginner's progressive set. I loved when you . . . you fucked my ass with your finger, and I wanted to be ready for you if you came after me."

Damn, she just kept the surprises coming. He ground his thick erection against the flat head of the plug, grinning as she moaned and cursed. "Your dirty language is improving, Kitten, and I love it. I also love the fact that, despite being on the other side of the country, you still felt compelled to please me. After your spanks, you will definitely be rewarded. What size plug is this, baby?"

"The largest one, Sir . . . Master."

She was going to be the death of him tonight. With practiced ease, he attached the restraints to her wrists, ankles, and waist, making sure none of them were too tight.

Eyeing the assortment of implements hanging from hooks on the wall, he spotted one he liked. Retrieving the leather-covered, oblong paddle, he rubbed it against her ass. "Just so you know, little kitten—before I found out you were in here waiting for me, I was ready to hop a plane to Oregon to beg you to come back to me. But now that you're here, I think you'll be the one begging tonight. Count for me, Kitten."

He drew the paddle back and let the first strike land hard on her right cheek. *Smack.*

"Ow!!! Holy shit! Holy . . . oh, fuck! W-What's happening?"

He was lucky she was facing forward and didn't see his evil smile. He knew exactly what was happening as he held his hand against the red mark left by the paddle. The pain was turning to heat and then to pleasure. Tilting his head, he saw she, indeed, felt gratification as more moisture coated her sweet pussy. "Pain then pleasure, baby. That's what's happening. Now count for me, or I might forget I gave you one."

"One!"

Not holding back his chuckle at her rushed response, he aimed the paddle again. *Smack.* This strike landed on her left cheek.

"Shit! Two! Holy shit!"

"Baby, I love how your ass looks all nice and red." As much as he wanted to warm her ass slowly, he wanted to fuck it even more. The next two spanks were on her sit spots, and the final one he placed over both cheeks just below the plug.

"Fuck! Five!"

Tossing the paddle to the side, he massaged her tender flesh, tapping the flat end of the plug, causing it to vibrate against the nerves inside her. Her moaning and panting were driving him crazy. He slid one hand between her legs, reveling in the juices he found there.

Two fingers probed her swollen flesh, then eased into her, urging her arousal higher. Using his other hand, he pushed his jeans down to his ankles, wanting to be ready as soon as he made her come. He continued to fuck her with his fingers as he reached over to a drawer in a nearby cabinet and felt around for one of the tubes of lubricant he knew was there. Finding one, he put it on the bench between her legs and sped up his thrusts. Her moans, curses, begging, and breathing all increased for him.

"Come for me, Kitten. Scream so everyone in the place hears you take your pleasure."

He found her G-spot and stroked it rapidly with his fingertips while tugging on her anal plug with his other hand. The combination of dueling sensations sent her flying over the edge, and he wouldn't be surprised if at least half the club heard her cry out. Her walls rippled against his fingers as he extended her orgasm as long as he could, flicking her clit with his thumb. Kat's screams faded to groans and then whimpers as he slid his fingers from her pussy and the plug from her ass.

"Damn, Kitten. I have to take your ass now before I explode. Can you stay like that, or do I need to take you over to the bed?"

As he spoke, he grabbed the lubricant tube, popped the top, and covered the tip of his cock with the clear liquid. Fuck, it was cold! Of course, the lube warmer was across the room, out of reach. Well, it wouldn't be cold for long. "Answer me because I'm ready to take you right now."

"Yes! Fuck! Now! Please!"

If he weren't so desperate to get inside her, he would have laughed at her one-word sentences, but he was sure he'd be in the same frame of mind in under a minute. Her asshole was still slick from the lube she'd used for the plug, and he lined his cock up with it. Pushing forward, he was relieved when she didn't instinctively clench. She was still open from the plug, and he slid past her sphincter with ease. "Holy fuck! Damn, woman, you feel incredible."

He was thicker than the plug, but by pumping in and out, he gained inches until he was far enough to give them both pleasure but not too far to hurt her. She was panting and gasping but hadn't complained at all. Still, he needed to make sure she was all right because as soon as he started fucking her hard, he wouldn't be able to stop. "Give me a color, Kat. Green is good, yellow is wait a minute, and red is stop."

He wanted to add, "Please, don't say red," but he wouldn't want her to lie to him just because this is what he wanted.

"Green, Master. If you don't start moving, I'm going to go insane. Please!"

It was all the encouragement Boomer needed. Grasping her hips, he dragged his cock out to the tip and then shoved it back in, making her yelp and moan. She was so tight that the friction had him seeing black and white spots before his eyes. Again and again, he repeated the slow-fast routine until she begged and cursed for more. Unable to deny either of them what they wanted any longer, he began fucking her faster and faster.

"Yes! Benny! Oh, God, yes! Please! Hurry!"

She was close, and so was he. Tingling shot from his lower spine to his balls, and he knew he had to send her over again before he came. Reaching around, his fingers searched and found her clit. The second he flicked it, she went off like a rocket, and her ass clenched with her orgasm as she shrieked her release. The pressure increased around his cock and sent him flying with her as his cum filled her ass. Bright lights appeared behind his closed eyelids as he forced his legs to keep him upright. His energy drained when the last of his orgasm faded, and he almost collapsed on top of her.

As much as he wanted to rest, he knew he had to release her from the restraints and carry her over to the bed, where they would both be more comfortable. He tilted his hips back and reluctantly slid from her body. After undoing the waist strap, he reached down to release her ankles. "Kat, baby? You okay?"

"Wonderful," she murmured, her voice raspy from screaming earlier.

Boomer chuckled as he freed her wrists. "Glad to hear it. Lift up for me so I can carry you to bed."

"I can walk."

Despite her protest, her limbs quivered like a bowl of Jell-O. Picking her up in his arms, he grinned when her head fell heavy against his shoulder. "That may be, but this is one of those things your Dom wants to do, and you shouldn't argue with him unless you want another spanking."

Exhausted, she cuddled closer. "'Kay. Love you."

"I love you, too, my little Kitten. I always will."

He placed her in the middle of the big bed before retrieving two wey washcloths from a warmer in the corner of the room. After cleaning Kat, he took care of himself, tossed the used towels in a hamper, and then joined her on the bed. She was almost asleep as he turned her on her side, his heart bursting with love for this beautiful woman. Spooning behind her, he finally gave in to the afterglow of the scene and closed his eyes.

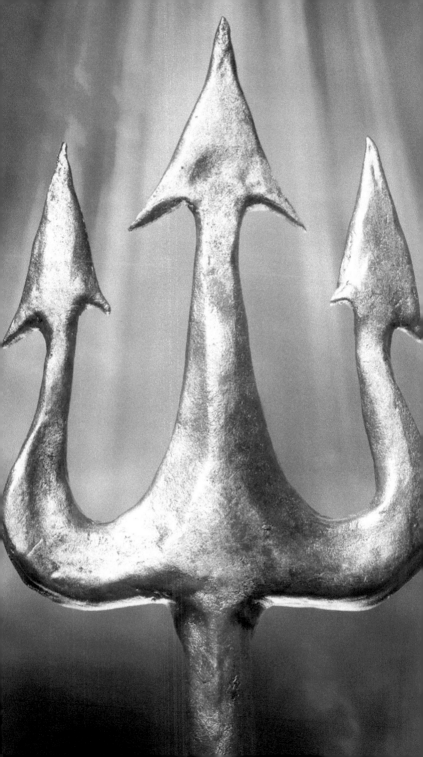

EPILOGUE

As the organ music started, Boomer stood tall in his Navy dress whites and watched Kat glide elegantly down the center aisle of the quaint little church. Damn, she looked stunning . . . and she was all his. It was three months since he first saw her in the Trident offices and fainted at the sight. He was still getting razzed for that, but he would gladly suffer through it to have her back in his life . . . for good. A ring on her finger and a permanent collar around her neck told the world she was spoken for.

The day after finding her in the club, they'd spent hours in his bed, having kinky sex, making sweet love, and talking about their future. They'd only showered and gotten dressed that evening to attend an impromptu barbecue at the compound because his mom had driven up to get his dad's bored ass out of the house for a while. His folks had also wanted to see Kat for themselves and reassure her they didn't blame her for things that had been beyond her control.

Instead of attempting to beat the crap out of Carter for kissing Kat, Boomer kicked his ass on the compound's basketball court in the parking lot outside the training building. He wasn't stupid enough to challenge a lethal black-op assassin to a sparring match, so he took the bastard down on the court. Of course, there were some scuffles, along with plenty of elbow jabs to the jaw, ribs, and gut, which were returned just as hard.

By the end of the game of one-on-one, both men had been sore, bleeding, and laughing, much to the women's horror. The female gender just didn't understand how men enjoyed beating each other up out of friendship and gratitude. Boomer was just thankful Carter had taken the initiative to get Kat back to Tampa, and he would owe the man his life . . . again.

With Reggie Helms' legal help and Dr. Marie Sawyer's contacts, Kat was setting up multiple large donations to a wide assortment of charities that would best benefit from the millions of dollars in the Cayman account. She was making all the donations in memory of her parents and brother, finally happy something good had come from their tragic deaths.

After they packed her things and shipped them by freight, then said goodbye to her friends in Portland, Boomer had taken the time off Ian had offered him. He flew Kat to the island of St. Lucia where they'd fucked like rabbits for a week straight, in between sunbathing on the beach and acting like tourists. On their last night on the scenic Caribbean island, they'd taken a moonlit stroll. Shaking with a mixture of fear and anticipation, he'd gotten down on one knee and proposed to her with his grandmother's antique engagement ring. His mother had surprised him and given it to him the night of the barbecue with her and Rick's blessing.

Gentle waves had lapped at the shoreline as a full moon

hung high in the star-filled sky. Taking Kat's left hand, he'd gazed into her chestnut brown eyes as they welled up with stunned but happy tears. "Kitten, I love you with all my heart. You're my sunshine, my moonlight, my past, and my future. My life was beautiful with you in it the first time, and it's beautiful again, now that you're back in my arms. I had a dream last night about Alex. I know it sounds weird, but he gave me his blessing and made me promise to take care of you forever. Whether real or imagined, it's a promise I intend to keep. Marry me, sweetheart. Grow old with me and make the rest of my life beautiful too."

He'd barely uttered those last few words before she shouted, "Yes!"

As he'd slid the ring on her trembling finger, a round of applause and whistles came from a small crowd of tourists who'd stopped to watch the romantic proposal. Ignoring them, Boomer had stood and scooped Kat up into his arms, kissing her with all the love in his heart.

"Benny?"

He shook the perfect memory from his mind and looked down at the petite woman standing next to him, holding his arm. Kat's Aunt Irina looked stunning in her simple, lace wedding gown. It was then he noticed the music had changed and the guests were waiting for him to escort the bride down the aisle. The corners of her warm brown eyes crinkled in amusement, and she grinned at him as if sensing where his mind had gone. "It's time."

"Right. Are you sure about this? You know I have a getaway car right outside if you're not," he teased her.

She squeezed his arm, then gazed toward the other end of the aisle where Ret. Major Harry Bernhard stood proudly, waiting for his wife-to-be. On the opposite side of the altar was Kat, the maid of honor, smiling back at Boomer and her aunt. "Oh, I'm very sure. Like the story of you and my little Katerina, I've been waiting for him all my life."

Continue the adventure with the *Not Negotiable*, now available.

Not Negotiable
A Trident Security Novella: Book 4

Mentally rolling his eyes, Parker Christiansen listened as his older brother droned on about life in Boston —a life Parker felt he never fit into and had left behind years ago. Dave was just like their parents—stuck-up, arrogant, and rich. He'd even followed in their father's footsteps and became a successful corporate attorney.

Meanwhile, Parker had taken his love for using his hands to build things and become an architect/builder/contractor. And no matter how successful he'd made his company, New Horizons, his father always managed to put him down. Nothing he ever did was good enough for the old man. Their family came from wealth and privilege, and Judge Alan and Janet Christiansen couldn't accept that their youngest son liked getting his hands dirty. They also didn't like that Parker was a Dom in the BDSM lifestyle—a fact Alan had found out by accident several years ago, and he never let his son

But his brother had always been curious about the life-style—not in front of their parents, of course. Dave had called him a few weeks ago, saying he was going to be in Florida on business this weekend and he wanted Parker to bring him as a guest to the club he belonged to. The Covenant was a private and elite BDSM club in Tampa and Parker had been a member since the doors opened over four years ago. His company had done some of the work on the club, as well as the other three warehouses in the gated compound.

He had converted one of the buildings into two apartments for the club's owners, Ian and Devon Sawyer, and was in the process of adding two more apartments in the currently unused half of the building. From what he was told, Ian's goddaughter, Jenn, was getting one, while their younger brother would be given the keys to the last unit for when he retired from the Navy. One of the other buildings was home to the Sawyers' company, Trident Security. The ex-Navy SEALs had a thriving business in both ventures, but their cousin Mitch Sawyer was the third co-owner and manager of the club. The club Parker and Dave were en-route to.

Parker had given Mitch his brother's name to get him cleared to be a guest. The Covenant was extremely strict with running background checks on potential members and visitors. Legally binding privacy contracts had to be signed to ensure what happened at the club, stayed at the club.

"Why do you want to check out the club again? I thought Carol was against the lifestyle."

Dave shrugged. "She agreed our marriage needs a little spicing up. I'm thinking about joining a club outside Boston, but wanted to check one out first with you, so you can fill me in on the lifestyle a little more."

Pulling off the highway, Parker drove down the private road leading to the compound. "Take your license out. You need to show it to the guard."

"There's a guard?"

"Yeah. The Sawyers take the security here seriously." He took the ID his brother handed him, rolled down the window, and gave it to the guard. "Hey, Murray. What are you doing here? Thought you only worked days."

The burly, armed guard swiped the license through his hand-held computer, compared the picture and name to the approved list, then handed the card back to Parker. "Just grabbing a little overtime. One of the guys called in sick. You're all cleared. Have a good night."

"Thanks. You, too."

Parker found a spot for his truck and killed the ignition. "Give me your cell phone."

"Why?" Despite his question, Dave handed him the device.

"They aren't allowed on the floor of the club." Well, they were if they remained in a pocket or purse. Any texting or talking on phones had to be done in the lobby or parking lot. But Parker didn't want his brother to be tempted to use it inside. He tossed the phone, along with his own, into the glove compartment. "All right. Remember. I'm responsible for you here. At the front desk, you'll get a yellow wristband that indicates you're a guest and not available for play. You don't do anything without checking with me first. When I introduce you to anyone, you ask permission from the Doms or Dommes to speak to their submissives. There's a two-drink limit for guests and anyone who is going to play. Don't ask for more than that because they keep track."

Waving him off, Dave climbed out of the Chevy Tahoe. "I got it. I read all the stuff you sent in the email. No worries."

Despite his brother's assurance, Parker still couldn't help but think this was a big mistake.

SHELBY WHITMAN WALKED OUT INTO THE MAIN ROOM OF THE club and let the pulsating music flow through her body. Ian's new submissive seemed nice. When they'd met a few minutes ago in the women's locker room, Angie appeared nervous, but that was expected for a sub's first time in a BDSM club. Shelby hoped she'd eased the woman's anxiety with her little pep talk.

Taking a quick glance down her body, Shelby grinned at her new outfit. Tonight's color was electric blue. Her bra, mini-skirt, which flared out when she turned, and wig with straight hair to her shoulders, all matched perfectly. What had started as a way to hide her thinning hair from radiation treatments years ago, had become a fashion statement that had remained long after her treatments for ovarian cancer were completed. Now, cancer-free for six years, she still wore a different colored wig to match her outfit every time she came to the club.

Glancing around, she tried to tell herself she wasn't looking for *him*, but her gaze still searched for those gentle brown eyes and blond crew cut. There were plenty of single, hot Doms at The Covenant, but something about Parker Christiansen always drew her in, making her libido wake up and take notice. Totally drool-worthy, he was continually tan from working outside. She knew he owned his building company, however, he wasn't the type of guy to sit behind a desk and let others do the dirty work. Parker got right down in the trenches with his employees.

But the Dom wasn't for her. He needed more than a

submissive . . . he needed a wife. Parker was the type of guy who should grow old with the woman he loved, spoiling lots of children and grandchildren. Something Shelby could never give him. It was part of the reason why she liked the lifestyle—well, besides the awesome orgasms she tended to receive on a regular basis from any of the other single Doms who wanted to play. She could hook up with anyone who wasn't looking for long-term . . . anyone who only wanted a relationship here at the club and not out in the "real" world.

Before her cancer, she had wanted a long-term relationship with a Dom/husband, two-point-six kids, a dog, and a house with a white picket fence. But that was before fate had been cruel. Now she had nothing to offer a man except sex and friendship. So, she came here, put on her best smile and the bouncy personality everyone loved, before going home . . . alone.

Taking a deep breath, she pushed Master Parker from her mind and headed over to the submissives' waiting area. Maybe Masters Brody and Marco would be here and willing to indulge her in one of their ménages. The two always left her sated and well-cared for without emotional attachments. And that was just fine with her.

AN HOUR AFTER THEY ARRIVED, PARKER WAS DYING TO GET OUT of there. It wasn't that he didn't want to be at the club—he just didn't want to be there with his brother. He knew this had been a mistake. While Dave had been asking a whole bunch of questions, it was obvious he still had no clue about the lifestyle and didn't belong in it. It was also pissing the Dom off that his brother was leering at every scantily dressed sub that walked by as if she were a piece of meat. Having him here was a recipe for disaster.

In addition to his brother issues, he didn't want to watch Shelby scene with the Masters of Ménage. Brody Evans and Marco DeAngelis were the popular tag-team duo for the female submissives, and a few minutes ago, he'd watched from afar as Shelby and the two Doms negotiated a scene. Well, mostly, Brody did the negotiating with the blonde sub. Marco was on Dungeon Master duty at the moment and had kept one ear on the other two and his eyes on everything else going on around him. The DMs were all experienced Doms or Dommes who took shifts to ensure no harm came to any submissive, whether intentional or not. And Parker was one of them.

Forcing himself to stop mooning over Shelby, who was chatting with a few other people in a sitting area designated for submissives, he bit the inside of his lip in frustration. She was probably waiting for Marco to get off his scheduled shift. Parker glanced at his watch. The DM would be free in about fifteen minutes. "Hey, Dave. Since you can't play and I can't leave you alone, why don't we go somewhere else and have a few drinks."

His brother tilted his head. "I'm fine here, but if you want, we can sit upstairs, have a few drinks, and watch from one of the balcony tables."

Not the response he wanted, but at least they'd be out of the "pit," as the members called the huge downstairs play-room. The entrance was on the second floor, where the bar was. The U-shaped balcony had numerous seating areas, with some along the railing so members could observe the scenes from above. He could pick the side over the spanking benches, so he wouldn't have to watch Shelby's threesome and dream she was his submissive—and his alone. He'd tried to negotiate with her twice in the past, and she'd turned him down both times. It was a single submissive's prerogative to play or not play with whomever they wanted, and a Dom had to accept it. He only wished he knew why she wanted nothing to do with him.

Parker stood. "Yeah, that's fine. Let's take a walk through the locker rooms. I need to hit the john."

Their table was not far from the submissives' waiting area, halfway between the grand staircase and the St. Andrew's cross on a small stage in the middle of the room. Usually, the stage was reserved for highlighted scenes or commitment ceremonies. Devon and his sub/fiancée, Kristen Anders, had their ceremony on it a few months ago, and Parker was glad his friend had finally found someone to love. He only hoped someday he could be so lucky.

Still eyeing the activity around them, his brother remained seated. "I'll wait here for you. No rush."

"I'm not supposed to leave you unattended."

Dave rolled his eyes. "Come on, Park. I'm a grown man and don't need a babysitter. I promise to wait right here."

Hesitating, Parker was about to say no way, but Dave gave him that stare that always made him feel like the idiot of the family. That fucking holier-than-thou look that said I'm better than you'll ever be. "All right, fine. But stay here and don't talk to anyone unless they approach you first. I'll be back in a minute."

He headed to the locker room, glancing over his shoulder once at his brother. The cocky bastard gave him one of those condescending waves like he was shooing away an annoying gnat. Parker winced and disappeared into the men's lounge. In there, the sounds of flesh, or leather, smacking flesh, and orgasms being reached faded away while the thumping music was muffled enough so he could hear himself think.

Why he agreed to come here tonight, he had no idea. It wasn't like he and Dave were the closest of brothers . . . hell, if it weren't for the blood relation, Parker wouldn't even consider him a friend. Four years younger than Dave's age of thirty-five, he had always lived in the guy's shadow. That was one of the reasons he'd moved to Florida . . . to get away from his family.

Brody stepped up to the urinal next to Parker. "Hey, man. How you doing?"

"Good. You?"

"Not bad at all. Especially since little Miss Shelby negotiated a scene with Marco and me for later. Damn, I love that little firecracker."

Parker clenched his teeth. He knew Brody didn't have anything but respect for the submissive. However, it irked him that the big bastard knew her in a way Parker had never experienced. The computer geek of Trident Security was a former Navy SEAL, as was each of his co-workers. He also had a heart of gold and seemed to be well-liked by everyone who met him. Brody treated every female submissive as they should be treated . . . like they were the most precious women in the world.

Zipping up his pants, Parker turned toward the sinks and tried to pretend it didn't bother him who Shelby hooked up with. "Well, then, have a good time."

"Hey, before I forget . . . can I call you during the week? I want to overhaul the master bath in my new place. Pink tile and I don't exactly go together, and the shower is way too fucking small." He finished at the urinals and stepped over to where Parker was washing his hands.

"Yeah, sure. Monday's usually a busy day, but I should have time Tuesday afternoon to swing by and take a look." Shaking the excess water from his hands, Parker reached over and grabbed a paper towel. He glanced back to see the other man was nodding.

"That should work. I'll call you Tuesday morning to confirm. Thanks. I appreciate it."

Slapping Brody on the shoulder as he walked by, he said, "No problem. See you later."

Wanting to get out of the club now more than ever, Parker strode back out to the pit, where two things hit him at once. One—his brother wasn't where he left him. And two—there was a large, loud crowd near the submissives' area, and it didn't appear to be for anything good. *Fuck!*

Shoving his way through the group, he wasn't expecting what he saw, although he wasn't too surprised. Dave was on the floor, being held face-down by a furious Marco, with one arm hitched high behind his back. His brother was no match for the security operative who worked out on almost a daily basis.

Parker had a sinking feeling in his stomach when he saw three women also on the floor a few feet away. Mistress China and a woman he didn't recognize had their arms around . . . *shit* . . . a crying Shelby. Wide-eyed, she held a trembling hand against her cheek while the Domme looked ready to spit nails.

With his fists clenched, he turned his attention back to the two men and barked, "What the fuck, Dave? What the hell did you do?"

"I didn't do anything. Now get this fucking gorilla off me. I'm going to sue if he doesn't get off me."

The whiny, pain-filled order didn't gain any sympathy from Parker. His gaze went to Marco, who growled and returned the questioning look with a pissed-off glower. "This asshole backhanded Shelby. I had people in my way and couldn't get here fast enough to stop him."

What? The bastard hit Shelby? My Shelby? A woman who wouldn't hurt a fly.

Parker was livid. Glancing back toward the crying submissive, his blood hit the boiling point. Through gritted teeth, he addressed the other Dom. "He's my brother. Let him up, Marco."

Marco's eyes flickered to Ian, who was standing next to Parker. Travis "Tiny" Daultry, the head of club security, and several other guards had pushed the crowd back to give the Doms some room. Ian crossed his arms and studied Parker's face. Parker knew his fury was showing, and he silently begged the owner to let him take care of this. Ian didn't say a word but nodded at Marco, who let go of the bastard and stood.

As Dave got to his feet, Parker couldn't believe he was stupid enough to say, "What's the big deal? Everyone is slapping women around here, and I get in trouble for what you all are doing."

Parker took a step closer to him, his voice low and barely controlled. "You okay?"

Obviously, not realizing how pissed his brother was, the idiot grinned. "Yeah, Park, I'm fine."

"Good." Without missing a beat, he reared back and punched Dave in the face, knocking him unconscious. He ignored the round of cheers from the crowd and hurried over to Shelby, crouching down in front of her. "I'm so sorry, Shelby. It's my fault. I shouldn't have left him alone."

He helped her stand, but Mistress China and the other woman stayed by her side for support. Parker gently pulled Shelby's hand from her cheek and growled, "I'm going to kill him," when he saw the red and swollen area, which starting to bruise. He'd known bringing the stupid prick here was a mistake, but the fact that harm had come to Shelby, of all people, had him wanting to wake his brother up, so he could knock him out again.

She grabbed his forearm, her eyes pleading. "No, don't, Sir. I should have grabbed Master Marco or one of the other DMs. He was trying to negotiate with me. I saw his guest wristband and knew he wasn't allowed to play, but he wouldn't take no for an answer. When I tried to walk away, he hit me."

Parker drew her into his arms and held her momentarily while everyone else looked on. He saw Ian cock his head at Tiny, who began breaking up the crowd with the other guards. The Head Dom then spoke quietly to Parker. "Let's take this to the office. What do you want us to do with him?"

Parker didn't answer him immediately—he had a sub to take care of first. She may not be his, but for now, he was responsible for her. He could hardly hold back the anger and guilt in his voice. "Go to the ladies' lounge and put some ice on your cheek. When I'm done with Ian and my asshole brother, I'll take you home."

"You—you don't have to do that, I can drive myself." Shelby's face flushed, and her eyes avoided him. Even though her trembling seemed to ease while in his arms, it appeared she didn't want to be there.

"I need to do this, Shelby, please. I need to make sure you're okay and get home safe. This is not negotiable." He tipped her chin up with his fingers until she looked at him. "Please?"

She bit her lip but nodded her consent. Mistress China wrapped her arm around the sub's shoulder and eased her from Parker's arms. Despite being a bit of a sadist, the Domme tended to be a mother hen to the submissives. "I'll take care of her. We'll be in the lounge when you're ready."

He murmured his thanks to her while Ian spoke to the

other woman with them. Parker figured she was the owner's new submissive, whom he'd heard someone mention earlier. "I'm sorry, but I have to take care of this. Please go with them and wait for me in the lounge. I'll be a few minutes."

"Yes, Sir."

The two women walked Shelby toward the locker room, and before he joined them, Marco gave Parker a heated glare he knew he deserved. He'd broken one of the club's rules—never leave a guest unattended—and the results had been devastating.

Ian asked one of the nearby waitresses to bring an ice pack to Shelby before turning to Parker, who still wanted to commit familial homicide. Handing his keys to Tiny, Parker asked, "Can you do me a favor? Toss him into my truck. And don't bother being gentle about it. He deserves every fucking bruise he gets."

The six-foot-eight, two hundred and seventy-five-pound, part-time bodyguard grinned. "My pleasure. We'll take care of him . . . you just make sure Miss Shelby is okay."

"I will." Parker then turned to Ian, his face filled with embarrassment, anger, and regret. "Let's get this over with."

Ready for the next book in the Trident Security Series?
Pick up *Not Negotiable* today!

Shelby Whitman has had a huge crush on the one man who deserves more than she can give him, so it's best to keep him at arm's length.

Dominant Parker Christiansen has been craving the perky,

petite submissive ever since he laid his eyes on her, but she's turned down his every attempt to negotiate with her.

When Parker finds out Shelby's hiding a devastating secret from her friends, he steps in to help, and this time he won't take no for an answer. Can he convince her he's fallen in love with her, and if they only have this time together, they should make the best of it?

For the best reading order of the Trident Security series and its spinoffs, check out the printable list on my website!

Also by

Samantha Cole

***Denotes titles/series that are available on select digital sites only.
Paperbacks and audiobooks are available on most book sites.

***THE TRIDENT SECURITY SERIES

Leather & Lace

His Angel

Waiting For Him

Not Negotiable: A Novella

Topping The Alpha

Watching From the Shadows

Whiskey Tribute: A Novella

Tickle His Fancy

No Way in Hell: A Trident Security/Steel Corps Crossover (co-authored with J.B. Havens)

Absolving His Sins

Option Number Three: A Novella

Salvaging His Soul

Trident Security Field Manual

Torn In Half: A Novella

Trident Security Series: Volume VI

USA Today Bestselling Author and Award-Winning Author Samantha Cole is a retired policewoman and former paramedic. Using her life experiences and training, she strives to find the perfect mix of suspense and romance for her readers to enjoy.

Awards:

Wannabe in Wyoming (co-authored by J.B. Havens) won the bronze medal in the 2021 Readers' Favorite Awards in the General Romance category.

Scattered Moments in Time, won the gold medal in the 2020 Readers' Favorite Awards in the Fiction Anthology category.

The Road to Solace (formerly *The Friar*), won the silver medal in the 2017 Readers' Favorite Awards in the Contemporary Romance category.

Samantha has over thirty-five books published throughout several different series as well as a few standalone novels. A full list can be found on her website.

Sexy Six-Pack's Sirens Group on Facebook
Website: www.samanthacoleauthor.com
Newsletter: www.geni.us/SCNews

facebook.com/SamanthaColeAuthor

twitter.com/SamanthaCole222

instagram.com/samanthacoleauthor

amazon.com/Samantha-A-Cole/e/B00X53K3X8

bookbub.com/profile/samantha-a-cole

goodreads.com/SamanthaCole

pinterest.com/samanthacoleaut